*Please turn the page
for more reviews . . .*

The
Termination
Node

Lois H. Gresh &
Robert Weinberg

A Del Rey® Book
THE BALLANTINE PUBLISHING GROUP • NEW YORK

A Del Rey® Book
Published by The Ballantine Publishing Group
Copyright © 1999 by Lois H. Gresh and Robert Weinberg

www.randomhouse.com/delrey/

Library of Congress Catalog Card Number: 99-90472

ISBN 0-345-41246-X

Manufactured in the United States of America

First Hardcover Edition: January 1999
First Mass Market Edition: November 1999

10 9 8 7 6 5 4 3 2 1

This book is dedicated in loving memory to my father, Sam Goldberg, a lifelong SF fan and a neverending source of inspiration. To Rena and Danny, with love. And to Bob: mentor, friend, and all-around great guy.

—LOIS H. GRESH

To Lois, talented beyond measure!

—ROBERT WEINBERG

CHAPTER 1

Judy Carmody's legs ached. It was three in the freaking morning, and here she was, still staring at some stupid computer screen in an office hellhole. The room left a sourness in her mouth. Not enough air circulation in this dump.

Certainly not enough for the beefcake hardware that controlled the money of half the population in Laguna Beach. This kind of beefcake required sterile living quarters.

Not dust on the tiled floors.

Not gray fabric walls enclosing it in a ten-by-ten prison.

She stroked the top of the monitor. Warm, too much heat. Beneath the desk, the disk drives whirred, emitting a nice low technothrum that rose to a whine. A sonata played on a broken instrument.

"These babies are at risk." Her voice came out scratchy, the words all frazzed.

"Could be," Jose said, "but you know management, they won't spring for better digs unless I'm a grade fourteen. Like that'll be the day."

Jose Ferrents. Senior security programmer at Laguna Savings Bank. One of Judy's best customers. She was stuck here until he was satisfied that she'd thoroughly checked the computer for security leaks. New passwords had been granted to marketing guys the day before. Like passwords would matter to some hacker. Jose was one paranoid quack.

He leaned back in his chair, waiting for her to finish the job. Thick black hair streaked with green Etch-o-Oil. Red lines painted beneath bloodshot blue eyes. Jose went in for the Dracula look.

The monitor flipped to the screen saver: swarms of infinitely regressing cubes and triangles, a neon blaze set against black. Dracula got off on the forever realm of fractals.

"Look, can we finish up? I'm really tired, Jose." It was creepy being cramped next to Jose in his lair, the gray walls plastered with posters of microchip circuits and lanky blondes in goth bikinis—like he really knew anything about circuits *or* bikinis. *Duh . . .*

"Sure. I have more important things to do, too." Jose graced her with a little smirk. She knew better. Jose never had *anything* more important to do than play with computers.

Judy shut her eyes, brushed her long, auburn hair out of the way, rubbed her neck. Damn, she was getting cranky. It was just too late to have to deal with Jose. She'd had one hell of a long day, grinding Internet security code for Steve Sanchez, fielding hysterical E-mails from that programmer at Widescreen DVD. But as a computer security specialist hanging five hundred dollars an hour, Judy could cope with a stiff neck a little longer and put up with Dracula.

He touched the screen. The fractals disappeared, replaced by the log of Internet transactions that had been executed by the bank's corporate customers.

Jose had done a good job on the bank's World Wide Web site. A customer entered a password, then processed debits and credits against authorized accounts. All transactions were encrypted before transmission, then decrypted at the bank. Crypto chips and digital cash. When Jose had first installed the system back in '02, Laguna Savings had quickly become one of the top Internet banks in the country.

Jose rolled his chair across the room to the other computer server. The clanking of rollers on tile cut into the disk drive whine and made Judy's body jerk. If only her nerves would settle, if only she could stay awake, if only she could find a method other than coffee, which she'd given up five years ago, or Methamorph, which she'd given up in high school.

But there'd be no drugs for Judy; not like Jose, twitching in his chair over there, nerves atwanging like snapped guitar strings, body gaunt, hollow eyes a million miles deep—tubular twin tunnels to nowhere.

No. She'd finish this job, then sack out for a few hours before facing another long day tomorrow—no, today.

She checked the first Internet transaction in the log, a withdrawal made by a small investment firm down by Laguna Beach. Jose checked the firm's account on the other server and confirmed that the withdrawal had been correctly subtracted.

They moved to the second transaction, and on down the list, until finally Jose said, "Two more transactions and we're done."

Her eyes shifted from the screen to the shelves over Jose's head. Micro Utility Corp—now a subsidiary of Sony—double-reinforced units, part number 3B12G14, the screws holding them together, part numbers 3B75I28 and 3C72I25. The shelves were crammed with Ethernet boxes and punchdown blocks.

Just two more transactions—crank 'em and get out.

One more.

"What the *hell* is *this*?" Jose's shoulders quivered more than usual.

The Methamorph freak. Jumping at ghosts. "Cut it out, Jose. It's late, and I want to go home."

"Penetration." One word, tight and low.

"Cut it *out*, Jose."

"I *said*, penetration. Big one. A half-million-dollar withdrawal from each of ten accounts, all made by Hirama Electronics."

What? Was he, like . . . *serious*?

She pushed herself from the desk, cringed as the chair rollers ground across tile, then stood and peered past Jose's shoulder. "That's a lot of money, but doesn't necessarily imply penetration," she said.

"Hirama transactions never come across the Net. They're always made in person by some top management guy in an Italian pinstriped suit."

He redisplayed the Hirama bank accounts. All ten had zero balances.

In the middle of the night, someone was wiping millions of dollars from Hirama's accounts. Penetration: *a hacker.* Judy grasped the back of Jose's chair. She was too close to the Dracula green-streaked head, too close to the new-plastic reek of Etch-o-Oil.

Jose massaged his right fingers with his left hand. His pupils were wider than Metha-normal, his forehead creased, his mouth trembling. "Fingers, can't move 'em."

Judy crouched beneath the blinking red Ethernet lights, the multicolored spaghetti wires dripping off the punchdowns. Her chin brushed against the Etch-o-hair. It was stiff, like scouring pad bristles. Mercifully, he rolled his chair to the side to give her space.

She closed the Hirama file, then accessed it again to see if the changes remained.

The accounts no longer had zero balances.

She had to be losing her grip. It was late; she was tired. Try again. She redisplayed the Internet transaction log. This time, it showed a huge transaction that had deleted several million dollars in Hirama funds.

A freaking break-in hacker at play in the black void of the Internet.

"A *superhacker*," she whispered.

Hot *damn.*

She hardly felt her legs move as she returned to the first computer, on the other side of the room. She was only faintly conscious of her socks padding across the tiles. Faintly conscious of the screen saver fractals. She touched the screen, kind of like touching God or something. Her whole body was numb. Brain in high gear. Ice-cold focus.

On the Laguna Savings Internet transaction page, real-time, right here and now, some freakzoid was deleting Hirama funds, then replacing them. What if this was no kid, out for a computer joyride? Breaking through a bank's firewalls was a federal offense and came with a mandatory jail sentence.

"Do a trace." Jose was behind her now, his breath hot on her neck. She hadn't even heard him cross the room.

She squinted and started typing.

```
powerman>finger -g
```

A short list of all system users scrolled down the screen. It showed no intruders.

```
powerman>netstat -a
```

A quick status check of all system sockets, every low-level software device feeding into the system. Nothing.

"Do it again," Jose said.

```
powerman>netstat -a
```

This time, the screen showed an established Internet connection coming from a foreign address called Helraze.

"I'd better call Naresh." Jose sounded scared. Naresh was his boss. Jose *never* called Naresh, who was a grade fifteen in the bank hierarchy. A grade fifteen who lived in a swanky house and reigned from a swanky cubicle on management row.

She'd spare Jose the agony. She'd handle Helraze herself. "Naresh lives fifteen minutes away. He can't get here in time."

"Yeah, guess you're right. Jesus, how the hell will I explain this to him? The bank's laying off people again. Next week."

The netstat command displayed its results again. This time, no connection from Helraze.

"Maybe you won't have to explain anything," Judy said. "The hacker's popping in and out of the system, removing cash, but replacing it. Could be he won't do any *real* damage."

"But why's he doing it?"

Damned if *she* knew.

One thing to do. Track the sucker. Discover the route he'd taken through the millions of Internet computer nodes to get to Laguna Savings.

```
powerman>traceroute helraze
```

He was far away, this Helraze, routing transmission packets through forty-seven other computers. Who the hell was this guy, and what did he want?

"Try tracing it again," Jose said.

This time, Helraze disappeared, simply disappeared as if he had never existed.

"The main password file," Jose said, "that's gotta be it." He pushed past Judy, touched an icon in the lower corner of the screen.

She scanned the encrypted MD6 file digest, which contained the main passwords, for security breaches. "Clean, all access codes in place and valid," she said.

"The syslogs are all clean, too, no breaches," Jose confirmed. "Hey, what's this? Fake syslog messages, Judy, as if dozens of superusers logged in tonight."

"Let me see." She gently nudged him aside, giving herself room again.

Superuser access was critical. It meant the hacker could get into all protected system files. He could bring the bank to its knees, destroy everything, transfer any amount of money, anything he wanted. So why wasn't he doing it, and *quickly*?

Both lastlog and umtp showed no indication of the hacker. She checked the syslogs again. They were wiped clean; all fake syslog messages had been removed.

Hopefully, their mystery hacker had screwed up. Rather than delete log entries that could be used to trace his system penetration, maybe he'd been in a hurry and had just replaced the entries with null characters. Blank lines, filled with nulls, would *prove* penetration—and right now, with all logs wiped clean and all accounts restored, there was no proof of a break-in. Judy's neck ached from the tension. Bank officials always *demanded* proof.

"Nothing," Jose said. "This guy knows exactly what he's doing. No authorization failures in /var/adm/messages. Nothing strange in the superuser log. No shell history. There's nothing to trace. It's as if the guy's never been here."

"If we don't get to the bottom of this, and soon," Judy said, "we'll have to notify top management. They may have to close the bank this morning."

"No proof. My God, Naresh will kill me."

Jose was right. Naresh *would* kill him. And management would never close the bank based on the statements by two programmers who *thought* they had discovered a weird system anomaly. Management never understood anything about computer systems anyway, even when there *was* proof.

"We're running out of time," Jose said.

Judy glanced at her watch; it was already four o'clock in the morning. In a few hours, bank customers all over the city would be turning on their computers and processing transactions over the Net. By the time management showed up, Net business would be at its peak.

"This hacker must have been sniffing the bank's Web page for weeks," Judy said, "just waiting for an opportunity to crack into the server. He got that opportunity when you sent the new password file to marketing."

Tap into a cable, intercept transmissions, pick up the new password file as it went from the central computer site to the downtown office. Simple enough. She said, "He hacked into the password file, added himself with privileged access to everything we have. Then he screwed with the Hirama accounts, deleted his fake password, erased all trace files. He's *fast*."

"And he may not be done," Jose said.

Judy trembled, hit by a sudden rush of fear. What if this guy had entered through the Web itself? Jose had coded some of the Web site using ControlFreak. What if the guy had hacked into the low-level software I/O routines, the system sockets? If so, he could be accessing bank files right now, writing to them, wiping them clean of money.

Judy stared at the monster machine: six parallel processors, all cranking with more than 400 megabytes of memory and tons of terabyte disk muscle. The latest crypto chips. All known Internet browser hacks plugged. From the Net, there was no way into Laguna accounts.

"He's doing something new, Jose. ControlFreak's clean at this bank. Remember, I'm the one who plugged all the holes. This hacker's cracked into the system using some method we've never seen before."

"We could rip out the wires leading to the punchdown blocks, cut his connection."

"That would fry the system. And if we just shut everything down, we'll never know who this guy is, or what harm he's done. Besides, if he wants to, he'll come back."

"I'm launching the agents," Jose said, touching the computer screen. The agents appeared, jiggling animations of bugs, real cute, but—

"Worthless," Judy said.

"Nothing else to do, not that I can think of." Jose touched the EXECUTE icon. The agents jiggled and the directory structure scrolled down the screen. The agents, artificially intelligent digital creatures mainly used for Net searches, were scouring Jose's Net files, seeking clues about the intruder.

```
System clean
```

Nothing.

"Waste of time," Judy said. Lack of sleep combined with tension had her head pounding. She stretched her back, raised her arms, tried to unknot her muscles.

The agents jiggled again. Then in metallic blue letters:

```
System compromised
```

Judy froze, arms still above her head. "What the—"

But, as her arms came down, the status changed:

```
System clean
```

Jose was quiet. He was staring at *System clean*, his eyes narrowed, his hair damp with sweat.

"Look."

The screen displayed all running computer processes. The hacker was back on the server. He was sending a terminate signal to the operating system:

```
powerman>kill -TERM 1
```

"He's shutting us down," Jose whispered. "He's deadlocking all programs, running in *s* mode."

"He's operating as the system console," Judy said. *"He's taking over."*

She stared at the screen, her heart racing, half from excitement, half from fear. In all her years of hacking, she'd never encountered anyone this bold and this well hidden. There was no way to trace him, no way to stop him.

The system knocked down to single-user mode, the single user being the hacker from Helraze.

"He'll destroy system memory." Jose's voice was thick with fright. "He'll destroy the operating system."

Then a new thought struck him.

"All my money's in there," he said, his voice practically a whisper. "How will I pay the rent? Landlord pulls it electronically from my Laguna account. How will I prove my digicard had five thousand dollars on it when—"

Judy cut him off. "Look—all of my consulting money's tied up in the bank, too. If this guy wipes out the system, thousands of people are going to be flat-dead broke."

Backups? Were the computer's backup systems sufficient to handle such a nightmare?

No. They'd restore only the transactions and accounts that existed as of last night. Better than nothing, but hours' worth of transactions would be lost.

And it would take forever to unravel the mess.

The screen flickered. A fireball appeared, followed by the large red letters DNS, then . . . nothing. Black.

Judy blinked. She shook her head, suddenly feeling dizzy. "He's gone."

The hacker had disappeared. Instantly, the system rolled over and rebooted back to multiuser mode. Soon the fractals glimmered into view, a forever wonderland of infinite penetration.

Jose stared at Judy. He had to be thinking the same thing she was: *No proof.* There had been no financial losses. No hard evidence of what had just taken place. Bank management would never believe them. The attack, the takeover, made no sense.

Unless, it had been . . . practice.

CHAPTER 2

Nine in the morning, and still in yesterday's clothes. The wrinkled orange shorts with the bleach stains, the faded lilac T-shirt over the blue bikini top. Same red socks that had padded aross the tiles at Laguna Savings last night.

Judy felt like a soiled clown.

Except nothing was funny.

"How long will it take to fix the mess at Laguna?" Steve Sanchez perched in the blue velvet chair behind his desk—fake-antique, oak-stained, laminated plywood. Kind of a bonzo desk for a guy who owned a computer security company that was worth megamillions.

But then, Steve always told Judy that old-time, cozy home digs relaxed his customers—and cast the illusion that Steve was an old-time honest businessman. That was the important part.

In Judy's opinion, there never *had been* such a thing as an old-time honest businessman.

Steve pried the cuticles off his nails with a paper clip. His eyes darted from the clip to Judy, from the clip to Judy. He was waiting for an answer, wanted a quick response, so he could get her out of the office and get on with his day. Jittery, as usual, too hyper—as if his blood pumped the morph without needing synthetic ingredients.

Dark chiseled hair, high cheekbones—Steve was a handsome man. His sharp black eyes sparked with excitement, intelligence . . . and total focus.

Aside from the computer on his desk, there was no equipment in his office. Just fake-antique plywood bookshelves, fake potted plants, his velvet throne—even the velvet was fake—and a plush reclining chair for visitors.

Judy didn't feel like sitting in the recliner. The seat was too high, made her feet dangle over the floor, made her feel like a midget or a little kid. Made her feel *diminished*.

The point of the visitor's chair, no doubt.

She stared out the window at a mutated banana tree: genetically altered so it wouldn't grow fruit. "What about DVD? When do we finish that?" she asked without turning.

"Rodriguez will be here any minute. The guard will flash a note on my computer. We pacify Rodriguez, then you go fix the Laguna problem. But I need a time frame, Judy."

Pacify Rodriguez without any sleep. Oh, great.

"Oops. Rodriguez is here earlier than I expected. The security guard just let him in. Guess it's show time. This won't take long, then I need to know about the bank."

There was a knock at the door, and Steve rose from behind his desk. At five feet eight inches, he was six inches taller than Judy. He wore a tan linen suit, complete with tie and cuff links.

By the time she moved from the window, Hector Rodriguez and Steve were shaking hands, rah-rahing each other like best friends . . . good to see you, buddy . . . how's the wife? . . . we gotta get together for that drink sometime soon . . . and blah blah blah.

Like either one of them cared.

Hector Rodriguez wore fancier clothes than Steve. Navy suit, white shirt, paisley tie, black polished shoes. Another handsome guy, charming actually, with a smile that almost made her feel like he was *real*.

But of course, he wasn't. He was executive vice president of the southwest region of Widescreen DVD, the second-largest video sales chain in the United States. He knew when to turn on the charm, and when to turn it off.

Rodriguez smiled at her.

He had come here to get something from her.

"Hello, Miss Carmody." He settled into the recliner and swept his eyes over her body. She had no idea what he thought of her. She could never tell with these guys. With Judy, there was never any of that rah-rah buddy stuff going on. She was a girl in a man's universe.

She sat on the edge of the windowsill, now glad to be wearing her mismatched, silly outfit. It gave her a twinge of power, allowed her a kind of twisted rebellion against skirt suits or anything remotely smacking of professional clothing.

When she didn't answer, Steve scowled at her, then walked around the desk and back to his throne. "Judy doesn't say much, she just *observes*."

"Observing is fine," Rodriguez said, casting her another dazzling smile. "I pay Miss Carmody to observe, and to fix. I'm interested only in results."

It was too warm in here. It was too warm everywhere. Why couldn't this meeting take place on a webvid? What were those freaking conference applications *for*?

Personal contact was the key to good business, Steve always claimed. If so, Judy was locked out.

She had to *say* something.

Rodriguez continued. "I must warn you, Steve, that I have only half an hour, then I catch a plane to that conference up north. So, please, not too technical—just straight talk."

Steve adjusted his tie. "Yes, of course."

They just continued without her. She *had* to say something.

"It's a delight to see you, Mr. Rodriguez."

Rodriguez shot a baffled glance at Steve. It was the look people always exchanged when Judy was around. As if saying, What an idiot.

From Rodriguez: "So. What *exactly* is wrong with DVD's security system? I didn't understand the technical jargon in Miss Carmody's report."

He was talking as if she weren't there . . . because she always said the wrong things. Or maybe because they didn't expect

friendly banter from her, just cold facts. Judy Carmody, the ro-
botic girlthing.

"Judy's tired," Steve said. "She was up all night on an emergency call with one of my clients. And she's been working
around the clock on DVD problems for the past week."

"Well, let's hear it then," Rodriguez said.

Time for TerMight. No more Judy. Just TerMight: technical
mistress of the Web. The one who ruled. The one who was confident, knew the tech, talked the lingo.

TerMight.

"Judy."

She stared at the recliner. A nice brown fake velvet. Soothing,
soft, molasses.

TerMight spoke.

"DVD's Internet security has at least one hundred and two
holes. The service pack was never installed to protect your
system from intrusion. Nor the required patches for the operating system, even though the OS patches are from your Internet
browser's competition."

She glanced up. Rodriguez was blinking at her. He was
baffled. Wasn't a technical guy like Jose. No matter how simply
she put it, it wasn't going to be simple enough for Rodriguez.

Give it to him in a way he'd understand.

She shut her eyes. "That is, Mr. Rodriguez, there are over a
hundred ways a hacker can break into your corporate files. Once
past the firewalls, this person could download all your sales
records for the past year. Or copy the purchase agreements you
have with manufacturers in the video field, complete with discount schedules and delivery dates. Or hijack all the passwords
to your electronic bank accounts, then withdraw any or all of
your corporate funds. One hacker, with a grudge against
Widescreen DVD, could bring your company to its knees."

There. Done. She sagged against the windowsill.

Rodriguez nodded. "So we plug the leaks. I understand. I just
need a time frame. How long will it take to fix the problems?"

Steve spoke before she had a chance. "Judy will supply a full
report on the necessary solutions within the week. Ten days at
most."

Rodriguez smiled. "Excellent. Now. How long will it take my guys to patch this thing up?"

"It makes more sense for Judy to program the fixes," Steve said.

"At *her* fees? Seven hundred an hour?"

It *was* amazing that anyone paid her fees. If it had been left to Judy, she'd be offering services to Rodriguez for two hundred bucks an hour, way below industry standards. But she knew enough to let Steve field the question. After all, he paid her contract fees of five hundred an hour, then pocketed the extra two hundred himself. He understood people and business. She understood only technology.

And Steve was one sharp smoothie. "Judy's the best. Nobody else comes close when it comes to Internet security. Face it, Hector, you need her. Your guys couldn't even *find* the problems."

"True enough." A pause. Rodriguez was considering whether he could bargain Steve's price down. Judy had witnessed this scene a hundred times. She felt ridiculous being called the best, being dickered over like a farm animal at auction. But Rodriguez gave Steve the response Judy always heard. "Done. In less than ten days, Judy fixes my security leaks. DVD is safe from hackers. It's fast; it's effective."

Great. Judy had only ten days to fix 102 security holes in DVD's Internet systems.

"Judy walks on water. She's a miracle worker," Steve said.

More like a girl who worked around the clock nonstop. She wasn't the best. She just worked like a dog.

"I have to run. Good meeting. Thanks, Steve." Rodriguez shook hands with Steve, nodded politely to Judy. Then he was gone.

Steve ran his hands through his hair, clasped them on his desk. "I hate justifying your fees like that. If you worked for me full-time, in-house, on my staff—"

"No way."

"—you wouldn't have to work under such pressure, Judy. My guys don't work half as hard as you do."

"Come on, you *know* how I feel about this."

"Be reasonable. Your fees are bleeding me dry. Besides, your name would add prestige to this place."

She didn't answer.

"Judy, you're not listening." Steve circled his desk, came too close, smelled faintly of soap and cologne.

She was keenly aware that *she* hadn't showered for two days. She backed away and edged toward the door.

"I go it alone," she said, "always have."

"You've been working alone too long, Judy." He almost sounded sympathetic—like Rodriguez had *almost* sounded charming. She wanted to believe that Steve was being real. But she knew better.

Nobody was real.

So why would she ever want to put up with them, day after day, face-to-face? She was an independent contractor. A loner. It was better that way. No company politics. No company rules. No small talk and drivel from personnel dragons.

Sure, Judy didn't actually have any close friends. Not off-line, at least. No boyfriend either. But that was the price she paid for independence.

She didn't like thinking about it.

Steve's computer beeped. He moved back behind the desk, said, "Private," then picked up the phone receiver on his desk-mate and started warbling to some customer. The phone icon on his screen shivered blue streaks as the computer transmitted Steve's words and received the customer's replies.

Judy was dismissed.

She left. Quickly.

Outside, the air was sweet with the scent from flowering shrubs that lined the parking lot. Hummingbirds jammed their long beaks into the petals and sucked moisture. A butterfly sat, folding and unfolding its yellow wings on the wide leaf of a banana tree.

This was reality. This was where Judy preferred to be. Relaxing, gazing for hours at the flowers and hummingbirds and butterflies, at the ocean as it glazed the morning beach.

Judy wanted reality.

But Judy was a Net girl. She lived where reality was a wash of phosphors, where sleep didn't fit in. Where physical distances—banks in Switzerland or Aruba or wherever—were irrelevant. Where she was everywhere, and nowhere, at all hours of the day.

She pressed together the Velcro straps on her Roller-blades, then cruised into the parking lot. Always alone, but at least she had freedom. She'd never work full-time for anyone. Even if it meant all-nighters forever, hunched over a netpad, as TerMight. Life was too short to play head games with the normal people, listening to their phony friendliness, returning their false smiles. Life was too short to be imprisoned in concrete walls.

CHAPTER 3

Rollerblades glinting, the street a blur of gray, Judy crouched low for maximum speed and tilted her body to the left, stared at the pavement as her blades flashed around the curve of Laguna Crescent. White gulls flapped their wings, eyes startled, heads cocked, and rose out of her way. She passed them, still hunched low, their caws reviving a distant memory of Mom getting on her case when she'd toyed with her laptop.

Mom. The word made her go faster, as if speeding down the Crescent would somehow help her escape the thought.

She flashed by a startled man in bathing trunks holding a green hose that dribbled water. A waft of roses billowed, then was gone.

Judy swerved around a pothole, warm air pressing her ears and stinging her eyes. One turn up ahead, past the red Ferrari, then an upward lift of her body, a spin of her skates, and a dip of her blades into the grass. She was home.

A shimmer of hair, auburn shot with gold and brown, cascaded down her face to her waist. She tossed it back, turned her head toward the sky, and shut her eyes. What a *rush*.

Judy dropped to the grass, ignoring the crunch of snail shells beneath her shorts, her legs long and tan and shadowed pink from the bougainvilleas hanging over the tiny fence. She wanted to stay right here, basking in the early-morning warmth.

But first, a quick call to Jose about the Helraze nightmare. Then, after a shower, a long nap on the beach.

Looping her skates over her shoulder, Judy climbed the stairs to the front porch. Once inside, she checked her mailbox, then started up the three flights, around the tiny landings, to her apartment.

At each level, four wooden doors sheltered residents from intruders. As if the doors would do any good. They were as thin as cardboard and offered about as much protection.

Hardly anyone was home this time of day. Trev LeFontaine's door, number 1-4, was half ajar, and a radio was blaring inside. Trev's voice, deep and full of vibrato, was singing to the music—some tune about dead flowers and lost dreams.

But there *were* no dead flowers in southern California.

Just a lot of dead and lost people. Like Trev, the superintendent who did nothing but putter around all day, fixing plaster and painting walls. Trev, who thought of nothing except surfing the waves at Huntington and Corona del Mar, and sometimes where the tides slammed the lagoon at Doheny down south.

But his lifestyle was none of Judy's business. He kept the place nice; that was all that mattered. The wine-colored tiles were cool beneath her socks. The walls were scrubbed white. Most important, Judy had ten phone lines, all supplied and secretly rigged by Trev one night while the other residents slept.

She slipped her key into door 3-2, entered her tiny apartment.

It was stiflingly hot. She hadn't been home in two days.

She carefully made her way across the living room to open the window. Minilamps, buzzers, batteries, and 9-volt clips littered the carpet, along with solar cells, wire leads, T-splicers, 555 timer chips, 3-volt power packs, capacitors, resistors, tangles of cables, and stacks of technical journals.

God, she could hardly breathe in here. She pushed aside the flowered curtains, yanked up the window. A slight breeze stirred. A warm breeze that did nothing to cool the sweat that coated her face and body.

She'd gazed from this window a million times. It was her window into the real world, where normal people went about their daily business: the neighbors chatting as they watered the pink and purple flowers dotting their tiny lawns—what *did* they talk about?; the neon convertibles, Jaguars, Fiats, and Mercedes lining the curbs and roaring off to places unknown; all the perfect bodies, all the perfect people.

It would be nice to enter their bodies, just for a day, to see what they saw, to talk to their friends . . . to hang out with *live* people.

How did they get the numbers out of their heads? How could they do *anything* with the work chores constantly grinding away, hounding them?

Yet, that's all her neighbors seemed to do: everything but work.

A car door slammed, then another. Down past the white stucco cottages and the silver-dollar trees with their paper-thin tinkling leaves, two men were getting out of a white Pontiac Velux Plus. The four-door hardtop was a strange car for southern California.

And the men weren't exactly California hunks.

The fellow on the driver's side was tall and thin and had a large bald spot fringed with gray hair. He was wearing a brown suit and white shirt: hardly appropriate when it was close to a hundred degrees outside.

The other man looked as if he'd walked off the set of an action flick. Also tall, he had the muscled body of a stuntman. Dark sunglasses hid his eyes. California enough, except for the black beard, which matched his hair: both were thick and long. Plus, this guy wore a navy blazer over a print shirt, with the buttons open halfway down his chest.

Probably corporate types from Vegas, hoping to make a big score in the computer biz. There were more slimy guys hoping to strike it rich in southern California than there were snails trying to mate.

The stunt hunk glanced at her apartment building. His face cocked briefly toward the third floor.

Her floor.

Judy darted back from the window. She hated being seen—*caught*—observing people.

Shrugging, she forced herself to concentrate on more

productive matters. She'd get some work done, then hit the
beach, where, surrounded by people, she could observe as much
as she wanted, and nobody would care. After all, they went to the
beach *trying* to be noticed.

She pulled off her T-shirt and tossed it on the floor. Then she
made her way to the tiny kitchenette, slurped down some water,
and splashed some over her blue bikini top.

The muscles in her legs were tight and sore from the Rollerblading. She rubbed them, but it didn't help. Forget the shower.
A warm bath would be much better, would unkink the muscles.

After she got some work done.

She circled the coffee table, a homemade job contrived from
old minitowers shoved together. They were tan and gutted. Perfectly lovely. Steve had given her the towers five years ago, when
she'd been twenty-one, new to town, and desperate for cash.
Inside the empty towers she stored her laptop case, the netpad,
and heaps of hardware junk.

As she sat on the left sofa cushion, exposed coils poked up on
the right side and dust wheezed from the green-and-orange plaid
upholstery.

She reached into her cache of goodies, pulled out her netpad,
and opened the slim case.

Home again, baby. Let's go.

She touched the tiny screen. Recognizing her fingerprint, the
netpad winked to life. At the top of the screen an icon identified
a cellular modem connection to her Net browser. At the bottom
her hacking passwords and utilities were listed, as were her direct links.

She said, "Jose Ferrents, Laguna Savings Bank." One of the
direct links. Voice-recognition software kicked in, and the netpad dialed Jose's number.

His computer voice mail picked up the call. Jose wasn't at his
desk. Rather than wait for him to return her call, she decided it
would be faster for her to dial into the Laguna Savings server
and see what was happening.

First, one more try. "Jose Ferrents, pager." No dice, he wasn't
picking up pager calls either. Pretty weird for Jose, who always
picked up Judy's pager calls, unless he was tied up in some intense session with Naresh . . .

What if Naresh was chewing him out? She pictured poor green-haired Jose, as sleepless as she was, squirming on Methamorph in a grade-fifteen management cubicle. Naresh, yelling at him for incompetence, threatening to fire him.

Nasty.

Jose didn't deserve to take the heat for some Helraze guy that even Judy couldn't track. She had to get into the Laguna server, maybe phone Naresh and save Jose's skin. The sooner the better.

She'd use the laptop. Its modem connections were much faster than the netpad's.

Shoving her soldering iron aside, Judy opened her laptop, touched the screen to launch the system. "ISDN." The machine kicked to the timesaving nethook that connected to her ISDN service.

"Gargon." The bank server. Her voice was enough to get her in. Her voice was her password.

The connection languished. No bank screen appeared.

She clicked her fingernails against the side of the laptop. The black-and-gold polish made her feel dark and mean—it helped her *be* TerMight when she was sniffing networks.

Finally, a message:

```
Connection attempt failed
```

The main server for Laguna Savings Bank was dead. Jose was away from his pager. Not exactly good omens.

A new thought struck. She tried a few more bank servers. "Samson."

```
Connection attempt failed
```

"Delilah."

```
Connection attempt failed
```

Everything had *seemed* stable when Judy had dragged herself from Jose's office at eight that morning. But now . . . Maybe Helraze had returned and destroyed the bank system. While Judy was wasting time with Steve Sanchez and Hector Rodriguez.

She needed something that would pump her up, help her think more clearly. Just to remain alert, awake. Trev had Methamorph, even had home-brewed hyper stuff that really jived. One spoonful of that clear, sweet liquid, and wham, she'd be racing.

But she'd been clean for a long time. Since she'd first become TerMight . . .

Seventeen years old, hooked on morph, five teaspoons a day. The stuff could keep her up three nights in a row, whenever she wanted. She had spent one stint building a Net-TV box for her dad. She'd modeled it after the Kmart Virtuoso I Web Box, but called her version the TerMight box . . . only because the trailer was overrun with termites, and insecticide was overpowering to someone under the influence of morph.

Dad had instantly become hooked on the vids, E-mail, sports, and comics. He spent every night glued to the box. For a month, he gave Judy more smiles, more hugs, and more love than she'd received from him in all the years since she was born.

The TerMight box was love.

But after three months, Dad no longer hugged Judy. And he stopped talking to Mom. Judy got her hugs from morph-fuzz. Mom just cried all night.

It had been cold, snowing. Judy in flannel pajamas and her Christmas-present robe, the pink fluffy one from Mom. Middle of the night. Judy had pushed open the back door. There was her father. Touching the box.

Behind his finger was an avatar, a naked man, having sex with a female avatar named Blushing Bimbo. Dad was saying disgusting things to Bimbo. And Bimbo was saying disgusting things to Dad.

He looked up, startled.

That was the last time Judy ever saw him. Mom went nuts: her husband had dumped her to fuck a computer. Mom became an antitech fanatic, a Barrington follower. End the Net, doom to computers, and all that rot.

Judy became TerMight. She cracked the computer security codes of the Pennsylvania Supreme Bank. Electronically shifted the family money somewhere safe, where Bimbo and Dad could never find it. On the Net, she found and cracked into her original

TerMight box, then crushed it with a mighty spray of electronic insecticide.

With Mom ranting on and on and breaking Judy's computer equipment with barn axes, Judy had to escape. She came to Laguna; she kicked the morph. The morph that created the Ter-Might that created the phosphor sex that destroyed her family.

But she would never escape from the TerMight box. It was with her forever, the memories popping up at any time and any place—on the beach, in Steve's office, while she worked, while she slept . . .

Nor was there any escape from Barrington, the old fart her Mom idolized. He was everywhere, on his Web-TV show, screaming about the evils of the Net.

It wasn't the *Net* that was bad. It was people like her dad who used the Net in perverted ways.

She hated the thoughts, hated remembering.

The only way to blank it all out was to be TerMight. Let the gears crank. Focus, focus . . .

With the Laguna Bank computers dead, nobody's digicard transactions would clear. Only the poor, who didn't qualify for digicards, used paper cash and coins. Everyone else—companies, families—would be in ruins. No income, no way to pay bills or the mortgage, no way to buy food. If the culprits were hackers, everyone would become a Barrington fanatic.

TerMight wouldn't let that happen.

She'd go to the bank's main computer, not hooked to the Net, but storing vital account stats.

"Big Cheese."

She scanned the log files, searching for some sign of a break-in. The logs were clean. No surprise there. She checked several large accounts, including Widescreen DVD. They were zonked: sums added, then deleted, computations all screwed up. She checked her own digicard account. Empty, no funds available, and fifteen thousand owed.

What a freaking mess. Judy's account should have shown well over fifteen thousand in *available* funds. She lived by her digicard, never carried real cash. Besides, digicards never had negative amounts. That was impossible.

Maybe she'd find some clues about Laguna Savings on Vile-
Spawn. Working round the clock on the Widescreen DVD project, Judy hadn't logged onto the underground bulletin board
system for nearly a week.

VileSpawn was *the* hangout for hackers. As her initiation, Judy
had been required to hack into VileSpawn before she was given an
account and a password. Once inside, people swapped code,
traded programming secrets, and compared cracking techniques.
Everyone used Internet handles—no real names.

She wondered if Griswald had finally used godcode to crack the
Internal Revenue Service's on-line site. Griswald was a hacker
who went places where Judy didn't dare to go. He'd even cracked
the CIA's server. Judy had never met him in person, but they'd been
swapping techniques for two years. Their communications always
centered around networks, never anything personal. Griswald still
thought TerMight was a guy.

Maybe today, Judy would tell him she was a girl. Maybe
today, she'd find out where in San Jose he lived. With this DVD
job and the Laguna Savings mess out of the way, she'd take a
little vacation, head up north . . .

No, she'd never have the guts.

The VileSpawn main window flashed to her screen.

@>>>>>---

A dead black rose. The symbol of death.

CHAPTER 4

Beneath the black rose there was a message:

```
Hailstorm dead from suicide. Yesterday, in
Seattle.
```

TerMight had never had any on-line contact with Hailstorm. He was just a name, a flamboyant superhacker. Odd that he'd committed suicide, though. Most computer guys wanted to live forever, always checking out the latest hardware. Nobody pulled the plug intentionally.

Judy punched in a search for recent messages from Griswald. No luck. He hadn't been on VileSpawn in ages. But someone had posted a message *about* Griswald.

```
Anyone hear from Griswald? He hasn't been
seen at his usual haunts, and his friends
are worried. If you've had any contact with
him in the past few days or know his where-
abouts, please post a message here. We're
not looking to make a fuss. We just want to
make sure he's okay.
```

A strange message with no signature. Judy read it three times, wondering what was going on. Hailstorm dead by suicide. Griswald missing. Weird.

She logged off VileSpawn and stared at the screen: sapphire blue deeper than ocean and swirling like a tidepool, white letters fuzzing like the flap of gulls' wings over Doheny lagoon.

"Shutdown." The laptop went to sleep.

No beach for Judy today. She had to return to Laguna Savings—in the flesh—and check on Jose.

Someone was hollering. Trev, the superintendent. "Hey, Judy! Open up!"

What did *he* want?

"Come on, Judy, *open the door!*" A fist banging wood, then a key grating, a knob twisting. Trev came storming into her apartment, clad in a red Speedo swimsuit. His skin was mahogany, his black hair crimped and long. His foot came down on a chip, and he winced as prongs drove into his sole.

"Damn, Judy, what have you done *now*? I was talking to my mother in Pasadena when the phone went dead. Did a quick check on the line in my bedroom and that's not working either. All the phones in the building are dead."

"Dead," Judy repeated, trying to make sense from what he was saying. "The lines are dead?"

"That's right. What did you do *this* time?" Trev stepped over the minilamps and buzzers, the batteries and volt clips: Judy's electronic carpet. He stared into Judy's eyes.

"Trev, I haven't done anything. How can all the phones be dead? They run on different lines."

"Don't know, Judy; just figured you did it."

Her phone lines were dead. One top hacker was dead. Another was missing. Some unknown hotshot had cracked into *her* Laguna server . . .

Judy knew the on-line handles of all the top hackers on the West Coast. There were only a few in her league. Who was Helraze?

Panic began to well up inside her.

"Don't understand. Don't understand. Have to go—"

She started scooping components from the floor, stuffing them into the pockets of her shorts. She grabbed a bunch of cable ties—nylon strips in different lengths. Closed her laptop, detached the cables, slipped the machine into its case along with the netpad.

"Judy. What are you doing?"

She heard Trev's voice, but she didn't look at him, didn't respond. She had to think.

First Helraze, hitting Laguna Savings.

Then Hailstorm, killing himself.

Then Griswald, probably the best hacker on the West Coast, just disappearing . . . poof.

Now TerMight's phone lines going out in the middle of a peaceful summer afternoon.

Four seemingly unrelated incidents—or were they? It didn't make sense.

She was getting out, taking everything that mattered—her laptop and netpad, her electronic gadgets, her Rollerblades . . . she draped them across her shoulder.

She reached for the door and swung it open.

Firmly planted on the landing, as if waiting for her, stood the two men from the Pontiac Velux Plus. Each held open a wallet containing an official-looking badge.

"Judith Carmody?" the stunt hunk said.

"Who wants to know?" she stammered.

"Tony Tuska, ISD. This is my partner, Paul Smith."

ISD. Internet Security Department. The government agency that handled computer crime. Judy had worked with agents from the LA office more than once, helping them track down Internet pirates. She didn't recognize either of these two, though their badges looked right. Maybe they came from outside the Los Angeles area.

Maybe they had found Helraze; maybe they were here to help her.

"Is this about Laguna Savings?" she asked.

Tony Tuska nodded. "Exactly."

CHAPTER 5

"What's going on?" Trev asked as Judy stepped back over the threshold, the two men following. He rose from the sofa, his feet crunching chip prongs. "Who are these guys, Judy?"

Tony Tuska frowned.

His partner, Paul Smith, shut the door, then crossed the room and leaned against the kitchen countertop. His elbow shoved paper plates to the floor. "Sorry." He retrieved the plates, put them on the pile of plastic forks and spoons.

"So who's the beachboy?" Tuska asked. "We thought you lived alone."

There was something wrong with these guys. They were too direct. Even ISD agents commented on the weather and gave Judy fake smiles aimed to charm her and loosen her up. And Tony Tuska, with all his muscles, didn't look anything like an ISD computer geek, though Paul Smith looked kind of nerdy.

"Trev, these guys are Internet Security. Maybe you should go."

"No," Tony Tuska said. "That won't be necessary. We only need to ask a few questions. Your boyfriend can stay."

"Trev's not my—" Judy began; then she shut her mouth. It seemed to her very odd that the ISD would send two out-of-town agents to talk with her, when she knew most of the LA staff on a first-name basis. Also, there was no reason for them to concern themselves about her personal life.

"No one else around, is there?" Tuska asked. "We're not interrupting a party or something?"

"A party—on Tuesday afternoon?" Judy said. "Not likely."

"Check around, Paul," Tuska said.

Smith nodded and went into Judy's bathroom. The shower curtain rustled.

"Hey, what the hell do you think you're doing?" Trev demanded. "Got a warrant? Are you charging Judy with a crime, or what?"

Judy's muscles tightened. There was an ISD agent who wasn't acting like an ISD agent in her bathroom, rifling through her tampons and deodorant.

"Sorry, Ms. Carmody," Tuska said. The wallet and badge were gone from his hand. Instead, he held a snub-nosed revolver, and it was pointed at her stomach. "Your boyfriend complicates an otherwise simple situation. Please don't be alarmed. We're here strictly on business. Just relax and no one will get hurt."

Judy backed against Trev, and he gripped her shoulders. She could feel the heat of his body behind her. His breath was coming in rapid blasts, his sweat slicking her skin all the way down her back.

Paul Smith emerged from the bathroom. His left hand smoothed some gray strands over his bald spot. His right hand reached into his pocket. "We're all alone. No problem." His hand came out of the pocket. It held a gun, just like Tuska's.

"A cozy little scene," Tuska said. "A pretty girl and her lover, spending a lazy summer afternoon together. Somehow, I expected better of you, TerMight. Your file led me to believe you had some class. Never expected to find you shacked up with a beach bum."

Judy couldn't speak, couldn't move. *He knew her handle.* She'd worked on projects for the government. NSA, CIA, FBI— she had top secret clearances with all the alphabet agencies. She was well known by members of the National Security Agency's Information System Security Organization, the FBI's National

Computer Crime Squad, and the Defense Department's Computer Emergency Response Team. Somewhere in D.C. there had to be a computer file covering just about every aspect of her life.

Tuska had to be government; nobody else had access to that information. Yet, for some reason, he was threatening her with a gun. It didn't make sense. A cold dizziness pounded her, and the men went fuzzy before her eyes, as if shot into a million bits of color.

"Who *are* these guys, Judy?" Trev's grip tightened on her shoulders, bringing her back. His body was a solid wall, tight against her, holding her upright.

"Don't know," she managed to say. They couldn't be from Internet Security. Judging from her own experience, ISD agents never carried guns. There wasn't much need for firepower when dealing with renegade computer operators or illegal porn site sponsors. If there was any chance of violence, the ISD just called in local cops for backup. So who were these guys working for? And what did they want with her?

Paul Smith said, "Beachboy complicates matters. Loose end. Doesn't fit the scenario."

Brushing his too-heavy beard, Tuska nodded. "Right. So much for nice and easy. Never occurred to me that TerMight would be shacking up."

If she weren't so frightened, Judy would have laughed. Finding her with Trev in the apartment, both of them in skimpy bathing suits, the two men had jumped to conclusions. She saw no reason to correct them. Hopefully, Trev had enough brains to keep silent, too.

"Forget suicide," Smith said. "Not with two of them."

"Robbery?" Tuska suggested.

A wave of fear swept over Judy. She shifted, the Rollerblade wheels digging into her shoulder. Immediately, Tuska shifted the gun so that it pointed at Judy's forehead. One squeeze of the trigger and her brains would be splattered across the apartment.

"Not a sound, please," Tuska said. "Just sit down and keep quiet."

Judy sank onto the sofa, pulling Trev beside her. The exposed cushion wire ripped into her shorts and raked her upper thighs. Judy eased the Rollerblades off her shoulder, dropped them to her lap. The strap of her computer case cut into her flesh, but she kept the machine beneath her right arm and close to her body. This computer was her life, and she refused to let it go.

Paul Smith laughed and kicked at the junk on the floor. "You're kidding, right? Robbery in a junkyard like this? How about fire?"

Tuska shook his head. "Arson's risky. Investigators are suspicious bastards. Must be something easier. I need to think."

He sat on the gutted minitowers that served as Judy's coffee table. His partner's gun, not wavering an inch, was pointed at Trev's forehead.

Gone now was any pretense of questions. As far as Tuska and Smith were concerned, Judy and Trev could have been pieces of furniture. Clearly, these guys had nothing to do with the mess at Laguna Savings. They were killers. And *she* was their target.

The only reason she was still alive was that Trev had seen them. They had to kill him, as well.

Judy had to *do* something . . . but *what*?

"Murder suicide," Smith said. "Beachboy shoots girl. Then kills himself. Nice and easy, no problem with motive. Lover's quarrel."

"Just *what* are you saying?" Trev said, his voice a harsh whisper.

Smith slanted his gun at Trev's waist. "Don't push, beachboy." His voice was flat. "This close, a bullet would blast a hole in your gut wide enough to drive a truck through. You'll bleed to death trying to keep your intestines from spilling over the floor. It's an awfully messy way to die. So don't make trouble. Understand?"

Judy's ears were ringing. She couldn't be hearing these words, *couldn't* be. Her hands shook on her lap. They were clammy, cold with sweat.

Dust swirled around the men; the sun cast shadows into the hollows beneath their cheekbones. Tall and thin, with an air of casual brutality, Paul Smith actually appeared bored, and Judy had no doubt that he was. He stared at them with empty brown eyes.

Tony Tuska seemed to be in charge. He still wore his sunglasses, but Judy envisioned that, beneath them, his eyes held no more emotion than Smith's. The images of the two killers seared into Judy's brain.

Her gaze dropped to her Rollerblades. They weren't much, but they were her only weapon. How long would it take to swing them into the men's faces and escape? Probably too long.

"Beachboy as the shooter?" Tuska said. "Then he offs himself."

Smith's eyes narrowed in concentration. "Need to be careful about the powder burns. With two deaths, cops spend a lot more time investigating than they would with an ordinary suicide."

"You can't get away with this," Trev said angrily. He started to rise from the sofa. "You're both crazy."

"Consider this a quick education, beach bum," Paul Smith said, a slight smile crossing his lips. He shoved the barrel of his gun under Trev's nose, so that steel pressed against skin. The building superintendent froze. "We *are* getting away with it. You've been screwing the wrong babe. She's too damned smart for her own good. Now sit down and shut up."

Judy grabbed Trev's wrist, pulled him back onto the sofa. Something wet seeped from her leg—blood—and she squirmed on the cushion wire, trying to shift closer to him.

"Girl first," Tuska said, dropping his arm so his elbow rested on his thigh and his gun pointed at Judy's stomach. "Beachboy we do with the muzzle in his mouth, his finger on the trigger. Neat and simple. Like the Navajo operation."

Judy laughed shrilly. She was running out of time, needed to make something happen. She had to jerk out of Judy mode, become TerMight. Had to say the right things. Had to *think*.

Her words came out in pieces. "Trev. Not beach . . . lover—" She broke off, unable to continue.

"Judy and I aren't lovers," Trev said. "She hasn't got a lover, and everyone in this building knows it. And that neither of us owns a gun. Police find us blown away, they'll know it's bullshit."

Tuska stared at Judy. "Muscleboy's right. According to Ter-Might's file, she's a strict loner." He raised his left hand and rubbed his eyes beneath the sunglasses. "I'm getting a migraine. Maybe faking an attempted robbery would be easier."

"Better than all this damned talking," Smith complained, glancing at Tuska. "I hate talking."

As Smith shifted his eyes to Tuska, Trev hurled himself from the sofa. Judy bolted upright.

Trev rammed his head like a cannonball into Smith's stomach. The two men tumbled back over the minitowers in a jumble of arms and legs.

Tuska swung his gun around, aimed it at Trev. His finger squeezed the trigger. To Judy, it seemed as if everything shifted into slow motion. He was *squeezing the trigger* . . .

"No!"

Judy's skates slammed into Tuska's wrist.

Something snapped, and Tuska shrieked.

"No, you won't kill anyone, *no!*" She smashed her computer case into his beard. She'd never been this angry in her life. Never felt the blaze of pure fury rising in her veins, pumping through her, taking control. She would kill Tuska. Kill Paul Smith. *Kill*.

Tuska's sunglasses fell and clattered across the minitowers, to the floor.

A few feet away, a gun went off. Plaster shattered, and the smell of gunpowder filled the room. Trev was on top of Smith, desperately struggling to keep the killer down. In one hand, flat against the floor, Smith still gripped his gun.

Despite his size and weight, Trev was waging a losing battle. His opponent was a trained fighter. Another few seconds and Smith would be free. Still holding a deadly weapon.

Judy raised her computer case again and slammed it against Smith's hand. Bones cracked. For an instant, Smith stopped struggling, his eyes glazed over with shock.

"Come on!" Judy screamed, grabbing Trev by the hair. With all her strength, she yanked him across the apartment. They stumbled through the door and onto the landing.

She charged down the steps leading outside. She was almost to the door when high above, a gun fired three times. Then there was a loud gasp behind her.

She glanced back.

Trev was staggering, his body jerking as if he'd been hit by an invisible hammer. He dropped to his hands and knees.

There was blood. Killers. Blood.

"Go," Trev whispered, his face ashen. "Run, Judy, run."

"I'll get you, bitch," Smith hissed from the third-floor landing. Two bullets cracked the floor, inches from Judy's feet. "I'm gonna blow your fucking brains out!"

Trev collapsed on his stomach. Blood trickled from the up-stairs landing like rain from a roof gutter.

Judy pushed through the door that led to the yard. Trev was shot, killers after her. She had to get away *now*. Death was sec-onds behind.

She scanned the street.

Their car.

Through a blur of bougainvillea pink, she raced toward the killers' car. Less than a hundred yards, it felt like miles. She felt weak, wanted to collapse, let it all dissolve away. But she couldn't stop running. She couldn't stop thinking of Smith, cursing, threatening to blow her head off.

Reaching the car, she grabbed the handle. It wouldn't budge. There was a keypad beneath the grip: the car was electronically sealed, protected by an encrypted password.

Judy wrenched the netpad from her computer case. With a computerized key, the car had to be on the Net. She touched the JUDY icon that brought up her secret crack page and fingered UN-LOCK. Instantly, the netpad dropped from graphics interface to command mode. The words *ping radius=1 dimension=m* flashed, and the screen showed all computer identification codes within a one-meter radius: the only one was the car's number, 29.555.22.3. The UNLOCK icon disappeared as it applied the cor-rect code. The door lock popped open. All in seconds.

Behind her, the door of her apartment building slammed open. She looked back. Paul Smith, his smashed hand tucked under one arm, face contorted in pain, stumbled into the yard. She was running out of time.

She yanked open the door and threw herself onto the front seat. Wrenching herself around, she slammed the door shut. A bullet pounded against the trunk. In the rearview mirror, she saw Smith staggering down the street.

Locks clacked shut as the car went on full security alert. She was safe for a moment, but even fiber-reinforced shatterproof glass wouldn't stop a bullet at close range.

The dashboard Net console flickered to life, displaying color pie charts about the car's operation, as well as Internet channels for weather, sports, and news headlines. "Good afternoon," a man's voice piped from the digital speakers. Judy hated these damned user-friendly cars. "If you state your next destination, I'll be glad to—"

Without a key, she would have to enter the password code—twice—followed by a sublevel code . . .

No time for tech.

She groped beneath the steering wheel. Plastic ripped. Two wires touched. The engine roared. For once, she was glad that she'd grown up in the rural sticks of Pennsylvania, that Dad had taught her . . .

No time for *that* crap, either.

She pressed the gas pedal to the floor. The car leapt forward, the digital voice bleating about the dangers of sudden acceleration. In the mirror, she caught a glimpse of her pursuer standing in the middle of the street. Then, the car careened around the end of Laguna Crescent onto Route 1, the Pacific Coast Highway, and he was gone.

CHAPTER 6

Pressure. Cal never worked well under pressure. People staring over his shoulder made him want to scream. He needed to be alone to finish this project. But privacy was the one thing he never got here.

"Okay, Nikonchik, we're down to the wire." Harry fiddled with his string tie. It hung from his usual stupid turquoise slide thing. His skin was like old leather, his breath like old meat. An ugly dude, with an ugly temper. Worse than the creeps who used to beat up Cal for being a nerd.

"Thursday's coming up quick," Harry continued. "We paid your asking price in cold, hard cash. It's time for results."

The asshole just never *let up*. Thought he was so cool, with his handlebar mustache and all his muscles. And that stupid Southern drawl.

Made Cal want to puke.

If the guy had any brains, then he wouldn't need *Cal*, would he?

But this was Cal's first real job, so Cal had to be careful. Didn't want to get fired, or anything.

Cal lifted his fingers from the keyboard, then rose from the black leather chair and turned to face Harry and his partner,

Greg. His stomach was churning. These two scared all hell out
of him. Like old clacker Morgan, the witch who had taught social studies back at Bonita High School.

Authority figures.

But Bonita High was history for Cal. No more Mrs. Morgan.
He was seventeen now, an adult.

And this job was his ticket.

"I'm working as fast as I can," he said, trying to sound laid-
back and all adultlike. "Swinging a transfer as large as you want,
without setting off all sorts of alarms, takes serious programming. That's why I'm running tests first. You want everything
done clean and fast. No entry traces."

Greg placed his hands on his hips and shifted his weight. Behind him, the bright desert sun poured through the bedroom
window. Though the air-conditioning was turned up full blast,
Cal was drenched in sweat. His long, blond hair hung limply
down his back.

The heat didn't seem to bother Greg, though. During his free
time, Greg exercised outside. He was a nutcase.

But he was smart. Cal could see it in his blue eyes: they reflected a cold, calculating mind. And Greg had that kind of coolness Cal had always wished *he* had. The kind of always-in-control
charm that made girls giggle.

Girls had always laughed in Cal's face.

"You gonna quit stalling, or what?" Harry said.

Greg gave Cal a smile that said, yeah, Harry's a jerk, but I'll
take care of it. He said, "Look, Harry, Cal hasn't been here all
that long, and he's been working night and day on this thing."

"That's right," Cal piped in.

"On the other hand," Greg continued, "Mr. Ingersoll needs the
project finished in less than a week. He promised the agency results by the end of the month. Mr. Ingersoll reports directly to
the head of the NSA, Cal, and we can't stall him much longer."

Mr. Ingersoll. The big bossman. A top dude in the National
Security Agency.

"It's not like I take any breaks," Cal protested. "It's not like
I'm hanging in a MUD, pretending to be a transvestite, or sitting
on my butt, watching vids on the commercial net. This computer
doesn't even have a drive for playing DVDs. I could use a little

music, you know. Comp Patrol, Millennium Plus Five, stuff that has a beat. How about that, at least?"

Greg shrugged. "I don't see why not. We can cover it under miscellaneous supplies and use a cash voucher. I'll pass along the request, but you know the problem, Cal. We've got a limited budget and it barely covers the day-to-day costs of the operation. Buying all the computer equipment you wanted was easy. That's top priority. Squeezing out funds for creature comforts isn't so simple. Damned Congress watches every penny we spend like they're personally guarding the mint."

"A DVD player and a few discs won't put a dent in the national debt," Cal said. "Write it off as a memory cache."

Actually, he couldn't complain too much. The place he shared with Harry and Greg was pretty fine. It served as the guest cottage for the big house on the hill, a few hundred yards away. It had a small living room, a kitchen, two bedrooms, and a fancy bathroom. It even had a whirlpool tub and a sonic shower.

There were prints on the wall, western scenes by some guy named Remington, and the furniture looked barely used. Whoever maintained the place apparently didn't have many overnight guests. The National Security Agency men shared one bedroom and did all the cooking. Cal was left free to spend all of his time with the computer.

Harry said, "We do for you; you do for us. Teamwork. Just no Net hopping. I don't want to catch you at that again. Focus on the job. If secrecy's broken, the project collapses. We hired you to plug a major hole in the Internet banking system. Once you're done, you get big bucks. Then you can go back to San Jose, buy the fanciest sound system you want, crank it up, and blow down your neighbors' walls."

He continued. "It's been a week already. Get it done, Cal, then you can head for the beach with nothing to do but pick up girls and ride the surf."

Cal nearly trembled at the thought. Yeah, that was what he wanted all right, what he'd wanted all his life. His own car, a top-of-the-line computer, and lots of babes chasing him. After years of being Cal the drone, Cal the hacker, Cal the guy you copied your homework from, he'd finally be someone important.

It sucked being such a social misfit. Tall, scrawny, gawky. All through high school his only friends had been computer geeks. He'd never even had a girlfriend.

But it wasn't Cal's fault. After all, he'd grown up on that stupid commune. Nobody else had been forced to live with parents who were poets and back-to-nature freaks.

And then there was his brother. Dan. Mr. Overprotective.

Don't bother Cal. He has homework to do.

Don't bother Cal. He can't be out late at night.

Like he'd get beaten up going to some movie or to a concert with a bunch of friends.

Like he'd ever *had* a bunch of friends.

"Why don't you just get back to work?" Greg said, almost gently. "I'll make you something to eat, to keep you going. What do you want? The usual?"

Yeah, the usual. Cal nodded.

"I'll ask the boss about the DVD player," Harry said, walking to the bedroom door. "No problem. Should have an answer after lunch."

"One sandwich coming up," Greg said. "Turkey okay?"

"Fine," Cal said. His menu for the past week had consisted of fat-free turkey, roast beef, and chicken. Just once, he'd really like an olive-and-tuna pizza.

With the agents finally gone, he shut the door and walked to the window. He parted the white lace curtains, stared at the rolling desert that stretched past the barbed-wire security fence. It seemed to go on forever, mounds of glimmering neon sand spilling into the huge white sun far beyond. Giant cacti poked from the sand. Squat Mojave yuccas, spiky and weird, looked like bones dripping with frail flesh, baking endlessly in the soundless sweep of neon haze.

Even with the climate control turned to maximum, Cal could feel the waves of heat pressing at the glass window. It was nearly unbearable.

He returned to his makeshift desk, a huge slab of plywood resting on gray cinderblocks. It looked strange sitting in the center of a fancy bedroom complete with leather chairs, blue throw rug, and lace curtains, but the guest house hadn't been furnished with a computer center. They'd improvised.

Except for the dedicated modem line, there wasn't even a

phone. Isolation and secrecy—typical NSA paranoia. Cal's computer didn't even have the software that would allow him to place simple phone calls. He could easily download what he wanted, or whip it up from scratch, but he saw no point. This government project was his big chance. There was no way he was going to get caught talking to his brother, Dan, or any of his friends. No way he was going to screw this up.

The agents didn't even use cellular phones—too easily tapped, they said. All calls had to be made on the secure line from the house on the hill.

Cal stretched a rubber band, then wound it through his hair, twisting the sweaty mess into a ponytail. When he got back to San Jose, he'd get a buzz cut. Always, in the past, he'd liked his hair long. To hide his face. After caking this heist, though, he wouldn't have to hide from anyone.

Mr. Ingersoll wanted to make the Internet Security Department sit up and take notice. Cal would have them falling off their chairs. He'd prove that hackers ruled the world. He'd prove that *he* ruled the world.

Make a name for yourself on the Web, and people in a hundred countries knew who you were. Cal was tired of being invisible.

Even the hackers on VileSpawn knew little about him. It cracked him up, really. A few subtle clues, and they thought he was in his twenties, a college dropout, a hacker with years of experience. Nobody but Jeremy knew he had just graduated high school and had no intention of *bothering* with college.

Even Jeremy, his only real friend, treated Cal like a little kid. Just because Jeremy was older and had all those degrees. Jeremy didn't mind using Cal, though—to pull off the heavyweight stuff on his big projects.

And Dan—he wasn't about to tell anyone about the code Cal had created for his business. Nor was Cal stupid enough to list *that* program on his résumé.

Cal was always invisible.

He settled into the black upholstered chair in front of the computer. The leather stuck to his skin, but he ignored it. His fingers danced across the keys.

He tried to bring up a Laguna Savings Web page, but failed.

Someone at the bank must be screwing around, maybe updating hit stats or something. The server was flaking.

No biggie, just a minor annoyance. Cal logged onto a computer at Newport Beach Financial. As superuser—god with total access—he popped to the main server, where he displayed a Web page. There was no risk of detection. No one would ever know he was there.

Despite all the software security used, the page still had plenty of holes. Years ago, Java had done the simple trick of cracking the server right off Web pages. Then had come ActiveX. Now there were dozens of new technologies that let Cal hack Web sites. His personal favorite was ControlFreak. That little baby had been a godsend to hackers.

ControlFreak applications ran all over the Web. *You can't enter this Web site unless you enable ControlFreak.* Who could resist a ControlFreak site? Everyone enabled ControlFreak.

Interactive, top-speed virtual reality, complete with voice chats, movies, sliding panels, dribbling goo, and awesome monsters. Cal had spent hours chatting with Jeremy in ControlFreak sites. Cal always turned Jeremy into a monster, who in turn attacked Cal's avatar—a muscled guy a lot like Greg—whenever Cal said something Jeremy didn't like.

ControlFreak also provided a simple way to break into a bank.

The Laguna bank had provided employees unrestricted outgoing Net access. It was simple to scan for a worker who had viewed an Internet ControlFreak page. All you had to do was imbed a one-bit by one-bit hidden ControlFreak blip on a jazzed site, then wait for a bank employee to hit the site. Then you could capture the employee's username and password, log onto the bank server *as* the employee. From there, it was baby play to capture bank account transactions.

But Cal didn't need ControlFreak to crack the Laguna bank server. And besides, at Laguna Savings, someone had plugged the Freak gaps a long time ago.

All Cal needed was a microslice of info, and he'd grabbed that last night. Sure, the bank had changed its passwords. Big deal.

He'd sniffed the raw Ethernet lines for packets with log-ins and passwords. Presto. Any jerk could get an Ethernet sniffer, free off the Net, by anonymous file transfer.

Decryption of the new password file had been simple enough. A few calls to the getpwent system program, and bam, Cal knew where the shadowed password was hidden. He decrypted the superuser password in the usual way, took two minutes.

People were so scared of stuff like ControlFreak. They just didn't realize the *truth*. They never had. No matter what method was used—even Rivest-Shamir-Adleman crypto, the so-called fail-safe RSA—hackers like Cal cracked it. Ethernet sniffing and password cracking: it was the easy route to millions. Siphon fifty cents from each of a million accounts, and what did you get? Five hundred thousand bucks. With nobody the wiser.

But that wasn't the way Cal operated. He was working for the government. Doing NSA business. Strictly legit.

And for now, no Net hopping. It wouldn't be a good idea to let Harry catch him at *that* again. Cal was only allowed to Net hop in the course of *government* business.

On the other hand, what harm was a little fun? Harry was a dweeb. And Cal wouldn't let himself be caught again.

On the Newport Beach Financial server, signed on as superuser, Cal inserted some fun stuff that mischievously changed customer buttons.

Enter account number became *Enter driver's license number per IRS regulation 25208-B*.

It never hurt to get license numbers. He could use licenses to get any information he wanted. About girls, for instance, like their full medical histories pulled from insurance files, their physical dimensions . . .

If only he could find his dream babe, someone like the virtual-Net star, Mistie Lane.

Of course, Mistie wasn't real, but who cared? She was an *awesome* piece of 3-D imagery. Programmed to look and sound and react any way you wanted her. Mistie was United Cable Network's hottest star, real *or* virtual.

A few minutes spent with Mistie wouldn't disrupt the NSA schedule, Cal decided. At least, not much. Dropping out of the Newport bank server, he typed *View United Cable Network publicity photos*. With the touch of an icon, he downloaded the Mistie 3-D library from the UCN publicity site. These were from Mistie's international hit show, *Beach Babe, Private Eye*.

Each library offered Mistie as a different nationality: Italian, Japanese, French, Cambodian, American, and so on.

Cal touched the American Mistie library icon. She appeared on his screen in classic Beach Babe form: tangled black hair falling halfway down her back, huge black eyes lit by raw sexual fire. Gyrating in a microbikini, cavorting on a beach, staring Cal straight in the eyes, begging him to touch her. He touched. She writhed. Then she giggled and scampered away.

He missed his personal Mistie library, which he had stored on his computer back in San Jose, filled with custom-coded Misties. There he could have *felt* her hot skin beneath his fingers. *Smelled* her. Drank her in.

Still, this was better than nothing.

The door to the kitchen banged open, causing the thin walls of the guest cottage to shake. "Lunch is ready."

Cal's heart nearly exploded. Lost in his dreams, he'd forgotten Greg was just down the hall.

He hit the CLOSE icon. Mistie's image disappeared. He jumped from the chair, his skinny body shaking like the plywood walls, as the NSA agent came through the door.

"Working already?" Greg asked as he set the turkey sandwich and two colas on the desk. Somehow, though, Greg seemed to know better.

"Uh, yeah, really pushing," Cal answered. He grabbed the sandwich and took a huge bite. His words came out muffled around the wad of turkey. "But the music would really help. And I need privacy, Greg. It's hard for me to concentrate when someone barges into the room."

"I'll get you the music, Cal. Promise. But no more screwing around. Time is tight." Greg lowered his voice to a whisper. "Probably I shouldn't tell you this, but we're buddies, right? They've been talking about finding someone else if you can't finish the job. Some other hacker, like TerMight or Mercy. The boss is starting to get nervous you're going to blow the big deadline."

Someone *else*?

"I'll do it, I'll do it," Cal said, nearly choking on his food. "Tell Mr. Ingersoll I'll get everything done."

"I've got absolute faith in you, Cal." Greg slapped Cal on the back, a man-to-man macho thing, then squeezed his shoulder tightly. "So don't screw up. Prove me right."

Greg grabbed an issue of *Sports Illustrated* from the night-stand. "You can have all the privacy you want, kid. I'll be in my bedroom if you need me."

With that, Greg left the room, and Cal found himself left alone once again, to consider what had been said.

As he calmed down, Cal was more acutely aware than ever of the isolation in which he was working. It was claustrophobic, being shut up like this.

Outside, the yucca trees baked. The sun caressed the sand. Shimmering waves of blast-furnace air rose off the desert floor. Not even a lizard moved in the intense afternoon heat.

Inside, the guest house was too clean, too neat, *too proper* for a hacker like Cal. It reminded him of the hospital he'd stayed in ten years ago, after the big fire. Antiseptic. Sterile.

Cal had to get out of here, and soon, or he'd go nuts.

It was time to get down and dirty, finish the job. Life had pushed him around long enough. Dan, Jeremy, everyone used him for their own purposes. They claimed they meant well, but Cal never got any of the benefits. It was time for him to get the rewards.

The sandwich sat on a sterile white plate, layered with turkey, lettuce, and tomato. Greg believed in healthy meals. Cal longed for greasy tacos and cheese fries. He needed a junk-food fix.

How much more of this could he take?

Over the next three days, he had to finish the first part of the project: arrange the transfer of a billion dollars, untraceable, to the numerous secured bank accounts set up by the government guys. Then, afterward, having proved the threat was real, he'd transfer all the dough back.

From his file of customer credit card numbers, Cal chose a few select ones belonging to people who had more money than they could manage. Millionaires lounging on Newport Beach in tight-security mansions. He withdrew five million from each of their bank accounts.

Child's play.

Boring.

It had taken only an evening's work to break the bank's credit card numbers. All cards still used the old Luhn Check Digit Algorithm. Any card with an even number of digits was easily cracked: Cal doubled every odd-numbered digit, and if the result exceeded nine, he subtracted nine. Instant credit card number.

The method he applied to cards with an odd number of digits was almost identical. And he could always spot a Newport Savings number. It contained the digits *4555*.

Digicards were just as easy to break. Hackers everywhere were breaking them and living the good life.

But that was a freaking bore chore.

And Cal was no thief.

What he'd done for Dan, well, that had been a special case. Dan was his *brother*, for God's sake.

"This isn't work for amateurs, kid. We need a real pro." That's what Greg had said when he'd first contacted Cal about the job. The government guys had E-mailed him through the VileSpawn bulletin board. Cal always hung out there, a guru's guru. "Not only do you have to beat bank security, but you gotta steer clear of ISD, too. We're out to give them a real test. Their programmers will treat you as the enemy, do anything they can to stop you."

Greg and Harry had met with him in person and told him about the job. They'd been standing near the volleyball nets on the beach at Santa Cruz. All around them girls had sauntered by—long-legged girls in tiger-print thongs, string bikinis that concealed nothing. The agents seemed not to notice. Their eyes, hidden behind dark sunglasses, never left Cal.

They flashed some fancy papers and badges for his inspection. Working for the National Security Agency, they were hyperlegit, cool dogs in shades, musclebrains. Big boys with big bucks to spend for the right talent.

"Sure, I'll do it," Cal had replied, even as he watched a girl smoothing lotion on her tanned stomach. "You came to the right man."

But now, despite his bragging, Cal was growing impatient. He wanted to finish the job and return to his apartment. He hated the desert, and Greg and Harry weren't his idea of great company.

And the guns bothered him. Both Harry and Greg carried

guns—sleek steely things nestled in shoulder holsters. Guns they cleaned a lot.

"It's part of the job," Greg had said. "Can't be an NSA agent and not carry a gun. We're just like cops. Required to be prepared at all times. Even in the middle of the desert. Nothing to worry about. We're not expecting trouble."

Nonetheless, Cal hadn't felt any better. The guns made him real nervous.

But what worried him most of all was the fact that Mr. Ingersoll knew all about the work Cal had done for Dan. Turned out, it was *that* code that had originally attracted NSA attention.

One word from Mr. Ingersoll, and Cal and Dan were toast. Even if it wasn't for the big money, Cal would have been forced to do this job. Whether he liked it or not, he was stuck here until the project was over.

It was time to get back to work. But first, he'd dial into VileSpawn. There he'd get a quick fix, a dose of superguru power that would help him forge through the long night of hacking off Helraze.

He logged on as Calvin, the handle he always used for idle hacks. It was the name he preferred, unless he was *super*-hacking. When he was in superhack mode, he was far more fierce, and used a handle nobody could trace.

ā>>>>- - -

A dead black rose scrolled onto the screen. Cal's fingers froze on the keys. He couldn't believe what he was seeing, a log-on message that proclaimed:

```
Hailstorm dead from suicide. Yesterday, in
Seattle.
```

Hailstorm? Larry Chomsky, the guy who along with Jeremy had helped Cal perfect his genetic code? He was *dead*?

Impossible. They'd been hanging out in a ControlFreak room just six days ago, the night before Cal had left for the desert. Larry had been fine, really cool. He couldn't be dead.

Cal scanned the rest of the messages. He blinked when he

came across one about Griswald. Someone on the Net was worried about Griswald. Who? Why?

Cal was Griswald. His alter ego was a Net scourge, a code-sniffing demon. Unbeatable, unstoppable, Griswald was a Net ghost, a hacker who did anything he wanted and got away with it, nice and clean, without a trace. There was no reason that anyone on VileSpawn should be searching for him.

No reason at all.

CHAPTER 7

Picking up speed, Judy gunned the Velux Plus down the wide, four-lane highway. It had been a long time since she'd driven a new car. She'd forgotten how fast they moved. "Good getaway car," she muttered, as she swept along the cliffs overhanging the ocean, speeding north toward Newport Beach. No reason to leave the area. By now, the shooting would have cops all over the place. It wouldn't be long before it was safe to return home and figure out exactly what this mess was about.

The local police were okay, the honest ones at least. They could manage drug busts and traffic tickets fine. But, Tony Tuska and Paul Smith had claimed to be ISD. No way, not with those guns. The truth would come out. Still, the two men had known her handle. The only way they could have learned that was from confidential security-clearance files. Was the government somehow involved? It would take more than the Laguna Beach Police Department to piece things together. In all likelihood, Judy would have to dig up the real story herself.

The air was cool, and it helped clear her head. The sky was warm azure, set with tiny pearl clouds. Down on the beach, bright bikinis and silk swim trunks glowed under the hot sun of the late afternoon. Mothers dug in the sand with their children.

She glanced at the car's Net console, reading the script as it scrolled across the screen. The sound was turned off, the way she preferred. She found it too distracting having a voice constantly talking to her, interrupting the news to warn her that she was driving too fast.

Weather:

```
Clear, 85 degrees and rising.
```

Sports: who cared? News:

```
Late-breaking report. Murder at Laguna
Crescent. Building superintendent shot by
tenant. Details to follow.
```

The car swerved, almost shot over the cliff into the ocean. Judy jerked the wheel, regaining control, trying to steer and stare at the screen at the same time.

```
Police are withholding the full details of
the shooting until the dead man's relatives
have been contacted. Currently, an all-
points bulletin has been issued for Judith
Carmody, a tenant in the building where the
shooting took place. She is a female Cau-
casian in her mid-twenties, five feet two
inches, with long auburn hair, last seen
wearing orange shorts and a blue bikini top,
driving a white Pontiac Velux Plus. Au-
thorities have issued a statement that she
is considered armed and dangerous.
```

Judy cursed as an empty pit formed in her stomach.

Tuska and Smith had killed Trev and blamed her for the crime. It was incredible, but true. And nobody put together a frame so fast without megatons of official cooperation. Tuska and Smith had to be FBI. Or NSA.

One thing was certain: she couldn't go to the cops.

Fear. Uncertainty. This wasn't a reality Judy liked. Smith, the crazy one, had said she was too smart for her own good. What had he meant? She needed time—to puzzle it through, figure out who was behind this lunacy. But time was the one commodity she didn't have.

Whatever craziness was taking place, Judy was entirely on her own. She'd always told Steve Sanchez that she didn't need anyone. Now she had to prove it. One mistake, one wrong move, and she was dead.

She could already imagine the headline: HACKER KILLED RE-SISTING ARREST. Judy had to disappear. She couldn't trust any-body. Especially those in authority.

She cut across traffic and pulled onto the shoulder of the highway. Just in case, she let the car idle in the gas-economy mode. There were plenty of other cars parked on the side of the road, their drivers relaxing in the sunshine, car CD players blaring. It was a typical California afternoon. Nobody had any reason to notice her as she sat hunched in her seat. She tried to look casual as she issued instructions to her netpad.

The netpad was all the muscle she needed to cruise the Internet, raiding very specific sites. With its cellular modem and high-speed CPU, the tiny computer really was a hacker's dream tool.

A sticker on the dashboard identified the car as having been rented from the Avis outlet at LAX. It took Judy only a few sec-onds to break into their main computer. A quick scan of records assured her that the Laguna Beach cops hadn't yet done a trace and search on her vehicle. Fourth Amendment paperwork took nearly an hour to file.

As a hacker, she wasn't bound by any such legal restrictions.

Three commands switched the ID numbers of her car with those of one that was in the shop for repairs. When the cops fi-nally did put out a trace, the trail would lead in the wrong direc-tion. It was a simple trick, but one that allowed her to use the car without fear, at least for a while.

Digging further in the rental files, Judy pulled up the vehicle's original rental form. It was criminal trespass, but that was the *least* of her worries.

The car had been rented earlier that same day by Tony Tuska, whose place of residence was listed as New York City. Judy downloaded Tuska's personal data, including his driver's license number and credit card info. That would allow her to run a check on both. She noted that he gave his occupation as independent contractor.

An attached file listed a second driver for the car. Paul Smith, of Baltimore, Maryland. His driver's license number was also provided. And his occupation, again independent contractor.

A tag at the bottom of the form caught her eye. The car had been rented at LAX, for three days. Point of return, however, was listed as San Jose.

San Jose. Where Griswald lived. Another hacker who had been reported missing.

Three days? Today was Tuesday. The car was due in San Jose on Friday morning. Less than seventy-two hours. Not much time, especially given the long drive north up the coast highway. Even inland, it took most of a day. Whatever Tuska and Smith planned to do, they meant to finish it quickly.

Judy pulled out of the Avis agency computer. Next, she did a credit search on Tony Tuska. As a security specialist, Judy had assembled a file of corporate passwords that enabled her to access the financial history of anyone who conducted business over the Net. That meant just about everyone in the world.

Anyone could access this sort of information, really. All it took was a quick and perfectly legal peek at the Securities and Exchange Commission's on-line database. There, any bozo could locate income tax files, salaries, bonuses, stock options, and even unlisted phone numbers for the top dogs who ran major corporations.

Even small bananas, like independent operators with government contracts, were listed in the SEC database. And if not there, they were definitely to be found—in great detail—on the pages that described government contracts.

Judy had removed her own personal data from the SEC and government contract pages long ago. Damned if *she* was going to have her private phone numbers, private statistics, and medical history laid bare on the wide-open, freak-haunted Net.

The information for Tony Tuska came up indicating a squeaky clean record. He lived in an expensive apartment in Manhattan, spent money in fine restaurants, did a good amount of traveling throughout the United States, paid his bills on time every month. His credit and digicard applications listed his profession as investment analyst. No employer was listed.

A steady thrum whirled above her car.

It was a helicopter.

The police.

She tucked the still-open netpad beneath her laptop case. Then she lowered her head, pretended to be napping in the car, like many of the loungers parked around her. She waited, fully expecting a loudspeaker to demand that she immediately get out of the car. She gazed at the steering wheel. Could she somehow elude the cops in traffic? With computerized dispatching, it seemed a worthless hope.

Ten seconds, twenty seconds, thirty seconds. Judy remained motionless, anticipating the worst. Nothing happened. Gradually, the noise overhead lessened, as the helicopter moved north. Peering through the windshield, Judy spotted the call letters of a local radio station emblazoned across the bottom of the helicopter.

She laughed from relief. She was getting way too paranoid.

Back to Tuska's credit report.

On the surface, everything read just fine. No bad checks, no late payments, not a hint of credit risk. The closest thing she could find to a lie was that Tuska's weight was listed at 195. Wishful thinking. The whole report was very amusing.

She didn't believe a word of it.

Reaching across the seat, Judy flipped open her laptop and turned on the power. A simple sensor hooked the computer to the netpad. With the touch of a key, Judy sent CreditCheck—a powerful Internet search engine—sniffing for Tony Tuska's financial profile. Created by the ISD to detect credit card scams, the program was the scourge of con artists throughout the world.

Twenty-three seconds later, Tony Tuska's credit history began to unravel. A vivid pattern of red lights, indicating false or unverified credit references, flashed across the screen. A string of green pinpoints identified large cash transfers from unidentified sources, all taking place within the past few weeks. On the surface, Tony Tuska may have appeared legit, but in reality, his identity was less than thirty days old.

This was standard operating procedure for freelancers who

did work for the government. Judy knew the riff. Accept an assignment, create an identity. Finish the job, wipe the slate clean.

Her real problem was discovering which department Tuska was working for. Unfortunately, all the big agencies knew the dangers of leaving electronic trails. They did their recruiting by personal contact.

Still, Tony Tuska was clumsy. He hadn't killed her, had he? He'd wasted a lot of time, gabbing with his partner, Paul Smith. The two were sloppy, had let a girl escape, a girl without weapons, while they had guns.

And Tuska hadn't wiped his on-line slate clean. There was plenty there for Judy to uncover. Kind of careless for a government agent, even for a freelancer.

Judy dropped his records from her screen. She'd confirmed that he wasn't working on his own. For the moment, she'd have to assume he actually was with some branch of the United States government. But why did the government want her *dead*?

She debated destroying Tony Tuska's credit, cutting off his digicards, as well as his driver's license. She could siphon all the cash from his bank accounts and even identify him as a deadbeat parent—one who owed thousands in child support. It wouldn't take more than the touch of a few icons. As a hacker, she had the power to destroy his life.

She shrugged. Unfortunately, Tuska wasn't real. He was a false identity, one that could be discarded whenever necessary. If she wiped out his credit, the bearded man would merely become someone else. If anything, he'd become more difficult to trace. Leaving him alone was best.

What Judy had to do, and right away, was fill her gas tank, change her appearance, get some food, and make it to San Jose.

She packed the netpad into her laptop case and stashed the equipment beneath the front seat. A few seconds fiddling with the dashboard computer changed the door password to *Ter-Might*. Then, she stepped into the sunshine, locking the car behind her.

A young boy tossed a pink rubber baseball to his father. The ball went wild, flew over the cliff toward the ocean. The boy started crying.

Nobody paid attention to Judy.

She walked quickly past the father and son, past the scattered sun worshipers perched on their cars, baking in the heat. She headed for a Discount Mart that sat across Route 1.

With the Laguna accounts all messed up, and her digicard useless, she had to find an alternative.

She had some options. Like old-time phone cards, digicards had identification numbers concealed beneath sealed plastic. And like old-time phone cards, digicards often were used as prizes to reward people for buying six-packs of cola, rival laundry detergents, and just about everything else—even hemorrhoid ointments.

Throwaway cards. Use them to buy ten bucks' worth of whatever, then toss them in the garbage.

Judy pushed open the steel and glass door of the Discount Mart. The clerk, a guy about her age, flashed a bored smile at her, then returned to stocking shelves by the register.

The store was pretty empty. Not many customers on a nice afternoon like this. One giggling and near-naked girl buying suntan oil. An old guy leafing through magazines.

The cola aisle was up front, too risky. Besides, the security cameras kept that area under constant surveillance. But there were no cameras in the hemorrhoid aisle near the back.

Judy strolled down the aisle, and quietly ripped open a few packages of Dr. Frond's Electrostatic Anti-Inflammatory Hemorrhoid Cream. Yeah, like it was electrostatic—but what the heck, people bought anything if it was advertised as revolutionary. And this junk cost a whopping twenty bucks a pop.

These were ten-buck digicards. She removed a few, stuffed them in her pocket. Then she moved to the cosmetics aisle. A portly old woman with blue-black veins was studying blue-black hair rinses. The woman, standing there in size 50 shorts and a man's Tiger Minileague baseball shirt, avoided Judy's eyes, probably embarrassed that she colored her hair. Ridiculous, as if anyone would believe that a seventy-year-old woman with blue-black hair was sporting her natural color.

Judy had never done a thing to her own hair, hadn't even cut it since she was a kid. She knew nothing about hair dyes.

"Need help, dear?"

Judy jumped, swiveled. The woman was standing a few

inches away, peering at her now. Her brown eyes seemed to say, I know who you are, I know what you're doing . . .

Paranoid. Judy was being paranoid again. She fought her nerves. "I want something razz, a new look," she said, trying to sound punk and silly. She even giggled, feeling absurd.

Trembling fingers, long and wrinkled, reached and stroked Judy's hair. "But you have beautiful hair, dear. Why do anything to it? I once had beautiful hair, too."

Judy grabbed a bottle of greenish-yellow something from the shelf and backed away. And for show, a bottle of green glitter gel. The woman grimaced and turned back to her blue-black dyes.

No cola cards. Make the purchase; get out of the store.

Judy gave the clerk a freebie digicard freshly stolen from the hemorrhoid packages. He didn't even blink. Just took it, zipped it through the register, announced, "Fifty cents left," and handed her the dyes in a brown bag.

No food, no cola, no gas, but she still had twenty bucks in free digicard dough to use later, farther up the road toward San Jose.

She crouched by a garbage bin behind the Discount Mart. Read the back of the greenish-yellow dye bottle. *Apply thoroughly, let soak into hair for an hour, rinse.*

She squeezed the goo out of the bottle and massaged it into her hair. That done, she hurried back across Route 1 to the stolen car. It was locked and secure. Getting in, Judy checked that her laptop was safe.

She noticed the boy and father were now staring at her. Must be her weird wet hair, all the goofy colors. Time to move on, head north.

Judy started the car and cruised back up Route 1, past the ocean and on top of the cliffs, watching the sunlight dancing on the sparkling sand, the kids playing on the beach, the loungers idling and flirting.

As she drove, she again pulled out her netpad and continued searching for clues about Tony Tuska. Using a carefully established search pattern she'd developed over the years, Judy shifted into the American Airlines flight records. Every airline saved passenger lists for thirteen months in case of medical and security checks. American ran a fly-and-drive promotion with

Avis. If Tony Tuska had arrived at LAX that morning, it seemed probable he'd flown American.

Again, searching through passenger lists was a federal crime. The airlines had invested billions in near-foolproof firewalls and encryption systems that were supposed to make sure their data was untouchable. But Judy had helped design dozens of similar systems. When necessary, she could break into files anywhere.

She ran a name scan on all incoming flights from Seattle. In an instant, her laptop beeped, indicating a match. Tony Tuska had arrived at 12:40 in the afternoon on a direct flight from Sea-Tac. Judy flipped through the seat assignments. He had sat in 14C. The passenger in 14B had been Paul Smith.

Judy wished she knew Hailstorm's real name. Still, how many suicides could have occurred in Seattle during the past few days?

Only two suicides had been listed during the past forty-eight hours. Judy pulled up the police reports on both. She instantly dismissed Natasha Hemsky, a sixty-seven-year-old widow, depressed by the recent death of her husband. Which left Lawrence Chomsky, a computer game designer, forty-eight, found dead in his apartment Monday afternoon, the victim of a massive Flash-powder overdose.

Chomsky evidently had a long history of drug use, with arrests dating back to the turn of the century. A former girlfriend, interviewed at the game design workshop where he'd been freelancing, claimed that Chomsky had been drug free for more than a year. Still, there had been enough of the deadly powder in his lungs to kill three people, and investigators had found a half-filled vial in Chomsky's pants pocket.

Since Chomsky had left no suicide note and had been in reasonably good health, the file officially listed his cause of death as accidental. Judy had a terrible feeling that the names of that accident were Tuska and Smith.

Most people booked all flights for a trip at the same time, generally on the same airline. Records showed that Tony Tuska and Paul Smith had first arrived in Seattle Sunday evening on American Airlines flight 149. Hailstorm had died on Monday. Today—Tuesday—Tuska and Smith had arrived in Los Angeles. On Friday morning, the Velux Plus was due to be returned in San Jose.

Judy flipped through the departure lists for Friday afternoon and evening. Tony Tuska showed up on a 6 P.M. flight back to New York City. Paul Smith was booked for Baltimore on the red-eye leaving at midnight.

Stay in town just long enough to get paid. A satchel filled with cash, in small bills. Judy knew the routine. Sometimes the government and the mob both handled covert operations in similar fashion. Judy held the exact same opinion of both organizations. Scum was scum, no matter who paid the bills.

This was like peeling an artichoke. Pull back one layer of leaves to reveal the layer underneath. Then rip off those fronds to display yet another row. And so on and so on until you finally reached the heart.

But this was no chef's chore. It was murder. Hailstorm had been first on the list. Judy had been second, but Trev had died in her place. Was Griswald third? Had he somehow discovered he was marked for death, and pulled a vanishing act? Judy didn't know. But she intended to find out.

She looked at the Net console, touched the NEWS icon. Big debate going on, a special report with top commentators from both the left- and right-wing strands of the news media:

```
Judith  Carmody,  murder  suspect,  still  on
the  loose.  Tied  to  the  underground  hacker
organization,  VileSpawn,  where  computer
felons  are  known  to  trade  pornography  and
tips  for  bombs  and  biological  warfare.
```

What a joke. Yeah, porno, bombs, poison—stock in trade for every hacker. Some people were so stupid.

Porno was for people like her dad. It destroyed families. If there had been any porno on VileSpawn, Judy wouldn't be there. And besides, VileSpawn didn't allow graphics, only text—fast information, no frills.

```
With  much  of  Laguna  Beach  in  chaos  due  to
bank  digicard  malfunctions,  businesses  are
desperate  today.  Top-selling  items:  six-
packs  of  cola  and  beer.
```

And what about Dr. Frond's hemorrhoid ointments? Free digi-cards in those, too. Fortunately, none of them came from Laguna Savings. Jose had sure screwed things up royally.

```
Digital Information Response Team has been
called in. White House DIRT czar Josephina
Shmidt joins Bradley Barrington in calling
the Laguna digicard mess "outright informa-
tion terrorism." Says Shmidt, "These people
stop at nothing. Organized crime outfits
are now our heaviest users of computer net-
works, pushing everything from live touch-
and-feel smut to drugs."
```

Yeah, the Net, an evil, carnal den of filth. So why did everyone in the world use it so much? Why did people buy stuff off the Net, watch television on the Net, make private phone calls on the Net, do all their banking transactions on the Net?

Next they'd be claiming that all hackers were into S and M and drove chip prongs into their scalps, just for fun. Or that all hackers were into acid rock and had neon hair.

Neon hair. She had to wash out the Etch-o, or she'd end up looking worse than Jose.

Judy pulled off the road again, and parked in a deserted nook overhanging the cliff. The sun was beginning to dip close to the horizon. She made her way down the steep incline, following an overgrown path of spiked weeds that sliced into her unprotected legs. Blood dribbled down her calves. Was this an S and M hacker, or what?

The beach was only a sliver of sand here, the ocean roaring right up to its lip. The water was cold, salty. She went down on one knee and ducked her head under, gagged, but flushed the greenish-yellow gunk from her hair.

Scrabbling back up the incline, she clutched the thorny weeds to pull herself forward. Her hands were bleeding and raw, and sticky with dye and salt water. She wiped them on her shorts. Fi-nally, she returned, panting, to the stolen car.

She peered at herself in the rearview mirror. Her hair was greenish-yellow. Already.

What the heck. Why stop halfway? She opened the bottle of green glitter and worked some in, did her hair up right. Let the anti-Net goons think what they wanted. Now, she looked like *all* hackers did to them.

Next step: run and hide.

There were plenty of hackers in San Jose, people she knew from VileSpawn. Somehow, she'd manage to hook up with them. With their help, she'd locate Griswald and discover if he knew the truth about Tuska and Smith.

It wasn't much of a plan. Still, it was better than nothing.

She flipped open the netpad, accessed an Internet outdialer, one of the thousands of modems freely available to anyone who spent the time to find the outdialer list on the Net. Fakeout mailer: that was the ticket. She did a telnet to port 25 of a university Web server in Michigan, called herself blahblah@blow.edu. Her message: *Need help. Innocent. On the run. TerMight.* Maybe somehow she'd luck out and a VileSpawn hacker would see her message and come up with a way to help.

She didn't know what else to do. At least, not for now. But she wasn't going to give up easily. There was no way Trev's killers were going to squash Judy Carmody and walk away free. No way.

She might be scared out of her mind, but Judy Carmody—rather, *TerMight*—never made promises she didn't keep. Tuska and Smith were going to pay.

CHAPTER 8

"Company's here," Harry announced, pushing open the door to Cal's bedroom. The big man grinned, white teeth gleaming against dark-leather skin. "How's this for results, Nikonchik? The boss himself's come to listen to your complaints."

Cal's head jerked up from the computer monitor. The last person he had expected to see today was Bob Ingersoll. The project chief rarely came to the guest house without advance notice.

"Hello, Calvin," the NSA agent said. Mr. Ingersoll was the only person who used Cal's full name. He talked like a politician: thoughtful, dignified, and, Cal mused, totally fake.

"Harry says we've been working you too hard," Mr. Ingersoll continued, walking across the small room to the lace-curtained windows. Pushing the dainty white cloth to one side, he stared at the desert. "He tells me you want a DVD player—for entertainment."

"If it's not too much trouble, sir," Cal sputtered. Nobody called Mr. Ingersoll Bob—not to his face. Not even Harry or Greg. He was always Mr. Ingersoll, or sir. Cal didn't believe in titles. All his life he'd called his teachers and his friends' parents by their first names. But here he made an exception. There was something about the soft-spoken man that gave Cal the creeps. He was definitely a *sir*.

Mr. Ingersoll drew in a deep breath. He never spoke quickly. Slender, a shade over Cal's own six feet, he had jet-black hair and deep brown eyes. He was always perfectly groomed, even on a sweltering day like today. He wore a tweed charcoal suit, a blue eggshell shirt, and maroon tie. Bob Ingersoll refused to sweat.

"I see no problem with your request. If it'll help you concentrate, it sounds like a great idea."

Still standing at the window, the project chief turned to face Cal. He had a thin face, a long nose, and skin that had been shaved so smoothly it seemed prepubescent. The guy looked like a grown-up choirboy. His lips parted in the slightest of smiles. "Seems to me you've been working awfully hard without a break, Calvin. Don't forget, I've been in this business a long time. I know it's tough to be locked into a project day and night. You start going stir-crazy after three or four days of constant pressure."

"I'm not used to the silence," Cal said truthfully. "No offense to Harry and Greg," he added hurriedly. "They're fine company. Just fine. But, this desert is driving me nuts. It's so . . . *quiet*. Not like my place in San Jose."

Mr. Ingersoll twisted the gold ring on his finger, the finger where most men wore wedding bands. But this ring had nothing to do with a wife. It was wide with a ruby set in the middle and letters—NSA—clearly etched in fancy script over the stone. He lifted the ringed hand, and let the curtains drop to cut the glare, blocking the view of Joshua trees and yuccas.

The shift in light cast strange shadows on the walls of the small room. Cal's head began to throb. He pressed his palms over his eyes, let a wave of dizziness rise and then recede.

When he opened his eyes, Mr. Ingersoll was standing behind him. "Have you been on VileSpawn lately?" the NSA agent asked. Despite the fact that he had moved closer, his voice seemed to be coming from a million miles away.

"Just for a minute today," Cal confessed, trying to keep his voice steady. "I needed a break."

Mr. Ingersoll nodded. "No problem. I understand. You saw the message inquiring as to your whereabouts?"

"Yeah," Cal said, "I sure did. Have no idea who posted it. Maybe TerMight. Wasn't Hailstorm. He's dead."

"I saw that, too," Mr. Ingersoll said. His voice, usually firm and tight, softened. He laid a hand on Cal's shoulder. "Sorry, Calvin, I know he was your friend. If you like, I'll do some checking. Call the Seattle Police Department for more information. Once they hear I'm with the NSA, they'll tell me anything I want to know."

"I'd appreciate that," Cal said. "Thanks."

"You understand, of course," Mr. Ingersoll said, "that you can't answer whoever was asking about you. I'm sure the ISD suspects you're our top gun on this project. If you break cover, they'll be on us in a minute. Squash the project flat. You need to stay underground until the job's finished. No communications, Calvin. Right?"

"Yes, sir," Cal said. "You're paying the bills."

"You're under a lot of pressure." Mr. Ingersoll settled into the adjacent black leather chair and swiveled to face Cal. "We can't afford to blow the heist. Internet Security is breathing down our necks. They consider this whole operation a waste of money. It has to be done *right*. No shortcuts, no screwups. What do you need to make that deadline three days from now?"

"The music?"

"Done. Anything else?"

"Maybe a few hours off-line. Go out for a pizza. Just hang out and relax a little."

"I don't see why not. As long as you keep quiet about your work. Sounds exactly like what the doctor ordered. Greg can take one of the limos."

"Then—then . . . it's okay?"

"Sure," Mr. Ingersoll said, rising from his chair and smiling. "Why not? We're not running a prison here, Calvin. Even hackers need a social life. Have a good time."

Excellent. A night on the town—away from the compound—a down-and-dirty, outright *mad* band, some live babes . . .

Maybe Cal had misjudged everything. Sure, Harry and Greg often treated him like a kid, or like hired help, but Mr. Ingersoll, the big dog, was treating him like a real professional.

Mr. Ingersoll *understood*. He wasn't just a field operative, pulling guard duty like his flunkies. He was an NSA encryption expert, a mathematician, a programmer. He'd been a key consultant to the Automated Systems Security Incident Support Team at the Defense Information Systems Agency back when they had developed i-Watch, the first Internet wiretap.

Suddenly, Cal felt at ease again, confident he was doing the right thing working for Bob Ingersoll. A few more nights on the genetics software program, just a few more nights . . . and then Cal would crack into banks all over the world, right off the Internet, leaving no trace that he'd been there.

He'd be a hero. He would have developed the *first* completely fail-safe method of Net cracking. The government would applaud him, mark him as a genius. His future would be certain. He'd be set for life, personally heading a team of programmers whose only goal was to create bleeding-edge code that prevented *real* bank heists.

Greg broke into his daydreams. "Come on, Cal. You better hit the shower before we head to town. Then the two of us can get going, grab a pizza, maybe a few beers. Kick back for a few hours. You'll feel a lot better. You're our key player, our main man. We need you in top working condition."

Cal's thoughts turned to Mistie Lane. Forget the pizza. Forget the beer. Cal wanted to find some *girls*.

"Yeah, get me into top working condition. That's the key," he said.

"Listen," Greg said, "I'm gonna put on some clean clothes, then get one of the limos. You be ready in half an hour, and we'll bust out of here and have some fun. Spend some of that government expense account." Greg balled a hand into a fist and socked Cal playfully in the back. "Maybe we'll get lucky and score with some ladies looking for a good time."

Cal couldn't believe his ears. It was like listening to his dreams come true. His brother, Dan, had always treated him like a nerdy teenager. He was never willing to fix Cal up with any of those hot waitresses who worked at the restaurant. Dan didn't believe in sharing the wealth. Greg didn't seem to mind, though, and he was a real studdog. He probably attracted girls like a dog attracted fleas.

It wouldn't take long for Cal to get ready. He jumped in the shower, punched in the water temperature and spray force—both tuned to his personal taste. Then he pulled on clean jeans and a zoid T-shirt. His blond hair, blown dry, shimmered in long waves over his shoulders. He looked *good*.

He sat on the sofa in the living room and waited impatiently for Greg to bring the limo. His fingers beat an incessant staccato on his knee. He couldn't wait to get off this compound, escape from the confines of the barbed-wire fences, the security guards. Sure, he could wander freely around the grounds, but what good was *that*, when wandering meant thrashing your way through prickled cacti and desert scrub, fighting off snakes and ugly lizards? During the day the heat baked all the moisture out of your body. And at night, no telling what desert creepies might trip you up.

Tonight he'd finally cut loose.

He left the living room and walked outside, stood on the bottom step of the front porch. He gazed up at the main house, which sat on a nearby foothill.

Cal wondered who had originally lived in the place; it was practically a mansion. Probably a senator or congressman. That would explain how the NSA had ended up here, with use of the cottage and free run of the compound, as well. Despite what Cal's parents had told him, power obviously did have its privileges.

After five minutes, a big white limo rumbled down the dirt road that connected the main house with the guest cottage. The car pulled up in front of the porch. The dark glass window on the driver's side slid down without a sound. "You ready to go, Nikonchik?"

It was Harry, dressed in a white shirt and sports coat. "I'm playing chauffeur. Tonight, you're getting the royal treatment. Get in."

Cal pulled open the rear door of the immense car and was slammed by a wall of noise. Greg, holding a beer in one hand, grinned at him from inside. He waved. "Come on, Cal. Climb aboard. We're gonna party."

The seats were leather—*real* leather. There was enough legroom for a basketball player. And the beer was ice-cold. "Dynamite sound system," he said to Greg, feeling obligated to make some comment.

"It's a muscle box," Greg said, "600 watts rms per channel; actually, 300 watts per channel, with each channel cycling into 8 ohms."

People always expected Cal to know everything about hardware, cars, stereos, and anything electronic. It was ridiculous. He was a hacker, not an electrical engineer. As it was, Mistie Lane probably knew as much as he did about 600-watt rms channels. But he nodded, pretending to understand.

As they started down the road, he stared out the UV-tinted window and tried to get a fix on where they were. All he knew was that the compound was somewhere south of Palm Springs and north of Anza-Borrego Desert State Park. There were no road signs. They weren't really even on a road; just a single-lane stretch that went from gravel to cement half-covered in dust and sand. There were no footprints in the sand, no landmarks, nothing anywhere; only foothills out beyond the desert, poking up like raw digital waves, dotted with bunches of brush that looked like lopsided binary trees.

He had no idea where the nearest town might be. This area was new territory to him. But Harry seemed to know where he was going. And Greg had mentioned pizza and girls. That was all that really mattered.

Cal settled back on the plush seat and gulped down some beer. He wasn't used to beer. A few sips, and his head started to go wonky.

"Want another?" Greg asked. "It's around twenty minutes to town. Roads are pretty rough, so Harry's got to take it slow. Can't risk breaking down in the desert. There's no service station on the corner. Especially one that can fix the chips they use in *this* car." He laughed. "No tow trucks in our neighborhood, either."

"Where are we—" Cal began to ask, but before he could complete the question, the limo bucked wildly, sending him flying. The beer can bounced, and he sprawled on the carpeted floor, landing in a puddle of fizz, barely missing the steel casing of the portable bar. The car jerked a second time, sending Cal's body slamming into the rear seats.

"What the hell?" Greg growled, grabbing hold of Cal's shoulder, steadying him. "Harry, are you crazy?"

The limo shuddered a third time and then came to a total stop. The engine sputtered for a moment more and died.

"Shit, shit, *shit*," Greg said, his face turning bloodred. "You okay, Cal?"

"Yeah, but what's wrong with the car?"

Greg pushed open the limo door. "I've got a piss-poor bad feeling about this."

They met Harry in front of the car. He already had the hood open. "Damned radiator's sprung a leak," he growled, a disgusted expression on his face. "Forget town. We ain't goin' nowhere."

"So much for a night of wine, women, and song," Greg said. He looked at Cal and shook his head. "Sorry, kid, but nothing much we can do about it. I'll use the Net phone to call the estate. Hopefully, someone can come in a Jeep and pick us up."

Cal should have guessed something like this would happen. Finally, he was getting away from the computer screen, the dust, the monotonous tan sand—away from the computer. His one chance to blow free for a few hours, and the freaking car had to break down.

They waited in silence by the side of the road. Cal was in no mood to talk. Neither Greg nor Harry were the talkative type. The two drank beer, passed around a tin of cashews Greg found in the portable bar, and stared at the moon. By the time the Jeep arrived, driven by a thin, tight-lipped man, Cal was more than ready to leave.

The trip back to the estate took ten minutes. No one said a word the entire drive back. When they reached the compound, Harry and Greg went up to the main house to report the details of the disaster to Mr. Ingersoll. Back in the guest cottage, Cal yanked off the beer-sopped zoid T-shirt and flung it into a corner. He scruffed up his hair, chewed on some pretzels, and tinkered with a stupid computer game—some idiotville shoot-'em-dead thing with goofy dinosaurs. The screen was dusty. He touched it, and static crackled. He should probably clean it, but he didn't feel like doing anything.

He was bored. Ticked off that his night out had been cancelled. Frustrated, he brought his genetics code up on the screen, played with it, watched the chromosomes break and join, grow and segregate. He tinkered with inversion, breaking chromosomes and rejoining them in reverse orders.

He could do anything with digital chromosomes. He could make them dance, make them kill each other, make them steal tons of money, leaving nobody the wiser. But right now, he didn't feel like playing with them.

His mind drifted . . .

Who lived in the house on the hill? No one ever said a word about the owner of the compound. It sure wasn't Mr. Ingersoll's place. Not on a government check. The head guy must be loaded to afford this sort of layout, complete with servants and security guards.

Maybe it was a safe house for intelligence agents who were on the run? Or a training center for NSA operatives? Anything was possible.

Cal wondered about the security net that protected the estate and how tough it was. It would be easy for him to tap into the setup and find out anything he wanted.

Not to do any harm, really. Just because he *could* do it. And besides, a little knowledge never hurt anybody.

He pulled his special cleaner from the desk drawer. It was his own invention. It looked like a wad of putty, but was actually a pliable, moisture-free blob that cleaned the computer screen using a combination of ammonia and antistatic agents. It also sharpened the screen colors a little, and imparted a soft 3-D glow to graphics. It cleaned; it was a viewing filter: it was *way* cool.

He sucked some salt off a pretzel, took a swig of ginger ale from the two-liter bottle he always kept by the desk. It was time for Griswald to come out and play.

First stop, the computer file of the compound's phone records. Years ago, he'd coded a dead-file sniffer, and based on that, he'd created a tiny executable that went beneath the surface of an operating system to dig out information about system calls. First, he ran a kernel debugger to determine system call numbers. Then through his code, he used those numbers to access secure files, disk caches, and anything else he wanted. He could see a list of all parameters passed—as in *phone numbers*—to any computer on the compound.

A few minutes later, dozens of phone entries from the past few days scrolled down the screen. Odd. Though Harry reported their progress to NSA headquarters every day, there wasn't any sign of calls to Washington. Maybe he just E-mailed the information as encrypted files.

Curious, Cal pulled up the billing reports. A dozen different business names appeared, each seeming to have no relationship to any of the others. It could take days to find a connection under normal circumstances. But he had the world's most powerful data bank—the Internet—at his fingertips.

It only took seconds to find the link. All of the companies were anonymous payment services. For a monthly fee, they paid bills for major corporations that wanted their financial records kept secret. It was a cumbersome but effective way of protecting itemized data from outside investigators. Whoever maintained the big house wanted his business to remain secret.

This was the perfect setup for Bob Ingersoll. Nobody would ever think of looking for an NSA guy out here, in a place so remote even the coyotes stayed away. That Mr. Ingersoll was one sharp whiz.

And Mr. Ingersoll wouldn't appreciate Cal sneaking through the phone records. Using system calls again, Cal erased the log entries that showed his tap. Griswald vanished back into the ether.

Who had posted that note, wondering where he was? Not Dan. His brother was clueless when it came to the Net. It had to be someone else, a hacker—probably from VileSpawn.

Cal took another swig of ginger ale. While he spent a lot of time on VileSpawn, he really didn't have that many close friends. Just TerMight, Hailstorm, JC . . .

Jeremy Crane. It must have been him. Cal and Jeremy had worked together for six months refining the basic concepts of the genetic algorithm. They made a good team. Usually, Cal visited him every week. He'd missed their last session because he'd been here in the desert. But he couldn't let Jeremy know where he was, and Jeremy probably thought Cal had been hit by a truck or something.

He'd let Jeremy know he was okay. Besides, Cal was *lonely*. And pent up, going nuts, no way to break free, even for an hour. Some minor virtual contact wouldn't do any harm. Though Mr. Ingersoll would have a fit if Cal sent a message that the ISD could find.

The solution was obvious. Cal would leave traces of himself somewhere on the Net, somewhere that only another master hacker could go.

He dialed into VileSpawn. From there, he opened his Internet browser and typed the address for a private CIA Web site. At home, he would have touched an icon. Here, he had to be more careful, couldn't have CIA icons on his screen while working for Bob Ingersoll, an NSA honcho.

A prompt appeared, asking for his CIA password. He typed it, then entered it again, as required by protocol.

Now *that* had been another fun time. Cal remembered it well. Right before taking Mr. Ingersoll's job, Cal had intercepted E-mail containing some CIA guy's public key. The boffobrain had been exchanging keys with another agent. Cal had sent his own public key to the second agent, who then encrypted her oh-so-secret private key with Cal's public key. From there, Cal had simply intercepted the second agent's transmission containing the secret key.

It was all so incredibly stupid, these encryption schemes. As long as encryption keys or passwords went over the Net, hackers could get them.

So here he was, nosing around in the CIA files again. As Griswald. Unbeatable, unstoppable, all-powerful Griswald.

He opened a text file in binary mode, inserted an end-of-file marker, then appended a second file to the first. The second file contained two words: his guru moniker, Fire, and his secret Griswald password. Nobody would ever see it, and even if they did, no one would recognize it for what it was—no one except another superhacker. Both Fire and his password were hidden, thanks to the end-of-file marker.

Finally, he ran a simple encryption against the word *fire* and inserted the code into an ISDN header packet that altered the destination of all subsequent packets.

That should do it. JC was sharp. Almost as sharp as Griswald. If Jeremy was searching for Cal, he'd find the trace. That would be enough. It would stop him from worrying. And Mr. Ingersoll wouldn't be the least bit upset.

What the NSA agent didn't know couldn't hurt him.

CHAPTER 9

The highway seemed like an endless black thread, broken only by jots of dashed and double lines that were illuminated by Judy's headlights. To her right rose cliffs, to her left, there was ocean. And everywhere, the fog, night's ghost roiling over the bang of water as the waves broke on rocks and sand. A steady beat, almost like the thrum of disk drives in Jose's cubicle at Laguna Savings, but more violent, as if all the disk drives of the universe were crashing and screaming their death throes.

Judy's neck ached to that beat, each crash of surf on sand the jab of a knife down her spine, radiating to her arms, numbing her shoulders, washing through her skull in slow-tangled spasms of pain.

She slowed the car, forced her right hand off the steering wheel. Her fingers were stiff; she couldn't unball them. Scabs crisscrossed her palms, and her fingers were stained the color of the thorns that had ripped them. She blew on her hands, the warmth of her breath easing the frozen tingle.

How easy it would be to stop the car, just pull off the side of the road and shut off the engine. Rub her legs, her arms, her neck. Rub the warmth back into her body. Then give herself up to the fog and the surf. Her legs wouldn't feel a thing this time as she stumbled through the thorns and weeds, down the slope of rock and dust to the edge of the ocean.

She would lie on the beach, wrapped in the arms of night fog, the cold mist caressing her face. And in the morning, they would find her, but not know who she was.

She wouldn't be TerMight. She wouldn't be Judy Carmody.

She would be free.

The gas pedal was slicing a groove in her bare foot. Only the pain, *always* the pain, kept her going.

Why not give herself up to it, finally, now, and be done with it?

Maybe because with the pain came the *fight*. She'd always been a fighter. Many nights, alone in her room in the trailer, she'd wondered why the other girls made fun of her. Why she'd never been invited to parties. Why she'd always eaten alone in the school cafeteria, pretending not to see how the other girls sneered, all gathered in clumps, heads together, *making fun of her*.

The dress she'd worn to the sixth-grade graduation ceremony: not good enough. Mom had made it from flowered soft cloth. The other girls had worn cutoffs and neon spaztek.

In junior high, they were already bedding down the boys. Only the curl of their hair mattered, their giggles, the tiny thrusts of their chins, the creases of their smiles, the flirtatious come-ons reflected in their eyes—

Eyes slathered in the lard of glitterglo gels and neon noir pastes that matched their short-shorts.

When Dad had fallen for that crap, dumped Mom for the fakeness of the glitterglo, it was just too much. No more fight in Judy. She'd died, become someone else, for the next year.

Now, she blinked back tears, but felt them burning on her cheeks anyway, dribbling salt into her mouth. She slowed the car again, this time to a crawl.

She hadn't felt this lost, hadn't had the fight so drained from her, since Dad . . .

She'd sworn, way back then, she'd sworn, that nobody—

that *nothing*—

would ever kill her like that again.

Drifting, alone, creepy guys coming on to her, half raping her till she beat them off. Lousy jobs, working at the local Wal-Mart as a checkout girl. Listening to the endless complaints of the customers. As if she cared.

Longing for the morph, the drug to pump her through the nights. Alone with her computer, her only friend.

She'd felt back then that if she only knew enough, learned enough, somehow, she'd dig her way back to the surface, be human again, whole and herself.

And it had worked.

She'd escaped to California.

It had *worked*.

Never again. They wouldn't beat her down like that again. If she could survive Dad and Bimbo, Mom going nuts, she could survive anything.

Bright stars were easing into the fog. The canopy of night was lifting. Soon, she'd be in San Jose, where she'd make things *right*.

She pressed on the gas pedal, urging the car back to top speed, ignoring the pain in her foot.

"Audio." The Net console sparked to life. The mechanical male voice warned her that gas was low, that the oil required checking.

The mechanical male—Grunt, she called him—was the only guy who didn't care that she dressed like a weirdo, had the body of a stick, and didn't giggle like some goo-goo girl off the vids.

Funny—she almost *liked* the mechanical male.

"News?" Grunt asked.

"News," she said. Friend to friend. "And thank you, Grunt," she added.

"My pleasure."

A gentleman, even. Now that was archaic.

But Grunt's news wasn't pleasant.

"Los Angeles authorities continue the manhunt for alleged killer Judith Carmody. Armed and dangerous. Advise extreme caution." And more: the announcer went on to relate stories about her unhappy childhood, her wild hacker exploits, the secret projects she'd done for the government. Taken together, the reports painted a frightening picture of a half-insane computer expert who had been driven over the edge by too much work and too little life.

Shut up, *mechanical man*.

"Computer: Audio off."

The mechanical man went away. She was frustrated, and wanted to take it out on the mechanical man. None of this was his fault; he wasn't even real.

She preferred his company to flesh men.

The main highway was dangerous; in daylight, she was sure someone would recognize her and call the cops. She had to find someone from VileSpawn. Quickly.

Route 1 branched into Route 17. From there, it stretched north past Lexington Reservoir, and eventually, the city of Campbell. She was getting close to San Jose, would be there by daybreak. Along with trucks, cars were starting to appear on the road. Workaholic slaves from the far distant suburbs were heading north and east on their long commute to the heart of the city.

At the top of the Net console, the orange picture of a gas pump flickered, warning that gas was low. Like she hadn't heard this already, from the mechanical man.

Like *he* would help her in some way, tell her what to do. If only . . .

But if she ran out of gas, and the cops got her . . .

As they dragged her from the car, the mechanical man would say, "My pleasure, my pleasure."

She had to *do* something.

If it ran out of gas, the car would transmit an automatic signal. The highway patrol monitored car signals so they could help stranded travelers.

She eased up on the gas pedal, hoping to coax a little more efficiency from the engine. Soon the car crossed Route 280, and by the time the tank was a notch above empty, Route 17 turned into 880, the last leg on the long road leading to San Jose.

No way she could buy gas. She had only three hemorrhoid digicards, worth twenty dollars and fifty cents. Buying gas would drain all her funds. And she might need money later, for more important things.

Like for food, bribes . . .

God only knew. She couldn't even guess anymore.

A white envelope flashed on the Net console: there was a message for the driver.

Weird.

According to all the records at the Avis agency, her car was in the Avis repair shop waiting for a new fuel filter. Who would be sending a message to a car that was being fixed?

"E-mail: Text."

The letter was encrypted and came from someone named grouch@out_back.com. Driving with her left hand, she flipped open the netpad, brought up her hacking links, and downloaded the E-mail. Then she decrypted it using the key known only by TerMight and her few select cohorts on the Net.

The message:

```
We know you're coming. Take 880E to 101S,
get off at Berryessa Road. Read second
letter for further directions.
```

They'd found her. The VileSpawn hackers had found her.

She'd never met them, but they were willing to help. *Amazing*.

On the other hand, if hackers had tracked down her car, so could the cops.

On the *other* other hand, hackers always stayed one step ahead of the groundhogs down at cop communications.

A few minutes later, a second message appeared on the car's Net screen. This one was also from Grouch, and this time he hadn't bothered to encrypt it.

```
Erase the EPROM. When you get to the street,
scan the phone poles.
```

What on earth was he trying to tell her?

It was already morning. The sky was turning from gray to peach. San Jose loomed before her, an immense cityscape: houses, glass buildings, dust and dirt, all crammed together between the coastal mountains and San Francisco Bay. The fastest-growing urban area in the United States, a gigantic sprawl of city and suburbs that stretched for miles into California's heart. And somewhere in this sea of humanity, Judy hoped to find a safe haven.

She steered onto Berryessa, parked on a remote side street.

Then she leaned her head on the steering wheel and desperately tried not to cry. It was so unfair. She hadn't killed anybody; she didn't even *know* anybody. All she wanted was an end to this nightmare, a way to retreat quickly into her peaceful, little world, a way to pretend that none of this had ever happened.

But it was all just beginning. And deep down, she knew that things would only get worse. Much worse.

She couldn't cry. She had to keep a grip.

Yet she had no idea how to find the hacker hideout from here. Look at the telephone poles? What kind of stupid clue was that?

She touched STOP CAR on the Net console. The car whined and switched off. The console remained on, fueled by software. The console wouldn't switch off until Judy physically left the car and pressed her password into the outside keypad. The software would run until she closed the network connection.

A few lights winked on in the surrounding houses. The lawns were classic for northern California: evergreens, flowering bushes, bright green grass that had to be watered regularly in order to keep it green. Ranch houses lined the street, each with plaster walls and dark-shingled roofs.

There were *no* telephone poles.

The phone lines must be underground, as they were in southern California, where Laguna Beach was, where her apartment was, where Trev was . . . used to be . . .

Again, she blinked back tears. Exhaustion was hitting her hard. She had to focus, remain clearheaded, figure out what to do.

Erase the EPROM?

She figured the Net console had an EPROM chip in it, since it was new technology and the browser company would want to upload the latest software to the cars every few months. Rather than programmable read-only memory, or PROM, that couldn't be erased, the EPROM allowed vendors to change code without having to manufacture new PROMs.

How could she erase the EPROM? The easiest method was to hammer at the Net console, expose the chip, and sear it with ultraviolet light.

She pulled a small screwdriver out of her computer case, and began hacking away at the console. It was simple enough to remove the plastic casing and expose the guts of the system. But she didn't know how to erase the memory. If she destroyed it using a screwdriver, she wouldn't be able to get out of the car; the door would jam on her. If she first opened the door, then destroyed the memory . . .

Yes.

But then, how would she drive to the hideout without a working car?

Well, she'd worry about the EPROM later. For now, she had to find the telephone poles.

Damn.

She scanned the street. Nothing. But there, over the houses on the next block, a long pole jutted into the sky.

That *must* be it.

She touched START CAR, waited a moment for the engine to whiz back into action, then drove slowly around the corner, past a row of bright roses. A man was collecting his newspapers, and a dumpy woman in jogging shorts was walking a yapping dog.

Witnesses. Now there were two people who could identify her, tell cops that Judy Carmody, the murderer, was in their neighborhood.

She glanced into the rearview mirror. Neither the man nor woman was staring at her. Neither had even noticed her.

Pushing herself lower onto the seat, hoping to hide her head a little, she drove to the lone pole and stopped the car again.

Two cables wound down the pole into the ground.

Two cables slithered *up* from a mound of dirt piled next to a garage fifty feet away. The house in front of it was no different from the rest on the block. A tiny brick ranch, but painted navy blue. A scraggly lawn. Dark windows.

This was it. Safety.

She touched STOP CAR again, clambered from the front seat, then stretched and touched her toes. Glad, so glad, to be out of that car. The Net console displayed the latest sports and weather in happy rainbow letters. It made her sick. There was nothing happy about this day.

She pressed the keypad, terminating her session with the car. The Net console winked off.

At last.

Goddamn freaking computers. They drove her crazy.

She ambled up to the house, clutching her laptop and netpad.

God, how her feet ached. She wanted some shoes.

A bath.

Food.

Sleep.

She peered through the living room window. Eyes on the other side of the glass met hers.

She jumped, cried out loud.

"Shhh . . ." The unknown guy motioned, his eyes bleary and red from lack of sleep, his hair clumped in greasy mounds around his face. He waved her toward the front door.

Once inside, she stood there, trembling, ready to collapse. Judy hardly saw her rescuer through the blur of tears.

His voice was low and soft. "It's okay, it's okay . . ." He led her to a sheetless mattress in a corner of the room, held her elbow, and gently sat her down.

She sank in a sea of comfort, her head between her knees, her body rocking from relief. Tears rolled down her cheeks, drenching her sweaty shorts. She smelled bad. She felt bad.

A collection of faces gathered around her. She was a blubbering mess. Someone handed her a glass of water. She gulped it down, asked for another.

Four guys, all wearing boxer shorts, and one girl. A room stuffed with computer equipment: PCs, cables, server towers, blinking modems. The place reminded her of home.

"You're TerMight?" said the guy with the greasy mound of hair.

"Yeah," she said weakly.

"I'm Grouch." He gestured at his friends. "This here's Tarantula; she's about as good as you are."

The girl blushed. She was a little younger than Judy, had short-cropped black hair and huge blue eyes. She was skinny, too, like Judy, and wore nothing but a man's large button-down shirt.

"Nobody's as good as TerMight," Tarantula said. Her voice faltered, sort of emptied from her lips, squeaked, and died.

Judy instantly liked her. No ego crowd, this; just a bunch of jack-'em-hack-'em geekoids.

People almost like Judy. And in the flesh. Not names flashed on a screen, names like void25 and wham42.

Yet, Judy didn't like to be called good, or the best. She didn't like anyone knowing she even existed.

Grouch waved his hand toward the three guys. "And these guys are just a pack of losers."

The *losers*. Weren't they all losers? Even in the flesh, Grouch didn't have a real name, just his Internet handle, grouch@ out_back.com.

And Tarantula was probably tarantula@out_back.com.

The three losers, two distinctly older than Judy, the other younger, shuffled their feet and looked away. One had blond curly hair cropped closely to his head, another had straight brown hair flipped behind the ears, and the third ate too many candy bars. Curly, Moe, and Larry, she decided.

"VileSpawn?" she asked.

"Working on it," Grouch said.

They weren't good enough to get in.

Then how had they found her?

"You . . . live here?" A stupid question. She waited for the laugh and the sneer.

But there was no laugh, and nobody sneered at her. Grouch answered. "Sure do. We develop Net applications. We're a business, you know? We call ourselves Outback, Incorporated, though we're not really *incorporated*, not yet, anyway. I'm the prez. My office is the bedroom in the back of the house."

Yeah . . .

She'd seen plenty of these operations. Programmers camping together in a house full of hardware. Not for her. She had to work *alone*. But still, she knew the type. They wanted to adopt the persona of Hellion Macho Computer Outlaw, but needed each other to make them feel that way. They didn't understand that flesh people were fake, that flesh people smiled at you when it served their purposes, dumped you when it didn't. They didn't understand that only the skills mattered, the hardware, the anonymity.

"It won't be good for your business, Grouch, to have *me* here," she said.

"On the other hand, it might be very good for our business."

Grouch sat down beside her. His eyes were serious; he wasn't kidding.

"How so? I'm wanted for murder." As she spoke, Tarantula left the room, trailed by the Stooges. Judy heard noises from what had to be the kitchen, sounds of water gurgling from a faucet into a pot, smelled the brew of fresh coffee.

Grouch ran thick hands through his hair. He was in bad need of a shave. He wore boxer shorts printed with images of cartoon characters doing cartwheels and whacking each other over the head with keyboards. His chest was hairless and concave, his arms and legs without muscles: he was so skinny he looked like the Gumby she'd played with as a kid.

Judy hadn't had many toys. Just Gumby and a laptop. Her mother had foisted some Barbie dolls and Raggedy Anns on her, but Judy had shown no interest in dolls, just stuffed them in her closet with the flowered dresses.

Still keeping his voice low, as if the cops could be hiding anywhere—outside in the bushes, in the closets—Grouch said, "Look, we all know you're Judy Carmody, wanted for all that stuff in Laguna. We don't believe it. The news has been screaming about TerMight—yeah, your Internet handle—so we know who you are, in the real. But your hacks are legendary—we study them—and none are built to crack the law. And you're no killer."

So the whole world knew that Judy Carmody was TerMight. So much for anonymity. Still, whatever Grouch had studied, it wasn't Judy's *real* stuff. Only Judy's Tinkertoys. These people were clueless about what she could really do; and the key, the thrill, was never letting anyone know.

"You'll help me?" she asked.

He nodded. "Of course. We figure you were framed. The feds have had it in for hackers since day one. They blame us for everything that goes wrong. *They just don't get it*—if we can break into the CIA and into banks, so can anyone else out there. An engineer, some guy in his basement, anyone with a programmer's head. We expose the bugs and security cracks."

It was a line Judy knew well. It was *her* line.

"If they bring you down," Grouch said, "how long till they start coming after all of us?"

Tarantula returned, this time wearing jeans and a halter top. She gave Judy a cup of coffee. The mug was chipped all around the lip. The faded image of a dog smeared one side. "What's with the dog?" Judy asked, settling back onto the mattress. She placed the cup on the floor. No way she was going to drink coffee.

"Garage sale," Tarantula said simply, twirling her hair in her fingers. Then she backed off to slide onto a stool with a ripped red vinyl covering. She turned, reached over, and pressed a switch. A computer whirred on, and in an instant, she was fixated, touching icons, tapping on the keyboard. With the sound off. To eliminate distractions.

These people were weird. Their equipment was banged together from bits and pieces, probably pulled from corporate garbage bins. No netpads, no laptops, just clunker PC skins stuffed with high-speed components and RAM. They drank from garage-sale mugs and sat on stools that years earlier had graced the suburban homes of 1990s housewives.

Tarantula kept her eyes on the screen, said, "New police reports coming in, Grouch. Judy's fingerprints were found all over the murder scene, of course—it was her apartment. And they traced the missing murder gun to her. Bought a month ago."

"What?" Judy leapt up, and the mug tipped. Hot coffee sloshed over her bare feet. "Ouch. Damn!" She staggered, winced, but made her way across the room to peer over Tarantula's shoulder. Grouch followed, shrugging as if he already knew what Judy would learn.

Somewhere in the house, a shower turned on and a male voice hummed a technobeat. Elsewhere, someone tapped a razor on a porcelain sink. The Stooges were cleaning up for the day.

As if nothing peculiar was happening around them.

"You want some eggs?" Tarantula asked.

"No!" Judy said.

The girl jumped and glanced up at Judy with big blue eyes filled with surprise at the outburst. And fear of . . . fear of something . . .

Judy knew the fear, had felt it all her life. It was the fear of being hurt, of being blamed for all the things that went wrong in life. It was the fear that made people withdraw, pull inward, deep

within themselves, that made them loners, geeks, hackers. She
wanted to say she was sorry, but didn't know how. She placed a
hand on Tarantula's arm. Too close, weird to feel the warmth of
someone's arm beneath her fingers. Much warmer than touching
her own arm.

Tarantula removed Judy's hand. "You're hurting me," she said.

Judy blinked. On Tarantula's arm there were four tiny cres-
cents where Judy's nails had bit the skin. Flakes of black-gold
nail polish shimmered on the upraised hairs.

Her polish was chipped. Her one concession to glamour, the
polish.

Tarantula was rubbing her arm and wincing. "Be careful,
would you? Say, what happened to your hand? And your hair, I
thought it was kind of red, at least according to the news."

Judy's green glittergoo hair. Stiff, still with a new-plastic reek.
Etch-o-Oil, like Jose. Her hand, scabbed with blood, fingers
swollen and cold and stiff.

Judy was a freakzone. "Doesn't matter," she said.

"Sure it does," Tarantula said.

"Yeah, right." Like: bug off. Like, why couldn't flesh people
be as easy to control as mechanical males? Just, Audio Off, and
they'd leave you alone. No fake smiles, no fake friendship. Hu-
mans were just too difficult.

Or maybe Judy just didn't know how to cope with them.
Maybe she was as bad as her father, only capable of mechanical
relationships.

"If you're hurt, it matters," Tarantula said.

Yeah? To whom?

But Judy didn't say it. Tarantula was young, still naive. Why
bust her belief in people? She'd either learn the truth on her own,
or maybe luck out and never have to know.

"I'm sorry," Judy said.

"Forgiven."

"My pleasure." Judy spoke the words of the mechanical male.

A hand rested on her shoulder, another on Tarantula's. Hairless chest. Greasy black hair. Whiskers. Grouch. The one in
charge, who knew how to talk, more or less. "Listen," he said,
"we're all under a lot of strain here. Judy's stressed out and for

good reason, plus she's in pain. She needs our help, so let's cut her some slack."

"I didn't mean any harm," Tarantula said, sitting on the stool again, gazing at the computer screen.

True enough. These people were just trying to help her. For no reason Judy could fathom. There had to be a catch, though. Could it be that Grouch and Tarantula hoped to claim hacker fame by helping the great TerMight? Would they want a payback from TerMight someday? Technical jobs, high-paying corporate contacts?

That's all anyone ever wanted from Judy.

Still . . .

To make Tarantula feel better, she said, "You must be pretty good to have found me, since you're not on VileSpawn."

"Your fakeout message hit more than VileSpawn," Tarantula said, her cheeks gaining color. "It hit every underground net on the planet."

"Tarantula figured," Grouch said, "that if you left the LA area, you'd head for San Jose. More hackers here than anywhere else. We ran a satellite scan on rental cars coming up the highway. There weren't many. So I sent the first message to all of them. Figured you'd be the only one who could break the encrypted letter. Once we saw the flag, indicating that you'd cracked and received the first letter, I sent the second one directly to you."

"Cool, huh?" Tarantula said.

"Very cool," Judy said.

"Look at the screen." Grouch tapped Judy's back, and she turned her attention to the police report that was scrolling in white letters down the blue screen.

```
Police believe the suspect is heading north
toward San Jose. She may still be armed.
```

Tarantula stared at Judy.

Judy stared at the screen.

"Incredible," Grouch said. "They're making you out to be Jack the Ripper. How did they pin this stuff on you so fast?"

"My God!" A shriek rang from a back bedroom.

Another shriek, from someone else. "The police tap—Jesus! Grouch!"

"The guys monitor police communications. They must have glommed on to something they don't like," Grouch murmured, dodging past Judy and toward the hallway.

Larry, Moe, and Curly barreled from the hall into the living room, almost knocking Grouch into the wall. He grabbed the fat one's shoulders. "What is it?"

"They—they're closing in—closing in *on us*!"

"What do you mean, man, what do you mean?"

"I mean . . . the cops, they're in helicopters, just a few blocks from here. Not just cops, SWAT teams!"

Grouch released the kid, who fell back against the wall. Then, he grabbed Judy's arm. "Go! Hurry!"

"Where? Where do I go?" It *couldn't* be true. She had to run *again*.

Grouch shoved her into the kitchen. A blur of filth: unwashed dishes, open cans of stew and slop, dirty towels, a hundred cola cans. He pushed her out the back door to a weed-choked lot, where computer cables snaked and an air-conditioning unit hummed. Grouch said, "Did you erase the EPROM like I told you?"

"N-no . . ."

"Jesus!"

The EPROM. She'd forgotten the EPROM. It held her password, the one she used as TerMight. It stored fragments of her download to the netpad. It stored fragments of Grouch's E-mails, the directions to his house . . .

Nonvolatile memory, used specifically to retain vital bits of data in case of system crashes.

They were all facing a bust, a big one.

Tarantula ran from the house behind Grouch and Judy. In the girl's trembling hand was an old car key. "Take it," she said, thrusting it at Judy.

"It's a wreck, but it can't be traced." Grouch grabbed the key from Judy, twisted it into the lock.

It was an old car, made in the early '90s, had no Net console, no keypad. Just a key and a door handle. Judy leapt into the driver's seat. She was on the run again.

She jammed the key into the ignition and jammed the stick on the floor into reverse. She hadn't driven a car like this since she was sixteen. Who the hell used cars with shifts on the floor anymore? "But where will I go?"

Grouch shoved her laptop and netpad through the window. He scribbled something on the back of some junk mail. "Follow those directions. Tell them I sent you. No way they can be traced back to me. We'll stall the cops the best we can. Now move!"

"Wait." Tarantula ran back into the house, returned a moment later, and thrust some equipment at Judy.

Wallet-sized hardware boxes.

Judy knew what they were. Mini circuit boards, old-time stuff.

The purple box would let her make free phone calls without a digicard; the green one would change traffic lights; the blue one would hide her dialing location.

"Get out of here!" Grouch said. He was already heading back inside, dragging Tarantula with him.

Judy stared at his scrawled words. Hostetter, Capitol, Morrill, and on and on, a maze of roads that led . . .

Somewhere.

She began to hear sirens; copter blades whirred.

Judy pressed her bare foot on the gas pedal. Cringed from the pain, as sore, coffee-burned flesh hit hard metal.

Cringed, because she was on the run again, dog-tired, with no idea where she was heading or what she would find when she got there.

CHAPTER 10

The phone icon on Bob Ingersoll's computer flashed red. Another interruption. Bradley Barrington, probably with another idiotic demand.

The bank accounts would have to wait. Again.

Ingersoll touched the icon, said as pleasantly as possible, "Yes, Mr. Barrington? What can I do for you?"

"Have you been watching the morning news, Bob?"

Barrington's booming voice filled the small office. Though the millionaire was probably the most brittle, uncaring, egocentric man Ingersoll had ever met, he insisted upon calling everyone by their first names.

"No, sir," Ingersoll said. "I've been working on finalizing the bank accounts for the transfer. I can't do that with distractions."

"Switch to the television, Bob," the millionaire said. It wasn't a request but a command. "Watch the news for a few minutes. Then, find out *exactly* what's happening in San Jose. Looks like your associates may have dropped the ball with that Carmody girl. I'll expect you in my office in a half hour with a full report."

"I'll check right into it, sir," Ingersoll said, and toggled off the phone icon. He stifled a curse. Looking at his watch, a Rolex digital, guaranteed accurate within microseconds, he noted the time. And his pulse rate. Both were racing too quickly.

Seemed only yesterday, at the NSA offices . . .

People listened to him there. They respected what he had to say. They *believed*.

Here, the carpet was plush and burgundy, and matched the satin curtains. His chair was executive black leather. His desk was mahogany, and every night, a maid polished it to remove his fingerprints.

At the NSA, the floor was old linoleum, and his office had no windows. His chair was government-issued steel on rollers; his desk, battered oak.

Yes, this project had its advantages—not that the fancy office mattered much. But Ingersoll couldn't wait to finish this job, get away from this estate, and most of all, get away from Barrington.

He terminated the Internet connection. A few hundred more bank accounts, then bingo, Nikonchik could cast his spell.

Ingersoll pushed back the leather chair, rose, and straightened his tie. The knot was perfect; the tie rose in a tiny ridge beneath it and swelled over his chest.

He smoothed the white shirt so it was sleek against his body and was tucked, without a crease, beneath his black belt.

Navy jacket over navy pants. Silver cuff links matching silver belt buckle. Hair trimmed to avoid the slightest curl. Face shaved so close, his skin was almost as smooth as the leather on his chair.

Self-control. Nerves never showing. No emotions.

Just business.

Bob Ingersoll was a leader, a successful man.

Soon, a wealthy man.

With the wealth would come big privileges.

He checked the Rolex again. Thirty seconds had passed. His heartbeat was still too high.

Olivia's fault. His first wife. She liked to nag, and she liked to spend money. It had cost him a fortune to unload her.

Then, Camille, another woman ten years his junior, another pretty face with flawless skin, big blue eyes, and long, sweet-smelling hair.

Both of his ex-wives . . .

Nags, flirts, spendthrifts; and once he grew weary of their beauty, there just hadn't been anything left. No brains. No real affection for him. Just beautiful shells who had wanted too much.

Ingersoll walked around the mahogany desk. The door was carved, intricate, a bas-relief of men in a boat, straining their oars against the ocean: raw masculine strength.

Doing the job. Whatever it took.

Ingersoll liked that door.

Weak men lost their tempers. Weak men let emotions get in the way. And Bob Ingersoll wasn't a weak man. His control had made him a top NSA agent for years. Still, staying at Bradley Barrington's desert compound was testing even *his* patience.

Barrington and his Luddite, antitechnology friends were among the most distasteful bunch of fanatics Ingersoll had ever encountered. Their lunatic theories made him sick. Barrington's weekly rage, broadcast on the webvid, was like watching a fruit-cake shriek in the loony bin. Ironic to find the old man's audience of millions *on* the Web. Though *The Barrington Fireside Chat* was also broadcast on plain old radio and television—to reach those who were too poor for Net access.

Hell. What did it matter?

Resourceful men formed unexpected alliances. In his long career with the government, Ingersoll had worked with worse. Private opinions didn't matter. Only results.

For a moment, he stared at the door. He didn't remember why he was there.

Barrington wanted to see him.

No. First, he was to watch the news.

Then see Barrington.

Ingersoll shook his head. Too much work lately. Long nights spent with the bank accounts. Handling Greg and Harry, and that kid, Nikonchik.

And all the field operatives.

He laughed at himself, and returned to the desk. Damn, he was letting this project get under his skin, and he never— *never*—let that happen.

Better be more careful. Chances were strong that his office

was bugged and rigged for video. Bradley Barrington was a paranoid SOB; he trusted no one.

Ingersoll understood. He was no different.

Wondering why the millionaire was so upset, Ingersoll touched the webvid icon on his computer screen. Instantly, the screen displayed channel 54, the all-news station from Los Angeles. He caught only the tail end of the lead story, but that was enough.

The newswoman was standing on the lawn of a seedy-looking home located, according to the banner on the bottom of the screen, in south San Jose. "Local authorities are holding the four men and one woman on a variety of minor charges," she said in clipped tones, "until they can determine if the group actually had any contact with murder suspect Judith Carmody. A lab team is now going over the rental car that was found parked in front of the house. If they conclude it was indeed the car stolen by the fugitive, the more serious charges of aiding and abetting a suspected felon will likely be lodged against the five."

A photo of Carmody, obviously taken from her driver's license, flashed on the screen. The reporter's voice rose a half octave. "No word yet as to what happened to the driver of the vehicle, who seems to have disappeared without a trace. Carmody remains on the loose and is described by police as potentially armed and dangerous."

The picture disappeared, and was replaced by a close-up of the reporter's face. She appeared intensely concerned. "We'll have more on this dramatic story as events continue to unfold. This is Charita Collins, reporting live from San Jose, for News 54."

Disgusting.

Ingersoll touched the webvid icon, and the news window closed. This story must be all over the news stations—even on Kmart Virtuoso TV, which broadcast for those who couldn't afford real computers. The media were devoting more time to the Carmody story than to the war in Indonesia. It was amazing how certain stories took on lives of their own. Carmody should thank him. Ingersoll had made her famous. She'd probably appear on the covers of *People*, *21st Century*, and *Time* within a week. Posthumously, of course.

Touching the phone icon again, he switched on the voice

modifier and the caller-ID scrambler. He was now officially Richard Nixon, calling via an unregistered phone in Washington, D.C. With a slight smile, Ingersoll dialed Ernie Kaye's unlisted number. He almost hoped someone was monitoring the message. Creating a new conspiracy theory these days came as easily as placing a phone call.

He wiped the smile from his lips as soon as Ernie Kaye answered the phone. "Ernie," he said slowly, letting the words roll one after another from his lips. "How are you? Expecting my call, no doubt.

"The news report this morning was an unpleasant surprise," he continued. "What happened? I thought you had this matter under control."

Ingersoll didn't mention his own name. There was no need. He listened as Ernie Kaye fumbled with an explanation. Gently, he tapped his fingers against the side of his computer, silently counting to ten as Ernie detailed the difficulties he'd encountered trying to locate Carmody.

"Ernie," Ingersoll interrupted. His voice cracked like a whip. *"Shut up."*

Ingersoll continued in precise, measured tones. "You made one serious mistake. I sent you all the data you needed to make it convincing. NSA personal-history files are wonderful tools. The frame's a good one. But—" Ingersoll's voice dropped to nearly a whisper. "—if that girl's arrested, brought in for questioning, the *whole fucking frame collapses*. On the run, she's fine. In custody, things get sticky real fast. Smart-ass lawyers will check into circumstances, want to know why Tony and Paul were at her apartment. Who do they work for? Why was the agency interested in Carmody? Pretty quick, the seamless story begins to come apart. And, as the point man for this whole operation, you start smelling like week-old meat."

On the other end, Ernie started chattering, but Ingersoll gave him no time for apologies.

"I don't want any more excuses, you stupid shit!" Ingersoll screamed. It was time to put the fear of hell into Ernie Kaye. "Your job is to find the bitch and kill her. Do you understand? *Do you understand! I want her dead."*

With the touch of an icon, Ingersoll cut the call. There was no reason to continue the conversation. He had made his point. A dash of movie-style psychotic behavior worked wonders. Time now to let Ernie sweat for a few hours. Later, in the afternoon, Ingersoll would call back with new instructions.

This time, there would be no screwups.

He glanced at his watch. Exactly ten minutes till his meeting. The scrambler and voice modifier were still in use. He dialed the phone number of the condo that was being used as a base of operations in Laguna Beach. As usual, Royce answered on the third ring.

"Tony Tuska here." His voice sounded muffled.

Royce had a fondness for double initials. Over the years he'd been Harry Henderson, Jack Jones, Mitch Miles, and a dozen others. Like all good field agents, he concocted legitimate backgrounds and electronic trails for each of his fake identities. He was an expert at being other people. But Jerome Royce, freelance contractor, left no electronic trail.

"Hello, Tony," Ingersoll said. "How's the nose?"

"The nose is broken," Tony replied. "And I have a badly bruised wrist. Of course, it could have been worse. At least the young lady didn't crack any of my fingers."

"Good thing Paul is ambidextrous," Ingersoll said. "How's he managing?"

"Other than wanting to rip a certain person into little pieces?" Tony asked. "You know how much Paul enjoys casual conversation. When he's angry, he talks even less than usual. Past twenty-four hours have been pretty damned quiet."

Paul Smith was a good agent; Ingersoll had used him for years in countless operations. He was ruthless, and he followed orders. But he was no leader, and there was always the chance that his temper would get the best of him at the wrong time. This kind of work was tough, though, even for the strongest of men. If you weren't careful, it could slip you over the edge. Ingersoll had seen it happen to others. But this job was too important for any risks.

"I'm not sure that I'm pleased. Paul's letting this assignment get on his nerves. Maybe I should send Greg and Harry to give you a hand."

"Nothing to be concerned about, sir," Tony said. "Paul's a

professional. You know that. Look at Seattle. Slick as could be. Accidents happen, even to the best of us. We did a nice job tying up a sticky situation yesterday. Put the frame together real fast, with Ernie's help. Today, we'll take care of our other objective, in Los Angeles. You'll see. Tight and clean, no mistakes. Then, we're off to our final destination, for the wrap-up."

"I'm not worried, Tony," Ingersoll said. "You guys are my best. That's why I gave you the assignment. I just don't want Paul doing anything stupid. There's too much at stake. Important people are watching over my shoulder. My career's on the line."

Ingersoll paused, then continued. "Actually, the situation as it stands may work to our advantage. The young lady offers a perfect hook on which to hang some of our dirty laundry. I need to mull over the possibilities. Continue as per your original instructions. I'll be in touch. And, make sure Paul keeps his temper under wraps."

"Okay, sir," Tony said. "Will do."

Ingersoll broke the connection. He checked his watch again. Two minutes. Time to move. Standing up, he straightened his tie, smoothed down his pants. Looked quickly around the room, made sure everything was neatly in place.

Leaving the office and walking down the long hallway, he considered the advantages of implicating Judy Carmody in the tangled web he was weaving. The notion appealed to him. Much like the Taiwan situation in '02. The more complications the better.

Jerome Royce was slick, professional. What he lacked in imagination, he compensated for through years of experience working as an independent contractor for the NSA and CIA. With Ingersoll's guidance, Jerome, aka Tony Tuska, would get the job done.

Ingersoll would miss Tony and Paul. They'd worked for him on NSA covert operations for nearly twenty years. He almost thought of them as friends. But, there was no room for sentiment in today's world.

The silent hallway that led to Barrington's suite had light brown carpet, antique wood furniture, more western prints by Eigenhofer and Bama. The old millionaire was obsessed with the frontier. An era when men took the law into their own hands.

Ingersoll passed a middle-aged maid who was dusting. She looked up, smiled. He nodded. To Barrington, roughing it meant living with six servants instead of twelve.

Brushing stray dust from his jacket, Ingersoll knocked twice on the door to Barrington's suite. Waiting a few seconds, he entered, exactly thirty minutes after the millionaire's call.

Gloria Simmons sat behind a huge cherry-wood desk, guarding the room's inner door. There was a framed photo poster of the Grand Canyon on one wall, a large aquarium fronting the other. A water cooler stood next to the second door.

Gloria looked up from a thick stack of reports as Ingersoll walked across the blue carpet. She was more than a secretary. She was Barrington's personal assistant, and as such, she handled Barrington's nutcase mail, the flood of fan letters that flowed into the office from all over the world. When necessary, she dealt with problem reporters. And managed the routine paperwork concerning the compound.

She glanced at Ingersoll now with her shrewd dark eyes. In her late twenties, she wore only a trace of lipstick and no discernable makeup. Her light brown hair was coiled into a knot on the back of her head. She was dressed in a tailored business suit and practical, flat shoes.

"How are you this morning, Mr. Ingersoll?" Gloria was all business. Cool and professional.

"I'm fine, Gloria. Enjoying the weather." He smiled as he spoke. It had been their running joke for the past week. The weather in the desert never changed—always hot and dry.

"Hard to tell in this office," she said, casually reaching for a notepad, scribbling a few words on it. "No windows. Recycled air."

She turned the paper around, so he could see what she had written. Four words. *Need to talk. Private.* The last word was underlined several times.

Ingersoll had read her NSA file. Gloria Simmons had clawed her way to her present position over a half dozen corporate rivals. Smart and ambitious, her only allegiance was to the mighty dollar. Her loyalty to Barrington was only skin-deep. Ingersoll wondered what she wanted to discuss. There was only one way he would find out.

"You need to get out a little," Ingersoll said. "Go for a walk on the grounds. Enjoy nature."

"Right," Gloria said. "Mr. Barrington says the same thing. Learn to appreciate the great outdoors."

"We should go for a walk," Ingersoll said, as he watched Gloria methodically tear the note to shreds. "It'll give us both a break."

"Sounds fine to me," Gloria said.

"Stop by my office some time," Ingersoll said.

"I'll do that," Gloria said. "Now, you better go in. Mr. Barrington's waiting. You know how impatient he gets."

"Indeed I do," Ingersoll said.

Walking past Gloria, he pushed open the door to Bradley Barrington's inner sanctum. The room was huge, a forty-foot square with a fifteen-foot-high ceiling. Almost as large as Barrington's ego.

As always when he was expecting company, the millionaire stood in front of a picture window that covered one entire wall. He was gazing into the desert. The old man liked to make a dramatic first impression.

"Inspirational, isn't it, Bob?" Barrington said, without turning, as Ingersoll approached. Tinted thermal glass reduced the sun's glare to a soft white glow. "The magnificence of raw nature."

Ingersoll, who cared nothing for cacti, lizards, and sand, knew better than to be honest. "A remarkable vision, sir," he declared, repeating a phrase Barrington often used in his video broadcasts.

"That's the truth," Barrington said. The old man stood silent for a moment, as if absorbing strength from the stillness, then shuffled to a black leather armchair that sat behind an oak desk covered with papers. Trivial papers: nothing important. Barrington left the real work to Gloria and the vice presidents of his numerous corporations. He spent all of his time trying to make his mark on society.

With a sigh of relief, Barrington sank into the comfort of the chair. The years hadn't been kind to the millionaire. In his prime, he had stood six foot three and weighed 230, all of it muscle and steel. His beet red features and tangled mane of white hair had been a familiar sight at high-profile conservative fund-raising events in the 1970s and 1980s. That had been before a series of heart attacks shriveled the flesh from his bones and left him a bitter, dried husk of a man.

And the evolving political landscape had been equally unkind. His detractors had labeled his harsh views on encroaching technology as . . . *demented*.

In addition to the beloved western prints, the walls were plastered with photos: all featured Bradley Barrington with someone famous. Most were personally inscribed. Barrington shaking hands with Richard Nixon. Whispering something to Ronald Reagan. Conferring with Pete Wilson. Standing with Pat Robertson in front of an American flag. There wasn't one picture of Barrington with his family. The wife who had died three years before. His two grown sons, successful business executives who, according to NSA files, wanted nothing to do with their father's vendetta against modern society.

"Well, Bob," Barrington said. "What's the good word?"

"Nothing to worry about, sir," Ingersoll said. "The situation is well in hand. The girl isn't a problem. She's a typical hacker, no close friends or family. There's no possibility of her causing us any trouble. In fact, I'm toying with the notion of shifting the blame for this operation on her. She makes a perfect scapegoat. By the time we're finished, Mr. Barrington, hackers will be as popular as child molesters."

"Perfect," the old man said. His eyes narrowed. "How's the boy holding up? More important, will he be able to deliver on time?"

"No question about it," Ingersoll said. "Your friends—the ones who told you about Nikonchik's code—were right. The kid's a genius. The plan remains on schedule, sir."

Barrington laughed, a dry wheezing sound. "Then let them tout the benefits of electronic money and unlimited Internet access."

Ingersoll smiled, said nothing. The old man was tiresome, but necessary. Covert operations needed an untraceable source of seed money, funds not connected with the government. Iran-Contra had proved that. Tony and Paul, Harry and Greg didn't work cheap, and they required half in advance. Ernie Kaye and his crew of cops weren't cheap, either.

Murder *cost*.

And why shell out the money required to set up thousands of bank accounts, when Barrington had resources to burn?

Besides, Barrington's compound provided a safe base of operations. Nobody would ever think of looking for a top secret NSA operation *here*.

Listening to the millionaire's ramblings would prove to be a small price to pay.

CHAPTER 11

By noon, Judy was ready to call Steve Sanchez and tell him she'd take his full-time job at any price. All she'd need was a hot computer and a chocolate Yoo-Hoo vending machine.

Her eyes burned from exhaustion; the road was a fuzzy blur. Twice, she nearly dozed off and had to jerk her shoulders against the seat to knock herself awake. Three times, the car drifted and almost careened off the road. She nearly ended up in a creek. The creek itself was blinding: the morning sun shooting off it in glittering prisms of white and orange.

She was desperate for food. Something to drink. And her fingers ached from clutching the steering wheel.

Her route began with a winding blast down Hostetter, Capitol, and Morrill streets: wide, broad avenues crowded with low-rise apartment buildings. The suburbs surrounding San Jose looked no different from those of Los Angeles, or any big California city. They were hot and crowded with life. Fifteen percent of the country lived in the long narrow stretch of land between San Francisco and San Diego. Millions of people searching for the good life, for the big payoff.

Judy had worried that the old beater she was driving would attract attention. Not around here. This was the low-rent district.

She'd continued east for nearly an hour, then north on Old Piedmont Road. The hastily scrawled map took her up into the foothills, past a huge reservoir, and after a half dozen twists and turns, through the area known as Poverty Ridge. Judy kept even with the traffic, so she wouldn't attract attention, and she paid close attention to street signs. If she got lost, she was finished. The car she was driving was so ancient it didn't even have an on-board navigator.

Finally, with an empty stomach and a near-empty gas tank, Judy steered the wreck into a dirt lot adjacent to her destination: a ramshackle wood cabin tucked into the forest at the base of a steep mountain. If nowhere had an address, this was it.

She kicked open the car door, and almost tumbled to the dirt. The air was even cooler here than back at Laguna Beach, and scented with pine. A stream gurgled somewhere to her left, and pine needles stirred, *whish whish,* gently.

She shut her eyes, sank against the car, her legs trembling. If she had to run again, she might very well turn herself in, just to get some food and sleep.

Again, it was a scruffy man about her age who found her, propped her up, led her into the cabin, and made her sit down. This time she was beyond trying to comprehend. His name didn't register, nor did anything he said. She was just too far gone.

He left her slumped on a scratchy blue sofa that made her legs itch. The sun filtered through a curtained window above the sofa, casting yellow dots on the rough-cut wooden walls.

She fell into a deep sleep.

When Judy awakened, the dots were gone, as was the sun. In their absence, the room was lit by a pole lamp and two large lamps that sat on end tables. Circles of light hit the walls. It was pitch-dark outside. Night had fallen.

Faces emerged from the light, faces linked to bodies, a guy and a girl, both a few years older than Judy. They sat together on another blue sofa across the room, separated from her by a coffee table and a short expanse of wood floor.

The guy was lanky, probably well over six feet tall: his knees jutted high off the sofa, hiding his waist from view; his arms were long, the cuffs of his flannel shirt unbuttoned and dangling well above his wrists. His face was covered in whiskers, and a thicket of black hair curled to his shoulders. Duct tape glued both sides of his glasses to the lenses.

The girl was whispering something in his ear. She was petite, looked five feet tall, at most. Her short blond hair appeared as if she'd hacked it off with a garden shears. She wore ragged jeans several sizes too large, topped by a man's green flannel shirt.

Well, the two of them *looked* cool enough—no skirt suits, no fancy stuff—just laid-back types, who didn't give a freak what they wore.

Yet, they were people *in the flesh*. Strangers. And Judy hadn't done well with Tarantula and Grouch. She'd been rude to Tarantula, and she hadn't exactly been gracious to Grouch; instead, she'd scrambled out of the place after insulting everyone, without so much as a thank-you.

If only there was a way to run somewhere, hide, get her energy back, her focus.

Her stomach was growling and gnawing at her insides, as if trying to nourish itself with her body. Her cheeks and shoulders were splotched with red hives from the glittergoo hair.

Freak on the run.

She rubbed her arms, trying to massage some warmth into them. Her knees were shaking from the cold mountain air. Her teeth, chattering.

"Looks like you're in bad shape." It was the guy. His voice was softer than she expected.

The girl rose, her hand on the guy's shoulder. "Judy, I'm Bren. This is my husband, Carl. Grouch E-mailed us that you were coming. Just before he was busted. You'll be safe here, at least for a couple of days. We're pretty far off the mainstream."

"Then . . . you know who I am?"

Carl stood and put his arm around his wife's waist. The two were pressed tightly together, both trembling slightly, their words soft and low. They seemed nervous, as if they weren't used to company. Carl said, "You're Judy Carmody, the one wanted for murder. TerMight."

Wanted for murder. Unbelievable. "So . . ."

"Nothing to worry about. We trust Grouch."

"But Grouch—"

"Was busted. Yes," Bren said.

"Don't worry," Carl said, "we have no direct connection to Grouch. We've never met him in person. Only on the Net. We give him technical advice; he does the same for us. The cops won't be able to trace you here unless they're psychic."

The only people Judy even half trusted were people she'd never met. People from all over the world. Technical people: programmers and engineers. Trading technical tips. As long as the power held and the lines were open, it was happyland for everyone.

Carl and Bren reminded her of Grouch and Tarantula. Only, this was a little different. Carl and Bren had real names, not E-mail address names. And they actually lived together; they were married. No avatars, no facades to hide the flesh behind the words.

"VileSpawn?" she asked.

Carl laughed. "Haven't cracked it yet." Same as Grouch.

"Your equipment?"

"In the bedroom," Carl said. "We sleep here on the sofa."

"Whatever." Bren poked a finger at the half dozen earrings dangling from her right ear. "We can talk later. Look, you take a bath—Carl will show you where—and then you can put on some of my clothes, eat, and tell us about everything. Okay?"

More than okay. For the first time since leaving Sanchez Electronics, Judy began to feel at ease. Carl and Bren weren't trying to grease her ego; they weren't carrying on about her hacker exploits. They didn't seem to want anything from her. "Food first?" she asked.

"Food. Yes. Of course. I'm sorry, Judy." Bren's eyes twinkled, eyes that were gray with flecks of violet, unusual and very pretty.

"I'll do it." Carl slipped past Judy and down a dark hallway. A light flickered on. She heard dishes clattering, the whine of a nuke, and within moments, he returned.

They huddled around the coffee table, sitting on the wooden floor. Carl served stale bread, Gouda cheese, and hot vegetable soup. "We're health nuts," he said, as if offering an apology for the meal.

As if Judy cared what she was eating. She would have eaten

fried toads right now, and pickled squid suckers. Stale bread was fine.

"We're happy, as is. You know—high on love." Bren's hand touched Carl's cheek.

Judy nearly choked on her bread. Had she not been there, no doubt the two of them would be rolling on the floor. Like, forget the *food*.

These two had to be newlyweds. Who the hell was "high on love" these days? As far as Judy knew, the only thing people did was work, then go home and drop down, half dead, in front of Net videos and sound systems. Those without human connections, like Judy, cruised the Net all night.

"I'd better take a bath now," she said, cramming a final wad of cheese into her mouth and swallowing it whole.

They both looked at her, then at each other. Judy's chest tightened: it was that look again, that old what-an-idiot look. Or maybe in this case, *what an idiot* was infused with pity, as well.

She didn't want anyone's pity.

"I can't waste time." Her voice sounded harsh. Her black-and-gold-painted nails, the black all chipped now, began clacking on the coffee table, betraying her nerves. She slid her hands to her lap, beneath the table, where Carl and Bren couldn't see them.

"Time's never wasted, Judy," Bren said. "It's just not always used properly. Relax. Everything's cool. Now come on; follow me and I'll get you comfortable."

Pity. Forgiveness. Why couldn't Judy just be normal? Say the right things at the right times. Not cause everyone to get so wigged out.

Bren led her down the hall to the bedroom.

No bed.

No nightstand.

But a flipping *ton* of equipment.

Three desks holding huge-screen monitors connected to hand-whacked towers. Netpads everywhere. Laptops open on the floor. Two printers. Four large filing cabinets. Six floor-to-ceiling bookshelves stuffed with computer texts. Cables hooked to the walls and running into ceiling holes. Plenty of wall jacks, indicating ample modem access.

"This is where the action is." Bren pulled a knob, and slatted folding closet doors swung out. "Pick what you want, Judy; we're pretty much the same size."

Inside the closet she saw old PC skins, their insides junked, stripped of parts—probably cobbled into the machines on the desks. A pile of external modems, big clunky things with switches, a cigar box filled with memory chips, empty software boxes for graphics and movie programs, tons of Web applications . . .

"The clothes," Bren said.

Yeah, the clothes.

Judy rooted around, pulling a pair of boxer shorts and a ripped flannel shirt off a box labeled LavaTalk/C++. She tried to make conversation. "Your background?"

"Computer science major, UC Berkeley, then some graduate work, got bored, and quit. Met Carl there, and we shacked up. We've been together ever since."

Judy straightened up, clutching Bren's clothes to her chest. Here was a girl much like Judy—a Web wizard, a techie—and Bren even had Carl, something Judy had often dreamed about, a flesh person to share her world. Or just someone to talk to . . . like, *real-time* talk to . . .

Someone to free her from the prison of her mind, open her up, let her finally emerge. Sure, Judy had experienced the physical stuff, like hunger, cramps, and headaches. But her body had never felt the good stuff, like warmth, touch . . .

What was it like to have someone love you? To gaze at you as if you were beautiful, to talk to you as if you weren't a freak, to touch your hair, to hold your hand?

Bren was drumming her fingers on the top of a nearby computer. Her eyes shifted toward the open door. "Well, uh, if you want that bath now . . ."

Bath. Yes. *No.* Judy wanted to talk to Bren. She wanted to ask about Carl.

What she really wanted to know was what it felt like to be in love, to *be* loved, to feel sex. But those were taboo subjects. Never to be discussed, not with anyone.

So what could they talk about?

Judy's mother and aunts had often gossiped. Judy wasn't into gossip. And when Judy overheard women talking at shopping malls or on the beach, their conversations had always been about men, makeup, and movies. How fat they were, what diets they were on, what kinds of clothes made them look thinner.

She knew there were businesswomen out there, but she had even less in common with *them*. Those kinds of women were her *customers*. They wore suits and heels. They talked about trips abroad, fixing up their houses, their children's activities.

"Judy?"

She wasn't good at small talk, didn't want to come across like a computer drone. Wanted some of Bren's coolness to rub off on her. Wanted to learn how Bren managed to be a techdroid *and* a girl.

Bren smiled, shrugged, and gave it up. "Oh well, you know where to go." She fingered her earrings and ambled off to find Carl.

Judy was alone again.

Time's never wasted. It's just not always used properly.

Giggles filtered down the hall from the living room. Bren was using her time the right way.

As she crossed the hall into the bathroom, Judy peeked toward the living room. Bren was lying on top of Carl—they were on the floor—and they were kissing.

She slipped into the bathroom, gently closed the door. The tub, with its four brass legs and rusted spout, was waiting. She turned on the tap; the warm water would loosen the muscles in her arms, thaw her hands, wash the bloody scabs from her palms.

She unhooked the bikini top, slithered out of the filthy shorts, and sank into the warm water. She lathered the stiff greengoo hair, then with her eyes shut, dipped her head beneath the water.

Soaking, she let herself drift into a familiar daydream. It was early morning, on the beach, the sun just rising, the ocean split into Picasso planes of warm color: pinks and blues and greens. She was naked, and there was a man with her—a Faceless Man. Somehow, she couldn't feel his skin. His face was by her right ear, where she couldn't see what he looked like.

The Faceless Man didn't say anything, and neither did she. They never said a word, no matter how many times she dreamed the dream. But he *wanted* her; she could feel it.

And now he was going to have her. She felt the slight shift of his body, but as if she were removed from her own body, *observing* the feeling.

And then . . .

The dream short-circuited, like usual. The Faceless Man disappeared into the bath water.

She tried to replay the dream, to capture the moment and crank it forward a little.

But, as always, the moment was lost, and she couldn't do instant replay.

Pathetic really.

She might as well get out of the tub.

She wrapped her hair into a scrunchie on top of her head, glanced in the mirror over the sink. Her hair was no longer greenish yellow. The dye had been cheap, had pretty much washed out with one shampoo. A good thing. Or was it another disaster?

Whatever. Who cared? There were more urgent considerations.

This time, she didn't peek at Bren and Carl as she slipped across the hall into the bedroom.

She shut the door, then switched on a computer. She scanned the notes taped to the wall, found a bogus password, and logged onto the Net as CJSmith from Deadwood, Idaho. She jacked up her netpad and picked a handle from her cracker list. CJSmith became Bill Jones from Los Banos.

She surfed the newsgroups, seeking details of Hailstorm's death. Occasional giggles and moans floated in from the outer room.

Time had to be used properly.

She snapped back to it. Not a word about Hailstorm anywhere. No hint of suspicion, talk that he might have been murdered.

Abandoning that line of thought, she decided to see if there was any news about Griswald. Maybe even a post from him, saying where he was. Or why he had vanished. Again, after twenty minutes of searching, she came up empty. Griswald had disappeared, and no one seemed to care.

The Internet browser was a hacked-up kludge made from the one used by 90 percent of all Net surfers. It incorporated some hand-coded patches that provided several nifty tools, such as an integrated search engine/code editor. The search/debugger tool allowed full on-the-Netfly debugging and disassembly of source code from multiple applications: virtual reality worlds, Control-Freak, even LavaTalk, one of the newest technologies to hit the Net.

Bren and Carl were *good*. It was strange that they chose to live seemingly impoverished in the middle of nowhere. They could easily make a fortune selling their browser code.

Judy brought up Griswald's hack page on VileSpawn. It was one of her favorite sites. Here she found his old stuff: memory-dump tools, dead-file sniffers, sneaky code that shipped E-mail to Griswald whenever anyone hit his Web page—though Judy had a way around that one. She tripped the Web using fake log-ins and scrambled user IDs.

With Griswald's page on the screen, Judy touched the icon that cranked up Bren and Carl's search/debugger tool. Then she opened the source-code file for the independent-agent search engine. She would use the tool on itself, just to figure out how the tool worked.

Bren had programmed it, and it was an awesome piece of code. Clearly, Bren didn't realize her own talent.

The agent ran in the background, scanning the Net for key-word combinations, displaying all results with hypertext links and brief notes about detected sites. It was artificially intelligent, weeding out Web sites that had a low probability of a hit. It also analyzed hit patterns; it would look for Web sites that known hackers had hit. Very useful.

She typed, "Griswald and/or Fire," supplying the keywords for both Griswald's name and the moniker he used for cracking.

The screen displayed:

```
Searching.
```

While waiting, Judy downloaded the independent-agent code onto her netpad. It was well worth keeping such a handy tool.

Then she uploaded some of her own tools to Bren and Carl's machine. One dug into low-level network files and retrieved the locations of Web sites that had been previously viewed by the

browser. It was her version of Griswald's dead-file sniffer, only
in this case, it sniffed network routes from hidden files.

While the search engine chugged, she ran her sniffer program,
found that Bren and Carl were frequent visitors to a private
server called dan_land.com. On her netpad, she ran her password cracker against Bren's password, then logged into her own
browser and moved to dan_land.com. It was some sort of virtual
reality restaurant site. The menu listed over twenty types of
batter-dipped fried chili dogs. An odd place for Bren and Carl to
hang on the Net; after all, they were health-food nuts, and what
could be more disgusting than battered-dipped fried chili dogs?

On the desktop computer, she returned to Griswald's Web
page and waited, the browser colors blending into a screen saver
of neon tropical birds.

The waiting was driving her crazy. She couldn't stay here forever, hiding from cops. She had to find out why Tony Tuska
and Paul Smith had tried to kill her. Why they had framed her.
More than anything, she wanted to prove them guilty and make
them pay.

The rental car had been scheduled to be dropped off in San
Jose early Friday morning. It was already late Wednesday night.
Actually, the start of Thursday. Tuska and Smith would be in the
city in less than twenty-four hours. They might be here already,
searching for Griswald, planning to murder him and make it
look like a suicide.

There were too many questions, too many unknowns, and not
enough clues.

Trev. Poor guy. He'd never done anything but surf and paint
and crack stupid jokes. And she was the reason he was dead.

The computer beeped. The independent agents reported,

```
Search Done.
```

There were two matches for Griswald and Fire:

```
Central Intelligence Agency. Private intranet.
URL: http://13.555.44.5/~private/NSA/per-
sonnel.html.
```

```
Networks: ISDN header packets.
No URL.
Encrypted string Fire found in destinations
of packets
from 99.555.12.3, 88.555.77.6, etc.
```

Wow. How had the search engine hammered into the CIA's private network, into personnel records for the National Security Agency? And how on earth could it find encrypted strings within network header packets?

More important, it had found an entry that had occurred in the past day. That meant that either Griswald was still on-line, or someone was using his codes. Judy knew the second possibility was extremely remote.

Interesting that the search engine hadn't succeeded in locating Griswald's Internet address, his surfing home spot. He must be generating random and *very* fake machine identification numbers. Either that, or he was surfing via a series of anonymous and very hidden sites. Something Judy usually did.

From the outer room, Judy heard more giggles: Bren and Carl, lost in their own world, oblivious to what they had created and what it was worth, just lost in some goofy blissland that made no sense.

As far as Judy was concerned, love certainly made no sense. It was ephemeral. Judy's mother had lost her father. Judy had never trusted anyone enough to let them get that close.

Yet, listening to those giggles filled her with sadness. Part of her wanted to know what it was like to feel loved, even knowing it would end. She was tired of the Faceless Man.

But such thoughts weren't for her, at least not *now*. They slowed her down. It was best to focus on the task, always the task, and move forward.

She had to discover the motive behind Trev's death. Find out why Griswald had dropped out of sight. And most important, save herself.

She rested her fingertips on the keyboard. The light from the desk lamp cast a soft blue tint on the screen, easy on the eyes.

There was no way Judy would break into the CIA intranet. It was enough that she knew Griswald had done it. Griswald had always been snooping into forbidden areas. It was good to know he was still okay. Now, the trick was to make contact with him.

Her second clue, the network header packets, didn't help much. With faulty header packets, their destinations rerouted to false locations, all high-speed ISDN lines would go down in the area where the 99.555.12.3 and 88.555.77.6 machines were located. Once ISDN hardware analyzed packets with improper destinations, it deleted not only the header packets, but all associated data packets. There was no reason why Griswald would tamper with ISDN lines. Except, perhaps, as a clue so someone like Judy would realize that he was still *around*.

"Well, what are you up to?" A soft voice, and Judy whirled.

God.

It was only Bren.

"I—I'm trying to find traces of someone who was reported missing the other day on VileSpawn." Judy's heart was pounding, her fingers shaking. She sat on her palms, trying to warm her fingers.

Bren was rumpled, her hair more disarrayed than before, shooting out at all angles; her flannel shirt unbuttoned in three spots; one earring missing. But she was smiling, and her eyes were deep violet under the glow from the soft blue lamp. She laughed. "Yeah, Griswald. Carl and I were the ones who posted that message about him on VileSpawn."

"But . . . VileSpawn . . . you said—"

"I know. We said that we hadn't cracked into VileSpawn yet. But we do have friends, you know. Ever hear of symbiont@nonoland?"

Symbiont was low profile; he rarely posted anything on Vile-Spawn. "Sometimes," Judy said.

"We went to school with him."

"Oh. Well, why didn't you tell me?"

"About what?"

"About Griswald."

"Never occurred to me you'd be searching for Cal—that's Griswald's real name, Cal Nikonchik. You never mentioned him. Carl and I just figured you were studying police reports about—about the murders . . . or maybe trying to clear yourself. We figured it was best to give you some space."

Space? Judy needed all the help she could get.

She rose from the chair, put a hand on Bren's shoulder, almost hugged her. "Two killers are after me. They'll probably be in San Jose tomorrow. Looking for Griswald."

"Yeah?" Bren looked confused.

"I have to find him, don't you see? They'll kill him."

"I don't think Griswald's disappearance has anything to do with you, Judy," Bren said. "Actually, we only posted that notice because Dan kept bugging us for help. We did it to get him off our backs."

"Who's Dan?" Judy said.

"Dan Nikonchik, Griswald's older brother. He runs a greasy diner called Dan's DiskWorld in downtown San Jose. Serves chili dogs on plates that look like ancient computer disks. Big hit with the Silicon Valley types. Griswald runs his Web site, does all his accounts. Kid's a whiz with financial stuff.

"Dan's really overprotective of Griswald. Raised him for the past ten years, since their parents died. Dan means well, but he drives Griswald nuts. Carl and I are pretty sure Griswald just left town so he could get away from Dan. Dan can't accept that. Thinks his brother's been kidnapped or something crazy like that."

News about Griswald. His real name: Cal Nikonchik. His brother's name: Dan. Judy had found people who *knew* Griswald. Her brain rolled over into TerMight mode. The words started flowing. "Not so crazy," she said. "Why doesn't this Dan go to the police if he's so worried?"

"Good question," Bren said. "We're not sure. Dan doesn't trust authority figures. His parents were hippies, thought the government was run by jackasses. Dan doesn't talk much to me and Carl, though. Personality clash."

Bren shifted her gaze to Judy's waist and legs. Judy's face burned. She must look pretty awful standing there in Bren's long johns. But Bren said, "You want to keep the clothes, Judy? They look great on you."

There wasn't time for this kind of chatter. No time to be Judy. Had to be TerMight. She was close to finding Griswald, felt it in her bones. "Can I meet this Dan guy? Or would he turn me in to the cops?"

Bren settled into the chair, tugged her shirt to hide bare skin. "Dan's a total jerk. He's loud, arrogant, and crude. But he loves Griswald. I don't think he'll do anything to hurt you, if he thinks you're the key to finding his brother. Dan will do *anything* for Griswald. Because of the fire."

"What do you mean?" Griswald's cracker handle was Fire.

"There's a reason for Fire, Judy. Their home—Dan and Cal's—their home burned down back when they were kids. They lived on some back-to-nature commune with their freaked-out parents. One day, somebody lit a joint the wrong way, and *bam*, it all went up in smoke." Bren hesitated for a moment then continued. "Killed the parents, burned them alive. Dan pulled Cal out of the flames, tried to go back for his mom and dad, but it was too late. That's why Dan's so overprotective. He's scared, scared of losing Cal."

Loud, arrogant, and crude. Judy hated people like that. But who would know Griswald better than his own brother? Perhaps Dan could be trusted.

She might not have any other choice.

Judy tilted the desk lamp so there was less glare on the screen, then stood behind Bren. With her head clear, TerMight would know what to do. "I have some more work," she said, "and then I need some more sleep."

"No problem," Bren said, rising, walking to the door. "Sleeping bag is in the closet. I make Carl sack on it when we have an argument. Call if you need anything."

The door shut, and after a few minutes the low giggling returned as background noise. Judy again turned to her netpad, this time uploading some of her hottest hack stuff to Bren's computer: reverse-engineered code for the CIA's file server. She hated cracking into the CIA, but there were times when caution didn't pay.

She had to assume Griswald's identity. He was too clever to use a password an ordinary hacker could crack through ordinary means. No, Judy would find the log-in he *really* used, not some stupid listing in a password file.

Using system calls that dug directly into the file system, she found a binary file that had been created by Fire, only last night. She couldn't read the file, since it was all binary code.

Concealing text files within binary files. Using cryptography for sending hidden messages.

She had just the program to deal with it. She ran her code, split the end-of-file marker out of the middle of the file, and copied everything after the marker to a temporary file.

There it was, text planted at the end of the binary file: the word *Fire*, followed by Griswald's hacker password.

For a moment, Judy felt dizzy, couldn't type. She had Griswald's secret encrypted password. It was as if he were talking directly to her, through some weird, low-level whacko-nerd language. He *must* have done this on purpose. To reassure someone he was okay. Bren? Carl? His brother? It didn't matter. The important thing was that, having his password, she could send him a message. One he was sure to receive.

As Griswald, she logged into VileSpawn, moved to his private account area. Then she used an old text editor to plant a message:

```
This is TerMight. Tell me where you are, why
you disappeared. Tell me what's happening.
```

She snooped into his files. Something weird here. Genetics programming of some kind.

She downloaded the genetics programming code to her netpad. Then she changed all file ownerships from Fire to Water, and created a low-level and empty directory called TerMight.

She erased all entries in the CIA network files, anything that showed her presence. Then all entries in VileSpawn that showed the presence of Griswald.

Satisfied that she was finally en route to becoming a free woman in charge of her own life again, she logged off as Bill Jones from Los Banos.

CHAPTER 12

"Did you sleep well?" Bren set Judy's breakfast on the coffee table. Gouda again, and toast with jam.

The sleeping bag had been soft enough—at least, after Judy had cleared the cables, screws, pliers, and strippers from beneath it. The Faceless Man had rolled through her dreams all night, rewind-play rewind-play, interspersed with images of Bren and Carl on the living room floor.

She lied. "Very comfortable."

From the bedroom came the clatter of the keyboard. Carl was already hard at work, coding a corporate Web site for a customer he'd never met.

The morning sun flicked its way through the pine trees and glowed softly through the front window. It was like fairy dust on Bren's face. "I didn't sleep much," Bren said. "As you might have noticed, Carl's a hardworking man."

A secret joke cast between two girls? What did Bren mean? That Carl worked hard at coding Web sites? Or that Carl worked hard at . . .

Car wheels crunched into the lot by the side of the cabin. A door slammed, and then someone cursed.

"Dan's here," Bren said. She moved to the window, glanced

outside. "Yes, right on time, it's Mr. Nikonchik in all his gory flesh." Her hair, tangled from God knew what she did last night, was a golden halo shot with white and reddish sparks.

Bren opened the front door before Dan Nikonchik could knock. He blustered into the room. Next to Bren, with her peaceful, I-am-in-heaven face, next to those violet-speckled eyes and that smooth white skin, Dan Nikonchik looked like a gargoyle.

The upper half of his body seemed elongated, because his legs, while muscular, were too short to be in proportion with the rest of him. His face was rough, his nose a bit too broad. His hair and eyebrows were blond—not the golden impressionist blond of Bren's hair, but rather, flat blond, maybe from a bottle. Small black eyes darted around the room, as if he expected a chainsaw-wielding lunatic to pop from behind the furniture.

This was Griswald's brother?

What on earth did *Griswald* look like?

Maybe it was a good thing Griswald thought TerMight was a guy.

"I came. What's the big deal, Bren? And *who* is *that*?" Even his voice was harsh. Sandpaper.

He slurped coffee from a car mug that proclaimed, *Dan's DiskWorld: For the Hard-Driving Man.*

Bren gestured at the blue sofa across the room from Judy. "Sit over there, Dan."

He sat, still slurping, his eyes still darting.

Judy pushed her plate of Gouda and toast farther back on the coffee table. She had lost her appetite. She crossed her legs, folded her arms across her chest.

"May I present Judy Carmody. TerMight in the flesh." Bren seemed to be enjoying herself, proud to have TerMight in the house, amused to be toying with Dan Nikonchik. She plopped onto the sofa next to Judy, and as the left cushion sank under Bren's weight, the one beneath Judy popped up, tossing Judy slightly to the side.

Judy suppressed a laugh. Bren made her feel like a little girl. She bounced on her own cushion, just once, making Bren pop up.

Dan Nikonchik didn't smile. Rather, he glared at them. Especially at Judy. "So this is the great TerMight, is it? Judy Carmody, killer at large. Bank robber, too."

Rude.

Bren's face hardened. "Judy's no killer. And no thief."

"Right. Sorry." He didn't mean it.

"Bren—" Judy started. She wanted this guy to *go away*.

But Bren cut her off. "I asked you to come here, Dan, because Judy can help you find your brother. She hasn't killed anyone. She hasn't stolen a dime. And she thinks Cal's in danger."

"TerMight knows about Cal?" Dan put his coffee mug on the floor, hitched his blue slacks up his thighs, leaned forward, and placed his hands on his knees. "How *much* does she know?"

Judy pretended Dan was Hector Rodriguez, shut her eyes. "TerMight knows Cal Nikonchik as Griswald. I've known your brother for the past two years. On-line. We trade—" She opened her eyes. "—technical secrets."

"Holy shit, Bren!" Dan rose, his face turning red with emotion, his fists clenched.

"Relax," Bren said. Sweetly.

"Relax? Are you crazy? This—this person trades technical secrets with my little brother. She knows! And on top of that, she's wanted for murder. It's no wonder Cal's disappeared. He somehow got mixed up with this—this older woman, this killer—"

Nobody'd ever called Judy an older woman. And all this ranting about her being a killer . . .

Bren clasped Judy's arm, then released it and stood, pointing a finger at Dan. Her face no longer looked so calm and peaceful. She was plenty ticked off. "Shut up, Dan, and sit down. And get off that high horse. You're no choirboy yourself. Your little brother did all your dirty work for you. And I bet you paid him peanuts. How about if you tell us, right here and now, what you paid poor Griswald to fancy up your accounting files, huh?"

Judy blinked. Accounting files? Had Cal juggled his brother's accounts?

"Listen," Dan said, moving to the window, his back to Judy and Bren, his voice going low, "I pay Cal's rent. I give him a weekly allowance. He eats at my restaurant, for free, all the time. *I take care of Cal.* In return, he helps with Dan's DiskWorld. So what if he designed some of my business software. So what? He's my brother."

"Maybe you should have given him one more thing," Bren said.

"What's that?" Dan said.

"His freedom."

Dan shook his head. "Cal's a dreamer. He gets lost in cyber-space all the time. Besides, he's just a kid. He needs me to watch out for him. That's why I have to find him."

Judy had to keep the conversation focused. Somehow, with Bren on her side, with Bren acting as if Judy was the normal one and Dan was the weirdo, Judy found the courage. "Do you have any idea why Cal left?" she asked. "Did he leave any indication when he'd be back?"

"Nothing," Dan said. "It's not like him to head off without at least calling me first. He knows I worry."

He was responding; he was talking to Judy as if she was a normal person. She was actually controlling the conversation. "Maybe there's something on his computer, mentioning what he was planning. Did you check his files? Look at his E-mail for the past week?"

"Me?" Dan said, staring at Judy. "Do I look like some sort of computer geek? Cal does all the programming in the family."

"Well, how about if you let me take a look, then?" she said. "You might be getting all upset over nothing."

"Search Cal's computer files?" Dan said. He shook his head. "Not in a million years. There's important business stuff on Cal's machine, private stuff. I can't let you examine that. Sorry. Besides, how do I know I can trust *you*? All I know is that you're wanted for murder in Laguna. That's not exactly a five-star endorsement."

Judy didn't know what to say. She had to see Cal's computer files. There was something illegal in them; that was becoming obvious. Maybe something that tied in with Tony Tuska and Paul Smith.

"Listen," Dan continued, "be reasonable. Bren says you're in-nocent. I suppose I trust her. If you help me find Cal, then I'll help you. But, forget the files."

It was stupid, egotistical. Dan was used to ordering people around and getting his way. He didn't believe in compromise.

Judy glanced at Bren, who always seemed to know how to act, but Bren was smirking, obviously enjoying Judy's first en-counter with Cal Nikonchik's big brother. Bren slipped off her earrings, one by one, and placed them on the rough-cut coffee table. Then she swabbed each earlobe with a cotton ball and rubbing alcohol, and pushed the earrings back into her ears.

Judy stared at the tiny decorations: a musical note, a bird, a dangling NOR.

Judy wanted to get rid of Dan, set off, *alone,* to find Cal.

She wanted to get her ears pierced, then plug all the holes with NORs, every freaking one of them.

But it was critical that she remain focused. Her life was on the line, and time was in short supply. With a little bluster talk, it was amazing how she could get this control-freak macho type to go mute. He could hate her all he wanted. It didn't matter. He couldn't terminate her, cut off her cash flow, like a Hector Rodriguez or a Steve Sanchez might.

"Well, if you want me to help you find your brother," she said, "give me his apartment address so I can check out his equipment. There's no reason for you to tag along."

From the bedroom, Carl was humming while he coded his corporate Web site. Talking heads that explained how to use a business reporting system.

Bren pushed another earring into place. This one was a golden bus, smashed at both ends, and on it were the words *memory bus.* "Judy, you can handle this," she said. "I have to go squash some data for Carl."

Judy *could* handle Dan Nikonchik. He was excess baggage, clueless, a baboon. And Judy was doing just fine. And Bren, well, Bren was cooler than a time-zone frazz in happyland.

Dan said, "What good would it do to take you to Cal's place?"

"I'm TerMight. I need his computer."

"You're a girl."

"I'm *TerMight.*"

"You're wanted for murder."

Damn, how this jerk went in circles. So thickheaded. Moronic. "Someone tried to murder *me*, Mr. Nikonchik. Because I'm TerMight. And they nailed my landlord instead. And they're probably after your brother, too. Do you *understand*?"

He nodded, slowly. "Yeah. I guess. Okay. You can see Cal's files. But don't snoop too much. Just what you need. Come on; I'll drive you there."

Judy hoped to God Cal wasn't as big a jerk as his older

brother. Growing up under the thumb of this guy, it was no wonder Cal hid in programming, became the gonzo hacker, the great Griswald. No wonder Bren assumed that Griswald had just left town. *Anybody* would want to escape from Dan Nikonchik.

Well, she'd use this bozo to get her into Cal's apartment, so she could access the computer files, see if there was any information indicating where he'd gone. Then she'd pump Dan for information: what Cal looked like, what kind of clothing he wore, his personal habits. And then she'd dump this jerk back into his chili dog palace, and get on with it.

"So . . . where did you say this apartment was?" she asked.

"It's at 1405 West Spruce Drive. It won't take long to get there."

"You have a key to the place?"

"Yeah, I have a key. Cal's my brother, a kid, for God's sake."

Judy hooked her laptop strap over her shoulder, tucked the netpad into the pocket of her flannel shirt, a nice royal blue and green shirt, gift from Bren.

"Okay, let's hike," she said.

She followed him from the house, into the chilly morning air. His car was blinding red, a Porsche. She wasn't surprised, though she wondered how he could afford it. Guys like Dan always drove ridiculously fast cars. They thought expensive toys made them irresistible. It was all macho crap, but it was none of Judy's business. She couldn't care less.

"What's this?" he screamed.

She glanced at him. He was probably whining about some mud on his shoes.

But he was pointing at the car. A long scratch, as if made by a nail, etched a silver trail through neon red. The line went from the front bumper to the back, straight across the door.

"What's this?" he screamed again. "Who's been at my car?"

Like, Judy would know?

His body was shaking. His voice lowered to a whisper. "Someone's going to pay for this."

"Look. Tire tracks." Judy pointed to the dirt leading from the road to the cabin. "Looks like somebody *found* you here, Dan, maybe even followed you. They scratched your car for a reason.

Why? Has this got something to do with your brother's disappearance? With me? Are you mixed up in all this somehow?"

"What are you babbling about?" he muttered. His finger slid across the silver scratch. He winced. "It's the books, the damned books. Without Cal, I didn't close them out on Friday. It's been days now. Damn!"

"What *are* you talking about?"

He flipped open the password panel, fumbled. "Just drop it. Has nothing to do with Cal."

But obviously it did.

And Dan's voice was shaking. "Forget it. It's not important. Now, give me a second, entry code always causes me trouble."

She'd question him later, after he'd calmed down. In the meantime, she'd play naive, give in. For all she knew, he might even be dangerous. "No problem," she said lightly. "I know what it's like to have car password hassles."

She did know. Standing there, waiting for Dan to open the door with his electronic key, memories hit her like a rock. Judy scrambling to get into Tuska and Smith's car. Trev: *dead*. She could see him, collapsed on the apartment landing, blood on his face. His last words, telling her to run.

She glanced at Cal's brother and felt a sudden surge of sympathy. Poor guy. He was probably worried out of his mind. His only brother, whom he'd protected for years, gone. Maybe dead.

He knew *something*, though, and yet . . .

Whatever Dan Nikonchik was mixed up in, it seemed unlikely he would knowingly harm his brother in any way.

The locks clicked open. "Climb in," he said. "Time to make like detectives."

She opened the car door. Inside, the car's Net console hummed. Nearly two dozen icons glowed on its screen. The Porsche offered total touch control. Hitching her laptop strap higher on her shoulder, Judy clutched the case tightly to her side and climbed in on the passenger side. The car seat shifted beneath her, molded to fit her back.

She remembered how Bren had touched Carl's cheek. Human warmth: touch, contact. Time to try it herself. She touched Dan's shoulder. "I'll find Cal. I promise."

But Dan glared at her. Like: don't talk to me and don't touch me; what's the matter with you?

Perhaps people were only allowed to touch those who loved them. Perhaps touching another person implied some sort of sexual thing, or in the case of another girl—like Tarantula—it was just *uncool*.

"How do you know I'm not planning to take you to the cops?" he said tauntingly. Dan just never *stopped*.

One touch from her, and he got the edge. Yet she'd managed to shut him up before and get her way. Maybe she could do it again. Bren's temper had flared. Maybe being quiet all the time wasn't the ticket. "Because," she said, "without me, your chances of finding Cal are zero. And, somehow, I have this funny feeling you don't want the police involved in your *business*."

"Hey, I was just kidding," Dan said, his face turning pale. "Can't you take a joke?"

He touched the ignition icon, raced the engine. On the dashboard, a 3-D hologram cube burst into life, projecting a four-inch-high image of a big-busted bimbo in a bikini. Sound sensitive, the figure swayed back and forth with the muted whine of the engine.

Judy felt like an idiot, riding in a stupid red Porsche with black leather seats, a macho jerk by her side. Judy, in a pair of Carl's boxer shorts and Bren's oversize flannel shirt. Judy, with her tangled hair, her face haggard from worry and lack of sleep, from too much squinting at too many computer screens.

"Mind if I listen to some music while we drive?" He didn't wait for her answer, just touched the console, and instantly, the speakers came alive while a rock video flashed across the screen.

Yeah, she minded.

Irritated, Judy reached up. She ripped the hologram cube off the control panel, and dropped it to the floor.

Dan laughed at her. Reaching into his pocket, he pulled out a pair of sunglasses and put them on. Then, without another word, he stepped on the gas and the car roared out of the dirt lot, spitting dust and debris as it departed.

CHAPTER 13

For what seemed an eternity, they listened to the pounding music, not speaking. Finally, Dan squinted at her from behind dark shades and said, "You ever actually *meet* my brother?"

He twisted the steering wheel and sent the car zooming past some gawking teenagers.

A blip of purple and pink hair, wide eyes, scruffy clothes—that's all Judy saw; then the car was speeding past sushi joints and taco places, hologram arcades and software shops. A late-morning smoggy haze drifted across the blue sky, the last of the marine layer. Fancy cars with fancy license plates zipped past: ELECTRO1. WHIZKID. SHEBANG.

Everyone trying so hard to be cool. Everyone failing.

Judy didn't care. She never went with the flow, never followed the crowd. That was one of the reasons she had liked Griswald. From his posts, she knew he was like her: quiet, shy, nervous around loud people.

He probably wore cutoffs and T-shirts. Didn't need or want a shiny new car or fancy shades to proclaim his greatness. And with a know-it-all control-freak brother like Dan, Cal was probably an introvert, maybe a slob, programming because he found it stimulating and challenging. He was an anomaly in these goal-infatuated days, where information technology departments pumped out graduates by the thousands, all of them pretty worthless in the slaughterhouse of real-world programming.

Cal most likely had sloped shoulders, a huge head for that huge brain, and a pile of pimples. For some reason, Judy found that comforting.

"Did you hear me, Judy? Ever *see* Cal?" Dan poked her arm, even as he swerved onto a freeway, cutting off three other cars.

Horns honked; lights flashed. Dan didn't seem to notice. He acted like he ruled the road. Laws were made for other people, not for him. Judy hated drivers like Dan, *hated* them.

"No," she said. "I have no idea what Cal looks like. Nobody on VileSpawn posts image files. We're more interested in content than glitz. Care to enlighten me?" Thinking, hoping, praying: man, I sure hope he doesn't look anything like you.

"Console: Sound off." At Dan's command, the blaring music stopped, though the screen remained alive with video. "Open the glove compartment. I keep some photos in there."

She twisted the latch to the glove compartment, and poked through the contents. DVDs of rock music, like what had been playing on the console. Buzz junk, synthetic noise for hyperaccelerated times. Breath mints, guaranteed to work all day; a large steel ring with tons of keys on it; a package of condoms.

Unopened.

A gold wedding ring decorated with what looked like interconnected tetrahedrons. She pulled it out of the glove box.

Seeing it, Dan flinched as though it might bite him. The car jerked from eighty miles an hour down to fifty. Behind them, a car honked and swerved.

His face twisted. His knuckles were white. "My—my mother's wedding band."

"Same guy who nailed your car?"

"Ring was in the safe-deposit box," he stammered. "In *my* safe-deposit box."

Her heart lurched. That was *enough*. "Okay, then, you tell *me*, Dan, who could get into your safe-deposit box, steal your mother's wedding band, and stick it in your glove box? And why? Why the scratches on the car?"

"None of your goddamn business."

"Yeah, it's my business. I'm in this car with you. And somebody's following you and leaving some pretty strange messages. You tell me what's going on. *Now.*"

"Nothing to do with you. Find Cal's photo. We have to find Cal. Then everything will be fine." He glanced into the rearview mirror. "My God, it's them!"

Now what? She looked over her shoulder. A beat-up green Volkswagen bus, some fifty years old, wheezed behind them, driven by an ancient guy with a white beard and no hair on his head. Beside the guy was an old woman, her white hair curled into a bun.

"You're afraid of that old junker?" Judy had to stifle a giggle.

"They always come in a green van."

"But *that* green van?"

He peered into the mirror again, relaxed a little. "Maybe you're right. That doesn't look like it. I'm letting it get to me. Gotta calm down. Look at my brother's picture. Get a move on, would you?"

Judy sighed. He was hopeless. She dug into the glove box again and found two photos, both of a guy who looked like a taller, thinner version of Dan Nikonchik. Like his brother, Cal had blond hair. Judy wondered if Cal's was real or dyed. Unlike Dan, he had intense blue eyes. Intense, as if he could read your mind, right from the photograph. Cal had long, slim fingers, arms that dangled at his sides, as if he felt awkward in front of the camera. Both shots were taken at a beach. He wore jeans and a zoid T-shirt. Around him clustered children in swimsuits, playing ball; mothers in sun hats, reading magazines; young boys in stud suits, ogling girls in string bikinis.

The only surprising thing about Cal Nikonchik was that he looked like a kid. A teenager, maybe fifteen or sixteen years old. She'd always thought Griswald was in his mid-twenties. On-line, his words were those of someone older, someone her age.

"He's *young*," she said.

"That's what I *told* you. My brother is a child. He just got out of high school. He's only seventeen, still underage. I'm his legal guardian."

"And you?"

"I'm twenty-eight. I became Cal's replacement father when I was practically his age, just over the legal limit."

Yes, Bren had mentioned the fire.

Two boys, orphaned, the older one taking care of the younger one.

Must have been a nightmare for an eighteen-year-old Dan to suddenly have to play father to a seven-year-old Cal. Judy imagined Dan, so young, losing his own parents in that fire—instantly having the responsibilities of parenthood thrust upon him, as well.

Poor Dan, never allowed to grow up himself. Having to become an adult before he had a chance to be a teenager. No chance for college. No chance to hang at parties, have wild nights with girls. Just work, work, work . . .

Same thing that had happened to Judy, just a different twist. A much more horrifying twist.

"He looks perfectly harmless, doesn't he?" Dan said.

She wanted to say, *Yes. I'm sorry, Dan.* But she was afraid it would come out wrong. It was one thing to handle a control-freak macho grunt for whom she had no respect, someone who wasn't even an employer. It was another to handle someone like . . . Dan.

His lips were tight, his forehead lined with worry.

She gazed out the window. The road was jammed with traffic. People everywhere looked bored and frustrated.

Some things never changed. Nobody was ever happy. Except perhaps for people like Bren and Carl, who ran away from it all and hid together in the woods.

No matter what people did for a living, even if they had lovers, wives, husbands, children—they were never satisfied. Blue-collar types wanted to climb the white-collar ladder. White-collar types wanted to control everyone, everything. Managers wanted to be vice presidents. And vice presidents and district chiefs, like Rodriguez, wanted to be CEOs. Even Steve Sanchez, with all his money, still pushing, beating, hammering for more. Always climbing the ladder, *never* satisfied. Never stopping to view the scenery.

At least she wasn't caught in *that* rat race. Judy's only goal was to be happy. Like Bren and Carl.

"Damn!" Dan pumped the brakes, jerked the car to a halt just before it crashed into the car ahead of them. Judy's intelligent seat moved forward with her, cushioning her back. Her seat belt pulled a little more tightly at her waist, then released her again. If Dan kept driving like a maniac, the air bags would pop out, inflate, and throw them both into the backseat.

She'd done better on her own in a dilapidated ruin with a freaking shift on the floor.

From her laptop case, she pulled out the green box that Tarantula had thrust at her. It was a gizmo well known to hackers, one created using schematics that were easily available, via anonymous download from the Web. With a flip of a switch, it would alter upcoming traffic-light patterns.

She flipped the switch, and all the way down the street, as far as the eye could see, they had green lights. Then she said, "I'm going on VileSpawn. Who knows, maybe Cal's posted a reply to that message."

"Sure. Anything would help," Dan said.

As she expected, there was no word from Griswald. But, there was something else waiting for TerMight:

```
@>>>>---
```

Another dead black rose. Judy read the words posted beneath it with growing horror.

```
VileSpawn reports: Larabee dead. Hacker
master. The man who put the Clipper chip in
its well-deserved grave. Cracker of the en-
cryption codes, published on the Net. No
friend to authority. Killed in a fire in LA.
```

Larabee, a guy Judy had never met, originally off a node somewhere on the East Coast. He was a hero in the underground hacker world, legendary for his exploits cracking federal encryption codes as fast as they were developed. He'd disappeared years ago, after having made peace with the government.

The black rose was a day-old posting. Tony Tuska and Paul Smith had talked about arson in Judy's apartment. She had a terrible suspicion that Larabee's death had been no accident. Only somebody with info gleaned from classified files could have tracked him down. But for what reason?

Why was the government killing hackers?

"Any news?" Dan asked.

"You want the truth?" Judy asked. "Or the candy-coated stuff?"

"If it involves Cal's disappearance," Dan said, "I'll take the truth."

"Two hackers are dead," Judy began, "and, if it hadn't been for a sweet, innocent guy named Trev, it would have been three." She spent the next twenty minutes filling Dan in on what had taken place over the past two days. Judy left out nothing, even describing the false alarm about Laguna Savings.

As long as she stated facts and avoided personal subjects, she was fine. The words just flowed. In return, maybe Dan would tell her about the scratched car and the wedding ring.

But he didn't. "And you think Cal somehow learned about these two murderers, and that's why he disappeared?" he said. "But you have no idea why they're killing people."

"Right," Judy said. "What do you think? Did he say anything about all this?"

He shook his head. "You're wrong. Cal wouldn't have to run. If some lunatics were on his trail, even if he thought there was the slightest danger, he'd tell me." Dan paused, seemed to hesitate on his next words. "I have friends, influential friends. They'd have kept Cal safe."

It wasn't very reassuring. Judy wished she knew a little more about Dan's friends.

Ten minutes later, Dan parked the car next to a curb in San Jose. They were on a main highway that cut straight through the heart of the city. It was tightly lined with dilapidated low-rise apartment buildings and cheap bars. Broken glass and beer cans littered the sidewalk. Definitely *not* a high-class neighborhood. Urban renewal had been here and walked away.

Pretty meager digs for a guy with Cal's talent. Judy wondered where Dan lived. Probably in some fancy condo surrounded by pesticide-drowned grass and man-made ponds.

Dan commanded the Porsche to switch off. Cars whipped on past in a blur of color and noise. It was early afternoon, and the only people visible were a couple of drunks who were sprawled in front of a bar half a block away.

"No sign of your murdering pals," Dan said, taking her elbow. "No cops, either. Come on. Let's look inside, see if you can find anything on Cal's computer. If you're right and those killers are after my brother, I'd prefer not to run into them."

They walked past the trash that was piled on the sidewalk, past some half-dead bushes with flowers that were shriveling in the intense sun, up the two stairs that led to Cal's apartment building. It reminded her of the place she'd rented in El Toro, way back when.

A dump.

There wasn't a video ID system. The hall door had no lock, and hung loosely on its hinges. She swung it open. Inside, the floor tiles were cracked and dirty. Brown and yellow, probably purchased by the landlord forty years ago at cut-rate prices. A lot were missing, and the gaps had been filled with cheap plaster. The walls were grimy, too, off-white plaster coated in dust and black soot. A lightbulb hung from a string that was hanging from the ceiling.

Trev could have fixed this place up. Trev could have painted it, patched it, cleaned it.

How many more would die? Trev, Hailstorm, now Larabee. And Judy felt certain Tuska and Smith were still after *her*. But why? Who benefited from dead hackers? How was Cal involved? Nothing made any sense.

To her left there was a row of ten mailboxes, each with a buzzer below it. Half the boxes were hanging open and vomiting envelopes and advertising leaflets. She found the one for Cal's apartment, number 2B.

Maybe she hadn't needed Dan for a key to Cal's apartment, after all. It would have been easy to crack into a place like this.

Dan was already halfway down the hall, passing beneath a brown-and-yellow arch and into the murk that lay beyond. She walked after him. Her skin tingled. Any second she expected Smith to jump from a doorway, gun in hand, screaming obscenities as he squeezed the trigger.

The arch separated the front of the building, the A apartments, from the back of the building, the B units.

"Here we go. Little brother's digs, number 2B." Dan twisted the key into the lock, and kicked the door open.

Poor Cal. His place really was a dump. One small room with a cot, two steel chairs, and a desk loaded with computer equipment. Industrial gray carpet, thin and dirty. In one corner she saw a sink, microwave, and small refrigerator. A half-closed door led into the bathroom. Suspiciously, Dan pushed it open, turned on the light. It was empty.

"Dismal place, but nothing strange," Judy said.

"His clothes are gone," Dan said. "He always piles them on the floor by the bed. So's his laundry bag."

A rumpled blue sheet covered the bed . . . *cot*. No blanket. A child's pillow, embroidered with his name.

Very dismal.

Two posters hung on the wall behind the cot. One was a life-size figure of a dark-haired bimbo in a bikini. In each hand she was holding a gun.

"Mistie Lane," Dan said, with a crude laugh. "Cal's favorite TV star. The lead character in *Beach Babe, Private Eye*. Loaded and ready for action. Some woman, huh?"

"If you get your kicks from liposuction and plastic surgery," Judy said.

"She's not even real," Dan said.

One of those create-your-own bimbettes. You could download them from joints heaped all over the Net. Mistie Lane and Dad's Blushing Bimbo.

Was Judy any better with her Faceless Man? He was a figment of her imagination, nothing on a screen, but still, he wasn't *real*. The Faceless Man couldn't hurt her. He enticed; he was a physical unit without emotional substance. She didn't have to talk to him. And even if she did talk to him, which she wouldn't consider, he would respond in any way she wanted. She could rewind-play, rewind-play him all night, for as long as it took, until his reactions were perfect.

So here was Mistie Lane: breasts like two giant mashed potato blobs pasted on an anorexic stick. Mistie Lane was a toy for macho pigs like Dan Nikonchik, for adolescents like Cal, for men who never grew up, like Dad. Only her outer skin surfaces were rendered. There was nothing inside her. She was a vacuum.

"Why do you get off on Mistie Lane?" Judy asked.

Dan laughed. "Because she's the perfect woman."

Clearly Carl thought Bren was a perfect woman. And Bren was alive, fully 3-D. Bren talked back; Bren had emotions, and a brain.

"I don't understand," Judy said.

Dan gave Judy the once-over. It was as if he thought, of course you don't understand, because you're not a real woman.

She didn't care to be appraised this way, scanned like an item at the checkout counter. As disgusting as Dan was, even *he* didn't think she was good enough. Maybe all men classified a certain subset of women as Desirable, and the rest of the women—like Judy—were lumped together as Work-drone Money-making Genderless Pack Animals. Would it be better to be a beautiful and desirable vacuum-headed playmate?

Bren didn't have to choose. Bren was allowed to be both: desirable, *and* a human being capable of thoughts, emotions, and intelligence.

"Judy, we have to get on with it."

She jumped, then said softly, "Yes."

"I didn't mean . . . I can't explain . . ." He reached to touch her, but she withdrew.

"It's okay," she whispered, but her voice was unsteady. Dan didn't have to explain his sexual preferences to her, and she didn't want to hear about them anyway.

She turned to the other poster. It was a chart of the human genome. On either side of the chart were intertwined DNA strands. Someone, probably Cal, had drawn black crayon lines, linking genes to the strands. The text was entirely in German.

"German?" she asked Dan.

His face softened. He seemed relieved to change the subject. "When he was twelve, Cal discovered the chart in the back of a health food store. Owned by a guy from Berlin who had moved to San Jose when the Cold War ended. Cal was fascinated by the diagram. The owner let him take it. He's had it ever since."

"He's interested in human genetics?"

"Beats me," Dan said. "We never talk much about science. It's all Japanese to me."

He pointed to the computer. "Why don't you do your magic? See if Cal left some clue where he went. Or why he's gone."

But when Judy turned on the machine, nothing appeared. Absolutely nothing. The disk drive was dead, the operating system gone.

"Looks like he's done an f parm, with 0:0 fff 0," she said.

"Whatever the hell that means."

"In short, he trashed his system."

They stared at each other, obviously thinking the same things. Had Cal done it? If not, then *who*?

CHAPTER 14

Silently, they emerged from the gloom of Cal's apartment, back into the baking heat and the soot that floated through the San Jose air.

Judy stared down the road at the bar, wondering if Tuska and Smith would stagger out, catch sight of her, and pull out their guns.

Dan circled his Porsche, checking for more damage. Then he lifted the hood to the trunk and peered inside. Looking for dead bodies? To Judy, his actions no longer seemed so ridiculous.

"Come on," Dan said, as they climbed back into the car, "do a trace on those two characters, Tony Tuska and Paul Smith. See if you can find out where they are. And let's make tracks."

Seemed like a decent enough plan. She would sure feel a lot better knowing Tuska and Smith *weren't* in that bar down the road.

Since Judy had stolen their car, they'd probably obtained a replacement. She nodded while Dan signaled and pulled away from the curb. "I'll check all the rental car places at LAX. Plus all motels in the area. They usually require a credit card number to hold a room. I already have one of Tuska's card numbers."

"Why not siphon off his money?"

"Because then *he* would track *me*. For now, he probably

doesn't even know I have access. I want to keep it that way. Besides, I don't do that sort of thing. Tell me, did *Cal* ever get really annoyed with someone and use his computer to retaliate?"

"Damned if I know," Dan said. He had developed a habit of staring at her whenever he spoke. At seventy miles an hour, Judy wished he would pay more attention to the road. "Like I told you, I'm just an idea guy. Cal handled all the high-tech stuff."

"Well," Judy said, "if you want some good advice, don't ever tick off a hacker. Meaning someone like your brother. Or me."

"So why don't you screw up Tuska and Smith, if it's so easy?"

"Because I don't know who they're working for. And if these guys get wind of where I am, they may very well send a hundred Tuskas and Smiths after me. If it wasn't for that, believe me, I'm mad enough to slap them with histories of polygamy, child abuse, and mental illness—time in some state mental institution. It'd be a pleasure putting them up to their ears in debt, giving them massive back taxes, and pegging them as wanted fugitives." She was getting fired up. It was easy talking about technology. About strategy.

"Well, calm down, why don't you?" Dan glanced nervously in the rearview mirror. Checking for the green van, no doubt.

"Just don't get a programmer mad," she added. "Not even a guy like Jose Ferrents."

"Who?"

"A programmer at Laguna Savings. Even people like that can destroy your life. *Accidentally.* This one guy screwed up the accounts of thousands of people and businesses all over Laguna Beach while trying to fix a security breach. Nice enough guy, smart, means well; but one innocent mistake, and *pow*, a programmer destroys it all."

Judy returned to the netpad screen. As she expected, there were no matches for Tuska and Smith at the rental car agencies. "The whole world's on-line these days. A really good hacker can break into any file, government or private, local or national, alter or destroy the information, and leave without a trace. It's a breeze."

She was on a roll. "In ten minutes, I can charge all your credit cards to the max. Donate all your money to charity. Brand you with a criminal record a mile long, so detailed your best friend would be convinced it's real. I can foreclose on your house, even if the mortgage has been paid off for years. List your car as stolen, invalidate your driver's license. Cancel your telephone services, electricity, and communications services. Or declare you legally dead and probate your will. And that's just the simple stuff."

"Anybody can do that by just obtaining a credit card number?" Dan asked. He was beginning to look positively green.

"Not anyone," Judy said. "But I could. And so could Cal."

"Hell," Dan said. "What a mess. What a goddamn mess."

Judy stared at him. "What are you muttering about?" she asked.

"Nothing," he replied. "Nothing at all. Just wondering how I got mixed up in all this junk. Any luck with your trace?"

"Not a peep," Judy said, turning off the netpad. "These guys aren't dumb. That credit ID was as phony as a three-dollar bill. Tuska probably has a dozen of them, completely separate, impossible to trace without days of serious hacking. And I don't have days. Not if they're in San Jose right now."

With a sudden twist of the steering wheel, Dan swung the car off the highway and down a single-lane road, capped by trees.

"Where are we?" Judy said. "This isn't the way to Bren's house."

"Woods between San Jose and Santa Cruz," Dan said. "We're making another stop. There's this guy, a close friend of Cal's, another programmer, who lives out here. I called him when I started worrying about Cal. Said he didn't know anything. But I know he doesn't think much of me. Just like Bren. Maybe he'll talk to you, though."

The road curved up the mountain, whipped to the right, then back to the left. Dan, obviously still preoccupied with what she'd said about hackers, didn't bother to cut his speed.

Judy's head filled with a stuffy dizziness; she got that sometimes from the smell of leather. The car swerved and her body jerked to the right. Her arm hit the door release and she let out a groan.

"Sorry," Dan said. "I'll take it slower."

"Could you roll down the window? Please?"

"Car has climate control. If I open the window, we'll be covered with dust."

"If you don't," Judy said, "I'll throw up. Take your pick."

"Gotcha," Dan said. He pressed the icon on the Net console to roll down the passenger-side window.

Despite the dust, Judy breathed the country air with relief. Her head began to clear. If she had her way, she'd live far out in the country, like Bren. Away from the pressures and stress of city life, away from people like Steve Sanchez, Hector Rodriguez, and Dan Nikonchik.

Dan pulled the car into the gravel driveway of a lone ranch house shrouded by trees. He told the car to raise the window, then turn off. He tapped his password into the console twice. Suddenly the air was still.

Judy peered through the windshield at the tiny home. One window bore flowered curtains, another had ape monster decals on it. This friend of Cal's had children. At least two, a girl and a boy.

The front door of the house opened, and the forest was no longer silent. Two boys, both about five years old, leapt off the front porch, scampered around the side of the house and behind some trees. A girl, hardly old enough to walk, tottered after them, wearing white shoes and a frilly dress. She clutched a Raggedy Ann doll and bawled for her brothers to wait.

But, of course, they didn't.

"If you can't guess, Jeremy has a family," Dan said. "Cal spends most of his holidays here. He and Jeremy are pretty tight."

The screen door banged open again and slammed against the siding. A woman emerged. She was round and flabby. Frizzy brown hair framed her face. She wore black, flat-soled shoes and a bland, washed-out dress, old-fashioned, that hung below her knees. "Get back in here, boys! We're going to Grandma's any minute."

The woman ran across the lawn and snatched the toddler into her arms. The girl cried and thrashed, but the mother only held her more tightly. "Stevie? George? Get back in here *right now*!"

Dan sighed. "It never changes. Reminds me of life on the commune. Why my brother *enjoys* hanging out with these people, I'll never know." He pressed the release to the car door and clambered out, brushing off his pants.

The woman looked up, startled. "Why, Dan Nikonchik, shows where my mind is today with these kids! I didn't even notice that bright red machine of yours in my driveway!" Still clutching the screaming girl, she walked through the sparse grass toward the car. The boys, Stevie and George, reappeared and raced after her, laughing. They looked like twins: same height, nearly identical features, and identical impish grins.

Judy opened her own car door, struggled to her feet. Her body still ached, and her arm was bruised from crashing into the car door.

Dan nodded toward Judy, then at the woman. "Judy, this is Jeremy's wife, Natalie."

The two women exchanged greetings, and Natalie explained that she was taking her children to their grandma's today for dinner and a birthday party. "Jeremy's in the house," she added, "plugged into his computer. He's staying home, working."

Of course.

Judy followed Dan into the house and through the living room, which was heaped with toys and unfolded laundry. The house smelled like onions and frying hamburger. Something sizzled in the kitchen.

Outside, Natalie screamed at her boys, who apparently had scampered back into the woods. The little girl howled. The noise dimmed, perhaps muffled by the clutch of trees, as Natalie chased her children into the woods.

Judy couldn't remember any time when her mother had noticed what she was doing or where she was, except late at night, when she heard Judy's computer keys clacking and yelled at her to go to bed.

Jeremy was in a bedroom at the rear of the house. As Dan and Judy entered the room, he turned, surprise appearing on his face. "Hey, Dan, what are you doing here? Hear anything from Griswald?"

"Not a word," Dan said. He waved a hand at Judy. "Jeremy Crane, meet Judy. Judy's a friend. She's helping me look for Cal."

Jeremy rose. Tall and burly, he wore a pair of bib overalls and a faded blue T-shirt. He looked more like his daughter than his sons, with light brown curly hair and large, innocent brown eyes. But unlike his daughter, who got plenty of exercise chasing her brothers, Jeremy was as soft and fat as his wife.

"Pleased to meet you," he said, stepping over an Ipex 14-gigabyte magneto-optical storage drive on which rested a High-Edge 8-megabyte VRAM circuit board the size of a business card. He held out a hand, puffy and white as a marshmallow. "You know Griswald?"

"Just from VileSpawn," Judy said.

"Really?" Jeremy said. "Who are you? I'm JC."

"TerMight," Judy said, recognizing Jeremy's nickname immediately. She smiled, suddenly feeling more at ease. Jeremy was familiar, safe. He was from her world.

"TerMight's a girl?" Jeremy said, grinning. "Griswald know that?"

"No," Judy said. "But I'd like to tell him in person. Do you have any idea where he might've gone, JC?"

Jeremy shook his head. "Not a clue. Like I told Dan, Griswald hasn't been around for more than a week. Nothing unusual. He's like that. Gets obsessed with a problem, forgets everything else until he solves it."

"Yeah," Judy said, "I know exactly what you mean. Story of my life, too. This time, though, we're afraid Griswald's being chased by some dangerous characters. We really need to find him. Fast."

"Antitech loonies?" Jeremy asked. "They're getting worse all the time. I watch them on the nightly news, demonstrating in the valley. Computers are dangerous, the Internet's destroying privacy, the usual junk. Guys like that jerkoff Barrington on his Web-TV show, talking how we should turn back the clock. Meanwhile, he's using the latest technology so his show is seen nationwide. What a flipping hypocrite."

"We don't know why these guys are after Griswald," Judy said.

"Sorry," Jeremy said, "wish I could help. But I don't know a thing." But there seemed to be something he wasn't saying.

A red phone icon flashed on his screen. "Yeah," Jeremy said to his computer, "JC here."

A gruff voice asked for Dan Nikonchik.

Surprised, Jeremy nodded toward Dan.

"How'd they know I'm here?" Dan said, startled. He grabbed a headset from the desk and barked the order "Private."

Good question, Judy mused. And if *they* knew Dan's whereabouts all the time, they knew her whereabouts. And if *they* were Dan's unusual friends with the ability to save people's necks, why weren't *they* saving Dan's and Cal's and Judy's necks?

Dan muttered, "Yeah, yeah, I understand. Friday. No problem. I'll take care of it."

Despite her curiosity, Judy's attention was caught up in the moving images she saw on Jeremy's computer screen. There were video clips of what looked like real people, only their faces and bodies were continuously shifting, changing dimensions, and transforming.

Adjacent to the keyboard she spotted a multimedia controller and some microphones, the kind used to conduct wiretaps. The wall behind the computer was covered by a huge sheet of wood paneling. There was a button beneath it. A sliding door. Instantly, Judy's suspicions rose. Here was a programmer who used microphones and video software, who changed people's images by using digitally recorded clips. A surveillance operator.

He was probably employed by the cops. Or the government. Or maybe some of Dan's *friends*.

Dan removed the headset.

"What was all that?" she asked.

He shrugged. "My bookie. I bet on the wrong horse."

A crook calling about a gambling debt, tracing Dan *here*?

Shaking, Judy took a step back. "I don't believe you. You're lying. What about the green van, the wedding band? I want the truth, Dan. No more crap."

"Don't get so damned hot," Dan said, raising his hands in protest. "I'm not lying. Ask Jeremy. He knows. I like playing the ponies. No crime in placing a few bets. Had a bad luck streak. Bookie wants his money. He's been tightening the screws until I pay up."

"He does like to gamble, TerMight," Jeremy said with a shrug. "Stupid habit, but nobody's perfect."

Judy stared at Dan in disgust. "You sleazeball. Griswald lives in a dump and you blow your money on horse races."

Still driven by her anger, she swung around and faced Jeremy. "You work for the police, JC?"

Jeremy's eyes bulged. Then, after a second, he laughed. "My equipment, right? No. Never. This setup is my big project. Something I was working on with Griswald. Object-oriented stuff—you know, changing various instantiations of the objects, as in change them to different faces and so forth."

Dan grimaced. "While the two of you blather about computers, I'm going to get something to eat. Okay with you, Jeremy?"

"Sure. You know where the kitchen is."

Seconds later, Judy heard him rummaging around. Drawers opened and closed, cabinets banged, dishes clattered. God, the man was *noisy*. You'd think he'd be better in a kitchen, owning a restaurant and all.

"Don't worry about Griswald, TerMight," Jeremy said softly. "He's been anxious to go it alone ever since he got out of school. Freedom from big brother. You can see why. I'm sure that's what happened."

"He could be in major trouble," Judy countered.

"No way," Jeremy said. "Who'd want to hurt Griswald? He's harmless."

Judy couldn't answer Jeremy's question. She had no explanations, only fears.

"Anyway," Jeremy continued, rubbing something squishy-looking across his screen, "I have tons of multimedia equipment here. I develop software for *legitimate* uses. Mainly, I'm into creating pliable environments for people."

That explained the microphones and the panel on the wall. She fingered the button on the wall, pressed it. The wood sheet slid up, revealing what she expected: an immense monitor.

"Here. Wear these." Jeremy insistently thrust a pair of sunglasses at her. They looked ordinary enough. She put them on.

Then he told his computer to turn on "The Room." His eyes were glowing. He was proud.

The screen popped to life showing the room in which they were sitting. There was an image of Judy, but all the clutter and the furniture had taken on cartoonish colors and rounded forms. In addition, she appeared plumper, and her hair was neat and glowing with gold highlights. She wasn't wearing the special sunglasses.

She looked rested and calm.

Judy reached out and saw her hand and arm move on the screen, as well.

"Populate," Jeremy commanded. Suddenly, cartoon animals and goofy aliens and neon swirling blobs appeared around her screen persona. She was fascinated, couldn't pull her eyes from the image.

She reached out and touched a fluffy green creature, which giggled and licked her fingers. She felt the moisture from its tongue, felt the soft warmth of its fur.

Felt it.

The creature said, "I'm Dozong from the planet Alphatrod." Its voice was high and squeaky.

She laughed. Without thinking, she replied, "I'm Judy from the planet Lost."

"Where's the planet Lost? It must be far from Alphatrod. And I know your real name. It's Judith Carmody, and you come from Pennsylvania, don't you? And you're a programmer."

The creature was talking to her, holding a real conversation with her. More, *it knew things about her.*

This was no mere virtual reality. This was much too sophisticated for fun and games.

"Who created you?" she asked. "How do you work?"

The creature snuggled up to her, wrapped six tentacles around her legs. They were as soft and cozy as the comforter she'd had on her bed when she was a little girl during the cold Pennsylvania winters. Unlike the comforter, though, Dozong's tentacles pulsed.

She could feel its heartbeat! In six separate places on her legs!

She pressed her hands to her cheeks, and gasped.

"Amazed, aren't you?" Dozong said. "That's why you've got your hands on your cheeks."

Smart. Very smart. And it could *see* her.

Suddenly, the screen blinked off. Hands removed her sunglasses. Jeremy's hands. "Pretty awesome, huh?"

She stared at him, dazed. Judy wanted the glasses back. She wanted Jeremy to switch his program back on and return her to the comfort zone of Dozong. To the most astonishing display of digital reality she had *ever* experienced.

"It's incredible," she finally managed to say.

"Artificial intelligence, artificial life: Griswald's babies," Jeremy said. "That's his specialty. He's a genius with this stuff. He developed most of the code. Some sort of genetic A-life routine. I'm more into hardware myself. I build the cameras, whack together cheap microphones, prime the CPUs, that sort of thing. Griswald and I make a great team. When we get the last few kinks out of this system, we're going to be rich."

Judy agreed. The Dozong project was worth millions. It was decades beyond the create-a-chick Net joints, where guys bought time with hand-tailored bimbos like Mistie Lane. A-life evolved on its own, without human intervention or structured programming rules. And Dozong even came with touch sensors—most likely part of the special glasses— feeding into her skin and triggering neurochemical transmissions right by her ears, eyes, and nose.

Dozong explained some of Cal's fascination with Mistie, or so Judy preferred to think.

But she was pretty sure the Dozong gig had nothing to do with Cal's disappearance, with Judy, Larabee, or Hailstorm. Or the murders. It just didn't seem to fit.

Judy knew little about technology that was *this* sophisticated. "How does Dozong—"

But she didn't finish her sentence. Heavy footsteps came down the hall. Dan poked his head into the room. He was holding a bag of nacho chips, munching on a handful. "I found these in the cupboard, Jeremy. Hope you don't mind."

She couldn't believe it. Walking into someone's house, and taking food from their kitchen. Dan must have noticed her expression.

"Well, I was starving," he said defensively, tiny flakes of nacho chips dropping onto the motherboards. He crammed another handful of chips into his mouth, crunching them noisily. "Didn't have breakfast this morning."

The computer monitor beeped. Bugs Bunny's voice announced, "Someone's at the front door, doc."

"Where's Natalie?" Jeremy asked, frowning. "She always gets the door when I'm working."

"She said something about going to Grandma's house," Judy answered.

"Yeah, I forgot. Probably just a delivery. I buy a lot of my equipment through the mail."

Dan dropped into Jeremy's chair as the big man headed for the front door. "Learn anything important?" he asked, wiping greasy hands across his pants.

Other than you're a slob?

She said, "No question, Cal's brilliant. But companies don't kidnap or kill computer geniuses. They hire them. This is a dead end."

"What the hell," Dan replied. "It was worth a try. We can drive back to Bren and see if she's had any ideas. At least now you can tell her I'm not imagining things. That Cal's in real danger."

"Sure," Judy said. "She owes you an apology. Of sorts."

Jeremy reentered the bedroom, carrying a three-foot-long cardboard box in his arms. His eyes were glowing with excitement. "Like I thought. New microphones for the system. Been waiting for these babies all week."

He looked at the two of them. "Anything else you need to know?"

He was anxious for them to leave so he could play with his new toys.

Dan took Judy's elbow. "Let's go. Jeremy's got work to do, and so do we." He steered her out the bedroom door. Over his shoulder, he said, "Jeremy, thanks for your time."

"Yeah, sure," came the reply. Jeremy was already searching through the clutter on his desk. He grabbed a pocketknife. "Just let yourself out the front door. Everything will turn out fine."

"Well," Dan commented as they walked across the grass to his car, "that was a total—"

A boom, roaring like thunder, cut off his last words. Gouts of red fire poured out the front door and windows of Jeremy's house. A blast of superheated air lashed at them.

"What the hell?" Dan yelled. He staggered, a look of total astonishment on his face. "Oh my God. *Jeremy!*"

He raced across the lawn back toward the wood house. Judy, her heart pounding like a hammer, followed.

There was no going inside. The blast had ripped the front door right off its hinges, blown the glass out of the windows. A blazing inferno raged within. There was no chance that Jeremy could still be alive.

Dan stood motionless in front of the building. His face was white. "Oh my God, oh my God," he repeated again and again, his gaze fixed on the little house.

In the distance, a truck's motor coughed. Someone was coming up the narrow road that led to what had been Jeremy's home. It was too soon for the police or fire department. Judy, her mind racing, knew who it had to be. Grabbing Dan by the arm, she started dragging him toward the forest.

"What are you doing?" he demanded, trying to pull himself free.

"It's them," Judy said, "the killers. *Don't you understand?* They're coming back to check on their job. And if they find us here, we're dead, too."

CHAPTER 15

They ran for the woods in blind fear. Judy's breath came in deep, ragged gasps. Her lungs felt ready to burst. Black dots swam before her eyes. Behind them, the fire crackled and roared, quickly devouring the wood-frame building.

"Get down." Dan dropped to the ground, behind a big pine tree, pulling her down next to him. She collapsed on the pine-littered soil, the needles scratching her arms and legs.

Behind them, a truck door slammed.

Twisting around, Judy raised her face from the earth. Two men stood in front of a brown delivery truck less than a hundred feet away. Motionless, they stared at the burning house. They were talking, but the roaring fire blotted out all sounds of their conversation.

Judy moaned. Though they were dressed in brown uniforms, she recognized both men. Tony Tuska: muscular stud body, black beard, dark sunglasses, his wrist wrapped in gauze, a strip of white tape covering the top of his nose. Paul Smith, tall and thin, sallow face, foul expression, his hand in a lightweight cast, where she'd hammered her computer case against his fingers.

Judy squeezed her eyes shut, trying to lock out the memory, the look on Trev's face. These men were killers. First Trev, now

Jeremy. She could feel a scream welling up deep inside her, a scream she couldn't control.

Cold hands gripped her shoulders, fingers that felt like icicles on her skin. "Don't panic," Dan whispered. Fear glazed his eyes. His face was dead white. "Stay down."

"Dan," she said, barely moving her lips, "those are the guys who killed Trev."

He nodded, but said nothing.

Smith was looking at the red Porsche. Smiling, he said something to Tuska. Both men laughed. Evidently, they thought the car had belonged to Jeremy. Old house, new car, the California way of life.

Still smiling, they climbed back into the big delivery truck. The motor coughed, then roared to life. Seconds later, they were gone.

A wave of relief rolled over Judy. She sagged against Dan, grateful now for the presence of his solid body beside her. His one arm was still wrapped around her shoulders. For a minute, neither of them said a word. Slowly, the tension drained away.

"We gotta get out of here," Dan said. "Fast."

Fear made her twist away. "Not yet. They might not be gone. They could be waiting up the road."

"I doubt it," Dan said, rising to his feet. He half pulled, half dragged Judy up beside him. "Sooner or later, the fire department will arrive. And with them, the police. We can't stick around this place very long."

"We can go back to Bren and Carl's house," she said. Jeremy was dead. Poor, sweet Jeremy, a man with a family, a man who got off on creating warm and cuddly creatures like Dozong, just to amuse people like Judy. "It's safe there."

"*Don't you understand?* No place is safe. Once they find Jeremy's body, the cops will contact Natalie."

Where was Natalie? Where were the children?

"Dan," Judy said, "how do we know that Jeremy's family, his children, are okay?"

He opened the passenger-side door and pushed her onto the seat of the Porsche. "Because the killers showed up after the explosion, just to make sure it had happened. Natalie and the children are safe, off visiting with Grandma somewhere. But," he added, sliding into the car beside her, "nothing will be fine this afternoon. The cops will locate Natalie. She'll tell them about our visit. She'll tell them about *you*. The police aren't dumb. We're going to take the blame for Jeremy's murder. The two of us. Now, we're both fugitives."

Judy sat—stunned—as Dan turned the car around and headed for the highway. He was right. Natalie hadn't seen the delivery truck, hadn't seen Tuska and Smith. She had seen only Judy and Dan. Poor innocent Jeremy, poor innocent Trev. Linked only by Judy. It wasn't fair. It just wasn't fair.

Fear was becoming like an old, familiar blanket. She had to resist. "This car's too easy to spot," she said as Dan steered the car back onto the throughway. "Even if I screw around with the computer registration, there can't be that many red Porsches in San Jose. We have to make a switch."

"Hell," Dan said. His hands tightened on the steering wheel. "I know you're right, but I hate abandoning this baby on the street for the cops to find. I bet they tear it apart looking for clues."

"No choice," Judy said. She remembered her problems from the other night. "Park it close to a cash station. You need to make a withdrawal. Your accounts aren't frozen like mine. Grab as much cash as possible. We won't have the opportunity later."

"Police will discover that quick enough," Dan said.

"Who cares?" Judy said. "Four people are dead and we still don't know why. More important, if we don't find Cal soon, it's going to be five."

Dan scowled. "How do we even know that? Maybe Cal's dead already. Maybe these two lunatics killed him first."

"He's alive," Judy said. "I know. Last night, on-line, I found Cal's password, hidden in a file. Posted there recently. No message, but definitely from him."

"Why the hell didn't you tell me?" Dan said. Angrily, he jammed his foot hard on the gas pedal. For an instant, Judy was sure they'd crash into the van directly in front of them. Then, Dan pumped the brakes, slowing them down. "I deserved to know."

"Sorry," Judy said. She had no excuse, so she didn't try inventing one. "I sent him a short message. Asked him where he was. Hopefully, he'll reply."

"Yeah," Dan said. "Do me a favor, though. Don't wait all day before letting me know."

Twenty minutes later, Dan's pockets filled with twenty-dollar bills, they were on a bus heading north. They needed another car, but Judy knew better than to steal it near the abandoned Porsche. A smart cop would link the two events. And she was taking no chances.

CHAPTER 16

Cal sat on the polished wood floor of his bedroom, his toes curled beneath the throw rug, his head by the air-conditioning vent. He ran his fingers along the grill, savoring the chill that crept up his arms, only to dissolve into heat at his shoulders. His hair was damp with sweat and sticking to his back. He ducked his head and let the vent blast cold air through the tangled blond mess.

Luckily, Greg and Harry weren't around. An hour ago, a messenger had summoned them to a meeting at the main house. Cal hoped the NSA boss had a lot to say to them. This was the first time in a while Cal had been left entirely alone. He meant to take full advantage of the situation. He would goof off, listen to his new DVDs, and chill out—so to speak.

As he ran his fingers along the grooves, felt his hair whip around his face, he reflected with an ironic chuckle that he'd never thought this way in San Jose.

Used to be, he stayed up all day and night, coding just to code, hacking just to hack. To be the best, the smartest, the one nobody else could outclass. Now, he wanted nothing more than to *stop* coding, get himself out of this bungalow, this desert, and back to bleak old reality.

Thanks to the new drive Mr. Ingersoll had purchased, Cal's all-time favorite music cranked. It was the DVD he'd always listened to back in his apartment whenever he logged onto the nets as Griswald. All digital, a great beat, post-techno stuff. Really *driven*. Songs like "Crackerjack Jive" and "Cursing Fibonacci: My Recursive Love."

On one of the lower grooves of the AC vent, his fingers touched something flat and round. Sweeping hair from his eyes, he peered into the vent. There *was* something round in there. He pushed it. Then, discovering that the thing *moved*, he pried it off the inside of the grill.

Tiny, it resembled a bug, an old-style microphone, a transmitter. And it was cold, like maybe it wasn't working right. How weird.

He'd always figured the room was bugged, but not with an old-fashioned gizmo like this. The best way to record his words would be through software on his computer. These NSA guys were *lame*. If they really wanted to monitor what he was doing, they could even watch him through his computer screen. Though Mr. Ingersoll and his employees probably figured—and correctly— that Cal would notice anything unusual on his computer.

Cal pulled a piece of the cleanser wad from his pocket and wrapped it around the transmitter. Then he cracked the transmitter against the floor. Good. A nice dent, candy-wafer split down the middle. He pushed the unit back into the air-conditioning vent, then pulled himself to his feet. The ammonia cleanser, coupled with the dent, would silence whatever remained of the bug. Cal didn't like people snooping on him. And things were bad enough in this desert dump, what with Greg and Harry breathing down his neck all the time.

He was wasting precious time. Not that he wanted to *do* anything right now, but if he had any hope of figuring out this NSA setup, he'd better get busy. He wanted answers for some questions that kept nagging him. For instance, why was the government running this whole operation from the desert instead of somewhere in San Jose? Mr. Ingersoll was nuts if he was concerned about Internet Security. The ISD could search all they wanted. When Cal used his code to surf the Net, he was invisible. It was impossible to trace him.

There had to be some other reason for being stuck out here. Dan had told him all about Watergate and Filegate and Chinagate. This whole operation probably violated a *bunch* of government regulations. As if he could care. He'd done worse jobs for Dan without even getting paid.

When this NSA project was finished, he'd be rolling in dough. That's what really mattered.

Still, he had no desire to go to prison for his country. He was no vid-screen patriot, just a hacker. If Mr. Ingersoll wasn't playing it straight with him, Cal wanted to know. Which was why he planned to search the bedroom that Greg and Harry shared.

He wound a rubber band around his hair, forming his usual ponytail, turned the music off, then slipped from his bedroom door into the short hallway that led to the rear of the bungalow. The sweat still dripped from his hair, down his neck and to his shirt. He was much too nervous to be a very good spy.

The guest house decor was simple, though posh. Even so, it was antiseptic, furnished with the kind of stuff rich ladies put in their living rooms, even in the twenty-first century. On the walls were framed western prints of cowboys riding the pony express. A tiny bureau of some kind stood at the end of the hall. It was a rich mahogany, all black with vibrant red glimmers, polished to a sheen.

He pulled open the drawers. Empty. On top of the bureau sat a vase of fake but very real-looking roses. They even had fake dewdrops on them. Very elegant, and ridiculous.

If Mr. Ingersoll was trying to make this dump feel like home, he was failing miserably. Home to Cal was a one-room dive on a main drag in downtown San Jose. A one-room dive stuffed with computer equipment and software journals and cables. Now, *that* was homey.

On the right was the door to the cottage's kitchen. To the left another door opened into Greg and Harry's bedroom. He pushed it gingerly. He'd never been in their room before. It was strictly off-limits. If they caught him here . . .

Best not to think about it.

He left the door wide open. Beyond his room, the house was

silent. If he heard anything, the slightest noise, he could slip out
of the room, pull the door closed, and enter the kitchen. In this
heat, a can of soda served as the perfect alibi.

Inside the room, he moved quickly to the dresser the two men
shared, pulled open the top drawer. Underwear, socks, steel
darts, black pellets of some kind. He dug through the second
drawer. Tan Levi's, two piles of shirts, nothing much here. Then,
in the final drawer, a photo of a woman wearing bikini lace underwear. A thin body, small chest, long brown hair. One of
Greg's babes? On the back there was an inscription: *To Greg,
thanks for the dirty work.* It was signed *G.*

In the air-conditioning vent was another microphone. Warm.
Whoever had bugged the cottage, it definitely wasn't Greg and
Harry.

Frustration burning through him, he left the room and shut the
door behind him. He went into the kitchen, grabbed a can of
cola. Popping the tab, he walked to the living room, slurping
down the cold drink as he went.

He dropped onto the sofa and contemplated his next move. So
far, all he'd found out was that Greg and Harry were obsessively
neat. And the whole cottage was wired for sound.

Maybe he should sneak up to the main house, peek in the windows. The ultimate would be snooping around Mr. Ingersoll's
bedroom. If only he could . . .

His mind whirled with wild plans, crazy schemes. But, before
he could settle on any of them, Cal heard male voices. Two men,
laughing. Coming closer. Greg and Harry were returning to the
bungalow.

With a final slurp of cola, Cal zipped back to his bedroom and
switched on the computer. He parted the curtains, peeked outside. Yeah, Greg and Harry were about thirty feet from the bungalow. In the heat, neither of them wore jackets. Their guns
gleamed in their shoulder holsters.

Cal's fingers wrapped around the ammonia cleaner/screen en-
hancer in his pocket. He squeezed. It didn't help ease the tension
much, but it was better than nothing.

Turning back to the screen, he touched the icon that executed
the bank-heist code in debugger mode. Mindlessly he watched it

run against a fake database on his machine. It was an exercise in nonsense. Only one bug remained in his code before he would be able to steal the money.

The code quickly determined all the best Net banks and Net corporations that were ripe for thefts, and it just as quickly executed withdrawal transactions, shifting the funds through dozens of computer nodes to secret locations that would be designated by Mr. Ingersoll. One problem had yet to be resolved.

The child chromosomes weren't killing their parents. At least, not rapidly enough to completely conceal the labyrinthine route the code would take to each bank and corporation.

Greg pushed open the door and walked into the room, Harry right behind. Cal turned, desperately trying to remain calm. Still, his fingers trembled on the keyboard.

"So how's it going, Cal?" Greg asked. His face was flushed, as if he'd just had a good time with some babe. "Close to that big breakthrough?"

"Everything's fine, real fine," Cal stammered. "Just one more bug, then I'm done." He paused. "How was your meeting? What's going on? More pressure from Washington?"

Greg laughed. He shook his head slowly. "You get rattled too easy, Cal. Only thing you should worry about is finishing the code on schedule. Mr. Ingersoll's tired of waiting. We all are. He wants results. Tonight's the night."

Harry twiddled with the curled ends of his handlebar mustache. For some reason, he looked a lot taller, a lot more muscular, a lot *meaner* than Cal remembered. "Listen to what he's sayin', Nikonchik," Harry said, slurring his words with that Southern drawl. "The boss is a bad man to cross. He's been pretty easy with you. It's time for you to earn your keep."

Greg settled into the black leather chair opposite Cal's, rested his elbows on his lap, propped his chin in his hands. "He asked me if you might be stalling, looking for more money, Cal. I assured him that wasn't the case. You're not that stupid, are you? Bad business, trying to sucker the U.S. government. Too many ways we can make your life difficult."

"No, no, no." Cal's fingers dug into the blob hidden in his pocket. His right arm began to ache. He hated pressure like this—reminded him of Dan, always bossing him around, trying to run his life. His brother meant well, but Cal needed freedom. He wasn't a kid anymore.

Greg continued. "You know, any work you do for the NSA is classified as top secret. This project is serious business, Cal. It's no game. And remember, the boss knows all about that stuff you did for your brother. That's why we recruited you, instead of some other hacker. You've got the goods, Cal. We're counting on you tonight."

"Yeah," Harry added. "Ingersoll runs a tight ship. Don't think just because he likes you, he won't press charges. One word to the FBI about the restaurant, and you and your brother are in deep shit. Stay focused, kid. No screwing around."

"I've been sweating my brains out trying to finish this code on time," Cal said. "Stop pushing me around. I'm working as fast as I can."

Old Mrs. Morgan at Bonita High was a charmer compared to Harry and Greg. All he had to do for her was keep his mouth shut, do essays, and show up for tests. Then he could let his mind wander, unscramble code, cook up new cracks.

Cal missed Jeremy, his best friend, and Jeremy's three kids. They were great. He was always happy when he was with Jeremy.

Not like with Dan, who was always bugging him, checking to see if things were okay, if he was eating right, if he'd met any girls. Dan was his only relative, and he tried too hard. He couldn't stop treating Cal like the little kid he'd rescued from the fire.

"Look," Greg said, "get back to that code. Finish it. Mr. Ingersoll's stopping by later. If you're smart, you'll have the job done before he arrives."

Cal didn't like the way Greg was talking. It made him even more nervous than he already was.

This time, the two men didn't ask Cal if he wanted a sandwich and cola. With a curt "we'll be back," they left him alone to slave away at his task. He heard them in their bedroom, chuckling over something. Beds creaked. Harry and Greg were taking it easy.

Well, pretty soon, Cal would be able to take it easy, too.

He'd have the dough from this job; he'd be on the beach; he'd be a hero.

He swiveled the leather chair, turned back to his computer. The genetics code could wait a little bit longer. It would take only a second to snoop into the compound's files again, search for some clue as to who was involved with this project. Cal had always been fascinated by spies, by the CIA. He'd spent many nights as Griswald, cracking into agency files, just to snoop around. And this operation had him curious as hell.

Thirty seconds later, Cal was logged into Mr. Ingersoll's computer in the main house. Using a simple utility, he ran a search that found and retrieved files that had been deleted from Mr. Ingersoll's disk drive. Any jerk could run a search and find deleted files. A long stream of file names appeared on the screen, and Cal mused once again how these NSA agents were simpletons when it came to technology. They used code, but they had no real idea how it functioned.

Selecting a recently deleted E-mail named *erniejudy*, Cal restored the file and shipped it back to his own computer. He removed any trace of his entry onto Mr. Ingersoll's machine, wiping out the log files in his usual way.

The *erniejudy* file was encrypted. When Cal tried to view it with an ordinary text editor, the file scrolled down his screen as gibberish.

No big deal.

Cal had plenty of decryption routines. He'd been in grade school when he cracked his first government code, not long after the fire on the commune.

And years ago, while in junior high school, Cal had cracked the code that Mr. Ingersoll was *still* using. It was awfully strange for the National Security Agency to use such an outdated method of encryption. Certainly, Mr. Ingersoll would have more modern versions of cryptography available at his fingertips.

After all, the NSA was the premier practitioner of cryptography in the United States. Its main functions were to decipher all foreign network communications that might impact U.S. security, and to stop the spread of cryptographic use. Everything the NSA did was top secret.

Cal remembered the outcry raised by all the net privacy hon-chos, back when *The New York Times* leaked the news that the NSA had purposely placed loopholes in the Data Encryption Standard language. The loopholes had let NSA spooks break anyone's DES-encrypted code.

Of course, DES had become irrelevant. Peter Krupland had cracked it in a day. Kind of interesting, though, that most major banks—like Laguna Savings—*still* used DES, albeit a more so-phisticated version.

All things considered, Mr. Ingersoll's choice of encryption really puzzled Cal.

It was Skipjack-Plus, a newer version of the algorithm that had been used on the old Clipper chip. Terrified that foreign powers would use crypto against the United States, the NSA had spent years trying to get everyone to install a Clipper chip and hand over their cryptocodes to the government. It had taken years for the computer industry to beat down any notions of using Clipper and Skipjack-Plus.

Talk about paranoid spooks.

So why on earth would Mr. Ingersoll use a crypto that had been passé for so long?

For the moment, Cal decided it really didn't matter. All that mattered was that he could easily read Mr. Ingersoll's encrypted *erniejudy* file in plain English. And here it was.

```
To: Ernie Kaye
From: I
Status: EYES ONLY
Subject: Judith Carmody aka TerMight

The following material is classified TOP
SECRET under the National Security Act of
2004.

Target: Judith Carmody aka TerMight; a lead-
ing hacker and independent computer contrac-
tor living in the Los Angeles area. Well known
in the industry as a major player in the bank
security field. Has cracked into all major
banks in southern California and recommended
```

cryptographic and Webmaster configura-
tions/firewalls; has cracked DES III, IDEA,
One Time Pad, PKP, Kerberos-A+, RIPEMD@-
260, MD4, MD5, MD6, and many other crypto
algorithms.

Home: 6905 Laguna Crescent, Apartment 3-2,
Laguna Beach, California.

Known hangouts: VileSpawn, hacking bulletin
board and newsgroup service; Sanchez Electronics, 1400 Digiton Boulevard, Laguna
Beach, California.

Physical stats: white Caucasian, five feet
two inches tall, approximately 90 pounds,
waist-length dark auburn hair, light brown
eyes, no glasses. Usually wears shorts,
bikini tops or T-shirts. Often seen with
Rollerblades and laptop.

Background: born and raised in rural Pennsylvania . . .

Cal gulped, stared at the screen. He couldn't believe what he
was reading.

For one thing, TerMight was a girl: Judy Carmody. But there
was something frightening here. Mr. Ingersoll was interested in
Judy Carmody. He had a complete file on her. Somehow, she tied
in with the secret project Cal was developing.

But how?

The report was sterile, written in typical NSA profile style. It
described Judy Carmody's parents, their divorce, her known personality weaknesses. But it wasn't hard for Cal to fill in the
blanks.

Lonely. Isolated. Just text, but the words resonated in Cal's
mind. He understood Judy's feelings, her emotions. It didn't require any great insight. In TerMight, he saw himself.

He skimmed several paragraphs about Judy's daily habits—
when she got out of bed, what she ate for breakfast, the kind of

music she listened to, her allergies, physical proportions . . . and on and on.

At the end of the file he found several encrypted binary files. Cal quickly decrypted them, as they were encoded using the same Skipjack-Plus algorithm. The first was a set of TerMight's fingerprints. The second, a complete DNA profile. The third, and most interesting to Cal, was an actual photo of Judy Carmody. Of *TerMight*.

She was tiny, all right, and very skinny. Her eyes were huge and very innocent looking for someone named TerMight. She had a wild expression, like an animal caught in the glare of head-lights. Her hair was thick and tangled, and indeed, hung to her waist. She was on Rollerblades, standing on a boardwalk, star-ing at the sand and ocean. A laptop case was looped over her shoulders. She didn't seem aware that she was being photo-graphed. Rather, she seemed lost, drifting, probably daydream-ing about a hack. Or perhaps, daydreaming about what she'd write to Griswald that night.

Ha, that was a stupid thought. She was almost Dan's age.

Cal's trance was broken by the beep of the front door's video ID system. Muffled footsteps hurried down the hall. Greg and Harry, heading for the living room. Someone opened and shut the door. It could only be Mr. Ingersoll. He had arrived earlier than Cal expected.

Cal's fingers hovered over the keyboard, his mind racing. Mr. Ingersoll was coming to see him. He'd better hide the TerMight file and bring up his genetics code on the screen, pretend to be working.

But there was a tiny blotch in Judy Carmody's photograph. A file hidden within the encrypted photograph. Cal *had* to find out what that hidden file contained.

Cal heard voices in the front room. More footsteps, this time in the hall.

Again, Skipjack-Plus decoding did the trick. Another memo appeared.

There was a polite knock on the door, and then, while Cal was still stuttering a reply, it opened. Bob Ingersoll stood in the doorway. He couldn't yet see the screen.

With the flick of a finger, Cal plunged the secret file into a hole in the deepest directory of his hard drive. But the contents of the hidden message, glimpsed only briefly, continued to burn like fire in his mind.

```
Carmody  represents  a  serious  threat  to
project. Make sure she does not interfere.
Use any means necessary.
```

CHAPTER 17

At exactly 3 P.M. Ingersoll arrived on the front step of the guest cottage. He could hear the video ID system beep inside. Harry opened the door immediately. Ingersoll smiled. His associates knew he was never late.

"Harry. Greg." He greeted the two agents as he stepped into the living room. "Did you speak with our friend, Calvin?"

"Yes, sir, Mr. Ingersoll." Harry stroked his handlebar mustache and grinned. "We put the fear of God in Nikonchik. You won't have any more trouble with that toothpick."

"Glad to hear it." Harry's Southern drawl irritated the hell out of Ingersoll; it seemed incongruous that a rough-and-tumble guy like Harry Barton would speak in such slow, curling sentences. The big man's flippant attitude grated on his nerves, too, and Ingersoll was sick of looking at those stupid turquoise cowboy slides and string ties.

Harry Barton was a brutal, unsophisticated thug, but he provided muscle necessary for the operation. Once Tony and Paul had finished the terminations in San Jose, Harry was scheduled to meet them at their hotel to deliver cash payments for services rendered. It was standard operating procedure for projects involving independent contractors. However, Ingersoll had rewritten the book on this assignment. Instead of green-backs, Harry would be carrying a gun. As the saying went, dead men told no tales.

Ernie Kaye would suffer a similar fate. Harry had been promised his victims' share of the loot. Ingersoll had no plans to honor that agreement, either. Hiring Harry Barton had been a challenge. Firing him would be a lot easier. Rid of three operatives, he saw no reason to pay their killer.

Tough as he was, Harry Barton was no match for a bullet to the back of the head.

Years at the NSA had taught Ingersoll all the rules of all the games. Ollie North was his hero. But Ollie had remained a golden boy to the end. Ollie had suffered the fool's fate. Ingersoll knew that only hard men who played very hard ball ever really won.

Keep the gold and ruby rings. Keep the pathetic retirement fund.

A life of devotion to the government.

An entire goddamn life of it!

Married to two women who had craved nothing but cash. Married really to his job, to his government, to the cause.

Ingersoll had the contacts and expertise to do as he wanted.

Cool. Always cool. Calm. In control.

And soon, very wealthy. Women like his ex-wives would be all over him. And he wouldn't have to marry them this time.

Ingersoll would be Ollie North's hero.

"You feel the same, Greg, that Calvin's ready to do the job, and tonight?" Though too much a ladies' man for his own good, Greg Larson was sharp. Ingersoll valued his opinion. "He's not suspicious?"

"Pretty much, sir," Greg replied. "Don't underestimate Cal, though. He's not very good with people, but that program he wrote for his brother wasn't used by a church social club. I'm willing to bet Cal knows more than we think."

"Who cares?" Harry sneered. "Greg overestimates the little shit. Nikonchik's scared of his own shadow. Slap him around and he'll finish the code quick enough."

"Much too dangerous," Ingersoll said. "We've invested a lot of time and effort, not to mention money, in this operation.

Everything depends on Calvin running the program exactly as designed. He's the one person we can't replace. Without his skills, we're nowhere. That means *no* violence." He paused, emphasizing his point. "Understand, Harry?"

"You make the decisions," the thug replied. He shrugged. "I follow orders."

Ingersoll nodded. He was the boss. Everybody else was just hired help. The entire plan belonged to him. And so did the payoff.

"I think I need to talk with young Mr. Nikonchik." He straightened his tie and brushed back his hair.

He tapped on the door to Cal's bedroom, then, not waiting for an answer, turned the knob and walked in. As usual, Cal sat hunched in front of the computer, his eyes fixed on the monitor. Startled, he looked up, then pressed the key that cleared his screen. Probably staring at those stupid publicity photos of that bimbo Net star he worshiped. Cal might be brilliant, but he was still a stupid kid.

Earlier in the week, the practice run at Laguna Savings had gone down perfectly. Tonight, the last hacker who might interfere with the heist would be dead. It was time to act, before anyone at the ISD started investigating the killings. The old man had cleared the way, had cut loose the millions that had been used to open accounts throughout the world. It was time to deliver.

Cal needed one final push.

"Good to see you, Calvin," Ingersoll said, settling in the black leather chair. "Ready for the big night?"

"Almost," Cal answered. His fingers drummed nervously on the edge of the keyboard. "I'm making progress. Taking longer than I thought. But I'm nearly done."

"You have the final code? We're scheduled to run the heist at midnight."

"Almost done," Cal said, slouching down in his chair. "There's one small section still giving me problems. Nothing to worry about."

Ingersoll frowned. Time to crack the whip. "I don't like what I'm hearing, Calvin." He leaned forward, resting his hands on his knees. "Harry and Greg assured me you were all ready. You knew the deadline. For days, it's been creeping closer. Tonight, we're scheduled to pull off the first run. And now you're telling me that it's *not* going to happen?"

Ingersoll rose abruptly to his feet. He paced, for effect. "Damn, damn, damn. I should've known better. Everybody in the agency told me I was crazy expecting a kid—a punk without any real programming credentials—to do a man's job."

He put his hands on the makeshift desk and stared at Cal. "It's *over*. The whole damned project's over. You blew it, Calvin. Spent too much time screwing around on the Net when you should've been working. My fault, too, for believing you'd come through when times got tough."

"I—I—" Cal began, but Ingersoll wouldn't let him get a word in edgewise.

"Too late for excuses." Ingersoll was talking fast now, keeping Cal off balance. "I've been under constant pressure to put up or shut up. The Internet Security Department has been trying to shut this project down ever since it cleared committee. Those sanctimonious sons of bitches refuse to accept the fact that their Internet safety measures aren't worth jack. Thanks to your goofing off, they win. And sooner or later, when the Urban Front or Chinese Triads or some lunatic fringe group with a grudge rips our banking system to shreds, the American public loses."

"But—" Cal was near tears. Ingersoll refused to let him interrupt.

"For years, I've fought for this project, demonstrating beyond the shadow of a doubt how vulnerable we were—*are*—to terrorist attack. It never got past the planning stages. Nobody would believe the threat was real. They accused me of seeing ghosts. Sure, there had been a few electronic bank heists, but nothing major. And the hackers were caught pretty fast. I had no proof, nothing concrete."

Ingersoll jabbed a finger at Cal. "Then, while doing routine checks on money laundering in San Jose, one of my sources ran across your code. The program you wrote for your brother's food joint. An undetectable method of filtering huge amounts of money, anonymously, to banks across the country. I could have arrested you and Dan for racketeering. Locked the pair of you in jail and thrown away the key. But I didn't.

"Instead, I offered you a job. A once-in-a-lifetime opportunity. Pushed a project through committee, put you on the NSA payroll at top wages. All I required was for you to modify your genetic code enough to help me prove my point. Show the world that Bob Ingersoll wasn't tilting at windmills. That my concerns about Internet security were legitimate. And now you tell me that, with our midnight deadline, the work's not finished!"

Ingersoll shook his head slowly. "What hurts the most," he declared, "is that I had complete faith in you. No other hacker could do the job. Not TerMight, not Larabee, not even Mercy. They lacked the proper vision, the necessary tools. Your genetic code was the key. But it's unfinished, and we're out of time."

"We're not out of time," Cal said, his voice wavering but still surprisingly strong. He pulled his little cleanser blob from his pocket and kneaded it beneath his fingers, as if drawing strength from the gummy material. "There's still hours to go before the deadline. The code's nearly finished. I'll get it done long before midnight. Don't forget, I'm Griswald. Mercy and Larabee and all the rest came to *me* for tips, not the other way around. Maybe I get nervous easy, but I'm the best. I know it, Dan knows it, you know it. After tonight, the whole world will."

Cal wiped the blob across his computer screen. "I couldn't care less about the ISD and the NSA. None of you care about the American public. That's not what this heist's all about. My brother taught me the truth about covert operations. This operation's just a power trip, a struggle between two departments. The rest of your patriotic talk is just bull."

"You're not as naive as I thought, Calvin," Ingersoll said. Silently, he was thankful for the lunatic fringe neo-hippies and their paranoid fears. "I should have realized you'd figure out the real motive behind my project. Budget cuts are in the air this year. One or the other, either the NSA or the ISD, is going to feel the ax. Your code will determine the winner."

"Sure," Cal said, sounding bitter. "Griswald rides to the rescue. I save Dan's restaurant business. I protect your retirement fund. But, when do I get my share?"

"Six hundred dollars an hour isn't a bad start, Calvin," Ingersoll replied, chuckling. "And once the project makes the newspapers and TV, you'll be famous. Companies will fight for your time. Cable stations will probably want to make a movie about you. This operation is the opportunity of a lifetime."

"It'll be done," Cal said. "I guarantee it."

"You'll have the code ready to run at midnight?" Ingersoll asked. "You're positive?"

"Yes, sir. A billion dollars, clean, just like the Laguna Savings run, deposited where you want it. Money gone, impossible to trace. Just like I promised."

"Good," Ingersoll said. "Very very good."

He stepped to the door. Reaching for the knob, he remembered Greg's warning. "Ever wonder what the *real* reason is for us hiding out in the middle of nowhere?" He grinned at the hacker's surprised expression. *Bingo.* "Because in the desert, nobody can catch you by surprise.

"It's war, Calvin, plain and simple. Between the NSA and Internet Security. The jerks at the ISD are scared to death of this operation. You can toss out the rules. They'll do anything to stop us—including sabotaging our lines, destroying our equipment, even commandeering our base of operations. They're mean SOBs. That's why Greg and Harry are here. To even the odds."

"Oh, sure," Cal said. "I figured it was something like that."

"Back to work, Calvin. Finish that last bit of code. I'll tell Greg to make you some dinner. And I'll stop back tonight to check out the results."

Opening the door, he stepped into the hall. Harry and Greg sat on the sofa, waiting. Raising a hand to his lips, Ingersoll motioned them to open the front door and accompany him outside.

"I've been thinking about our patron," he said softly, standing in front of the cottage. "The old man's a suspicious bastard. Wouldn't surprise me at all if the place is bugged, that cameras are focused on Cal in the bedroom. When you get a chance, see what you can find. Rip the stuff out. We're close to finishing up. I don't want anyone to know too much. Doubt if they could do anything with the information, but who knows. It never hurts to be extra careful."

"What about Nikonchik?" Harry growled.

"Calvin's going to do just fine," Ingersoll said. "Greg, bring him a sandwich and a drink a little later. Let our young friend work. No interruptions. Definitely no threats. I'll be back."

He looked at his watch. "Time for me to check in with Tony and Paul. I'll see you gentlemen later."

CHAPTER 18

A short time later, there was a knock on the door.

Ingersoll frowned. It was a few minutes past four o'clock. He wasn't expecting anyone, had no appointments scheduled except a return to the guest house.

Barrington was getting restless. He was pushing, wanted to see some return on his investment. It was time tonight for some concrete results. A billion dollars should satisfy the old man.

"Enter," he called. Probably the maid. Or one of the old man's flunkies, bringing news of a change in dinner plans. The old man lived like a king, and it was a lifestyle Bob Ingersoll could appreciate.

"Hello, Mr. Ingersoll," Gloria Simmons said, opening the door halfway and sliding through. She wore a maroon skirt, a beige cotton shirt, and navy pumps. She looked like she was draped in an American flag. All-American Gloria, the girl next door: the thought made Ingersoll chuckle.

Her dark eyes glowed with cold intelligence. "What are you laughing at?"

He scanned her body, letting his eyes pause at the correct places. She responded with an appropriate shiver.

He almost laughed again, but held himself in check. Instead

he said, "No reason in particular. Just pleased with the company. You look quite attractive in something other than a business suit."

Gloria smiled. "Why, thank you. How nice to be appreciated."

She settled into the plush burgundy chair across from his desk and crossed her legs. Her skirt rose to her knees. She made no effort to smooth it down.

Gloria Simmons was coming on to him.

Her legs were firm, tanned, and muscular. She noticed him looking at them. She bobbed a navy shoe, reached down and massaged her ankle.

No doubt about it, Gloria Simmons was a masterpiece of calculated manipulation. Ingersoll wasn't fooled. She could run through his office nude and it wouldn't mean a thing. Sex was a bargaining chip with Gloria, nothing more. From everything he had seen or heard, the only thing that excited her was money. Barrington must have talked, told her something about the operation. She wanted in. What did she have to offer?

"So what brings you to my humble office, Gloria? A message from your boss?"

Gloria uncrossed her legs, rose, and walked to the large window across the office. She walked slowly, stopped, then— her back still turned to him—ran her hands down the green satin curtains.

"The glare bothers me. I prefer it darker, more intimate." She pulled the curtains half shut, looked at him over her shoulder, smiled, then closed them all the way. Without being obvious, she glanced several times at a spot directly over one of the Remington prints. "We never went for that walk yesterday. Get outside, enjoy the beauty of nature."

Ingersoll nodded. The office was bugged. Evidently under video surveillance, as well. No surprise. "Sorry," he replied. "I was so busy the rest of the day, it slipped my mind."

He doubted that, under ordinary circumstances, Gloria could be bought. Barrington paid her plenty. That she was here meant she must have some idea of just how *much* money was involved in this project. Annoying that the old man had talked. But not likely to be terribly important.

Still, she was no fool. Gloria knew something she felt was worth big bucks. Ingersoll had to know what.

"I thought we could take a nice stroll," she said. "It's my afternoon break. Exercise keeps the body in shape, you know?"

Ignoring the burgundy chair, she perched on his desk, crossing her legs, then dangling them over the side. This time, her skirt slid up high on her bronzed thighs. A thin bead of sweat trickled down Ingersoll's back.

Nicely done. Better than some of the field agents he employed. But he wasn't tempted. Nobody in the world was worth risking these stakes.

Nonetheless, he decided to play along for a while. He pushed back his chair and stood up. He stretched, raised his arms over his head, then hitched up his slacks, smoothed the white shirt beneath the belt. Straightened his tie. Decades of lifting weights and jogging had kept him in top physical condition.

"I could use a break, too," he said, "though taking a stroll isn't exactly my idea of exercise."

"Mine, either," she said, "but what else is there to do?"

The answer was implied.

"I stay in shape with long workouts," he said. "We'll have to exercise together," he added, "when we have more time."

"Sounds like a great idea," she said. "Soon."

"Ready for that walk?" he asked. Flirting with Gloria was fine for the microphones, but in truth, he'd be safer sleeping with a rattlesnake.

"I'm ready," she said.

"I can't be gone for more than half an hour," he said as he pulled open the door to his office. They stepped out into the hall. "I have to finish these reports before supper."

"The gazebo's nice during the afternoon," Gloria replied, hooking her arm under his, drawing him close, so that her breast pressed against his biceps. "It's close by, and quiet. Okay with you?"

"Perfect," he answered. The old wood building was located on the north side of the compound, far from the guest house. There, Cal wouldn't get so much as a glimpse of Gloria, which was definitely wise. "Lead on. I'm in your hands."

She chuckled—a deep, throaty laugh—but didn't reply.

As they exited the house via the rear door, the heat wrapped itself around them. The gazebo was located approximately five hundred feet away from the building, in the center of a stunning flower garden. Inlaid gray stones marked the path. On either side of the rock, the desert brush grew wild and thick: flowering succulents, prickled cacti in all shapes, thorny weeds.

He donned sunglasses to fend off the glare of the sun. Ingersoll, who normally walked with a quick, determined step, let his companion set the pace. She meandered, not in a rush, maintaining a firm grip on his arm. From time to time, her hip brushed against his.

About a hundred feet from the house, she leaned her head against his upper arm. "Your office is bugged," she said softly. "The old man records every word you say."

"Tell me something I don't know," he replied. "Video monitor above the Remington print. That the only one?"

Gloria laughed. She peered up at him with wide brown eyes. "My, aren't we the paranoid one."

"Is there another?" he said, his voice steady despite her closeness.

"No," she said. "Too much trouble for the effort. The only room in the mansion where he wanted to post more than one camera was my bedroom." She grinned. "I told him he wasn't paying me enough for the privilege."

"The tape would melt," Ingersoll replied, only half in jest.

"The old man doesn't use tape," Gloria said. She had shed the sex-kitten persona. She was all business. "He prefers digital images. They allow him to play with the pictures, zoom in for close-ups."

"Amazing. I thought your boss hated modern technology. Or don't video cameras count?"

"When you're in his position," Gloria said, "you don't have to be consistent."

He pulled away from her. Talking about videos made him nervous. For all he knew, Gloria was carrying a digital microbug on her now. She could be recording their entire conversation, videotaping his every expression for Barrington. This whole episode could be a trap, set by the old man, to check if Ingersoll was planning a double cross.

Gloria seemed to catch wind of his doubts. She took one of his hands, and heat shot up his arm.

"I'm not wired in any way, if that's what you think," she said. "You can search me if you like."

"Tempting," Ingersoll replied. "But you're the one who wanted to talk to me. So talk."

"You don't trust me," she said, pressing both her hands on top of his.

Ingersoll laughed and pulled his hand free. "I don't trust anyone. Not even myself."

"I could earn your trust." Gloria started walking again, periodically searching him with her eyes. Watching his reactions. "The old man likes to brag. Tells me things. I know his secrets."

"Sounds very interesting," Ingersoll said. "Keep talking. I'm listening."

"Information costs money," Gloria said. "And I have expensive tastes."

She turned onto the path that circled the gazebo, walked past the flowering cacti that huddled in the dry brush that edged the gray stones. Ingersoll followed. A horned lizard, sunning itself on a rock, stared at them with an insolent glare.

"I think we could come to a settlement you'd find acceptable," he declared. Ingersoll was enjoying their conversation. Gloria was wonderfully direct.

"The more money I earn, the more I seem to spend. I never have enough."

"A common ailment," Ingersoll said. "But, there is a vaccine."

"There is?" Gloria settled on a bench on the perimeter of the flower garden, still far from the gazebo. Ingersoll sat next to her. Rose bushes blossomed and dripped dew, watered by sprinklers that had been buried in the soil. Jasmine sweetened the air; pink and orange azaleas were ablaze. Sprays of white and purple flowers dangled on vines that flowed over arched trellises. A gopher snake peeked at them from beneath a clump of prickly pears, then disappeared. "What medication do you recommend, Mr. Ingersoll?"

The late afternoon sun sizzled. Even the wood bench was hot. Ingersoll loosened his tie. He wiped a thin layer of perspiration off his forehead.

"A major financial transfusion," he answered. "Enough money to make you rich beyond your wildest dreams."

"That's impossible. I have very vivid dreams."

"I'm not surprised," Ingersoll said. "But I'm not exaggerating."

"The gazebo's wired for sound," Gloria said. "So is the guest house. Every time you go there, your conversation is monitored from the office."

"No surprise," Ingersoll said. "Good to know, though. Are there any video cameras planted in the guest house? Truthfully?"

Gloria pulled her hair onto the top of her head, wound it around her fingers, arched her back, released the hair. Crossed her legs, rubbed them with long fingers. She stared at the horizon, where the foothills rose out of the sheet of endless sand and marched to the sky.

"How much money?" she asked, smiling.

"Information like that isn't worth anything," Ingersoll said. "I can have Greg and Harry search the place. If that's all you have to offer, we can head back now."

"Why are you so worried about video cameras? Nothing digital is admissible in court. Too easily altered. Same as audio. Nothing's real anymore."

"I don't give a damn about trials," Ingersoll said. "If anyone's looking over my shoulder in the cottage, I'd like to know. Today."

"Afraid someone might steal your secret techniques?" she asked.

"You're quick," he replied. "This project has certain well-defined goals and objectives. The government can't risk having someone trying to duplicate the results a few months from now. That could lead to disaster."

"What if I told you Barrington's planning exactly that? He's setting you up for a double cross."

"He wouldn't dare," Ingersoll said. "Nobody screws the NSA. Not even your boss."

"You underestimate the old man. He hates the Internet. Would do anything to bring it down. Anything."

"My superiors feel the same way," Ingersoll said. "With good reason. The Net, with all its dangling, wide-open security holes, spells ruin for our country. At the NSA, we have all the facts and

figures. For years now, half the attacks on U.S. defense computers have come from supposedly friendly foreign governments. They're trying to break our codes, learn our security
keys. We're faced with total economic, financial, and social war-
fare, fought entirely by computer. If the Net's not brought under
government control, our country is heading straight to hell.
Nothing will be secret—not military communications, not orders from the president, *nothing.*"

"I've heard the lecture," Gloria said. "Many times actually.
Barrington's obsession. That's why he's paying one of your operatives big money to leak your secrets."

Damn, he couldn't trust anyone, not even his own staff, men
he paid *well* in return for loyalty. His wives had screwed him for
money; the NSA had jerked him around for years. All the NSA
had given him was hard work and double-talk . . . and a gold ring
with a ruby. Not much for a lifetime of devoted service.

"You're lying," Ingersoll said.

"Am I?" Gloria said. "You know what Barrington's like.
That's why you came with me on this little stroll. With a billion
dollars at stake, anybody can be bought."

"A billion," Ingersoll repeated. This was worse than he'd
imagined. "How much do you know?"

"In the words of Bradley Barrington," Gloria said, " 'tonight
the American public are going to be taught a lesson they won't
forget. They'll discover the dangers of an unregulated Internet.
And that's just the beginning.' "

"Who's the traitor?" Ingersoll asked. "Greg? Harry? That
crazy bastard, Paul?"

"You mentioned enough money to make me rich." Gloria's
eyes glittered. She cared nothing about security, nothing about
the Net. "How rich?"

"Ten percent? A hundred million, tax free. Should do wonders for your dreams."

For a moment, she stopped breathing. "Harry—Harry
Barton. He's been the one making plans with the old man."

"That dirty son of a bitch," Ingersoll said. "Him and his stupid
string ties. No surprise. He's a greedy bastard. What's the plan?
When's this going to happen?"

"I don't know," Gloria said. "Barrington hasn't said, and I can't be too curious. Don't want him suspicious."

"Well, if you want your money," Ingersoll said, "you damn well better find out. I need to know before tonight. Understand?"

"You'll know. For a hundred million dollars, I'll find out. Barrington'll tell me." She grimaced. "If I'm sweet enough to him, the old man will tell me anything."

"Harry," Ingersoll muttered. The arrogant SOB. Secretly working for Barrington. Not really a surprise. Like all the ops, Barton was in it for the money.

Things could be worse. He'd always planned on offing Harry anyway. All this meant was a slight change in his timetable. A smart agent took advantage of shifting circumstances. And he was the smartest agent around.

"Do whatever's necessary," Ingersoll said. "But find out by tonight."

CHAPTER 19

First, the stolen Velux Plus. Then Grouch's beat-up junker. Then the red Porsche. As if that weren't enough, now Judy was in a bus with Dan, heading out of San Jose toward the northern suburbs.

It was Thursday afternoon. She'd been on the road for days and was sick of it. Constantly on the run, scared for her life, and trying to save somebody she'd never even met. Working for Steve Sanchez would be like a vacation, once this nightmare ended. *If* it ended.

The bus wasn't too crowded. A half dozen exhausted men, clad in filthy jeans, heading home after odd work shifts somewhere. The driver looked bored and rarely even glanced in the rearview mirror.

The seat vinyl was ripped, the walls streaked with garish graffiti, the floor littered with dirty tissues and assorted garbage. Beyond grimy windows that were scarred with gang marks, evergreens poked up like fluffy cones looming over shacklike houses.

And the bus was old and belched gas. A battered blue wreck, salvaged from some corporation, like every bus these days.

This kind of bus took only paper cash, no digicards. Judy and

Dan, scruffy, exhausted, and smelling like sour milk, fit in just fine with the other passengers.

Sitting in the back, trying to stay unobtrusive, Judy used the netpad to scan incoming police reports. Small as it was, the laptop might be noticed.

"Fire's out," she reported. "The cops found Natalie and she told them about our visit. They're searching for the Porsche. No word about Jeremy's death. Cops are keeping a tight lid on the story. No talk about the murder in any newsgroup, either, and nothing on VileSpawn."

"Great," Dan said. "Well, at least we've lost the creeps who were following me. Soon as the police find my abandoned car, they'll run a DNA analysis on it, figure out that you were in it. Then, along with wanting me for Jeremy's murder, they'll be after me for aiding a fugitive. In a little while, they'll be at my restaurant, hunting for clues. Won't that be great for business? Buy your chili dogs from Dan Nikonchik, arsonist."

"Your restaurant," Judy said. "Why didn't I think of that? Dan, Cal's code is still there, right? It runs the restaurant. I've got to see it."

"Why?"

"Tuska and Smith are in San Jose. Hackers are dying. Cal's gone. The code's gone, too—wiped off his computer. I'm convinced that's no coincidence. Not much of a clue, but it's better than nothing. Somehow that code's tied in with the killings. I'm sure of it."

Dan shook his head. "Forget it. I've been using Cal's program for years. Why would it suddenly become so important?"

"You tell me," Judy said.

"I don't know what you're talking about," Dan replied.

"There has to be a tie-in," Judy said, packing up her equipment. "I'm sure of it. That's why Cal disappeared, why he crashed his system before he left. If it wasn't him, then who? The code is the answer. I've got to examine it. We have to go to your restaurant."

"Too late for a visit," Dan said. "Like I said, the cops are probably on the way there already. I'm sure they'd be thrilled if we dropped in."

"No reason for us to make a personal appearance," Judy said.

"Your place is hooked up to the Internet. I'll use the netpad to break in and swipe the code."

"You can do that?" Dan said.

"There's not much I can't do, using a computer," Judy said. "Let's get off the bus at the next stop. I need some privacy."

WELCOME TO SUNSHINE ESTATES. The sign sat in front of a tract that was covered with tiny one- and two-story prefab houses, all crammed together. A few blocks distant, dark smoke billowed from brown towers that poked skyward.

"Perfect spot," Dan said, rising from the bus seat and signaling for a stop. "Blue-collar area. They collect garbage in San Jose and the surrounding communities and recycle it in that factory. Work around the clock. It's a perfect place to find us some wheels again. Ready for a walk?"

She wobbled to her feet, followed him down the aisle, and lurched as the bus ground to a halt with a smoky belch.

Three men rose and followed them. Dan glanced nervously over his shoulder. "Come on; hurry it up, Judy," he murmured under his breath. "One of those guys looks a little funny to me."

She didn't bother to turn and look. It was just Dan, being paranoid.

On the sidewalk, she paused in a daze and tried to focus. Before her stood a boarded-up building made from wooden slats, surrounded by garbage. A coin-operated phone booth huddled by the ruins. Judy could imagine a whore slouched against the booth, or a wino. But nobody was there.

Next to the boarded-up building stood another shut-down dump, this one with a sign nailed to the door: FISH. Fish to eat? Fish for bait? Who knew.

The sky was hazy with gray smog that burned her eyes and nostrils. The air smelled vaguely like an outhouse, reminding her of the brick factory back in Pennsylvania. The sun sizzled through the haze, breaking it into shimmering clouds of color.

Two men shuffled off the bus, passed them, headed for Sylvie's Bar on the corner, a few dumps down the road.

A third man clambered from the bus. This one was tall and beefy, with clean brown hair, dark eyes empty, like bullet holes in a leathery, creased face. As he came close, his hand moved quickly into a jacket pocket.

"Dan," she whispered.

He swiveled, but too late. The man whipped his hand from the jacket, thrust a hard brown-wrapped package at Judy, and swung his fist at Dan.

The punch hit him solidly on his left cheek. Eyes wide with shock, Dan fell to the pavement.

"A gift for your boyfriend," the man said calmly to Judy. "Tell him to take care of the money by Friday. No more warnings. If he can't manage his brother, someone else will." Then he turned and kicked Dan in the ribs.

Dan grunted loudly and rolled to his side, clutching his stomach. His face was already bleeding.

A van, green and battered but no old Volkswagen, pulled around the corner where the drunks were entering Sylvie's. It screeched to a halt at the bus stop. The man gave Dan another kick, then said to Judy, "Tell him we expect things to be back to normal by tomorrow." Then he climbed into the van.

The van. The one Dan had worried about on the highway. But this time, it was real.

Judy dropped the package. It fell to the pavement, hit with the sound of breaking glass.

Dan had curled up into a ball, and was moaning in pain. Judy crouched next to him. His left eye was swelling and starting to turn purple. Blood dribbled from the top of his cheek to his jaw, splattering red drops on the pavement.

She helped him sit up, then propped him against the bus stop pole. It was rusty, BUS spray-painted orange to read BUSTED.

"No broken bones." Dan managed a weak smile. Shook his head as if to clear it, grimaced again, and held his stomach. "Guy kicked me hard, but the swipe to the face was a warning, not meant to do any permanent damage."

"Just a warning? Look at you! What's going on, Dan? Don't tell me that was your bookie. Who are these guys?"

"It was the van, wasn't it?"

"The van," she said. "Yeah."

"God, that hurts. I need something to stop the swelling, maybe some ice." He tottered to his feet, clinging to her for support. She almost fell backward. She wasn't exactly built for this sort of thing.

"Dan. Tell me about the package. About these guys."

"Not now. I'll tell you later. Nothing to do with your problems. I swear. Later." Then, "What package?"

She picked it up from the pavement, held it out to him. "This one. Guy said it was a preview, a reminder that you'd better get things fixed, *or else.* Something about taking care of the money by Friday. And if you can't manage your brother, then someone else will."

"Oh, shit . . ." He slouched against the fish building, sank against it. The boards strained and splintered under the weight of his back.

She sat down beside him. Made sure her legs were up, off the trash and grime. "I want the truth, Dan. No more lies."

"How the hell did they find me?" he muttered, ignoring Judy. He pulled apart the brown paper, which was held together by a few pieces of tape. A smashed disk platter fell in shards onto his lap. He wiped them from his legs, and they joined the rest of the trash piled up by the wall. Rotting orange juice containers, beer bottles, cigarette packages, rags.

"From your place, right?" Judy asked.

"Yeah," Dan said. He laughed abruptly. "Subtle, huh? Very subtle."

"Stay here. I'll get some ice. Then, we're going to talk."

He nodded, laughed softly again. Was he losing it?

She left him with the laptop and headed for Sylvie's. She was no longer Judy, no longer TerMight. She had to take care of Dan, had to find Cal, had to survive. Nothing else mattered.

Already, she'd dyed her long auburn hair a glittergoo green, something she'd never considered doing in the past, not for any reason. She'd escaped from Tony Tuska and Paul Smith, two *killers.* She'd been handling Dan Nikonchik for what seemed like centuries. She could do anything. Scared as she was, she would manage.

Inside the bar, it was all gloom and cigarette smoke. The two men from the bus sat, alone, on stools at the far end of a bar. The bar itself snaked in a semicircle over a dark-tiled floor, and a bartender slumped on a stool behind it. She was in her forties, brittle blond hair, amped into coils, held in place by two pink barrettes.

She sipped from a small glass, laughed at something one of the men said.

They all looked up as Judy entered. Judging by their reactions, they weren't used to strangers here. And Judy was nothing like their usual crowd.

The men eyed her. Raw meat, she guessed. Pigs.

Judy fixed her gaze on the blonde.

"What'll it be?" Her tone made it clear that the bartender knew Judy wasn't there for a drink.

"Ice," Judy said. "In a clean cloth, if you have one."

"Listen to her." The blonde shot a sarcastic glance at the two patrons. "She wants ice and a clean cloth."

"I'll pay."

"Yeah, you'll pay with *what*?" the woman challenged.

The men answered with leers and snorts.

The cash was with Dan. Best not to go back and ask him for some. They'd both be mugged. Judy pulled out a hemorrhoid digicard. "Ten-buck digicard."

The woman took the card. Her fingernails were long, squared at the tips, bright pink. Fake. She read the ad printed on the card.

"Hemorrhoids? Yeah, right, you little punk." She snickered, but relaxed. Judy had stolen the digicard; that made her okay. "Yeah, I'll get your ice, honey, but no cloth. No clean cloths around here." She stepped back from the bar and lifted her miniskirt. Tucked the digicard into a pouch on her underpants. Tiny thing, black, already containing a few digicards for the day's hard labor.

Happens to me every day. All cool. No problem, Judy thought to herself.

"Got another card? I'll give you a bar rag."

"How about half a card?" Judy asked, trying to stay in character. "All I got left."

"Give me the whole card, get the rag. That's it."

"But I gotta eat," Judy whined. "Half a card for the rag. Come on."

The men were enjoying the free show. "Come on over here," one said. "Do me a little something. Earn the rag, what say?"

"Knock it off, Crank," the blonde said. "The kid's young; give her a break. And you—" She pointed at Judy. "—give me the digicard, get your rag, and get out of here. I'm not sure how long

I can hold old Crank back. When he's horny, he's *really* horny, catch my drift?"

Judy handed over the digicard, and the woman rummaged behind the bar. A moment later, ice and greasy rag in hand, Judy made for the door.

She found Dan, bruised, right where she'd left him, propped among the debris. The blood was drying on his face. The ice was melting in the sun, and as the rag soaked through with water, Dan would be able to wash the blood from his cheek and jaw.

"Now," she said, "give. What's all this about?"

"Later," Dan replied. "I swear, I'll tell you, but not now. When we're safe. The cops are hunting us both. No time to stand here and chat.

"How'd they find me?" he continued. "How the hell did they track me even on the damned bus?"

"Good question," Judy said. "Needs a good answer. When all else fails, try the obvious."

She reached out and pulled his sunglasses out of his shirt pocket. *"Hey,"* he cried, as she snapped the frames in half.

"Hey yourself," Judy said. She pointed at the black microchip nestled in the hollow plastic noseguard. "I'm in security, remember? Your friends must not trust you, Dan. They've probably been keeping track of you for a long time. Probably bugged your Porsche as well."

"Shit," Dan said. "Those bastards."

"Still sure these goons aren't mixed up in Cal's disappearance?"

"Positive," Dan said. "They want him back. They want Cal alive. They're holding off killing me because I'm the only one who might know where my little brother is. I'll tell you the whole story, I swear. When we're someplace safe."

Finding such a spot, Judy mused as they started walking, might not be so easy.

CHAPTER 20

The recycling plant, a few blocks from Sylvie's, resembled a blue elephant with multiple smokestack trunks. The place was huge, covered four square city blocks. Every few minutes, a garbage truck drove into the huge, dark maw of the beast, delivering its sacrifice of paper, glass, and plastics to feed the ever hungry monster.

The people who worked in the blue elephant had probably absorbed enough toxins to kill them. One day in that place was probably equal to smoking four packs of hard-core FDA-approved cigarettes each day for a month.

The parking lot held few cars. There were no guards, no gates. This wasn't exactly a prime target for thieves, since the cars were mainly junkers. They were interspersed with pickup trucks on large wheels, and even those tended to be falling apart.

Dan motioned them over to a car that was in relatively good shape. "Take this one. It looks in better condition."

Right. Break into the car. Judy sighed, turned on the netpad, brought up her secret crack page. She touched the UNLOCK icon. A flash of *ping radius=1 dimension=m*, and the screen displayed the car's code. The UNLOCK icon disappeared, and the locks popped. At least this time no one was shooting at her.

The interior smelled like stale booze. The front seat was littered with newspapers, many folded back at the horse race pages.

Judy dropped onto the passenger seat. A tap on her keyboard brought the car to life. The radio blared a Top 40 tune. Judy slapped at the radio dials and the music died. She smiled at Dan. He stepped on the gas, and smiled back.

It felt good to smile at someone and not be insulted for it. Just as it had felt good, back in the woods by Jeremy's house, when Dan had propped her up with his body. He was constantly touching her—in little ways—holding her elbow, steering her this way and that.

It was too bad Dan Nikonchik was so bad tempered, so hooked on bimbos, and so physically . . . repugnant. Oddly enough, she was growing *comfortable* with him.

She put a hand on his shoulder. This time, he didn't glare at her. "Come on," she said, "let's get this thing on the road. I'll change the car's registration numbers and program the ignition to start on your touch."

"Next stop, food," he said, as they sped away from the recycling plant, away from the toxic air.

Judy opened the netpad, executed the wireless comm program. High speed and top of the line: a cellular digital packet data link that would sniff for voice frequencies and slip data packets into empty channels. Encrypted—big deal—and supposedly secure, it was the same method the cops had used to track her Avis rental car, the one she took from Tony Tuska and Paul Smith.

"Done," Judy said. "The car's safe. Now I'll tap into your Dan's DiskWorld computer and get Cal's files."

The car grunted up a dirt road on a foothill, the larger mountains looming in the distance. Scrub brush drifted in balls over rocks and weeds. The smog had lifted up here; the air was fresh again. Judy manually cranked the windows down, and felt much better. Awake again.

They rounded a curve, dust flying behind them. Dan flipped his hair off his face and jerked the wheel. Below them, the hillside dipped at a sharp angle, fell to a dry rocky ravine far below.

The car swung back down the hill, following the twisting road. Wooden cabins appeared, then a paved main road. They drove past dilapidated white buildings, store signs announcing fresh milk and vegetables. A few men in tight jeans loitered outside San Pueblo's Eats, some wearing cowboy hats. None afforded Judy and Dan more than a casual glance; they were probably used to seeing junk cars here.

On the edge of town, Dan parked in the lot of a chain grocery store. Anywhere in California, you could always count on finding a Ven's. Here, nobody would notice them, even parked for half an hour or more.

There was a sign in the store window: WE ACCEPT CASH.

"You still have money, right?" Judy asked.

"Yeah, enough for some food, ice, antiseptic. But I'm not going to spend too much. There's no more when we run out."

There was a huge cardboard stand-up in the window, too. Judy recognized the bimbo from the poster in Cal's apartment. Mistie Lane. Dressed in an orange string bikini, she held a gun in each hand. Printed across her ample chest in bold red letters were the words BEACH BABE, PRIVATE EYE. THURSDAY NIGHT AT 8 P.M., CHANNEL 36.

Noticing Judy's stare, Dan grimaced. He looked tired. His left eye was a white jot in puffed purple lids. He wiped the sweat off his forehead with the back of his hand. "Cal and I always watched that dumb vid, every week. It was one of the few things we did together. Didn't mean anything, really. Just something to do. Last Thursday, when he didn't show up at my place, I knew something had happened to him. Hard to believe it was only eight days ago. Seems like forever."

Dan's pants were rumpled, his yellow shirt brown with grime, stained with blood. Two twenties from his pocket went into his wallet; he deposited the rest of the cash from the money machine under the front seat.

There was no need to discuss Mistie Lane. Judy concentrated on the netpad screen.

```
Welcome to dan_land.com
Log-in:
```

She logged in as Griswald, using his secret password. Without looking up, she said, "Plain food for me, Dan. Bread's fine. None of those chip thingies. And some bottled water. No bubbles."

"Sure," he said.

She found Griswald's directory, noted some files that were stuffed with genetic code. Each file was prefixed by the acronym DNS—as in Domain Name Server? That had to do with how companies registered for Web site addresses. What did it have to do with genetic programming?

Whatever. She downloaded the whole mess to her netpad.

The download box appeared on her screen:

```
Downloading DNS1015 . . . 1% . . . 5% . . .
```

"It'll be five minutes," she said, pressing the palms of her hands to her eyes. She needed a break. Time to relax. But, there was no time for rest, not with Tuska and Smith on the loose.

"I'll be back in less than that," Dan said. He slid out the door, and she watched him skirt around the car and walk across the parking lot. He moved as if he had all the time in the world. Dan might not know anything about computers, but he understood something about human nature. Everyone noticed a man who was in a hurry.

```
Downloading DNS1015 . . . 25% . . . 27% . . .
```

With the netpad on the seat beside her, Judy leaned against the ripped cushions. Something Dan had said bothered her, but she wasn't sure what. It couldn't have been anything about Mistie Lane . . .

By the time Dan returned with a bag of food, the download was done: several header files, containing definitions and code that Cal would use repeatedly, plus a whole truckload of source files. Judy, though her eyes were open, didn't respond when Dan pushed the groceries onto the front seat then took his place on the driver's side. Her thoughts were whirling, going nowhere.

"Chow time," he said, pulling a bag of chips from the brown paper sack. Fire-spiced Mexican potato curls. He ripped open the top, stuffed a handful of chips into his mouth. Flakes of red powder, presumably pepper and chili powder, instantly ringed his lips.

He gave her a loaf of bread. She balled up a piece, chewed on it slowly. "Thanks. Anything to drink?"

"Pure spring water for you," Dan said, handing her a cold bottle. "Cola for me."

Judy glugged down half the bottle. She felt as dry as the desert. Another piece of bread followed.

"Feeling a little better?" Dan asked as he munched on a piece of beef jerky. The man had the worst taste in food. "Got all the code?"

"Yes to both," Judy said. Dan was a slob and a jerk, but he wasn't that terrible. "Much better, thanks. How about that story now?"

"Not here," he answered. "Too long to tell now. Later." She gave him a disgusted look, but didn't push it.

Pushing the last sliver of dried beef into his mouth, Dan reached into the bag and pulled out a tin of something called Dr. Reynold's Cure-All. Most likely, Dr. Reynold was the same guy as Dr. Frond: didn't exist. Dan twisted off the lid, dipped his fingers, and smeared yellow goo on his cheek.

"Got a bag of ice, too. Just in case." He turned on the ignition, let the car idle as he finished chewing.

Judy stared at the cardboard stand-up again, desperately searching for some hidden truth. Not that much could be hidden in a tiny swimsuit. Only a few lines of advertising fit across the bikini top.

THURSDAY NIGHT.

"Dan, when did you first ask Bren to post the message on VileSpawn, asking about Griswald?"

"Friday morning. After Cal didn't show up the night before to play with Mistie. But Bren's friend didn't post it until Monday."

"So he's been gone more than a week," Judy said. "Hailstorm died Sunday, four days after Cal vanished. Your brother left before the murders started."

"Maybe somebody threatened him. Tuska and Smith?"

"Why only Cal? No one else received a warning. At least, *I* didn't. Jeremy never mentioned a threat. Besides, the killers tried to make the deaths look like suicides. Pretty clear they didn't want to attract undue attention."

Judy was grasping for the answer. She knew it was very close. "Maybe Cal's disappearance isn't tied in with the killings. Maybe Bren's right, and Cal just left town on his own."

"A coincidence?" Dan said. "Remember what you said about that? My brother takes off without an explanation, wipes his computer clean, drops out of sight. Doesn't say a word to me, though he knows I'll worry myself sick. A few days later, two maniacs start killing the other top hackers on the coast. Sure as hell makes me suspicious."

"Paul Smith told Trev that I was too smart for my own good," Judy said. She started to tremble. "That's the reason he and Tuska came to kill me. I'm a hacker, Dan. I handle Net security. I'm no threat to anyone. Not unless they're planning some operation so big, so spectacular that there's no way I'd miss it. And maybe, because I'm not a crook, they're worried I'd try to stop them."

"What do you mean?" Dan said.

"Tuska and Smith are killing top hackers as a precaution, Dan," Judy said, knowing as she spoke that she had hit upon the truth. "That's why Hailstorm and Larabee and Jeremy died. The murders are insurance, guarantees that nobody will stop their big plans."

"But what about Cal? He disappeared before the killings started."

"I know," Judy said. "Don't you see? Cal's the key, the catalyst. Once he vanished, the murders began. Not until then. There's only one explanation. Whoever's employing Tuska and Smith has Cal—and his code. Cal's not a target for the killings. He's the cause of them!"

CHAPTER 21

Dan broke the silence. "Cal's no criminal, Judy. He'd never do anything to hurt anyone. Especially Jeremy."

"Cal probably doesn't know a thing about the killings," Judy said. "Most likely, someone has your brother stashed somewhere. Maybe it's even the CIA or the NSA, feeding him a line about national security and all that crap. Keeping him on ice until the gig goes down."

"Judy, are there other big-time hackers in San Jose? What about Bren and Carl? Tony Tuska and Paul Smith might not be finished."

A chill hit her. She hadn't thought of *that*. Who was left? Who might be the next victims?

"Mercy," she whispered.

"Yeah, right. Not likely," Dan muttered.

"No, no. Mercy. That's her name. She lives here in San Jose. Mercy's a top gun, Dan. I worked with her on a Sanchez project about a year ago, a major bank security setup. Bren and Carl are good, but they're not into real hacking, cutting into accounts, stuff like that. Mercy's the only one left around here—other than me. I have to call her, warn her about Tuska and Smith."

Judy pulled the blue box from her laptop case. Much like the box she had used to change traffic lights, this one was a kludged bit of circuitry that would hide her dialing location. It used a looped pair of phone numbers typically employed by phone companies for testing. They were also used by hackers who wanted to talk in guaranteed privacy.

Anyone could build one of these boxes. There were circuitry blueprints for *hundreds* of box types, all over the Net, all free for the download.

A touch of the phone icon on her netpad, and Judy dialed one of Mercy's numbers.

Judy wondered what to say to her. It had been months since they last talked. Anything she might say would sound crazy. Nobody killed over *code*. But somehow, Judy had to convince Mercy that she was telling the truth.

The phone rang once, then buzzed off to a voice-mail pickup.

Next they heard Mercy's voice, barely audible. The girl wasn't much of a conversationalist. "Yeah, it's me. Drop me a message. I'll be in touch."

Bad enough trying to think of what to say had Mercy actually *answered* the phone. But what the hell could Judy say into the voice-mail void that wouldn't sound completely insane? The machine beeped, and she stumbled for words.

"Uh, yeah, hiya, Mercy. This is Judy Carmody. TerMight. Maybe you've seen me on the news. I know this sounds freaked, but you gotta believe it. Somebody's killing hackers and trying to pin the blame on me. You may be the next target. I'll be there as soon as possible. Stay cool and watch out for a couple of thugs. They're real killers. No matter what excuse they give, no matter what credentials they flash. Believe me. Please, Mercy. I'll call again later. Leave a message on your machine if you can."

Well, that had sounded stupid. But, Mercy wasn't some naive teenager. Working in computer security, she'd dealt with plenty of crooks. Still, she might find it hard to believe anyone would go around killing programmers. The best thing would be to get to her as soon as possible.

"Get onto the 5, Dan. Head northwest, toward San Fran. Mercy's got a place on the edge of town. Meanwhile, I'm calling Bren, just in case. Maybe she can help."

A moment later, the phone rang, and a familiar voice answered. "Hello, this is Bren."

"Bren! It's Judy. You have a chrome box hooked up?" A chrome box disabled all FBI and cop taps on any phone/modem line.

"*Judy*. Sure, I have the box on. What, you think I'm crazy? Where are you? At Dan's place?"

"No. We never made it." Judy paused, wondering how much she should tell Bren. "Listen, I can't say a lot. Things have gotten way out of hand. Cal's friend Jeremy is dead. The police think Dan and I are involved. There's no way we can come back there. You need to watch out, avoid strangers. Two guys—they're the ones who killed Trev and Jeremy. We think they're after Mercy. Can you warn her? I need to know for sure she's safe. Then Dan and I gotta find a place to hide."

Judy spelled out what had happened, briefly outlined the possible explanation. She described Tuska and Smith in detail.

Bren said she'd try to contact Mercy, then send scrambled E-mail to Judy.

It arrived a few minutes later, a mix of good and bad news. Judy read it aloud.

" 'Tried contacting Mercy. No luck. She must be out of the house. Will keep trying. Checked the news. You and Dan are all over the place, wanted for questioning. But CBS in LA reports a possible witness in Trev LeFontaine's murder. So now you're just a possible suspect, instead of an escaped killer. Frame might be falling apart. Suggest you stay out of sight for a few days. Hide.' "

"Great advice," Dan said. "Hide. She suggest where?"

"Yes, Dan," Judy said. "She does. Let me finish. 'There's a shack southwest of San Jose, near the big Redwoods park. On the western slope. Abandoned by its owners. Carl and I go there to chill after a long job—our own hideaway. Off the beaten track. Cops will never find you there.' "

The rest of the E-mail contained detailed directions to the cabin.

Dan actually sounded pleased. "A place to rest and figure out Cal's code."

"First, we have to hightail it to Mercy's place," Judy replied.

Where was Mercy? Working alone, in a cubicle in some dimly

lit office in Silicon Valley? Alone where Tuska and Smith could break in and murder her?

Still on the Net, Judy went to the MapWizard site and typed Mercy's address. In seconds, the computer displayed the quickest route to her house. Estimated travel time was forty-five minutes. Not allowing for rush-hour traffic.

Would Mercy die because of rush-hour traffic?

No. Because Tony Tuska and Paul Smith were probably stuck in the same mess. While traffic crawled, Judy returned to the problem of Cal's code.

"You making any progress?" Dan asked.

She stared at her screen. Gibberish. The restaurant code was a more complex version of the program she'd downloaded from VileSpawn. Weird stuff—genetics programming of some kind, written in a language she didn't understand. How could she make sense from clutter?

"It's like trying to understand double-talk. None of the words make sense."

White letters on blue: Cal's code. Just words, something to decipher. Nothing more than that.

Words.

A dynamically allocated structure of nodes, defined to supply as many links as the program needed. Links to what, though? Credit records? Stock transfers? *Bank routes.*

Laguna Savings. Someone had broken into their Web site. On Monday. Days after Cal disappeared. Maybe it had been real. A test. A good programmer always tested code before putting it into operation.

Each structure of bank route nodes was created within function-driven objects. Each object was doing something. *But what?*

Judy peered at the code again.

Each object analyzed patterns, trends. Each object included a complex array of bits, encoded almost like an image file. Each object deleted—that is, killed—previously created objects.

Judy's frustration boiled over. "What was your brother *doing*?"

"Don't know, but whatever he was into, it kills people."

"Code can't kill."

"This code does."

They were sliding through the clean, quiet, suburban sprawl of Mercy's neighborhood with agonizing slowness, past the cement dump bungalows, lights mellow in their windows. People probably watching television, oblivious.

It was already drifting into night, the evening coming down like a murky hood. For Judy, fear was everywhere. In the dark green bushes, lurking behind pink and purple flowers, cowering in every shadow.

The air was turning cool, the chill coming down in a mist. Judy pulled on Bren's flannel shirt, but shivered nonetheless.

"Here we are," Dan announced, pulling into a short gray driveway. Directly in front of them stood a standard north California garage: brown door, tan concrete walls, shingled roof. A sidewalk wound along the side of the garage, beneath hanging cypress leaves, to the front door. Behind the cypress tree was a tiny window.

Dark. Mercy wasn't home yet. Or she was dead.

Dan helped Judy from the car, then looped an arm around hers, moving them quickly toward the front door. "Two friends," he whispered. "Here for a visit. Just in case the neighbors are watching."

He knocked on the brown-painted wood. No answer. He tugged on the handle. Locked. Leaving Judy standing in front of the door, he ducked behind the cypress tree, peered in the window. "Nothing," he muttered. "Looks like we got here before she did. Don't want anybody to see us. Come on."

Dan pulled Judy to the side of the house, unlatched the fence gate, and they slipped into the dark backyard. The trees were heavy with fruit. Fallen branches crunched beneath their feet. Together, they scooted past a row of perfumed cherry trees. Judy reached for a red berry. Dan caught her hand. "Don't eat that," he said. "The cherries are bitter. You'll get sick."

Judy dropped her hand, nodded. "You got that from the commune, right?"

"Yup," he said.

A solid wood fence five feet tall hid Mercy's yard from her neighbors. The hacker valued her privacy. From somewhere on the other side of the planks, a dog barked.

Dan tugged on Judy's elbow, pulled her over the patio. She almost tripped over a hose. The latch to the patio doors didn't budge. He jiggled them in frustration; the glass rattled, but a wooden pole stuck in the bottom groove kept them from opening.

A lizard, late to bed, blinked up at her from the patio cement. A cat's eyes were yellow on the far fence. The dog was howling. The evening moaned.

Dan muttered a curse and steered her farther down the patio to a small window.

Judy looked back over her shoulder, stared at the cat eyes, expecting to hear Dan swear again because yet another entrance was barred. But this time, he didn't curse. Rather, he hissed, and she felt his body freeze.

She whirled. Saw what he saw, and gasped.

The glass of the tiny window was shattered. Shards glistened on the cement, lit by the moon.

"They've been here, already," he whispered.

No. They had to save Mercy. They had to save *someone*.

Blood rushed to her head.

That vibrant gold hair, the warm blue eyes, the laugh. The tiny body, lithe and always darting about. All that energy. Mercy?

"Stay here. I'm checking the other side of the house." He ducked away from her, disappeared behind a pink azalea bush. She stared at the cat again. Had it seen anything? Did the cat *know*?

Then Dan was back. "Another door, come on," and he pulled her again, this time around the side of the cement structure, along a narrow walkway, where a wooden door stood ajar by mere inches.

More cautious now, Dan took off his shirt, wrapped one sleeve around his hand. He pushed open the door, far enough so they could enter without their bodies so much as grazing the wood: "Don't touch anything," he cautioned. "We don't want to leave fingerprints. Or DNA traces."

Shaking, Judy followed Dan into Mercy's bedroom. Computers, three of them, none of them on. The intruders weren't after Mercy's equipment. The bed was unmade, a robe draped across the bottom, computer journals open and draped over the pillow. On the nightstand there was a voice-mail box, with a light flashing. Mercy had messages waiting. It had to be Judy's call and Bren's follow-ups. None of them received. Perhaps Mercy still *hadn't* returned home.

Dan, his fingers still swathed in the shirt sleeve, switched on the bedside lamp. He stepped into the adjacent bathroom, pushed the shower curtain aside. "Nothing," he said.

No sound in the house, except a clock ticking somewhere.

They inched down the dark hallway. The living room held a beat-up sofa, a few end tables with lamps, posters on the walls. An assortment of hardware was scattered across the tabletop. Judy hardly noticed it. Maybe Tuska and Smith had come and gone, hadn't found Mercy.

Beneath a high arch, green vines dripped from a shelf.

Closer to the ticking clock.

They moved into the kitchen. Dan flipped the light switch. Dazzling white countertops, steel stove, and there, on the floor, there . . .

Judy collapsed against the archway, her fingers brushing the dangling vines. There . . .

Mercy. Gold hair matted, wet with blood. Blue eyes glazed. Lying on her side, arms sprawled in a sticky red pool on the kitchen floor. Sticking out from Mercy's back, a *knife*.

Dan was on the kitchen floor, down on his knees, tears dripping between his fingers. "Too much, too much," he was gasping.

The knife. Judy didn't move from the archway, stood there as if turned to stone, her heart ringing in her ears. *The knife in Mercy's back came from Judy's kitchen.*

"We gotta get out of here," Dan said, wobbling to his feet. "The cops could arrive anytime. If they find us, we're finished."

"The knife," Judy said, having a difficult time forming the words. "It's from my house. They used one of my knives."

He wiped his tears off the floor using his shirt sleeve, then bent and wiped the handle of the blade. His voice quavered. "Get rid of your fingerprints. Best we can do. We can't remove the knife."

"Why, *why?*" She couldn't think.

Dan rose to his feet. His face was gaunt, haggard. "If the cops find the knife on us, Judy, the game's over. We switch back from wanted for questioning to suspected of murder."

Outside, the dog howled again. A man's voice called; a screen door banged. Dan's head jerked around. "Time to move. Nothing we can do for Mercy."

Holding each other up, they slipped down the dark hallway to the open door—on the run again. The dog howled as if lamenting Mercy's death, or to warn them that they would be next.

CHAPTER 22

Dinner usually was served at 7 P.M. in the main dining room. Tonight, with only five hours till the project, Ingersoll preferred to eat alone. He apologized to Barrington by phone, citing last-minute details that required his attention. The old man didn't sound upset. All he worried about was the money. And destroying the Net.

Sitting in his office in his stocking feet, Ingersoll nibbled on a roast beef sandwich and reviewed foreign bank account numbers. During the past week, he had set up more than five hundred new accounts, already prepped with millions. All were located in credit exchanges that asked no questions. According to NSA files, most served as repositories for drug money and syndicate profits. He didn't care.

Once deposited, the money from tonight's operation could be withdrawn only via a digital key. And he was the only one who held that code.

Turning on the scrambler and a voice modifier, he touched his PHONE icon and dialed the San Jose hotel where his three operatives were staying. With the heist scheduled for midnight, he wanted assurances that there would be no outside interference.

Three rings. "Roy Reed."

"Hello, Roy," Ingersoll said. "How goes the job?"

"Exactly as promised, sir," Tuska said. "Paul and I completed the last assignment on schedule, late this afternoon. We used the proper tools, as instructed."

"I'm pleased to hear that," Ingersoll said. Though there was no reason to suspect a police tap on the phone line, it was best to remain discreet. "Anything to muddy the waters. The more confusion the better in this situation."

"No motive, though," Tony said. "That's the missing ingredient."

"A good point," Ingersoll said. "I'll take care of that this evening. Meanwhile, any word on our female friend? The one who broke your nose?"

"We've not seen her," Tony said, "though I gather from certain reports that we were closer to her than we realized, earlier today. Paul's damned annoyed that we didn't stay and check the surroundings. I reminded him we were on a tight schedule, and had no reason to suspect she was in the neighborhood. He understands, but is still anxious to find the young lady."

"He sounds obsessed," Ingersoll said.

"The cast on his hand serves as a constant reminder," Tuska noted. "Paul's a professional, sir, but he's still looking to even the score."

"Well, I'm not thrilled with his attitude," Ingersoll said, "but I'm not opposed to his objective. I'd be willing to up your fee twenty percent if you could eliminate the problem by tomorrow morning."

"Twenty percent?" Tony said. "That's a substantial amount, sir."

Ingersoll had promised Tony and Paul two million dollars each for killing five hackers without raising suspicions. Twenty percent was another four hundred thousand, just for terminating one security specialist—who so far had eluded their best efforts.

"I'm in a generous mood, Tony," Ingersoll said. "But I require results."

"You'll get them," Tuska said. "As per your orders, Ernie drove up with us yesterday. He's been pulling a few strings, knocking on a few doors. Only a matter of time before he finds a lead."

"Call me when it's done," Ingersoll said. "No matter the hour. I'll be awake."

"Will do," Tony said.

A soft beep let Ingersoll know someone was approaching his door. He felt sure he knew who it was. "Harry will meet you tomorrow," Ingersoll said. "As arranged."

"I look forward to seeing him."

"Good night, Tony," Ingersoll said. "And good luck."

He switched off the phone and rose to his feet. Harry Barton was scheduled to meet Tony, Paul, and Ernie tomorrow afternoon in the airport parking lot. But instead of millions in cash, he was bringing them a different sort of payoff. So much for generosity.

As he had expected, it was Gloria Simmons at the door. Not saying a word, he motioned her to wait in the hall.

"Just a minute," he said loudly. "I'll get the tray."

He walked back to his desk and lifted the wicker serving tray that held the remains of his dinner. Odd to see a roast beef sandwich and sweet potato chips on hand-painted china. As out of place as the gold-leaf silverware he used for mustard and ketchup, and the cut-crystal glass goblet for his cola. Barrington had money to burn. Ingersoll wanted to know that feeling.

Platter in hand, he turned and bumped into his chair. He stumbled, fell to one knee, as the contents of the tray dropped to the floor. "Oh, hell," he said for the microphones, as he grabbed the table knife and used the rubber heel of his shoe to shove it into the electric outlet on the wall behind his desk. With a loud pop, the room went black.

"Enter," he said to Gloria, ushering her into the dark office. He closed and locked the door behind her. Curtains wide open, there was still plenty of light this early in the evening.

"Your boss needs to upgrade his circuit breakers," he said, dropping back into his black leather chair. "Microphones and camera are off. We should have five or ten minutes before anyone comes to see what's wrong. You get Barrington to tell you his plans?"

Gloria settled into the chair facing him. She still wore the skirt and blouse from the afternoon. They looked wrinkled. Ingersoll didn't ask. She didn't offer. No attempt at seduction this time. No big smiles, no playing with her hair. She was all business.

"You promised outside to tell me all the details about the operation tonight."

"Like hell I did," Ingersoll said. "You find out about Harry?"

"Sure," Gloria said. "I said I would, and I did. Disgusting old bastard. Harry's supposed to cut a disk of Cal's code, but not tonight. Barrington's worried there still might be bugs in the program. He's waiting for the final code, the second run."

No problem. There would never be a disk cut of Cal's software. All so stupid—Ingersoll had all of Cal's code on backup, on the server right here in his office. Why would Barrington require a disk?

Still, Barrington could cause problems if he wasn't watched. Better to string Gloria along until after the big heist. The more she knew about the project, the closer she'd watch the old man, make sure he did nothing to jeopardize the outcome. Gloria wanted that cash.

"Most people at the agency think I'm paranoid," Ingersoll said. He had to be brief. "Too suspicious of new technology. Fortunately, my superior knows different. He realizes the Net's an atomic bomb waiting to explode. When I came to him with Nikonchik's code, he authorized this covert operation. Time to wake up the president and Congress before it's too late."

"By stealing a billion dollars," Gloria said.

"For starters," Ingersoll said. "Tonight's just the dress rehearsal. Using Nikonchik's genetic code, I'm plundering one billion dollars from banks all over the country. The money will be transferred over intricate computer network routes, passing through hundreds, maybe a thousand computer nodes each, into secret accounts in Net banks, trading houses, and investment firms. That's mine, as repayment for years of faithful service to our great country. Ten percent was going to Barrington, for allowing us to use his estate, his cash. No more. Double cross gets reversed. You collect his share."

She stared at him as if hypnotized. "I didn't know the government was so generous. Even with covert operations."

"What my boss doesn't know won't hurt him," Ingersoll said. "The next step takes place over the weekend, once I'm convinced the code performs to expectations. Like any plan, you proceed carefully from one step to the next."

"The final amount?" Gloria asked. "How much?"

"Fifty billion dollars."

Gloria sank deep into the plush chair, her eyes wide.

"Fifty billion dollars," she repeated, as if reciting a prayer. "That's a hell of a lot of money."

"Just a couple of new Stealth bombers for the air force," Ingersoll said. "Or a new battleship for the navy. Not really that much in the general scheme of things. The public doesn't notice when a billion's wasted on a new weapons system that doesn't work. Or a satellite system that goes a few hundred million over budget. It doesn't make an impression. But I'm going to change all that. I'm going to make it *personal*.

"What makes my plan so effective is that I'm taking the money from the United States banking system. One morning, a few days from now, thousands of ordinary people across the country are going to wake up and find their savings accounts empty, stripped bare. Businesses everywhere are going to find themselves in a cash crunch, their digital cash reserves gone. Overnight, billions of dollars are going to disappear without a trace. It's going to send a major shock through the entire system.

"Blind panic's going to ripple across this nation like a tidal wave. Imagine the 1929 stock market crash, magnified twenty times over, fueled by today's headline-dominated media. Talk about a circus. Newslink banners, TV special reports, thousands of rumors on the nets. Mass hysteria, maybe even runs on banks as people realize that their life savings are vulnerable. If it happened once, it could happen again."

"The old man's talked about this stuff for years," Gloria said. "But everyone thinks he's nuts."

Ingersoll smiled. "Barrington wants to alert the nation to the dangers of technology. After this weekend, his claims will be taken as gospel. This is going to convert a lot of people. Congress, the president, the news media are all going to demand answers. Immediate answers from the ISD, NSA, FBI, CIA. We're going to witness the biggest, most intense manhunt in U.S. history. The witch-hunt to end all witch-hunts."

Gloria frowned. "What's going to happen when the politicos

discover that the NSA, a government agency, is behind the mess? They'll crucify you."

She almost sounded as if she cared. But Gloria wasn't that good of an actress. Ingersoll knew she worried only about herself. And the money.

"That," he answered, "is the beauty of the whole operation. There won't be any evidence linking me, your boss, or the NSA to this theft. Not a single clue. At worst, the Internet Security Department, working day and night, using their top programmers, will trace fragments of code back to a pair of hackers. Two rogue programmers, nowhere to be found. They'll take the fall, not us."

"Two?" Gloria said. "That kid, Nikonchik, for one. Who's the other?"

"A young lady named Judy Carmody. Nicknamed TerMight. She's the perfect mark. A flaky, offbeat, brilliant computer hacker, with the reputation for being a rebel. All points on the ISD security risk profile. We get the money; she gets the blame."

"But, if she's taken into custody, claims she's innocent," Gloria said, always practical. "What then?"

"After this heist," Ingersoll said, "Judy Carmody and Calvin Nikonchik will vanish off the face of the earth. Disappear. Neither of them will ever be heard from again. Except for sightings reported in the scandal sheets."

CHAPTER 23

Cal glanced at the clock in the corner of his computer screen. Nine o'clock. Finished. The code was done, with three hours to spare. He'd told Mr. Ingersoll there would be no problem. And there wasn't.

Tonight, at midnight, the heist went down. A billion dollars, routed to bank accounts all over the world. Untraceable.

With a sigh of relief, he settled back in his chair and watched his code traverse the Net:

```
Cosworth's Tradex
/USauto/accounts/1487a9b042 . . .
Amount withdrawn: $14,683.43

Bank of New Zealand
/Tradex/debits/acct0143019 . . .
Amount transferred across node: $14,683.43
```

The program was working well. Pirating millions of dollars from accounts all over the world—from people's personal accounts, from large corporate accounts, from trading companies, from stock holdings, even from the federal treasury.

It was pretty nifty. He'd worked out this scheme to handle his brother Dan's shady restaurant dealings. Of course, Dan never dealt with amounts like this, but still, the method was much the same.

Start at a main computer node, Cal's computer here at the compound. Execute the code that creates the first two objects, the parent chromosomes. Then sit back and let them do their thing.

Each digital chromosome would incorporate both code and data. The code would force the chromosomes to combine, swapping genetic subtrees for a more optimal route—in this case, a well-hidden Net path. Then, after the parent chromosomes created child chromosomes, the children's code executed, and the first thing it did was delete the parent chromosomes—kill them off completely. No trace remained that the parent chromosomes had ever existed.

As the chromosome objects executed, they leapt from one computer node on the Net to the next, following increasingly ideal routes to take when stealing electronic funds and hiding them.

Artificial life.

This made old-time cops and robbers look like kids playing with toy guns. This was felony done with style.

Cal reached down and pulled the two-liter bottle of ginger ale off the floor. He swigged a drink. No more worries. The code was finished.

Satisfied there were no glitches in the program, he touched the RESET icon.

The screen displayed:

```
Bank of New Zealand
/Tradex/debits/acct0143019 . . .
Amount   transferred   back   across   node:
$14,683.43


Cosworth's Tradex
/USauto/accounts/1487a9b042 . . .
Amount added: $14,683.43
```

Within moments, all the accounts were restored to their original balances; all traces that anything had happened were removed. The chromosomes had killed each other off, all the way to the top level, the parent chromosomes who had spawned the rest.

The hard work was over. All that remained was for him to run the heist tonight, check out the results, then once Mr. Ingersoll was satisfied it worked as expected, set it up for a second pass on Saturday night.

That was the demonstration that counted, the greatest robbery ever committed. All the top NSA and ISD honchos would be present. Where Cal finally got his chance to show off. Rip fifty billion out of accounts all over the international banking system, spin them into secured stashes overseas, then reroute the money back to where it belonged. After seeing that show, nobody would doubt the power of his code. Ingersoll would prove his point, alerting everyone to the lack of security on the Internet. And Cal would be able to return home in style.

Home. Good old San Jose, where it wasn't always a hundred degrees in the shade. And he could munch tacos and hamburgers to his heart's content.

Greasy food. By now, Dan was probably worried out of his skull, wondering what had happened to him. Cal felt a twinge of guilt for keeping Dan in the dark. But there hadn't been much choice. Mr. Ingersoll had made it clear—no contact with the outside world—and the NSA agent's word was law.

Besides, it wouldn't hurt if Dan started realizing Cal wasn't a kid anymore. Dan needed to understand that he couldn't keep watch over Cal for the rest of his life. Cal wanted his freedom, and this job offered a real chance to stand on his own two feet.

Someday, Dan would understand. Hopefully, it wouldn't be too painful.

The code, fast as lightning, impossible to stop, was a masterpiece, born of Cal's ingenuity and interest in genetic engineering. He hadn't lied when he'd told Mr. Ingersoll that no other hacker could have designed the program. Not Hailstorm, not TerMight . . .

TerMight. Judy Carmody. In the rush to get the code finished, Cal had almost forgotten the mysterious message from Mr. Ingersoll to someone named Ernie, about making sure Judy Carmody didn't interfere tonight. Wiping the monitor screen with his green blob cleaner, Cal wondered about TerMight's connection.

Could she be working for the ISD, trying to track down Cal? The more he considered the idea, the more plausible it seemed. Thinking back, he remembered an E-mail from TerMight, describing some of the security work she had done for Laguna Savings—the same bank he'd used for the preliminary test of the genetic program, just a few days ago. If bank security had spotted his incursions, they might have called TerMight to investigate.

Cal shook his head. What a bizarre coincidence. Hard to believe that his first major job would lead him into battle with one of his best friends from VileSpawn. He hoped TerMight wouldn't be *too* upset when she discovered he had beaten her at her own game.

Still, who was this Ernie guy? And why had Mr. Ingersoll sent him TerMight's NSA profile? That transmission made no sense. There was only one sure way to find out. Cal would do a little snooping.

Greg and Harry were in the living room, playing cards, laughing over something. Sooner or later, Mr. Ingersoll was due, coming to make his last check, to see that the code was done. Cal had some free time, private time, to surf the Net, read the news, relax, and play detective.

He logged on to VileSpawn as Calvin, and was greeted by a black rose. *Another dead hacker.* Larabee, a guy Cal had never met but had heard lots about. It was a bad week for computer gurus. Two prime talents in the field gone. If he were superstitious, he'd be worried about the heist. But, he didn't believe in omens, and the code was going to work fine.

He moved to his private Griswald directory. Someone had downloaded his prototype genetics code. One hit, one read, by one person. And rather than by Fire, all the code was owned by Water. The intruder had found his private password and used it. Someone had been on VileSpawn as Griswald.

Maybe Jeremy. Cal smiled. If Jeremy knew he was okay, then word would get to Dan. No reason to feel guilty about making his brother suffer, after all.

He read the simple text message. It wasn't from Jeremy.

This is TerMight. Tell me where you are, why
you disappeared. Tell me what's happening.

Cal laughed. So much for the mystery of TerMight's connection. She was *obviously* working for the ISD. Exactly what Mr. Ingersoll had warned him about, over and over. The Internet Security Department wanted to stop this heist, wanted to maintain the illusion that Net banking was safe.

Unable to track down Mr. Ingersoll, knowing Cal was involved, they were grasping at straws. Sending him messages, asking for information, thinking he was so stupid, so incredibly naive, that he'd answer without hesitation. Damn, they must really think he was a geekoid.

He didn't blame TerMight for trying. She probably was getting paid good money by the ISD. She had managed to download his prototype genetic code and send him a message. Proof that she had tried her best, earned her salary. But, it meant nothing. In a few hours, the NSA operation would go off as scheduled. And there was nothing anybody could do to stop it.

Still grinning, he typed a reply to TerMight's message:

09/14, 24:00, DNS, Bank of Maine, Fire.

There was no way she could thwart the heist. Why not let her watch, invite her to the show, dazzle her with his brilliance? No harm. Fun, actually, knowing one of his VileSpawn friends was watching his entry into the Hacker Hall of Fame.

Logging off VileSpawn, he entered Judy Carmody's name into his search engine. In less than a second, his filter registered 417 entries. An awful lot of mentions for someone who kept her identity private. Maybe there was another Judy Carmody on the Net, someone more famous than TerMight. A quick scan of the first few hits would show him what they were about.

Ten minutes later, he emerged from a boiling sea of facts, rumors, and speculations, and one thing was crystal clear.

Bob Ingersoll was a mean son of a bitch.

He'd do *anything* to insure the success of this project. Even go as far as frame the ISD agent who was trying to track him down.

It was all there on Cal's monitor. Judy Carmody, bank security

specialist, wanted for questioning in the murder of her landlord.
Fleeing to the San Jose area, hiding among the hacker community. Still searching for him? Cal wondered. The ISD must have
paid Judy a fortune to stop this heist. She deserved every penny,
considering how dirty Mr. Ingersoll had fought back.

Cal assumed without hesitation that TerMight was innocent.
Though he had only chatted with her on the Net, Cal knew she
hated violence. It was impossible to imagine that she would
murder anyone. Absolute nonsense. The only thing Judy had
done wrong was to join with the losing side in a war between
rival government security agencies.

He had no doubts, none at all, that once the big heist went
down on Saturday night, once the ISD brass had admitted Mr.
Ingersoll was right, the charges against Judy would be dropped.
By the time Cal returned to San Jose, Judy would have been
cleared, a sincere apology issued by the police. Just a case of
mistaken identity caused by an error in the police computer
system. Everything explained neatly by the officer in charge of
the investigation, Captain Ernie Kaye.

It was all rotten, vicious, underhanded, and unethical. Cal felt
really bad for Judy, but there was nothing he could do to help her.
Mr. Ingersoll paid the bills, and Cal wanted the money. TerMight
was on the run because of the work he was doing, but he was just
a cog in an important NSA project.

Besides, it wasn't as if Judy was in any real danger. At worst,
she might spend a few days in jail. With her ISD connections,
probably not even that. In any case, it would all be over soon.

The laughter from the living room died down. Cal heard the
door of the cottage open, then a third man's voice. Mr. Ingersoll.
He had come to see if the code was ready. Footsteps clunked
down the hall.

Greg. Harry. Mr. Ingersoll.

No more time to worry about Judy.

The floor outside the bedroom squeaked. He doubted Mr. Ingersoll would appreciate his surfing the Net. He couldn't log off,
no time, so he just crashed the comm program down to its guts. It
winked off the screen.

He'd fix it later.

CHAPTER 24

Judy and Dan zoomed southward on Saratoga Way toward Bren and Carl's abandoned cabin in the mountains. Far past San Jose and back within the coastal range, they exited off the highway onto a narrow service road that swung upward into the forest coating the eastern slope. Finally, they came to a dirt road, barely noticeable among the undergrowth, and turned onto it.

Tall trees merged together far over their heads, shrouding their path in total blackness now. Using only the parking lights, Dan steered the car around several corkscrew curves as the road rose toward the mountain's summit. Finally, it came to an end. Nestled in the heart of the forest, they found themselves in a clearing with a small cabin in the center.

Dan parked the junker thirty feet from the house. Judy followed him, ducking beneath low-hanging branches that scraped her face with pine needles. The scent flooded her with memories of Jeremy and his family, where they had lived, what had happened to them.

By now, Natalie knew she was a widow, and probably, the kids knew they were fatherless. And as for the grandmother, Jeremy's mother . . .

She had lost a son.

If Judy didn't hustle and track down Cal Nikonchik, Dan might lose a brother.

Everyone was losing too much.

All because of *code*.

The cabin had two steps leading to a tiny front porch and the door. On either side of the porch, yews and junipers snarled together, as if wrestling for the better position. The cedar planks and chinked logs were moldy and splintered; the roof shingles covered maybe half the top of the cabin. The tiny window set in the front wall was covered by something dark and dirty.

Dan rattled the doorknob, but it didn't budge. "Did Bren say it would be locked?"

Judy shrugged. "She didn't say one way or the other."

"Yeah, well, it's locked. Gotta find the key or knock down the damned door." Dan stooped and wedged himself between the shrubs and the front of the house, inched to the window, groped on the sill. "Nothing," he said, returning to the porch.

Judy got down on her hands and knees in front of the door and stretched her fingers beneath the rotting wood panels. She felt something cold and hard, attached to a loop of some kind.

The key. She scrambled up, holding a long leather loop with a steel key on one end. She smiled, dangled the key in front of Dan. "Just like my mother used to do back home."

He took the key, twisted it in the lock, then pushed the door open. It swung back with a loud thump—evidently hitting something inside.

"Millionaires in the valley build these places for retreats," Dan said. "Use them to get away from the city life. After a few years, they get bored and abandon them. Squatters, like Bren and Carl, move in. Police usually ignore them unless the original owners return and make a fuss. This place looks safe enough."

Judy chuckled grimly. When was the last time she had felt *safe*? Not since the meeting with Steve Sanchez and Hector Rodriguez. When had that been? Months, years, decades ago. It felt like she had lived an entire life over the past few days. Never *safe*.

Would she ever feel safe again? Judy doubted it. *Safe* was a word that no longer had any meaning. Even under normal circumstances, it had been replaced by dozens of rules, practical guides for avoiding trouble.

Lock your cars; keep your doors bolted. Don't leave anything valuable on the beach. Scratch identification numbers into every possession, though that did nothing to stop determined thieves. Beware of angry people at fast-food joints. Never argue while driving. Stay out of neighborhoods you don't know. Don't download files from anonymous sites. Always travel in groups at night. Never give your real name. Encrypt a few times before using a digicard on the Net.

Safe was a thing of the past, right up there with disco, a chicken in every pot, Pentium chips, and *Seinfeld*.

Unfortunately, few people paid attention to any of the warnings. It was like listening to the Pope. Yeah, we hear, we obey; but hardly anyone really follows the rules. Besides, who wanted to spend their entire existence in fear? Everything always happened to the *other* guy.

She stepped into the cabin, following Dan, and they fumbled, looking for a light. Finally a string brushed Judy's forehead. She pulled it, and an overhead bulb blinked on. It was dim in here, and stuffy. Wood floor, bare wood walls, no decoration of any sort. The one window on the front wall was covered with tar paper. Dust everywhere: on the oak end table, the pole lamp, the floor.

"Nobody's been here for months." Dan looked like a zombie: eyes bloated and red, skin sagging, hair grimy and stuck to his forehead, pants rumpled, shirt untucked. He sniffed. "Smells like mold. Brings back all the bad memories of my teenage years on the commune."

The front door had cracked against a heavy pine dresser. Over the door there was the battery-equipped emergency light. The only other furniture was a battered old sofa, the end table, and the pole lamp. There wasn't even a cot, just a couple of badly worn sleeping bags. "How can they have electricity in here?" Judy asked, pointing at the lamp. "No power lines in the forest."

She slid onto the dresser, her legs dangling over the front, where the handles were cold against her calves. The skin on her face hurt, stung from the scratches inflicted by the dangling tree limbs and pine needles. A couple of old scratches had opened again. She wiped off some blood with her hand and rubbed her wet fingers on her boxer shorts.

"We need some air," she said. "Think it's safe to open the window?"

"Sure," Dan said, hardly listening. There was a flashlight on the end table. He picked it up and headed for a door just beyond the sofa. "Nobody knows we're here. Open the window. Be back in a minute."

He disappeared into darkness. A few seconds later, something clicked. A loud chugging noise filled the cabin. The pole lamp glowed with light. A mixture of dust and gas fumes filled the tiny room. Judy sneezed. She had to get some fresh air.

She jumped off the dresser, crossed the room, and tugged on the window. It refused to budge, frozen in place. So she opened the door a crack, just enough to stick her head into the night air.

Then she heard Dan's footsteps, his breathing, behind her. She turned and flashed him a weak smile.

"Yeah, it's pretty nasty in here, all right," he said. "Look what I found, though." Along with the flashlight, he held a portable radio. "There's a kitchen back there, if you can call it that. A bathroom, too. Well, sort of. It's more like a filthy toilet set into the floor, outhouse style. Through the rear door there's a portable generator. Nothing major, but some electricity's better than none. We can turn off the emergency light. The storage shed is filled with a hell of a lot of filled gasoline cans. I have a feeling this place serves as a fuel drop for the underground railroad."

"Underground railroad?"

He laughed. "Guess you had to grow up around here to know about this stuff. Illegal workers, coming up from Mexico. There's a big demand for cheap labor in San Francisco and San Jose. They drive up the coast by car. Don't like using gas stations, being noticed. So they set up fuel stops in the mountains, hiding places for their caravans. Like this place. It's an ultra-easy way for Bren and Carl to earn some extra dough. Nothing to worry about. This isn't the safest setup in the world, but there shouldn't be any problem as long as we don't start lighting matches."

Underground railroad. Interesting stuff. Judy'd been on her own underground railroad circuit since leaving Sanchez Electronics. The hackers' underground railroad. Grouch and Tarantula's house, where she picked up hardware that enabled her to change traffic signals and jam phone taps. Bren and Carl's place, where she'd picked up the kludged Net browser and teamed up with Dan Nikonchik. And now this, an underground railroad cabin for fugitive workers, or for fugitive computer programmers wanted for murder.

What could come next?

Dan turned on the radio. Scratchy rock music issued from the speaker. Reception was terrible. Grimacing, Dan shut it off. "So much for entertainment."

"That generator stinks." Judy turned again to the front door, grabbed a small chunk of wood from the ground, and wedged it between the door and frame. A cool breeze whistled through the opening, sending dust flying everywhere.

She slid back onto the dresser. "You seem to know your way around this place, Dan. Funny, I never figured you for the Boy Scout type."

"Who's a Boy Scout anymore? Sure as hell not *me*. My parents were back-to-nature freaks. They really believed all that junk—helped build their own home, raised their own food. First twenty years of my life were spent in a place pretty much like this. I hated every minute of it, but I learned the basic survival skills. Had to."

Dropping the radio and flashlight on the end table, Dan flopped onto the sofa, ignoring the cloud of dust he raised. "Man, what a day. I'm zoned. I need some food. And sleep."

"Here, eat all you want," Judy said. Along with her laptop and the netpad, she had brought the grocery bag from the car. She tossed it to him. Though all she had eaten was bread and water, Judy had no desire for anything more. Tension had destroyed what little appetite she normally possessed.

"All the comforts of home," he noted. Reaching inside the bag, Dan pulled out the loaf of bread and a package of bologna. He stuffed several slices of bologna into his mouth and chewed hard. He sighed with contentment. "Want some?"

Judy shook her head, wondering how Dan could eat so much cheap junk. The bologna probably reminded him of chili dogs. "Why do you make chili dogs?" she asked. "I mean, of all things, why batter-dipped fried chili dogs?"

She kicked her feet against the dresser. The oak was smooth and cool, felt good on her heels. The sensation kept her awake.

One of Dan's legs was crooked over the side of the sofa, and he was stretched across its length, with his head on an armrest. Bread crumbs littered his shirt and pants. Still eating, he eyed her, as if deciding what to say. But he didn't answer.

Why were the chili dogs such a big deal?

Obviously avoiding her question, Dan swallowed again, wadded four pieces of bread together, and took a huge bite. She turned away; watching him cram food into his mouth, watching the crumbs fly, seeing the grease on his chin, was practically making her sick.

She scanned the walls. Only one outlet, and the floor lamp was plugged into it. Not that she cared. No way was she going to rely on some ramshackle old generator for power. There was still plenty of charge in the laptop and netpad batteries. All she needed was room to stretch out and get comfortable.

Peeling herself off the dresser, she ambled past Dan, and grabbed one of the sleeping bags. Unzipping it, she stretched the bag across the floor near the sofa, next to the floor lamp. Nothing special, but it was a lot better than sitting on the bare floor. Settling into a lotus position, Judy flipped open her laptop, starting it up. Time to work.

Here, in the middle of nowhere, it seemed so peaceful, so calm. She could finally stop thinking about murder and robbery. How could anything horrible happen way out here, where nobody lived?

A pleasant thought, but not very realistic. And, in the past few days, Judy reminded herself, she had been forced to face reality and deal with it.

The laptop beeped. It was awake, ready for her to tell it what to do. From where she sat, only the back of Dan's head was visible, that greasy mop of black-rooted blond hair. As if reading her mind he turned, stared at her with dark eyes.

She looked down, typed her password, brought Cal's genetic code up on the screen. A file named DNS0923. Chromosome objects. Each object was made up of variable-length character strings. Each character string was made up of four components: *route, loot, source, dest.*

"What's all this DNS stuff that your brother's doing?"

He blinked. "DNS? I don't know. All I know is what Cal told me. That I should never, under any circumstances, screw around with those files. He said they had something to do with the restaurant accounts he set up for me."

Judy shook her head. Like it or not, it was time for Dan Nikonchik to fill in the blanks. Later was now.

"Okay, Dan," she said, "this is it. We're safe here. Time for the whole story. Enough stalling. You're the only one who can save your brother. Not me, not Bren, nobody but you. By tomorrow, it may be too late. You swore you'd talk. I'm waiting."

"How much do you need to know?"

"Everything. All about this DNS stuff. What kind of restaurant requires complex genetic programming for the accounts? What's the real purpose of the code? Who are these mysterious weirdos chasing you around in green vans, attacking you, threatening you? Your life makes no sense."

She looked him straight in the eyes. "The DNS stuff is the reason the government recruited Cal. That much I've figured out. I'll bet someone working for one of the national security agencies saw the program, realized its potential. That's how this whole mess started. And if you want it stopped, I have to know the truth. All of it."

His voice trembled. "Ten years I've spent raising Cal. Wasn't easy. I never wanted to be a parent. But I didn't have any choice. Cal's the only relative I got. He's my responsibility."

He paused, making a futile effort to compose himself.

Judy crawled over to the sofa, though the dust from the cushions made her cough. "Just tell me what you know, even if it seems irrelevant."

"Yeah . . . Cal and I . . . well, when our parents died in that fire, I was just—I don't know, I was just so *furious*. That they would leave me, without much going my way, to fend for myself—and for Cal. He was such a goofy little guy: awkward, a social screwball, so quiet I wanted to *scream* at times."

She nodded, urging him on.

"Judy, I didn't know what to do. Cal and I were left with nothing. We bummed around the state for a few years, me working any job I could find, Cal getting hooked on computers.

While I was working as a waiter, I heard some programmers talking about how much they loved pizzas, hamburgers, cola, chips. Lots of greasy stuff. I did some checking. Silicon Valley had lots of junk-food places and trendy health-food restaurants. But I wanted to try something new. I figured that, if I came up with some sort of fast food that was different, well . . . then, computer jockeys would flock to my place. So I opened Dan's DiskWorld."

He smiled wryly. "Besides, it was sort of sick revenge, serving fried junk after growing up on a commune filled with health nuts. Only problem was, starting a restaurant costs money. And paying our living expenses ate up what little money I was earning.

"I tried the banks. No luck. They only loan money to people who don't really need to borrow it. So I went to one of the more shady outfits. They loaned me the money. When the restaurant got successful, they came to me with the catch.

"Nothing dangerous, they said. Just filter their cash through the restaurant. I had no choice. It was cooperate—or else."

"Okay, so you use your business to launder money for punks," Judy said. "But how does Cal's code fit into this?"

"It wasn't too difficult at first," Dan said, "because the amounts weren't huge. But, they kept demanding I funnel more money through the accounts. All the transactions had to be kept hidden. No taxes, no traces, definitely no names. And since most people use digicards to pay their bills, it was getting harder and harder to understate my receipts. If I kept double books, sooner or later the IRS would catch on, and arrest me for income tax evasion. Finally, I told Cal what was happening. I wanted him to know the truth, in case anything happened to me. He told me not to worry, that he'd find an answer."

"Cal concocted the code, this DNS stuff, to conceal illegitimate profits?"

"Right," Dan said. "The program routed the income that came from my silent partners—and a lot of *my* income, too—into accounts all over the country. The money vanished, disappeared completely from the restaurant receipts, then reappeared in out-of-state banks, without any links connecting it to my business or the loan sharks. Every few weeks, Cal updated their files. That's why they've been putting the squeeze on me. They know he's disappeared. Without him to manage the program, the money just sits there. Last few days, they've grown impatient."

Dan's loan sharks clearly weren't professional mobsters; they were just lowlifes who had found a good thing in a young and desperate Dan Nikonchik. Certainly nothing compared to Tuska and Smith and the people who had Cal.

Suddenly, her mind clicked into gear: *route*, *loot*, *source*, *dest*, as in *destination*.

Cal had invented a program that rerouted money to banks all across the Net without a trace. Someone had broken into Laguna Savings accounts on Monday night. Judy's mind flashed to the German poster in Cal's apartment.

"That's it: *DNS*."

"I don't understand."

"It's Cal's little joke. DNS stands for the Internet Domain Name System. But it's also German for DNA—some really long German word. I can't remember it off the top of my head. Cal must have learned it from the genetic chart in his apartment."

"Yeah, so?"

She explained. "Cal's been using DNA code—genetic programming—to route this dirty money you've been receiving, sending it to bank accounts all over the world in untraceable ways. He's using these chromosome objects, whatever they are, to route the loot from one computer node, one DNS location, to another. I suspect the chromosomes replicate at each computer location, Dan. They know how much money to transfer—the *loot*. They know only the last computer on the Net that sent it to them—the *source*. They know where to send the loot next—the *destination*.

"I suspect Cal's code is artificially intelligent, some fancy new kind of independent agent that finds the optimal overall route for the sleazy money."

He nodded wearily, didn't seem to get it. Judging by his expression, she could imagine what he was thinking: Yeah, whatever you say. I don't care how code works. I want out. And I want my brother back.

He might be clueless, but it was becoming very clear to *her*.

With minor modifications, slight changes in the code's basic instructions, Cal's program could be used to take money from any electronic account on the Net, send it across an untraceable maze of paths, and deposit it in a new location known only to the user. It was the most sophisticated robbery scenario ever invented. And unless Judy unraveled the genetic code and figured out exactly how it worked, there was no way to stop it.

"I'll explain more later," she said. "Right now, I have to concentrate."

"What I can't understand," Dan said, as Judy rose from the sofa, "is why Cal's cooperating with these government guys. Doesn't he realize they're killers?"

She shook her head. "Of course not. Why would he? I'm sure Cal thinks he's performing a vital service for his government, and he's probably getting paid very well. No reason he'd suspect the agents he's working for are murdering people."

"Cal's not completely naïve," Dan said. "Our parents taught us that politicians can't be trusted."

"Lots of people don't trust government officials," Judy said, "but most don't assume they're killers. Cal isn't naive. Just normal."

She left Dan on the sofa and returned to the floor and her laptop. After a few minutes, he wandered back into the kitchenette. She heard him rummaging through the cabinets, just as he had in Jeremy's house.

The guy was *always* hungry.

Dan returned after a few minutes, resettled onto the sofa. He handed her a glass of water, and slurped from a glass of his own. "Bottled stuff," he said. "Nice and pure, no minerals."

She drank the water, thankful for anything that would wash the dust from her throat. Then she returned to the job at hand.

All the scares about the Net were true. Judy had known it for years. Apparently, so had Cal. Not that they, or any of their friends, would do anything illegal. But if they could figure out how to rip people off, so could someone with a lot less scruples. Lowlifes who wanted to steal, screw up the government, kill people. There was no such thing as privacy. Every bit of data was stored somewhere on a computer. And, nowadays, every computer was hooked to the Net.

The key was getting to data in a way nobody could detect.

Cal had found that key. She understood his approach. But, beyond theory, she had no idea how he was doing it.

She logged onto VileSpawn using Griswald's secret password. Perhaps he'd left a message for her. It was worth a check.

She dug into the Water directory she'd set up, found a new file.
It was simple, just one line.

```
09/14, 24:00, DNS, Bank of Maine, Fire.
```

What did it mean? A date, a place, a time—midnight *tonight*?

Something was going to happen to the Bank of Maine site at
midnight. Something to do with Cal's genetic code, his DNS
files. Her head snapped up. "What time is it, Dan?"

"Huh?" He was dozing. He glanced at his watch. "Around
eleven-thirty."

She'd been drifting, her mind wandering, for what . . . fifteen
minutes? More?

Time was running out. She had only half an hour left to unravel this mess.

CHAPTER 25

The door to Cal's room opened. Mr. Ingersoll, jacket and tie neat as ever, walked in, followed by Harry and Greg.

All three men looked grim. Worried.

"Well, Calvin," Mr. Ingersoll said. "Tell me some good news."

"The code's finished," Cal said. "I plugged the final holes an hour ago. It's all set. Got the Internet locations—for the banks we're testing—all loaded. Same with the accounts where you want to deposit the cash."

"You're sure the program works perfectly?" Mr. Ingersoll asked.

"I ran a quick check a few minutes ago. Runs like a dream. We're ready. The transfer should work nice and smooth."

"Excellent," Mr. Ingersoll said. "I knew you could do it. We'll keep to our original schedule. Midnight tonight for the first run. Bank activity should be at a minimum then. Be prepared for company, though. The compound manager wants to watch. Since we've used this place for the past week, I couldn't say no. Nothing to be concerned about. The old man won't say a word. And he has the highest-level security clearance."

"Whatever you say," Cal said.

"I have to return to the mansion," Mr. Ingersoll said. "I'm expecting an important phone call. From Washington, of course. They want confirmation that the heist is on for tonight."

That was why Cal hadn't found any record of phone calls to the capital. It made perfect sense. Incoming calls weren't listed in the compound phone log, only in records at the telephone company. NSA headquarters called here, probably routing the messages through several other cities, making the source impossible to trace. Thus, no hard evidence existed linking the facility with the government. Mr. Ingersoll was sharp.

"Shortly before midnight," the NSA agent continued, "I'll return to watch you make history."

"I'll be here," Cal said.

Mr. Ingersoll turned to the door, then hesitated. "Oh, one last thing, Calvin. I know your program leaves absolutely no trace as to the identity of the user. Well, I'd like you to modify that a bit. I want you to plant a few footprints during the heist. Not yours, of course. We'll pin the blame for this operation on another hacker. I'll supply you with all the necessary information when I return."

"Who?" Cal asked.

"A young lady who's given me a headache the past few days," Mr. Ingersoll said.

"T-T-TerMight," Cal stuttered, catching himself just in time. He almost said *Judy Carmody*. "Because of the work she's doing for the ISD?"

Mr. Ingersoll appeared startled. He stared at Cal with narrowed eyes. "Yes, TerMight." He spoke slowly, as if weighing each word carefully. "How did you know she was helping Internet Security?"

"She—she does jobs for them all the time," Cal said. Mind racing, he covered his tracks as best as possible. "Plenty of instances. She's posted on VileSpawn some details of her work."

"Well," Mr. Ingersoll said. "TerMight's the one they hired to track you down. Fortunately, she's been unable to find us. But, I'd like to make her life miserable in return. Nothing serious. Just make her squirm."

"TerMight's my friend," Cal said. "I don't want her in trouble."

"I understand. Don't let it upset you. She'll be fine once the details of this operation are released to the public. No arguments, Calvin. I want this done. *Understand?*"

"Yes, sir," Cal said. "I understand."

"Good," Mr. Ingersoll said. "I'll see you at midnight."

He turned and left, Harry and Greg following in his wake. The two men hadn't said a word the entire time. They were hired muscle. Mr. Ingersoll was the boss.

Cal grimaced. Mr. Ingersoll was a vindictive son of a bitch. Using that cop, Ernie Kaye, he'd framed Judy Carmody for murder. Now, he was going to pin the electronic bank heist on her, as well. Sure, she'd be proven innocent within a few days, but it still was damned mean.

For all of his cool, calculating ways, Mr. Ingersoll had a vicious streak a mile wide. This project was his baby, his reason for living. But, once the heist took place, as inventor of the code, Cal might be the one who received all the attention. The NSA agent might find that upsetting. Which could be dangerous.

Mr. Ingersoll was the one man who knew all about Cal and Dan's involvement with the loan sharks, as far as Cal could tell. He had promised never to reveal their secret, as long as Cal cooperated. But Cal was relying entirely on the agent's word.

Now that worried him.

What he needed was a written guarantee from the NSA that he and Dan would never be prosecuted. Cal felt certain Mr. Ingersoll could provide the document, if pushed. But, what could Cal use as a bargaining chip?

Speed.

The NSA agent was obsessed with speed. He insisted that the main heist, for fifty billion dollars, occur within split seconds. He wanted the code to run so fast that the withdrawals could never be detected. Speed was essential to his argument proving the evils of the Net.

The sample heist would operate with blinding quickness. Perhaps, if Cal slowed it down, he could strike a bargain with the NSA agent. Mr. Ingersoll wouldn't know why the heist took five minutes instead of one. All he'd know was that it wasn't fast enough.

Then Cal could promise to find some method to increase the speed. His price would be the written guarantee of immunity.

Cal inserted a simple loop in his code, one that used the system timer to slow the code for a few minutes.

What if Mr. Ingersoll didn't care that the program ran slowly? Cal needed a fallback option, another card to play if his first gamble didn't pay off. Was there any other glitch in the program that he might exploit?

He reviewed the entire operation. Following the first heist, they'd inform the ISD of their success. Then demonstrate the code in an even bigger heist in front of various government officials. But the second time around, they'd reroute the money immediately after stealing it, put the dough back in the original accounts. Then, there would be nothing left to do but return the cash from the first theft.

That would be the most difficult task. By its very nature, his code wouldn't list the accounts from which money was taken. That information would have to be determined via a search program that would review the withdrawal records of every bank they had hit. *Very tricky.* Once the looted accounts were identified, the correct funds would be returned.

It shouldn't take more than a few days, assuming it ran exactly as planned. Cal grinned. What if there was a minor problem with the system? A lot of people, waiting for their money to be returned, would be pissed off at the person in charge of the operation. No doubt Mr. Ingersoll would do anything to fix the mistake. Sign anything.

It was a nasty backup plan. But, considering Mr. Ingersoll's own dirty tricks, Cal felt no pangs of remorse. Typing quickly, he added one final instruction to his code.

Satisfied he had found the key to success, Cal leaned back and closed his eyes. For years, Dan had been protecting him, keeping him safe, making sure he stayed out of trouble. Now, the roles were reversed. Cal was the one saving Dan—from prison. Life was crazy sometimes.

There was a soft tap on the window. Startled, Cal looked around, saw a face outlined in the moonlight. A female face. One finger pressed to her lips, signaling for silence.

A girl? Here, on the compound? Who?

Cal leapt from the chair, knocking it over, and grabbed it right before it crashed to the floor. Barefoot, he padded to the window. Stood behind the curtain, looked at the face.

Not a girl but a woman. Good looking, with light brown hair flowing down to her shoulders. He'd never seen her before. Of course not. He'd had no idea there were any women at the compound. She had to be from the big house up the road. An NSA agent? Or Mr. Ingersoll's girlfriend? He wasn't sure. Didn't know what to think.

She gestured for him to open the window, at the same time glancing over her shoulder, as if ready to run. She was watching for someone. Who?

He considered, hesitated, then turned the lever that opened the window a crack.

The woman leaned close, whispered, "The screen, kid. Pop the screen."

Why not? What harm could there be? Besides, it was exciting. Like spy stuff.

He turned the lever more, till the window swung as far out as it would go. The woman stepped back as the panes swung toward her.

Then, he could see her clearly. She was the woman in the photo in Greg's dresser. The one who had written, *To Greg, thanks for the dirty work.* She was *G*.

"Hurry up," she whispered, glancing over her shoulder again. "I only have a second. Someone might hear us. The old man'll notice I'm gone."

What was she talking about? Who was the old man? Mr. Ingersoll?

He unlatched the prongs that held the screen in place. Twelve damned prongs. His fingers were sweating and shaking so much he had a hard time.

"Hurry it up," she hissed.

He hurried, fumbled some more.

"You're Calvin Nikonchik, right? The genius?"

The genius. Sure. And supreme jerk, who turned into a geek when he saw a chick. She called him Calvin. Mr. Ingersoll must have told her about him. The NSA agent was the only one who used his full name.

He nodded, unable to say a word. His nerves were popping. Any second he expected a big hand on his shoulder, Harry screaming at him.

"Listen," the woman said, "I want you to do me a big favor. Don't ask why. No time to explain. Just do it. Whatever Ingersoll's promised you for pulling this heist, it's not enough. He's out for himself, nobody else. Help me and you won't be sorry. Together, we can be rich. Incredibly rich."

What was she babbling about?

He unchinked the last prong, carefully and quietly slid the screen from place and set it on the floor. From the adjacent bedroom, Harry grunted again, Greg laughed. They were chattering about something, but he couldn't make out the subject.

The desert air was cool at night. The air conditioner thrummed beneath the sill, whining to keep pace with the onrush of desert breeze.

The woman's brown hair lifted on the breeze, fluffed around her face. Her skin was pricked with goose bumps. She shivered, moved closer to the window, held out her hand, uncurled her fingers.

"Take this, Calvin." She held out something small and dark. "Use it to record everything. Make sure you get *everyone* in the picture. Especially Ingersoll. We'll make him sweat."

He reached, took the object from her palm.

Her voice turned low and sultry. "Remember, Calvin. Tape everything. Do it for me. I promise, you won't be sorry."

He nodded, a weak little motion.

Then she turned and slipped away, gone in the black silent desert.

Cal eased the screen back into place, relatched it, cranked the window shut. He slid back into the black leather chair. He looked at the object the mysterious woman had given to him. It gleamed on the plywood desk.

It was a DC109: a microcamera with built-in audio chip. The latest in vidcam equipment. Cal used one when he worked with Jeremy. Together, they'd recorded people in the city, then uploaded the movie images to Jeremy's computer, tinkered with faces, bodies, and scenes. Had created whole new worlds.

Using a camera just like this one, they'd created Dozong and given him life.

Why had the woman given him a DC109? Why did she want him to tape the robbery? Something about a lot of money. It made no sense. But, what harm could there be recording the heist?

Cal gulped some more ginger ale.

Then he slipped off his watch, removed the back, and snapped the DC109 into place. The front of the microcamera looked like an ordinary digital watch. He wrapped the leather strap back around his wrist, secured it. As soon as Mr. Ingersoll walked into the room, Cal would press the tiny button on the side, and would start recording.

Cal looked at the tiny clock on the bottom of his screen. It was now 11:40 P.M. Twenty minutes till show time.

He touched the icon that brought up the launch program on his screen. One more touch, this time of the EXECUTE icon, and he'd steal a billion dollars.

The door opened, and Cal jumped.

It was Harry. With the sneer, the rough Southern drawl, the ugly face.

"Get your stuff ready, Nikonchik. Mr. Ingersoll and the old man will be here in five minutes for the big show. Make it good, kid. I'm tired of living in this dump, baby-sitting you. Time for the big payoff."

"I'm all set," Cal said.

It was time to show the world what Griswald could do.

camera just like this one. Hewell created Oozone and Nak—

CHAPTER 26

Sweat dripped from Judy's forehead and burned in the partly clotted scrapes from the pine tree branches. She mopped her face with Bren's flannel shirt.

Fifteen minutes, no, *twelve,* and Cal would enter the Net to execute his code. Perform the first major, untraceable Internet bank robbery. She had no idea how much, but five people had *died* to insure the operation's success. It had to be millions. Hundreds of millions.

With those stakes, the killers would never give up. They were out there, in the night, hunting Judy, murder on their minds.

"Dan. *Dan.* Wake up." She reached and shook his shoulder.

He stirred, mumbled. "Wha-what—"

"Get up. I need you to keep a lookout."

He pulled himself to sitting position. His shoulders drooped. His head drooped. His eyes were unfocused and bleary. "Lookout? Wha—"

"Get to the door, Dan. If you see anything, even one small light, we gotta get out of here, *fast.*"

She rose from the floor, grabbed his shoulders, and shook. His head jerked up; he pushed her away. "What are you talking about? Nobody can find us here. It's safe."

Judy had no time for chatter. She grabbed her laptop and started for the tiny kitchenette out back. "Nowhere's safe," she said. "You know that. Stand watch at the doorway, *now.*"

"Doorway . . . doorway . . . the doorway . . ." He climbed to his feet, wobbled, then staggered to the front door. Holding onto the frame, he peered out the narrow opening into the night. "Nothing. Don't see a goddamn thing."

"Good. If you do, holler, then hightail it into the kitchen. Understand?"

He was clutching the oak dresser to maintain his balance. "Don't worry about me," he said. "I'll be fine. Just need to wake up. Didn't realize I was dozing off."

The kitchenette was practically the size of a closet, with one small counter, some pots and pans, and a broken stool. She moved the stool to the counter, set up her laptop. The gasoline fumes were a lot worse here. So was the noise from the generator. The rear door stood open a notch, so Judy pulled it completely closed, muting the noise and cutting off the fumes. She was tempted to shut off the generator, but she needed the kitchen lights. The air quickly grew stale, but she'd survive.

Judy glanced at her laptop. Two minutes until midnight.

Two minutes . . .

Maybe, just maybe, Cal had sent her a message. No time for her to check on the laptop. Didn't want to run the risk of missing the heist. No need, she had the netpad. Dan was useless with computers, but he had eyes.

Grabbing the netpad, she raced to the living room. Dan stood slumped against the front wall, blinking hard as he tried to keep his eyes open.

"Dan? Anything?"

His head turned slowly. He was soaked in grime, and his shirt clung to his chest. His hair looked like a mop that had washed one too many filthy floors. "No, nothing," he mumbled. "I told you. We're safe here."

"Good." She turned on the netpad, then thrust it into his hands. "In a few seconds, any mail sent to me will turn up on the screen. Check it out. All you gotta do is read what's on the screen. I doubt if anything's there, but can't hurt to look. There might be something from Cal."

She hurried back to the kitchenette, to her perch on the broken stool, which wobbled beneath her weight, then placed her fingers on the keyboard.

Any time now, Cal. Go, baby, go.

As TerMight, she logged onto the public Internet, switched on visuals for full graphics. She waited in the Trancor/holdings/89443010 directory of the Bank of Maine, an anonymous watcher.

She waited.

Thirty seconds to go. Thirty seconds until midnight.

And when he arrived, when Cal arrived, she was shaking so hard the stool wobbled violently on its chopped-off legs. Lurching to the left, she grabbed at the counter, kicked the stool back, and stood.

Watched. Frozen in place, there in the back closet of a hidden cabin in God knew where, frozen, with the night buzzing around her, the white letters merging into blue, into black . . .

She watched in terror as Griswald arose and took over the world.

```
Bank of Maine
/Trancor/holdings/89443010 . . .
Current status: read/write
Ownership: water

Federal Reserve
/treasury/notes/16a87b00199 . . .
Current status: read/write
Ownership: TerMight

Hal's Hotspot of Girls
/gallery . . .
Current status: read/write
Ownership: water

Cosworth's Tradex
/USauto/accounts/1487a9b042 . . .
Current status: read/write
Ownership: TerMight
```

```
Bank of New Zealand
/Tradex/debits/acct0143019 . . .
Current status: read/write
Ownership: water
```

He was playing God of the Net. These weren't Web pages he was hitting. They were protected directories, secured files, sitting on computer servers all over the world. Though a bank or trading house might set up one server to hang off the Net, all their other computers were *linked* to that server. If someone like Cal broke into the server itself, from that server he could go anywhere, access all of the computers that were linked to the server.

And all computers were automatically linked to servers. Had been for five years or more.

He erased nothing. Instead, he *added* ownership to every freaking score, every freaking movement of money across the Net. Ownership that indicated that she, Judy Carmody, TerMight, was the one pulling down the big heist. The hacker who was accumulating some immense sum, preparing it to be sent . . . elsewhere.

And she couldn't do anything about it.

She had to focus, remain calm, unravel this damned code, *stop* it.

She opened her favorites page, slammed from the public Internet past several security firewalls, and crashed into the superuser account of a major Net bank, International Bank of Lincoln/Manhattan.

Here, she lurked in the bank's classified intranet, where only top bank officials could go. She'd coded the security setup herself, last year, with Mercy.

Mercy. Poor, dead Mercy . . .

Judy knew all the passwords; she knew all the algorithms used to change those passwords. She'd constructed them herself.

The intranet was heavily protected from outside access. But it didn't matter. Nothing could really be protected these days.

Had she wanted to, Judy could have been a very rich woman anytime she chose. She could have used the bank's projections of future earnings to make a fortune in the stock market, then raced off to the Bahamas or Switzerland, anywhere, the French Riviera . . .

But Judy Carmody was no thief. She was just a paid hacker, a drone for the computer firms that littered the southern California beach like garbage dropped by tourists.

And Cal—Griswald—he was one of her kind. A slave to people like Dan Nikonchik, Steve Sanchez, and all the others. A workdrone. A guy who'd never pull a score like this, much less pin it on one of his fellow hackers, on Judy, on TerMight.

The thought infuriated her. This could not be. She wouldn't *allow* this to happen.

No.

The bank's welcome message appeared, red letters on a black backdrop:

```
International Bank of Lincoln/Manhattan
Welcome. Your password is correct.
```

In the top left corner of the screen, the bank's logo appeared, a tiny red *L/M* throbbing and growing larger, then fading back to pinpoint size. She'd coded it herself, thought it very cool at the time.

She pressed a function key to capture everything she saw on the screen.

"Tell him we're here."

She whirled. He was behind her; Dan was staring over her shoulder.

"I don't have time to argue with you, Dan. I'm not typing a thing. You want *them*—you want the people who've been killing hackers—to know we're watching their big score? What are you, crazy?"

"Look!" He pointed at the screen.

The red *L/M* splintered into stardust.

A tiny flash of fire, like a match lit by an inept Boy Scout, or perhaps the spark of a firefly: it flickered, then died by the throbbing *L/M*.

Cal. It *was* Cal. He was here. He and Judy—alone—in the black silken corridor of the bank's innermost Web.

"Quiet," she ordered. "I have to concentrate. Quiet."

Dan cowered. His eyes dimmed momentarily, then flashed again. "Just help him, Judy. Do whatever you can."

A labyrinth of virtual reality mazes, woven in strands of two-pixel blue, appeared on the screen. The tiny red *L/M* throbbed. Judy touched it. Her laptop was rigged to instantly translate her screen touches into fingerprints for the user identity under which she had logged in. The bank's software, assuming she was the head honcho, the bank president himself, flashed the message:

```
Access Granted
```

The mazes split into thinner strands.

Dan squinted, rubbed his eyes. It was hard to look at one-pixel strands of color. But Judy was used to it. She zoomed in for a larger shot of the images. The screen refocused, displayed the strands in close-up.

She continued to press the throbbing *L/M*—once, twice, three more times—to give herself full access to everything that was happening on the bank's computer server. Everything: system resources, access times, withdrawal amounts. Numbers rolled on the bottom right corner of her screen. Right next to the clock: two minutes past midnight.

The blue strands coalesced and re-formed into three-dimensional helixes. Slow, very slow, as if Cal had slowed down all his code, just so she could see it.

Helixes. The old Watson-Crick formations of chromosomes, genes, DNA. Judy's heart beat with the pulse of the throbbing *L/M*.

The programmed chromosomes unfurled, then recombined. Their strands crossed between chromosomes.

Cal's code was mutating. It was reproducing.

Before her eyes, Cal was creating *digital life*.

Surely, he *was* the computer underground's equivalent of God. And if indeed this was the underground, were the right-wing, anti-Net morons correct in their fears? Was a hacker of Griswald's caliber really the Devil?

She watched, unable for the moment to do anything to stop him. Her only hope was to capture everything as it went down, so she could study the captured data later.

Within minutes, the amplitudes of the humps that formed the helixes shifted. The frequencies of the curves stretched. The cycles of current shortened; the phase differences tightened.

Judy had never seen code like this before, never in all the years she'd been hacking.

"Like watching the birth of a baby, from the moment the first cell splits right up to the fetus," she said softly, mesmerized by what she saw.

From behind her, Dan said, "Artificial intelligence, isn't it? Cal was always into that."

Artificial intelligence combined with genetic software—wherein an energy dip or a slight change in phase, even if it occurred randomly, could serve as an attractor, pulling bits in a seemingly chaotic direction. In standard artificial life programming, patterns would arise from the chaotic flow over time. The digital creatures would *evolve*, become more intelligent, adapt to their surroundings. The AI would analyze the patterns and set a new course: different frequency, different amplitude, *different genetic recombinations that altered the meaning and direction of data.*

The direction of data. The routes that would be taken by the accumulated stolen cash, on the way to its ultimate destinations.

The chromosomes crossing, transferring route, loot, source, and destination information, finding better ways to steal and hide electronic funds.

On her screen, the DNA strands looked like sine waves—voltage patterns—twisted into chromosomal formations. Where there should have been pyrimidines—thymine and cytosine—and where there should have been purines—adenine and guanine—instead, there were hexadecimal codes. Four of them. Yeah: route, loot, source, and destination.

The strands were splitting so much that they were beginning to look like upside-down trees with massive subgrowths and dense branches. The subtrees moved from one part of the screen to another, quickly, so fast that Judy couldn't see them—they were totally blurred—and then when the screen was blanketed with them, they faded.

The subtrees lost their branches, filtered into pixel dust, and vanished.

The original chromosomes were gone. New ones had cannibalized them in order to survive and grow. And now, only a few remained on the screen, the final ones, the most intelligent ones, the ones that knew where to direct the stolen cash across the network.

The accumulated amount flashed in red beneath the *L/M*:

$999,238,491.32

Filtered, absorbed from hundreds, maybe thousands of customer accounts. Lumped into one grand sum, ready to move elsewhere. A tiny fire appeared in the upper left corner, then flickered off. Having stolen the money, Cal's chromosomes were most likely shifting the funds into secret accounts throughout the world.

In seconds, Cal was gone.

Judy gasped, sank back against Dan. He clutched her around the waist.

It had all happened within minutes. The clock on the screen displayed the time: five minutes after midnight.

And nobody knew where $999,238,491.32 had gone. The very code that had taken the money and rerouted it had killed itself off, leaving no trace of entry, no trace of destination.

The only trace that did remain—on the computer server of the International Bank of Lincoln/Manhattan—was that someone named Water, someone named TerMight, had entered that night and committed the biggest theft in history.

CHAPTER 27

"Nearly a billion dollars," Judy said finally. "A billion. Now at least we know why they were willing to kill so many people."

They sat on the beat-up old sofa, both of them exhausted, shocked by what they had witnessed.

"What do we do now?" Dan asked. "Now that the theft's taken place, will they kill Cal? Is it all over? Have we lost?"

"Cal's not dead," Judy said. "It's a typical programming situation. Preliminary test first. Then, once the code's proven to work, push it to the max. There's still a chance to stop them. And save Cal."

"A billion dollars, and that's only a *test*? How much are they after?"

"I don't know, Dan. With Cal's program, these guys can steal as much as they want. Ten, twenty billion . . . who knows?"

"But if they're planning another heist, like you say, there's still a chance to save Cal."

"A small chance," Judy said. "I don't know how to cope with a mess like this. Your brother just stole close to a billion dollars, and I have no idea how he did it, where he hid the money. I suspect nobody does."

"Why did you ask me to check for E-mail?"

"Long shot. Just in case Cal got in touch."

He frowned. "Sorry. He didn't."

"Yeah, I figured. Wouldn't be stupid enough to send me freaking *E-mail*. Anybody can crack that rot."

"Yeah."

Damn. It was so bleak, the two of them sitting there, dead tired and at a dead end. After a few minutes, Judy broke the silence.

"Well, this is a waste of time. It's back to the programming. I have to figure out where Cal transferred all that money. I *refuse* to give up."

She returned to her position on the floor by the pole lamp. He returned to his position on the sofa and closed his eyes.

Judy had faced nightmare deadlines before, customers wanting software in a week that should have taken six months to code, others wanting major changes overnight, but she'd never faced a deadline like this one. This was flat-out a Dead Line. If she didn't think fast enough and code fast enough, she was dead.

She opened the captured graphics transcript from Cal's weird genetic bank heist code. Scrolled through it, noticed how the child chromosomes were formed, how they killed the parent chromosomes. Each chromosome represented an ideal destination for the transfer of digital cash. The destination was coded into elaborate binary trees, hence the dense jumble of tree limbs she'd seen on her laptop screen during the heist. The chromosomes reproduced by crossing subtrees—parts of the elaborate binary trees.

During this crossing of digital subtrees, the chromosomes swapped genes—the encoded route, source, destination, and transfer amount—until, many chromosome generations later, a final and perfect route existed. The entire process repeated at each computer node along the Net route that led to banks where money was stolen, then to where money was deposited.

More interesting, the child chromosomes acted as parasites on the older generation. They replicated, swapping subtree genes, but only after *stealing* gene subtrees from their parents. Without a complete genome of data, the parents died, leaving no trace of where the money had come from. As soon as the path went from one computer on the Net to the next, the path disappeared: it died.

Cal had created digital parasites. Intelligent. Almost like *cannibals*.

Unfortunately, Judy's transcript had captured only the code as it executed on one computer node. There was no way she could trace the ultimate destinations of all that money.

But if she was dealing with parasites, perhaps a counterattack could be devised that would include digital creatures that *killed* parasites. Or maybe, there was some way to force the parent generation to become *immune* to their parasitic children.

Judy stretched out on the sleeping bag. Put her hands beneath her head. The chugging of the generator, coupled with the gas fumes, was making her drowsy.

She shut her eyes. It almost sounded like a technobeat: the churning of the generator chugs. A tiny digital voice played in her mind: *I am your computer. I calculate. I calculate.* An ancient technotune she used to listen to as a teenager while coding late into the night. *Beep beep beep. Chug chug chug. I calculate. I calculate.* An image of digital sums flashed across the back of her eyelids. Actual amounts from that security job she'd done with Mercy. She remembered it well. Once the tally hit $999,999.99, the addition of any further amount caused the whole sum to hit straight zeroes: $000,000.00. She saw the numbers rolling in her mind, as if they were stored in little digital boxes on the bank's computer:

$$
\begin{array}{r}
\$999,999.99 \\
+\qquad .01 \\
\hline
1,000,000.00
\end{array}
$$

Eight storage slots, add a penny, and the amount suddenly needed nine slots; but only eight storage spots had been allocated, so the one was dropped and the sum was stored as straight zeroes. Some stupid bank programmer had been jacking a million bucks out of the bank's main accounts until Judy and Mercy learned his secret.

If only Cal's code were so simple to unravel. Funny how Cal

always flashed that fire on the screen when he entered and exited. Funny how she and Cal seemed to think alike.

Even closed, her eyes were stinging from the fumes. She rubbed them, then sat up again and stared, half awake, at her laptop. Fire. Maybe Cal had left another Fire message for her on VileSpawn.

She logged on as Griswald, figuring it was a wasted effort—how could Cal leave her messages on VileSpawn *while* pulling an Internet bank heist?—but still, what the heck, anything was worth a shot.

And her hunch paid off. Down deep in the Griswald directory, where she and Cal had left their earlier messages, Judy found a new message, one much longer than the previous ones. Not wanting to loiter and take a chance she might be spotted, she captured the file to her laptop disk, then left VileSpawn. The message had been created an hour ago, a text file. She browsed it. Then:

"Dan, Dan!" She leapt up, shook him awake, stuffed her laptop into the case.

He rose from the sofa, eyes bleary, his voice thick as if drug-hazed from psychopsilo-D: "Unh . . . uh, what? What is it?"

Judy turned off the pole lamp, motioned him toward the kitchen. "Come on. Hurry. We have to get out of here. They're coming!"

He staggered after her. "Who's coming? Judy! Who? Hey, wait up!"

"No time to explain." She raced into the kitchen and toward the back door. "We gotta run. Tony Tuska and Paul Smith, the killers. Bren told them where we are."

"*Bren?* What are you, crazy? Why the hell would Bren send those lunatics after us?" Dan scrabbled after her, then grabbed her shoulders. He held her tight, not letting her move. "Calm down. Don't get hysterical. No time to panic. Tell me quick. Where did you get this?"

Judy shook Dan off. "We have to move, Dan, *now*."

He leaned on the countertop. "Sorry. You tell me, or I'm not going anywhere. Tell me quickly, if you have to. I need to know what's going on."

Judy grabbed his elbow, urged him toward the open back

door, spoke as quickly as she could. "Bren left me a message in Cal's VileSpawn account. A police detective came to see her tonight. Barged into a party, shook everyone up. Flashed his badge. He was from Laguna Beach, up here on my trail. One of Grouch's flunkies had dropped Bren's name. That's how the cop found her. Threatened to throw Carl in jail. Lock him up with the druggies and gangbangers. Scared the hell out of Bren. Guy really meant it. Had cuffs on Carl. So she told him about the cabin."

Dan started moving toward the door after her. "*Hell!* What about the killers? How do they fit in?"

"Bren knew the cop was crooked. Said he had witnesses who saw me kill Trev. He left in a rental, with two other guys in it. One of them with a beard.

"Cop knew there's no phones up here. She's afraid he's monitoring my E-mail. Bozo figured there was no way for Bren to warn me. He'd never look for a message posted in Griswald's VileSpawn account."

"Damn it. Judy, don't panic. Even driving fast as possible, the trip from Bren's place to here would take more than an hour. We've got a little time. Not much, but enough. Come on; we gotta get busy."

She dragged him toward the door again. "Get busy? What are you talking about, Dan? We have to get out of here. And I mean *now*."

Dan shook his head. His expression was grim, determined.

"We can't keep running, Judy. These guys'll never give up. They want you dead. Don't you see? The killers want to pin the murders on you. To blame the bank heist on you, too. No way they can let you live. These guys are pros. Sooner or later, we won't run fast or far enough and they'll finish us. Only thing to do is fight back."

"Fight back? You said it yourself. These guys are killers. They're not punks like the ones who've been hounding you. These guys will swat us like flies. They have guns and know how to use them. Dan, we can't stand here arguing crazy stuff like this. Please, please, can't we leave before it's too late?"

"Judy, listen to me." Dan no longer looked so goofy and disheveled. Not comical or weird. Just angry. "These government guys just stole a billion dollars from a bunch of clueless people. They're the ones who killed your friend Trev, killed Jeremy, killed Mercy. I'm not leaving. You go if you want. I won't stop you. But, I'm staying. There's nowhere else we can run."

She released his arm, slumped onto the wobbly kitchen stool. She was dead tired. Her stomach was tied in knots, and her head hurt. But, she knew Dan was right. Tuska and Smith would never stop chasing her. With them on her trail, she'd never be free, never be safe. There really wasn't any choice. She had to fight.

"Okay," she said. "What do you want me to do?"

He moved toward the back door, without her. "You keep watch. Outside, by the car. Stay low; keep out of sight. They won't drive right up to the cabin, don't want to scare us off into the woods. They'll come on foot. Three of them, right?"

"Right," Judy said. "Dan, this is crazy. How can we fight three killers who have guns?"

"We have a couple of advantages. First, and most important, we know they're coming. Gives us the element of surprise."

"What else?"

"Gasoline, and lots of it. Now go keep watch. I'll join you in a few minutes, hopefully long before they arrive. But, if you hear them before I get there, come tell me. We can hide in the back just as easy. Now, move."

Carrying her computer gear, she headed for the front room again. But Dan's voice stopped her. "Wait," he said, "there's one more thing."

"What?"

"Your hair." He rummaged through the kitchen drawers. Found a serrated knife. "I need to cut off your hair."

"Huh? Are you *nuts*?"

"Trust me," he replied. "Please."

"Go ahead," Judy said. "Cut it."

He lopped off large sections of her hair, cutting it so short that it barely touched her shoulders. She'd always had long hair; it hurt to think of it *gone*. But Dan must've had his reasons, and there was no time to sweat over a hunk of hair.

Thirty seconds later, she was crouched behind the car, watching the road. She had absolutely no idea what Dan was doing inside the cabin. Though the door was closed, she could hear the faint sounds of the radio straining over the chugging of the gas generator.

It felt good to be outside. The air on the mountain was crisp and clean, with none of the city pollution. Judy had spent too many hours the past few days cooped up in cars, unable to breathe, choking on fumes. The night breeze caressed her cheeks, made her shiver. Her stomach was strangely calm.

And she no longer felt sleepy or ready to collapse. The fact she might die in the next hour had her adrenaline pumping. She was actually wired.

High clouds drifted across the night sky, making it difficult to see very far down the twisting road. Still, the moon was full and bright, periodically bathing the clearing in a soft white light. Judy tried listening for the noise of an automobile engine, but the clattering of the generator drowned out all but the loudest noises. Mentally, she counted thousands, trying to keep track of how many minutes were passing.

Dan opened the front door about five minutes after she began counting. Turning, he backed out of the entrance. In each hand, he held a five-gallon gasoline can. Carefully, he poured gas onto the base of the door. Then slowly he spilled the gas across the porch, the yews, the junipers, and the ground in front of the entrance, until one can was completely empty. Still walking with his back to Judy, he made his way to the parked car, leaving a trail of gasoline in his wake. Judy gagged from the fumes as he drew close.

He crouched beside her. "Don't worry," he said. "The breeze will take care of the smell quick enough. Inside the cabin, it's pretty strong. But they won't have time to notice."

"What's going on, Dan?" She continued staring down the road. Nothing moved.

"Trap's all set. I stuffed the two sleeping bags with sofa cushions. Your hair is sticking out of one of them. Looks almost real. Then I soaked them with gasoline. Covered the floor with the stuff, as well. Even left a few open containers behind the sofa and on the dresser. Place is a pyromaniac's wet dream. I barred the back door. Lights are off except in the kitchen. Just enough glow to make it look like we're sleeping. Left the radio going as a distraction. Not very elaborate, but remember, they think we feel safe and secure, think the element of surprise is on their side. No reason for them to suspect a trick."

Dan pulled a box of old-fashioned kitchen matches from his pocket. He test-lit one, then blew it out. "Found these in one of the drawers. Final ingredient to our trap. Only thing, once they enter the cabin, I gotta set the fuse instantly. Gas ignites fast, but it'll take a few seconds for the place to blow. When it goes, they're history. *Boom!*"

Judy gasped, the image of Jeremy's house etched in her mind. As if reading her thoughts, Dan nodded. "Seems only fair, considering what they did to Jeremy. Mercy, too. These guys are scum."

Judy nodded, unable to speak. She wasn't a killer. Violence made her sick. Despite everything Tuska and Smith had done, she knew there was no way she could condemn them to death. Dan would have to light the match.

They waited, each deep in thought, wondering when the killers would arrive. Dan muttered softly to himself, reviewing all the pitfalls. The three might split up, leaving one with the car. Or they might wait till morning, figuring it would be safer to attack at daylight.

Judy kept her mouth shut. Dan had been right. Running would have done no good. Unless they changed their circumstances, they were screwed.

"Listen," Dan whispered. "You hear that?"

Judy nodded, her stomach muscles tightening. Far down the road, the sound of a car. An instant later, it stopped.

"They're here. Stay as low as you can. Under the car if possible. Gas fires are explosive. There's a slight dip in the land a few feet away. I'm gonna throw some dirt and leaves on me, like I did when I was a kid. Nobody'll notice. Don't talk; don't say a word. Just watch and wait."

Judy hugged the ground. It was coarse. Gritty, tiny stones bruised her flesh. There were pine needles everywhere, again reminding her of Jeremy. And flames, and death. Pulling her computer with her, she crawled beneath the steel frame of the junk Ford. For once in her life, being skinny paid off.

Once settled, she turned her head and looked for Dan. He was nowhere to be seen. There was a slight mound of leaves and dirt a few yards ~~away~~: had to be Dan, covered in forest debris. The chili dog king, the loudmouthed, short-tempered jerkoid, really knew his stuff.

They came quickly, silently, outlined in the moon glow. Three men dressed in dark clothing, carrying guns. Immediately, Judy recognized two of them. Tony Tuska, muscles and a bushy beard, shirt half open, but *not* wearing dark sunglasses. Paul Smith, the nerdy-looking baldo idiot. He held his gun with his left hand. His right fingers were still wrapped in a plastic cast.

The third man she had never seen before. A beefy guy, with a big nose, as if from too much drinking, and with dark hair. He had to be the cop Bren had mentioned. Most likely, this guy was the one responsible for framing Judy for Trev's murder. He was as guilty as Tuska and Smith for the wave of violence that had washed across her life.

They walked without talking, using hand signals. Judy's muscles stiffened as she saw Tuska wave the cop over to the parked car. She shuddered, held her breath. As he approached, his body disappeared so all she could see were legs and feet, then just feet. The killers were only being careful, she knew, but that didn't stop her from wanting to scream.

Death stood less than six feet away. The cop was so close Judy could almost reach out and touch his brightly polished shoes. One noise—a sneeze, a cough—and she was finished. Her stomach twisted with fear. Sinking her teeth into her lip, Judy stifled a moan. An eternity passed in the course of ten seconds.

With a soft grunt of dismissal, the cop walked back to his companions. Feet turned into legs, and then legs turned into his whole body. All three men were very close to the cabin now. Tuska pointed at the window, covered with tar paper. Even from this distance, Judy could see he was grinning.

Tuska stopped ten feet from the front door, then turned his head, as if listening. The radio still played inside, barely audible over the *chunk-chunk* of the generator. The bearded man motioned to Smith, who disappeared around the side of the cabin. No doubt checking the back door. He returned in less than a minute, shaking his head. Tuska nodded. The only way in or out of the cabin was the front door.

Raising his gun, Tuska beckoned his buddies forward. He was

in the middle, Smith on his right, the cop on his left. Ten steps to the front door, seven, five, then they were on the porch. None of them seemed to smell the gasoline on the ground. They were fixated on their prey within.

As soon as the killers entered the cabin, Dan had to set the place ablaze. She wondered if all of the matches still worked, weren't useless from years of damp storage. Too late now to worry. If the matches were dead, so were they.

Gun held close to his body, Tuska raised a leg and slammed it into the wood door. With a thump, it crashed open. Instantly, Smith flung himself into the dark cabin. The cop followed, with Tuska barreling in behind them.

Dan was on his knees, matchbox in his hand. Judy could see the wood match in his fingers. His face was fixed on the cabin, but his hand wasn't moving. He seemed frozen, unable to act. Desperately, Judy started wiggling from beneath the car.

"Goddamn it, Dan, do *it*!" Her voice cracked like a gun.

She saw his face in the glow of the match—a face lit by terror, by anguish, by the memories of parents who had died in such flames . . .

He tossed the match. The flames caught . . . raced . . .

And then, the world exploded.

The blast threw Dan backward to the ground. Above Judy, the old junker shuddered, and suddenly she realized she was hiding underneath a car filled with fuel. Fire spewed from the cabin, spurting from the walls, the open roof, the solitary window. A huge blossom of red fire engulfed the entire structure, roaring with elemental fury. Even thirty feet away, the heat was intense.

A thin finger of flame stretched from the raging inferno, coming close to their hiding place. Judy scrambled from beneath the car.

A few feet distant, Dan was rising to his feet. There was a horrified look on his face. "My folks . . . the fire . . ."

"No need to expl—" Judy began, then stopped in mid-sentence. Out the front door of the cabin, through a curtain of flame, staggered a man. His clothes and hair on fire, he screamed in terrible agony. He crashed to the earth twenty feet from the holocaust, rolled on the ground, trying to extinguish the flames that held him in a deadly embrace. Muscular, gold chains looped around his neck, burning into his flesh: it was Tony Tuska, the last man into the cabin.

Dan was on his feet, running forward, even before Tuska fell. Judy followed. Though horrified by the blaze, she was surprised to find that she felt no pity for the burning man. What pity had there been for Trev? Or for Mercy?

There was no sign of the other two killers. Judy refused to think about them. Their own viciousness had brought about their deaths. Justice had been cruel but effective.

"Can't let him die," Dan was muttering. "Can't let him die."

Judy stared at Tuska, who rolled his head back and forth, moaning in pain. His clothes, what remained of them, clung to his body, charred bits of blackened ash. His skin was bloody, much of it seared right down to the bone. One eye was completely gone. His cheeks were charred like burned paper. A large plastic bandage on his nose had melted in place. His chest, under the fragments of shirt, looked like a piece of cooked meat, still broiling. His flesh was snapping and crackling from the fire.

Dan, on his knees beside him, looked up at Judy. "Can't we do something? Can't we do *anything*?"

Judy didn't really want to save Tony Tuska. She hated him. Still . . . "I can try reaching a burn unit on the Net. But by the time they get here—"

"Paul, Paul." It was Tuska, his voice barely audible, his one eye fixed on Judy. "Damned temper. Went berserk. Wanted to get you, TerMight." He coughed, blood frothing his lips, seeping out from the plastic over his nostrils. "Help me. The pain, please, the pain."

Judy dropped to her knees, the netpad in her hands. "I can call for help. They might get here in time to save you. But, only if you talk. Tell me who's behind these killings. Where's Cal Nikonchik?"

Tuska didn't move, didn't say anything. Judy wondered if his hearing had been destroyed in the blast.

"Help him, Judy," Dan said. "We can't just let him die. Do something."

She stared at the dying man. Help him? Why? He had killed her friends.

"Judy!"

Judy switched on the netpad. She executed a search for the nearest burn unit in the vicinity. The closest one was more than thirty miles away. Tuska coughed again, his whole body shaking. "Any second now," she said, touching the icon for emergency service.

"Don't bother," Dan said, with a deep sigh.

Judy stared at Tuska. His unblinking eye glared at her. His mouth gaped open; his chest didn't move. There was no question he was dead.

Something moved in the woods. Judy's head jerked up, and she saw a small bird fly overhead, clearly visible thanks to the flames. It was black, with a white head topped by a fire-red crest. Would Judy always see fire, everywhere she went, for the rest of her life? Is this what Dan saw in everything, every day of his life?

"A pileated woodpecker." Dan broke into a hysterical giggle. "Yeah, I sure know my way around these forests. I know which berries to eat in people's backyards. I know which snakes kill, which are harmless. And more than anything, boy, do I ever know how to blow up cabins and burn people to death. Have them die, just like my parents."

Judy skirted around Tony Tuska, forcing herself not to look at the dead man, and she crouched beside Dan. The poor guy, forever blaming himself. No escape from the memories. She wrapped her arms around him. The coarse whiskers on his cheek grazed her neck. "Oh, Dan, I'm sorry." She rocked him in her arms. He was shaking, muttering gibberish about birds.

"Ever see a red-naped sapsucker? It sounds like a cat. Lives in places like this. I should have saved this guy, Judy, never should have killed him—"

"No, Dan," Judy said. "He had to die so we could live. So we can save Cal. Your brother, the one you *did* save from the fire. You did what was necessary, Dan. Stop blaming yourself for not being able to do the impossible."

His body sagged in her arms. Then he nodded, and lifted his head. He pulled back from her. "I don't want any more fires, Judy. I don't want any more death. I just want Cal back, alive."

"We'll do it, Dan." She smiled, remembering their first conversation. It seemed like it had been years ago. "We'll do it together."

Dan laughed. Not very deep, but a laugh. "Yeah. Partners."

They both rose slowly to their feet. Dan stared at the roaring fire. "Look at those flames. There's no way I could have gone into that, to save anybody."

Judy wondered if Dan was talking about the other killers. Or his parents. In either case, it would take him a long time to come to grips with the truth. But, at least he was on the right track.

And she'd hugged someone for the first time since that last hug from Dad. She'd hugged someone she hardly even liked, simply because he needed human compassion, the real thing from a real person.

He turned. "We'd better get out of here. Forest rangers will spot the fire quick enough. Or the highway patrol. We don't want to be around when they arrive."

Judy swayed, groggy now—her energy nearly gone. The trap was sprung, their enemies dead, the rush over. She felt ready to collapse.

Dan swung an arm around her. "Sorry, but into the car, Judy. Don't worry. Things are gonna work out fine."

She was aware of Dan starting the car, driving down the road. She must have dozed, for it seemed only a few minutes later when he was shaking her by the shoulder, urging her to get up.

Groaning, she opened her eyes. They were still in the forest. Only a few hundred feet from the cabin. Behind her, she could see the fire still burning. They had driven only a short distance from where Tony lay dead on the ground.

"Their rental car," Dan said. He already had his car door open. "Left it unlocked. Just need you to change the records so we can't be traced. And find the ignition code."

Judy's head hurt. Her eyes hurt. She was in no mood to steal another car.

"Here," Dan said, pushing something in her hand. Judy looked down. It was a turkey sandwich.

"They got all sorts of snacks and junk in the backseat," Dan said. "Bottled water. Even cash. One of them left his coat. Thousand bucks in small bills inside his pocket. Come on, Judy. Get this baby started. Once we're out of the area, we can stop some-where. A motel, even. Sleep in a real bed. Take a bath."

A bath. Judy swallowed a chunk of sandwich. A bed. Wearily, she opened the netpad and went through the necessary ritual.

Dan switched on the ignition. The car roared to life.

"Did you say something about a coat?" she asked. She was dead tired, needed sleep, but couldn't rest yet.

"You cold?" Dan asked. "It's in the backseat."

Judy pulled it forward as Dan steered the car along the service road, heading for the highway. Anxiously, she searched the pockets. Smiled when she found what she was searching for. Held it up for Dan to see.

"Hotel key," she announced. "Room 208, Airport Ramada, San Jose."

"So what?" Dan said. They were on the highway now, heading south. Away from the fire, away from the city. But they still had no idea where Cal was.

"Small operation, Dan," Judy said. "Couple of hired guns, a crooked cop. Not exactly the full resources of the government behind it. Supervisor in charge, skeleton crew."

"Okay," Dan said. "I get the drift. What's your point?"

"Boss wants to frame me for the billion-dollar heist," Judy said. Though exhausted, her mind was clicking as logically as ever, maybe more so. "Can't do that unless he knows I'm dead, that I won't be around to prove I'm innocent."

"I still don't see what you're driving at."

"Tony Tuska must have told him they were on my trail. Gonna finish the job they botched in Laguna Beach. Boss is going to be waiting for confirmation."

"He's going to wait forever for that message," Dan commented wryly.

"Right," Judy said. "Sooner or later, he'll start worrying. Won't like calling, but he has to. He needs to find out what's wrong. That's when we'll locate the bastard."

"Locate him? How?"

Judy shook the key. "Using my laptop, I'll hack into the hotel switchboard. Reroute all calls coming into room 208, to me—right here. Remember, I did consulting work for Internet Security. Got their trace code on my laptop. It's used to locate kidnappers. Damned program eats telephone scramblers for lunch. It'll grab the big cheese's phone number as soon as I answer."

"Like magic," Dan said.

"Hackers rule," Judy said.

The call came an hour later, while they were parked at a rest stop overlooking the ocean. Judy let the phone ring several times, then pushed the key that completed the connection.

Silence on the other end. Not a word spoken. A few seconds passed, then the line went dead.

"He was waiting for a voice," Judy said. "Wouldn't identify himself without Tuska or Smith speaking first. Smart."

She looked at the display on her laptop. "But not smart enough. The call came from a place listed as Barrington Industries, in the desert east of LA."

Barrington. The nutcase who hated hackers, who hosted *The Barrington Fireside Chat*. Her mother's hero. Weird for an antitech lunatic to be mixed up in a computer heist.

She indexed the map of California on her laptop. "Not far from Lake Bristol. That's where Cal is."

"And that's where we're going," Dan said.

Judy crawled onto the wide backseat. "Wake me when we get close," she said, nestling her head in her hands. "I'm going to sleep."

"Sleep," Dan said, turning the car around and starting it down the road to the highway. "You've earned it."

"Dan," Judy murmured, as she drifted, her eyes closed. "This government guy's no fool. After that call, he knows Tuska and Smith are either dead or in custody. His time's running out. He's gonna pressure Cal to pull the big heist right away. We need to stop him before that happens. Or Cal's dead."

CHAPTER 28

Bob Ingersoll stared at the clock. Eight A.M. Hours since he had called Tony Tuska's room and had the phone answered by . . . whom? He didn't know. But he wasn't fooling himself. The news wasn't good.

Impossible for the police to trace his call, not in that amount of time. Not with the caller-ID scrambler in use. Still, he had no illusions. If that had been TerMight, she knew where he was.

It had been nine hours since he had last spoken with Tony. Together, Tony and Paul and Ernie Kaye were heading off to finish Carmody. They'd been instructed to report back as soon as the job was done. Their failure to do so, the open line at their hotel room, indicated to Ingersoll that his agents had somehow been neutralized. Perhaps killed. And chances were good that Ter-Might was still alive.

Sitting motionless in his chair, he evaluated the situation. There was no reason to panic, but at the same time, he recognized the need to act fast. Events were beginning to spiral out of control. There was no room for any more delays. Or mistakes.

Carmody was still a fugitive. She couldn't contact the police without being arrested, questioned. That would take hours. The wheels of justice moved extremely slow. Assuming the worst, that she went to the cops, he had a day. But no more.

He accessed a cable news station, watched the headlines for a few minutes. Not a word so far about bank problems. Ingersoll wasn't surprised. Banks were notoriously secretive about reporting shortages or data management problems. Under normal conditions, it would be several days before any of the original targets would make it known that a robbery had taken place.

After the heist tonight, that scenario would change drastically. Too many people, too many corporations would suddenly find themselves without funds. Their banks wouldn't be able to conceal the problem. Hysteria would rage across the country. The greatest crime in history would be front-page news across the globe. All the while, Bob Ingersoll would rest in a quiet resort village on the coast of the Mediterranean, and plan what to do with his fortune.

The intercom on his desk buzzed, shaking him out of his daydreams. It was Barrington's line. "Yes, sir?"

"There's trouble in Laguna Beach and the old man's freaking out." It was Gloria Simmons. "Word leaked out to the media. An old woman across the street from Carmody's apartment saw a man firing at her. The cops kept her under wraps until now.

"Evidently, Ernie Kaye was already under investigation by Internal Affairs. Authorities claim they were just giving Kaye enough rope to hang himself. Newspeople in LA are up in arms, claiming a police cover-up. Already Carmody's boss is back to saying she's a saint."

"Tell Barrington there's nothing to worry about," Ingersoll replied. "I'll give Kaye a quick call and tell him to disappear. Without him on stage, the story will simmer, but the smoking gun will be missing."

"You're sure you can trust this cop to keep quiet?" Gloria asked.

"He won't say a word," Ingersoll said confidently. "He's been doing dirty jobs for the NSA for years. Ernie won't talk."

"I hope you're right. My dreams don't include prison," Gloria said.

He broke the connection. Time for him to pay Cal a surprise visit.

When he stepped outside, the desert heat hit him in the face like a sledgehammer. It was blistering hot, a furnace of a morning. Normally, the temperature didn't bother him. However, after an entire day and night without sleep, Ingersoll could feel the first stirrings of a tension headache. He needed some rest. Even he wasn't invincible. But first there were a few loose ends that needed his personal attention. He headed to the cottage.

Greg answered, though after a half dozen impatient knocks. Harry was nowhere in sight.

"Sorry, boss," Greg said, staring at Ingersoll with bloodshot eyes. "Little too much celebrating last night after the heist. Harry and me hit the bottle pretty good. He's still sleeping it off. Didn't think you'd be up and around this early. Figured Barrington would babble on most of the night."

Ingersoll nodded. "I've yet to make it to bed. The old man spent hours on the same litany, raving about the dangers of technology. I refrained from mentioning that these horrible machines—the ones that are destroying modern civilization— had just netted us a billion dollars. Thought that might dampen his spirit."

"Is Calvin awake?"

"Yes, sir. Heard him in the kitchen a while back, wolfing down a fruit pie. You want to talk to him?"

"Definitely. Wake Harry. I may require your services."

"Will do, sir. Just shout and we'll be there."

Ingersoll knocked on Calvin's door, then entered. The young hacker sat slumped in front of his computer, fiddling with his watch. He wore a pair of shorts, no shirt.

"There's been a sudden change in plans, Calvin," Ingersoll said. His head throbbed with pain now. "The second run, for fifty billion, happens tonight, not Saturday. Midnight. Make sure your code's ready."

"Tonight?" Calvin said. He appeared stunned. "But—but, we can't do it tonight."

"Why not?"

"The NSA bigwigs? The top guns from the ISD? They won't be here till the weekend."

"All lies, Calvin," Ingersoll said. "Forget them. Forget, too, the part of the code that reroutes the money back into the original accounts. That's not going to happen. The fifty billion gets transferred to the same locations as last night's heist, and stays there. No refunds, no returns."

Calvin stared at Ingersoll, his eyes wide with shock. "But—but—but—"

"You're a nice kid, Calvin," Ingersoll said, "but naive. This project's a hoax. We're not testing bank security. Nobody cares about that. The truth is the NSA is out to destroy the Internet. That's why I've been working in secret with Bradley Barrington. No doubt you've heard of him. Deep cover, so none of the other departments know what's happening. The old man's put up his own money to finance this venture. In return, we're making his dream come true. Turning hackers into criminals, crashing the Net. The robbery last night was real, Calvin. I have no intention of returning a penny. That money belongs to me. The same goes for tonight."

Calvin's face was bloodless. "But, what about the NSA?"

Ingersoll laughed. "Government pay is lousy, Calvin. It would take me ten thousand years to earn the money we're stealing in two nights. Everybody gets something. The NSA and Barrington cripple the Internet. I become rich. Seems like a fair trade to me. I'm no Ollie North, going down for Uncle Sam. I've paid my dues. Just like Ollie. But I intend to go out *my way*.

"And, Calvin, your code runs much too slow. Fix it. I want it to operate at a much higher speed. Otherwise, it'll take maybe ten minutes to finish tonight's job, and that's too long."

"I won't do it. You're *crazy*. Everything you're saying is crazy."

Ingersoll looked Cal in the eyes. "No, Calvin, I'm perfectly sane. I found an innocent young man with incredible code, recognized the possibilities, and acted on them. That's not crazy, that's smart. And you will do exactly as I tell you."

"Not in your lifetime," Cal said.

"Greg was right," Ingersoll said. "You're not a coward. I never really thought you were. No matter. Violence is the refuge of the incompetent, Calvin. But sometimes it has its uses."

Ingersoll reached into his coat pocket, pulled out a white handkerchief. Carefully, he wiped the sweat off his forehead. "I'm not stupid, Calvin. You're my golden goose, the one with the power. Killing you would be insane, and I never act irrationally. Put on your shirt. It's time for you to learn a lesson about real life."

Cal pulled on a T-shirt, black with a red design. Ingersoll smiled, recognizing the kanji symbol that stood for *the best*.

"Greg, Harry, come in here," he called.

The two agents entered. Harry, his usual harsh features paunchy from sleep and drink, appeared barely awake. "Yes, sir," Greg said. "You want us?"

Ingersoll nodded. His head burned with pain, needles of white agony cascading through his skull. He didn't care. He pointed at Cal. "The schedule has undergone some revision. Second heist takes place tonight, not Saturday. No time to wait and check for bugs in the system. I want results, not excuses. Mr. Nikonchik feels I'm being unreasonable, refuses to cooperate. He needs to be shown the error of his ways."

His voice turned harsh. "Bring him into the living room. We don't want to damage the computer."

"What, *what*?" Cal cried as Harry and Greg grabbed him by the arms and dragged him through the hallway into the front room. Ingersoll followed, still dabbing his forehead with his handkerchief. The pain was intense.

The two agents tossed Cal onto the high-backed lounger. "You can't do this. You're crazy. Stop it, *stop it*," he screeched.

"Too late for talk, Calvin," Ingersoll said. The throbbing in his skull added a note of savagery to his voice. "Greg, hold his arms tight. We don't want his precious fingers damaged. He needs to be able to use them to modify his code. Harry, give me your gun."

"My gun?" Harry's face twisted in surprise. "Uh, I'm not packing it, Mr. Ingersoll. Didn't think there was any need—"

"Get it," Ingersoll said sharply. "No excuses. I don't have all day. Just get it."

Ingersoll's eyes hurt, as did his teeth, the back of his head. He continued to smile. There was no reason to be upset. Sometimes even the most annoying setbacks worked for the best.

Cal was no longer shouting. Harry had been wrong, and Greg had been right. Nikonchik wasn't a wimp. He was naive and trusting, but he had guts. Still, he needed to understand exactly who was in charge.

"What are you planning to do, boss?" Greg asked. The agent had his hands wrapped around the hacker's wrists, which he held at the back of the chair. Cal's back was arched with pain, his face frozen in a mixture of fear and defiance.

"Calvin needs to understand I mean business," Ingersoll said. "One picture is worth a thousand words."

Harry hurried into the room, the gun clutched in his hand.

"Give it to me," Ingersoll said, reaching for the gun, his own hand wrapped in his handkerchief. "I assume it's loaded? Safety's off? Fine. That's more like it. Now, grab the kid's ankles. Hold them tight, so he can't move."

"Whatever you say," Harry mumbled, dropping to his knees. He wrapped his arms around Cal's feet. "Gonna blow off one of his kneecaps?"

"No," Ingersoll said. "Much too painful. Calvin wouldn't be able to work for weeks. There's an easier and much more effective way of making a point. Like this."

Ingersoll stepped close to Cal, his finger on the gun's trigger. Hand moving in a swift, smooth arc, he raised the muzzle of the gun to Harry's left ear and pulled the trigger.

The explosion rocked the room. Harry's head exploded like a ripe piece of fruit, blood and brains cascading over the floor, splashing on the far wall. Cal shrieked. Face green, he gagged up his breakfast. Even Greg, unflappable under most situations, squawked in surprise and released the hacker's wrists.

"Hiring that stupid son of a bitch was a terrible mistake," Ingersoll said, kicking the twitching body at his feet. Blood pumped from the gaping hole in Harry's head, soaking into the wooden floor. Ingersoll turned and waved the gun at Cal. "I kept him around to handle some unfinished business on the coast. When circumstances changed, he became unnecessary. Killing him was a pleasure."

He pointed the gun at Cal's forehead, aiming it a few inches above the bridge of his nose. Cal's body went rigid. His heels dug into the floor, his hands flat against the chair cushions. "No, please!"

"Nobody," Ingersoll said calmly, his hand steady and

unwavering, "*and I mean nobody,* fucks around with Bob Ingersoll. Do you understand?"

Cal, his face ash white, nodded his head. His eyes were squeezed shut.

"Good," Ingersoll said. "Very very good. Now, be a good boy and have that code working at top speed tonight, okay?"

He smiled at Greg. His head felt much better. Harry had been a major annoyance. The world was a much better place without him. "Take this garbage," he said, dropping Harry's gun onto the dead man's chest, "and dump it in the desert. Another unsolved mystery for the highway patrol to investigate. Then clean up the mess. We can't have Calvin working in a house covered with blood. Besides, Barrington would complain that the red clashes with the furniture."

"Yes, sir," Greg said. "I'll get to it immediately."

"Fine," Ingersoll said. "No reason for you to be afraid, Calvin, as long as you cooperate fully. I like you. Killing you would serve no purpose. After tonight, I'll be gone and you'll be free. You can head back to San Jose, forget this whole adventure ever took place."

He paused. "Remember, nothing in these heists links me to them. Or implicates the NSA. It's your code, used on Barrington's estate. The only trace left during the robbery leads to TerMight. You can tell the cops anything you like, but I doubt they'll believe you. Especially when they learn of your brother's involvements. The NSA wouldn't be happy, either, with you running off at the mouth about their covert operations. It's not wise to make the government angry. My advice to you, son, is to keep quiet, stay out of sight, and pretend none of this ever took place."

"What about the money?" Cal said, his features still a pale shade of green. "Billions of dollars gone, people's savings wiped out, businesses destroyed, the whole Net ripped to shreds."

"Barrington and his antitech lunatics are right, Calvin," Ingersoll said. "The Net is a threat to our country. Unfortunately, making a point requires some sacrifice. That's life. Mr. Barrington expects a cut from the robbery, but I'm afraid he's going to be disappointed. Greg gets a digital key to one of the accounts. I keep the rest. I'm not a big fan of partners."

Ingersoll yawned. "I'm going back to the mansion for a nap.

Don't do anything foolish—like sending E-mails to the police or FBI or ISD. Try something like that, and you'll end up like Harry. I want that fifty billion, Calvin, but if necessary I'll settle for the billion we've already taken. Now, get to work fixing that code. I want it to hum. If there are any problems, let me know. Otherwise, I'll return tonight."

Walking back to the main house in the sweltering heat, Ingersoll realized his headache had disappeared. Amazing how tension dissolved when treated correctly.

CHAPTER 29

Lying on his bed, stunned by what he had just witnessed, Cal reached several important conclusions.

Dan had been right. The government was run by monsters who didn't give a damn about the American public. The NSA, CIA, FBI, and ISD were no better than the loan sharks who terrorized Dan's restaurant business. They were worse, because they wrapped themselves in the flag.

Dan was also a jerk. He meant well, but he was stupid. He should have let Cal out, to experience the treachery and double-dealing that existed everywhere. At least, then, he wouldn't have been so easily deceived. Cal had willingly cooperated with Ingersoll and Barrington in their plot to destroy the Net, never once suspecting he wasn't on the side of the angels. He'd been blinded by promises of fame and fortune. No question about it. He was an idiot.

Bob Ingersoll was crazy. No doubt about *that*. The NSA agent had smiled after killing Harry. He'd been lying to Cal ever since their first meeting, never once telling the truth. Still, he expected Cal to believe him when he said that he wasn't going to kill him after the second heist. Cal might be stupid, but he wasn't *that* stupid.

At least now he had some idea what the woman had meant when she had whispered about huge sums of money. She was no better than the others, anxious to make a big score, share in the billions.

Still, she had supplied him with the microcam. That could prove to be useful.

Cal glanced at the clock on his computer screen. It was already past 11 A.M. He'd spent hours lying here, trying to sort out his course of action, some way of saving his life, maybe even putting a crimp in Ingersoll's plans. The stream of late-morning sun formed a haze of glittering dust in the room. Greg was still out, burying Harry's body somewhere in the desert. If Cal was going to act, he'd better do his stuff before the agent returned.

Getting the code up to the speed Ingersoll wanted was easy. All Cal had to do was remove the loop, and he'd steal fifty billion dollars within minutes. All to be deposited in accounts only Ingersoll could access, using his special digital keys. Speed was no longer an issue. But access was.

Griswald, hacker supreme, was still alive and kicking. Cal had been naive and trusting throughout the entire project. However, so had Bob Ingersoll. No matter how good he claimed to be, he had no real grasp of the power of a computer keyboard. Ingersoll was a ruthless, cold-blooded killer. He wanted billions. But getting them might not be as easy as he expected.

The biggest problem, Cal decided, was implicating Ingersoll and Barrington in the robbery without taking a fall himself. The NSA agent had been right about going to the police. Start explaining things, and quick enough the truth about Dan's money-laundering operation would emerge. Cal wanted to be safe from Ingersoll, and he didn't want to end up in prison.

And, even though Dan had been the one who had originally screwed up their lives, Cal didn't want to see his brother arrested either. The cops and the feds were out. Any rescue operation was strictly Cal's responsibility.

Cal swung his legs over the side of the bed, slowly sat. He was still wearing the jeans and the kanji shirt from early that morning. *The best*. It was time for him to prove it.

Already the sun was beating through the window, soaking him in sweat. And the shirt was crusted with spattered blood.

Harry's blood. It smelled like rust. Cal pulled it off, threw it to the other side of the room.

He reached for the watch on his wrist, unbuckled the leather strap. Hidden beneath the dial, there was the microcam he had used to videotape last night's robbery.

As a hacker, Cal knew most everything there was to know about digital images. According to the law, as long as the video remained in the microcam, sealed and unopened, it was legal evidence. However, if Cal uploaded any of it to his computer, the pictures were no longer admissible in court. It was too easy to manipulate digital images. In the digital age, any picture, document, or file on a computer could be altered with minimal effort. There was no truth, once computers were involved, but sometimes truth wasn't as important as appearance.

Cal didn't care. Having taken the video, he wasn't in it. Only Ingersoll appeared, along with the computer screen that showed the entire heist taking place. Their voices were the only ones heard speaking. Cal hadn't said a word. He was a ghost, a silent observer, safely hidden from view.

Cal logged onto VileSpawn. He shuddered as the opening message flashed onto his screen.

```
@>>>>---
```

A dead black rose. The symbol of death.

```
VileSpawn report: JC dead, master image
craftsman, killed yesterday by a fire in his
home in San Jose. Police investigating.
```

Tears filled Cal's eyes. Jeremy dead? Jeremy couldn't be dead. His best buddy, the guy who had invited Cal into his home for the holidays, who had made him feel like one of the family. It couldn't be true. *It had to be a lie!*

Eyes aching, Cal stared at the unchanging screen. What the hell was going on? His whole world was collapsing. The Internet under attack. Hailstorm and Jeremy dead. It made no sense.

Cal leapt off VileSpawn and did a quick Net search for information on Jeremy Crane. In seconds, he had a dozen articles, all with the same information. Random facts that jumped from the screen and assaulted his already numbed mind.

```
Incendiary device in Crane house. Dan Nikon-
chik wanted. Accompanied by Judy Carmody.
Unexplained tire tracks. Police refuse to
discuss.
```

His brother, Dan, with Judy Carmody? Together, visiting Jeremy's home? Had they been searching for Cal?

Cal concentrated, trying to connect the data in some logical fashion. TerMight, hunting Cal for the ISD, came to San Jose, found Dan. Together, they went to visit Jeremy, hoping to find information. But, Jeremy didn't know where Cal was, couldn't tell them anything. They left. Right after, Jeremy died.

Under ordinary circumstances, based on the police reports, Cal might have wondered if Judy Carmody had flipped out, gone bonkers. Unlikely, since he knew TerMight from the Net and trusted her. Hard to believe, but he might have been swayed by the evidence.

But his big brother, Dan, involved with Jeremy's death? Never. Unthinkable. Dan knew of the bond that existed between Cal and Jeremy. He was aware of their work on Dozong, their dreams of striking it rich. Dan murder Jeremy? Impossible.

Who, then? Most likely, the guy who had framed Judy Carmody for the death of her landlord. The person who probably had arranged that murder. A man without scruples, totally without morals, willing to do anything to accomplish his goals. Robert Ingersoll.

Not him in person, of course. The NSA agent worked through hired thugs like Greg and Harry, that policeman Ernie Kaye. They did the dirty work, while he sat back and tricked Cal into stealing billions. And made him pin the blame on TerMight.

Were Judy and Dan still alive? Cal hadn't heard anything from TerMight since the brief message, yesterday afternoon, asking where he was. It seemed unlikely that a hacker and a chili dog maker could stay clear of Ingersoll's paid killers *and* the police. Yet, something had spooked Ingersoll into moving up the final

run to tonight. Could it be that TerMight was more trouble than
Bob Ingersoll could handle?

Cal didn't know. He could only hope. In the meantime, he'd
do some hacking on his own, try to save himself.

First, he'd upload the entire video of last night, spray it all over
the Net, and at least get people thinking. It wouldn't throw Ingersoll or Barrington in jail, but it would help.

He moved into his programming directories on VileSpawn.
Perhaps his work on Dozong would come in handy. Jeremy had
been using UCLA computers to test a lot of the major functions
of their artificially intelligent creation. The department chair-
man and several professors knew Cal, were people he trusted,
who trusted him. Their first instinct most likely would be to assume Cal hadn't been responsible for the bank heist.

He took the watch, set the infrared sensor next to the matching
sensor on his computer, and uploaded the digital video. Then he
sent a quick message to the professors, along with the microcam
documentary, asking that they spread the images all over the
Net, where everyone could see them.

They'd know what to do. Within hours, the video would be a
major headline on all Net news services, would display as soon
as people accessed Web pages for all the major magazines.
Bradley Barrington would find himself famous on the Net he so
despised.

Next, Cal went to his file containing all of the digital keys to
the NSA bank accounts Ingersoll had established. Did what was
necessary.

Finally, almost as an afterthought, Cal left TerMight one more
message in his directory. Ingersoll's name, Barrington's name,
NSA, and the time of the next heist. He added a black rose to the
end of his message. In case Griswald never returned to Vile-
Spawn again.

CHAPTER 30

A gurgling, then the buzzing of a saw. People chattering some-where, cars gunning, trucks thundering past. Judy opened her eyes, blinked.

Where was she?

Something warm moved by her back. She turned in the . . . bed? Oh, man, it *was* a bed, and beside her lay Dan Nikonchik, snoring loudly.

She bolted upright. "Dan!"

He gurgled again, sputtered, blinked at her. "Judy."

"Where are we? What are we doing here?"

He pulled the ratty blanket off his body, swiveled to sit. Rubbed his face, smoothed back his hair: it was damp, it was *clean*.

Dan groaned. He clicked on a light, then reached for a sack of chips on the metal nightstand. Washed down his breakfast with a slug of cola from a giant bottle. "Hotel 86," he said, "on the out-skirts of town, half an hour outside the compound where Cal's being held."

Hotel 86? Just what kind of dump was this? She looked around the room, pulling the blanket securely over her body. The blanket smelled vaguely of cat urine and cigarettes. It had burn holes in it. They looked like bullet holes.

The room was sparsely furnished and filthy. A metal washstand stood in one corner, dripping water. The wallpaper was tattered and stained, a geometric blitz of brown and gray parallelograms. The black desk lamp on the nightstand shed a dim light, maybe forty watts, illuminating dusty brown carpet.

"It's cheap," Dan said, rising and stretching.

He was wearing white underpants, and nothing else. She felt her face burning. He made his way to the washstand and turned the water on full blast. It trickled in a yellow stream from the rusty faucet.

"I figured," he continued, "that nobody would recognize us here. They're used to transients, truckers, one-night stands. You slept all the way from San Jose. I didn't want to wake you. The directions on the car computer were clear enough. So here we are. I paid cash for the room, then carried you inside. Don't worry. Seeing the cash, the rental car, they think you're a one-night stand."

So the owners of this dump figured she was shacking up with the likes of Dan Nikonchik, for what? Twenty bucks?

She groaned. What a nightmare.

"It's no big deal." Dan was soaping his face. He dried off with the white towel that hung from the metal bar over the washstand. The towel was also stained yellow and had burn holes in it. It probably hadn't been laundered in weeks. Dan didn't seem to care. He tossed the towel onto the bed, slid on his pants, zipped them, and pulled on his dirty shirt.

"Maybe you should wash up, too, and get to work," he said. "Want something to eat first?"

"How can you be so casual about all this?" she asked.

"What's the alternative, Judy?" He crunched on some chips, settled back down on the bed. "We had to get some rest. I was ready to collapse."

Her head felt light. Physically light. Cool, actually. She touched her neck, remembered suddenly the events of the previous night. Cutting her hair to fool their pursuers. She felt ready to cry. She'd had long hair ever since she was a little girl. Hadn't done anything more than trim it for at least ten years. How could she live with it short?

"Sorry," Dan said, following her thoughts. "You had beautiful hair, Judy. Prettiest hair I've ever seen. But, it had to be done. No choice."

She jumped up. There was no mirror in the dump, no way to see what she looked like. She fingered it mournfully. Three men dead because of her beautiful hair. It was a horrible thought.

A truck roared. Judy went to the window, and with two fingers barely touching the brown-stained filthy curtain, she peered outside. Nothing but desert. A few trees standing alone, a fierce sun, and a long stretch of highway. A woman walked past the window. She was staggering, wearing three-inch spiked red heels, a vinyl miniskirt, and a blue lace bra. Her breasts were huge and saggy. So were her thighs. Her face was lined with wrinkles, her lips hard with bright red lipstick. A prostitute.

Geesh.

For a moment, the two women looked at each other. The prostitute's eyes dropped to Judy's chest, and she snickered. Probably thought Judy was a whore, too. Judy looked down. Her own bikini top had slipped while she was asleep, and now nearly exposed an entire breast. She jerked it back into place. Then she noticed a potbellied old guy with a trucker cap leering at her, and she yanked the curtains closed.

"This place is a disgusting dive," she said, turning to look at Dan.

He laughed. "Like I said, it's the perfect place to hide. Nobody will ever think that a chick like you is here to unscramble AI genetic code that steals billions of dollars off the Net. So let's get to it. Food first?"

He offered her a sandwich from a sack on the nightstand.

"After I clean up," she said. "You have any peanut butter and jelly?"

When he nodded yes, she smiled. Dan was crude and loud, but sometimes he managed to do things right.

She took a quick shower in the tiny stall, a hole in the wall that splashed yellow water onto the grimy tiles below. When she emerged, Dan was pacing across the littered carpet, bored and restless. Judy was almost glad to have the programming to do.

Otherwise, she'd be as pent up as he was, unable to help, unable to save them, trapped like a caged animal, awaiting almost certain death.

Chewing on her sandwich, sipping a bottle of natural spring water, she flipped open the laptop and netpad again. Cal's code appeared on her screen.

Dan dropped next to her, settled cross-legged on the bed. He kept silent, apparently afraid to disturb her concentration.

With a good night's sleep behind her, Judy felt much calmer, and very focused. Like her old self again. No more tears and worry.

If anything, she was steaming mad. She would outthink her enemies, outmaneuver them. They'd killed her friends. They'd framed her for murder. She had run long enough. Now, it was time to get even.

"No way they're getting away with this crap," she said. "No way. You just sit tight, Dan, and let me do my thing."

"What if Cal's program can't be stopped?" Dan asked. "What then?"

Judy stared at him. "Do you know how long, how many years, *I've* spent screwing around with code, Dan? Your brother may be a genius, but he's met his match. Just watch. I'm telling you, if these guys push me just one step further, if they try to kill one more person, make me run just one town farther, so help me, I'll show them what a really pissed-off hacker can do."

He smiled. "You told me already, remember?"

"That," Judy said, "was the simple stuff. Tricks any decent hacker can pull off. If I have to, I'll shut down the whole West Coast. I'll kill all the power in southern California, so Cal's computer won't even run."

"You can do that?"

Judy nodded. Hopefully, she wouldn't have to resort to such radical tactics. If the power blew at Barrington's estate, Cal's captors would panic for sure. Who knew what they might do.

Though she talked tough, she had one huge concern. Could her skills outmatch Griswald's? In a head-on combat, which one of them would win?

Had to be TerMight. *Had* to.

She logged onto VileSpawn. The welcome message popped

into view, and a tremor hit her. Jeremy's death. Too many inno-
cents killed in this deadly billion-dollar duel. Judy felt her anger
growing again, hotter by the second. If it was the last thing she
ever did, she would get these guys.

They weren't after just her, or Griswald. No, they were framing everyone, hackers everywhere. They were screwing with the
professions, the lives, the integrity, the endless hours of work,
that millions of programmers had put into the Net. They were
destroying people's faith in banking systems, financial institu-
tions, the government.

These were Luddites at their worst, people who hated technology and progress of any kind, people mired in a past of cops
and robbers and lawless greed. They would stop at nothing.

But they hadn't faced Judy Carmody yet. Not the real thing.
No, just let them wait.

She had to get off VileSpawn. No doubt, the cops already had
a trace that proved she'd been there. She checked quickly for another message from Griswald, found one.

"Another heist," she murmured, "tonight, midnight again, this
one for fifty billion dollars. Ingersoll's the name of the bastard
behind it all. NSA. In cahoots with Bradley Barrington."

"Fifty billion!" Dan exclaimed. "My parents were right. The
biggest crooks of all are in the government. They make the mob
look like angels."

"Cal's life is in terrible danger. We're fugitives from justice
and Barrington's a big cheese. Ingersoll's with a government
agency. Nobody will believe us if we tell them what's happening.
And if the cops start investigating, Ingersoll will kill Cal to sever
his only link with the original heist."

"Even if he pulls off the second robbery," Dan said, "what
makes you think this guy Ingersoll will ever let him live?"

Judy said, "Ingersoll wants that fifty billion. At midnight,
he'll have Cal run the code. Somehow, I'll stop it. Ingersoll
won't give up, not with fifty billion at stake.

"Meanwhile, I'll create some sort of major disturbance at the
compound. Something to pull Ingersoll away from Cal, keep
him occupied. In the confusion, you and I can sneak in and
rescue Cal. Not bad, huh?"

"Why won't Ingersoll kill Cal the moment this disturbance of yours begins?"

"Because Cal's the only one who can snag that fifty billion," Judy said. "He's the last person Ingersoll would jeopardize. And this emergency will occur while the robbery's taking place. With so many cops on the grounds, we have to hope Ingersoll won't dare harm Cal."

"Emergency?" Dan said. "Cops? Judy, what are you planning?"

"A surprise for Mr. Barrington and Mr. Ingersoll," Judy said. "I'll explain later. Now, listen. This scheme only works if I discover a method to stop Cal's code. Without that, the heist runs smoothly and all of my great ideas are just smoke."

"Stop the code?" Dan said. "Yesterday you said it made no sense. How are you going to stop it?"

"Great question. Wish I had an answer. I have a few ideas. Listen, and tell me if they make sense."

He stared at her like she was crazy. "I don't know anything about computers. Nothing."

"But you're smart, Dan."

"No, I'm not."

"Trust me, you *are*. And if I just talk it through, maybe that'll be enough."

"Whatever you say."

"First," Judy said, "let me spell out the data structure used to store each chromosome. Listen carefully, and try to follow along.

"The chromosomes seem to have receptors, Dan, which tell them what's happening in their environment. In this case, the environment reflects all possible Net paths to the computer nodes where the money can be transferred. And in addition, paths to all the best computer nodes—those with weak security, those in places where taxes are low or nonexistent—for stealing money."

"Well, okay. Go on."

"There's executable code here, near the receptor bytes—that is, near the bytes storing the information about the environment, the computer nodes, the routes. That code allows the chromosomes to manipulate the environment."

"Manipulate the environment?" Dan said. "How?"

"Not sure. It isn't explicit, Dan. My guess is that the chromosomes get into the system memory of the computer nodes that they infect. They're kind of like larvae, which settle into a life-giving substance—in our case, maybe CPU time and system memory—then use that substance to reproduce. Once the larvae grow strong, breeding new rules for their children, the children take over and kill off the original . . . shall we say, digital crea-tures. The children erase any system registers that could possibly show traces that the parents ever lived."

Dan shook his head. "This is much too heavy for me. But go on; I'm listening."

Judy was thinking aloud, hardly paying attention to Dan. "Computer researchers back in the 1990s created digital organisms by using CPU time and system memory. The organisms then competed for those substances. The ones who won, lived. The ones who lost, died."

Outside, a truck roared, and men started shouting. Dan zipped over to the window, peeked between the curtains. "Truckers yelling at each other about dinner plans," he said. "Nothing to worry about."

"You need to learn how to work under pressure, Dan." She smiled wryly to let him know she was teasing. "Nobody will find us in this garden spot."

"Maybe I'll have something to eat," Dan said. He dug in the bags on the nightstand, pulled out a sandwich, grabbed the bottle of cola, and returned to the bed.

She ignored the chewing sounds, the slurping of the cola. She'd worked under worse conditions. People shouting at her to hurry it up, people screaming at her about bugs in her code. Even people trying to outsmart her, to make her work less hard, to slow her down, to *beat her down*. Let Dan chew and slurp. Let the crumbs fall. Judy no longer cared.

"The child chromosomes are like parasites," she continued, remembering her thoughts from the night before. "They steal genome information from parent chromosomes in order to repli-cate. Become cannibals. It's my thought to somehow make the parent chromosomes *immune* to the parasitic attacks of their children. In other words, enable the parents to essentially starve their offspring."

Dan shook his head, his mouth full of sandwich. His eyes looked glazed; he was totally lost.

"Here, I'll draw it for you." She launched a vector-based drawing program on her laptop, hastily slapped together some lines and circles.

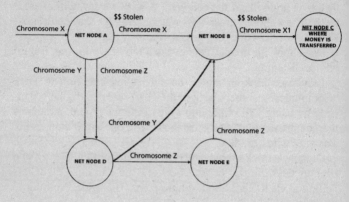

"This is the best I can do," she said. "Take a look. Here's how I figure it. Let's say we're at bank node B, hanging off the Internet. At B, the X chromosome is deemed the strongest. Why? Because it's taken the shortest path so far from bank node A, the starting point, to bank node B. Both chromosomes Y and Z have taken longer paths to get to node B. So, as I see it, the X chromosome is more fit. Remember, evolution means survival of the fittest. So X is best suited to take the trip to bank node C. Thus, in Cal's code, chromosome X beats both Y and Z for system memory and CPU time. X is allowed to reproduce more than Y. And, as a side note, Y is allowed to reproduce more than Z.

"There's probably even more involved. I assume that Z has taken not only the longest path to bank node B, but that Z has yielded the smallest amount of stolen cash so far and has hit bank nodes with the tightest security."

Dan nodded. "I'm following, but who knows how many rules Cal coded into this thing to figure which chromosomes reproduce and which ones get killed off."

"Exactly," Judy said. "I'm just guessing. But it makes sense.

And remember, this is artificial *life*, not mere artificial intelligence. Artificial life tends to evolve on its own, and thus create its own rules for survival. Probably even Cal doesn't know exactly what's happening from one node to the next. All he knows is that he's created a digital species that sets its own rules, all triggered from his original parameters. Anyway, as I figure in our simple case here, Z is terminated at bank node B and doesn't even reproduce. In the meantime, X *is* allowed to reproduce. Its children—for simplicity, we'll name just one, call it X1—*steal* the X chromosome's genome information. And having been cannibalized, literally eaten alive by its own children, poor old X dies, too."

"And the children, X1, X2, and so forth, continue to bank node C," Dan finished. His face was glowing. "My kid brother's a genius."

"He sure is," Judy said. "This stuff is absolutely awesome. *However,* I think I know how to stop this mess. The genome material is what feeds the offspring, right? So if the children can't steal genome information from their parents, they can't grow from larvae into full-fledged chromosome-based digital organisms. Obviously, they'll die. And the bank heist will terminate."

"*Damn.* Well, good luck." Dan chewed on his sandwich, his face screwed into a puzzled grin.

Judy turned away from him. It was time to test her theory. She slapped together some code, simple stuff. All she did was comment out the part of Cal's program that let the parents give genome information to their children. She touched the COMPILE icon, then after a clean result—no bugs, she'd only commented some stuff out—she touched the RUN icon. Of course, it worked as suspected. The children formed, but then didn't grow, and so they died. Simple.

But what could she do with this knowledge? There was no way to alter Cal's source code as it ran from Barrington's estate, especially with the code zipping over the Net so fast. She drummed her fingers on the edge of the laptop.

Time was running out.

Some crumbs fell from Dan's mouth onto the smelly blanket.

Crumbs. Tiny fragments of something.

Crumbs.

She needed something small, a tiny fragment. Maybe something at the one-gene level.

Coupled with a massive counterattack, the flooding of the Net with her own army of digital chromosomes.

A crumb. Just one.

It hit her like a flash of fire. *She knew exactly what to do.*

Judy pulled up Bren's independent search engine, the one she had copied onto her computer at Bren's home Wednesday night. Remembered how it had found a text file, something about personnel records for the National Security Agency, in the CIA's private network.

"Barrington and/or Ingersoll and/or Fire," she said, supplying all keywords she could think of that might lead her to Cal's hiding place on the Net. Dan squinted at her, baffled by her actions.

The screen displayed:

```
Searching
```

Then, a few seconds later:

```
Search Done
```

There were thousands of matches for Barrington, nearly a hundred for Ingersoll, in spite of security. Judy skimmed the first few for each man. Lots on Barrington, the right-wing crackpot who secluded himself in a desert compound that was minutes from the Hotel 86. And she learned that Ingersoll was an encryption expert employed by the NSA, a major fighter for U.S. government control of the Internet.

But there were too many matches for her to wade through. Time was precious.

"Barrington *and* Ingersoll *and* Fire," she said. The independent agents would scour the Net, seeking any location that had traces of *all three* words: *Barrington*, *Ingersoll*, and *Fire*.

This time there was only one hit:

```
Bradley Barrington Estate
IP Address: 32.555.11.9
```

```
IP Address Ghost: 82.555.26.9
IP Address Ghost: 35.555.17.1
IP Address Ghost: 44.555.81.6
IP Address Ghost: 99.555.42.3
IP Address Ghost: 64.555.33.8
IP Address Ghost: 22.555.12.9
```

She'd slept all the way to the Hotel 86. No time earlier to hunt for a hit using Barrington's name. But now that she knew that Cal was at Barrington's estate, finding Cal's network node was easy. Clearly, he was on the Net, using a series of ghost addresses, randomly generated to hide his true location. But Bren's search engine was too sophisticated not to pick up on multiple IP ghosting. Without the ghost clue, it would have taken Judy perhaps only a few minutes extra to hit each ghost and learn it was fake.

Knowing Cal's real Net node, Judy cracked into his computer—it took only a few seconds—and stole his password, then slipped back out without a trace.

"Perfect," Judy said. She smiled at Dan, who obviously still had no idea what she was doing.

"What's perfect? You found a way to stop Cal's code?"

"That's old news," Judy said. She pointed to the screen. "I found the Net node for Barrington's compound. Got the password, too. And I know exactly how I'm going to use them."

CHAPTER 31

It was midnight. Cal's code was set. He could only hope his one special modification would save his life.

Ingersoll and Greg stood behind him. Bradley Barrington hadn't come. Again. Cal suspected that Ingersoll hadn't told Barrington about the sudden change of plans.

Cal flexed his fingers. The AC unit thrummed. He was sweating anyway. Hair pulled into the rubber band on the back of his neck, ginger ale bottle on the floor by his feet, he was ready for action, ready to be Griswald. Perhaps for the last time.

"Let's go; execute the code," Ingersoll said.

Cal could sense the two men behind him, watching the screen over his shoulders. Greg, smelling sweaty from a day that had started by burying Harry. Ingersoll, calm and cool as ever, showing not the least trace of anxiety. Fifty billion on the line and the NSA agent didn't blink.

"Back off. *Please.* I can't work with you two standing over me," Cal said.

The two men moved a few steps back. Cal pictured them behind him, their eyes glittering with greed.

He rubbed his hands together, then settled his fingers on the keyboard.

It had been a long, frustrating afternoon. Setting his code back to its usual speed had taken only a minute. Then had come the waiting.

Though he kept zipping on and off the Net, he'd found no trace of his microcam video. Nowhere. Not even a mention.

Finally, hours gone, he had received notification of bounced-back E-mails. His transmissions to the UCLA professors hadn't reached their destinations. He'd re-sent the vidcam material nearly five hours ago, but there was little chance anyone would see it until morning.

"Come on, Calvin, *do it,*" Ingersoll said.

Yeah, he'd do it all right, he'd steal the fifty billion, but, man, was Ingersoll in for a shock when the code finished executing. And then Cal would tell him the really bad news.

That's when the bargaining would begin. With the prize, Cal's life.

He touched the EXECUTE icon. The chromosomes sprang to life—two parents—and quickly, they began to swap genes and reproduce.

```
Bank of Spain
Commstat/holdings/47396583 . . .
Current status: read/write

Federal Reserve
/treasury/notes/46e91f44129 . . .
Current status: read/write

Billington Securities
/Stocks/accounts/32f1c061 . . .
Current status: read/write

International Bank of New York
/accounts/acct12432329 . . .
Current status: read/write
```

Cal could feel the excitement radiating from Ingersoll and Greg. They were breathing more rapidly, watching the heist progress. He hardly noticed them. He was too focused on the stream of accounts continuously scrolling down his screen in the left Execute window.

Years ago, all those hotshot politicians and corporate bozos had claimed that digital money was to be the wave of the future. They hadn't realized that digital money meant standard transaction units: no more rubles, no more yen, no more U.S. dollars. Everything would convert instantly to the correct denominations, as determined by the various countries and economic boundaries. It made international business a lot simpler. And it made crime much easier.

Cal's little babies were multiplying at lightning speed. Blue strands, three-dimensional helixes: splitting, recombining, strands from adjacent chromosomes crossing and swapping, the chromosomes killing off any traces that they had ever existed. Artificial life, evolving naturally, based on intelligence and the fitness to do a particular job: to steal and hide electronic cash. Cal felt a glow of inner pride. This was Griswald's big show. Today Griswald was God—though nobody would ever know.

The transfers shifted from one computer node to the next, so quickly that the screen was a blur of blue chromosomal patterns.

"How much money have you taken? How much longer before we're finished?" Ingersoll asked. He'd moved closer again; his breath was hot on Cal's neck.

"Maybe twenty-five billion accumulated so far, maybe two minutes left before the code starts depositing the cash into the destination accounts," Cal said.

```
First International Bank of Switzerland
corporate/holdings/87825473 . . .
Current status: read/write
```

There was no way to stop it. In five minutes, fifty billion dollars would be stolen. By morning the financial world would be in flames. Chaos would reign. People would wake up, find their mortgages in ruins, their savings gone. Forget work; forget play. Banks would be flooded with mobs of angry patrons. Corporate leaders would be screaming, wondering how they were going to pay their debts, bankroll their expenses, figure out how much their customers owed. The U.S. government, and governments all over the world, would be reeling in shock.

Judy and Dan sat in the rental car on a small hill overlooking the Barrington estate, not far from the dirt road leading to the estate but not close enough to be noticed. The sun had set, and here, in the middle of the desert, the compound was a brightly lit oasis in a sea of darkness.

Displayed prominently in the right-hand corner of their windshield was an Internet Security Department sign with the official logo. Both of them now carried ISD identification cards. Having done plenty of work for the government agency in the past, Judy still had all their graphics stored on her laptop. Late in the afternoon, the two of them had made a nervous trip to the local computer workshop, where, for two dollars, they had run off hard copies. The IDs weren't perfect, but they would pass casual inspection. And Judy didn't expect anything more.

Judy had a cheap blanket wrapped around her legs, taken from the hotel. On her knees rested the netpad, connected by sensor to her laptop. She was already on the Net. It was ten minutes to twelve, and TerMight was busy.

Using Cal's password taken directly from Bradley Barrington's 32.555.11.9 computer, she set up a 1,000-pass loop for transmitting emergency signals. Instantly, a thousand messages flew across the Net, as if coming directly from Barrington and Ingersoll. Within seconds, all thousand would land in the police, fire, FBI, and Internet Security Department computers in the Los Angeles and adjacent areas. The messages screamed of a major explosion at the private compound of millionaire Bradley Barrington. The message would repeat several times before stopping. It was a distress signal that could not be ignored.

"Ten, fifteen minutes at the most before the cavalry arrives," Judy said. "Let's hope Ingersoll is a stickler for promptness. The heist should start in five."

Dan sat quietly, his hands gripping the steering wheel in a death lock. Judy suspected he was imagining his fingers around Ingersoll's neck.

"How could my brother do this?" he muttered, thinking aloud. *"How could he?"*

They both knew the answer, or hoped they did: because Cal had no choice.

"He's still alive. Keep that in mind."

Midnight. No time for distractions. "*Quiet* now," she said.

The previous night's bank heist had swept across the computer node occupied by the First International Bank of Switzerland. The bank had vast holdings and meager security. The perfect target for a hit. That node was somewhere in the middle of the heist route. It seemed very likely that Cal's intelligent chromosomes would cross that destination again tonight. If not, they were truly screwed.

On the Net, as Alfred Kosstater, president of the Bank of Switzerland, she had access to all information that hit the bank's computer server. Cal would be arriving very soon, his code running at incredible speed.

She touched the window that displayed the captured images of last night's chromosomes. She played through the genetic swapping, in slow motion, watched the unfurling of the chromosomes and their recombination over and over, mentally checking her theory for one last time.

Bren and Carl's debugger was ready. Judy had programmed the incredibly fast system in the motel room, using her captured sample of Cal's code as her test subject. The debugger was now loaded into the Bank of Switzerland's server, waiting to act. As soon as Cal's chromosomes appeared, Judy would strike back.

In the bank window, the blue strands appeared, started unfurling. Amplitudes shifted. Curve frequencies stretched.

The automatic debugging code went into action.

It would capture the executable code running on the server. It would run that code in full debugger mode. Judy would catch a data variable, at hexadecimal level, and change it.

She waited, excitement pounding in her chest. Then, *bam*. The debugger captured a fragment of genome information from a parent chromosome, and on the bank server itself, flipped the small series of gene bits. Those that had been a 1 bit now flipped to a 0, and those that had been a 0 bit now flipped to a 1.

It took only an instant, and it was done.

The strands split. In a blur of blue, the subtrees moved from one part of the screen to another. The subtrees shed their branches, filtered into pixel dust, and faded into nothingness.

"I did it, Dan. I changed Cal's chromosomes. Look at the playback. *Look!*"

Dan stared at her screen, dazed, confused by Judy's sudden outburst. "What? What have you done?"

She showed him the captured playback of what had just happened at the First International Bank of Switzerland.

"I knew your brother would hit here. So I waited for him. I took his parent chromosomes, Dan, and I changed them. I flipped the gene bits. I made digital alleles: other forms of the same genes."

"So—so what does this mean?"

"*Look.*"

Together, they watched the playback again in slow motion. As Cal's chromosomes entered the bank server, the gene bits flipped, creating new patterns that defined the source, destination, amount of cash transferred, and the optimal route.

"What does this mean?" Dan repeated. "I don't understand. Have you stopped him?"

"Yeah, I stopped him all right," Judy said.

Cal couldn't believe what he'd just seen.

"What the hell happened?" Ingersoll screamed. The usually stone-rigid face was twisted in anger. His cheeks were red. He looked like he was having a heart attack. Cal only hoped it was true.

"Goddamn!" Greg grabbed Cal by the shoulders.

"Calm down. Let him go," Ingersoll said. His voice was steady once more. "He's not responsible."

Greg released his grip. Cal stretched his back muscles, rotated his shoulders to ease the pain. "I don't know what happened. I really don't know," he said.

The heist had been stopped, literally dead in its tracks. Right there, at the First International Bank of Switzerland.

He scrolled through his captured trace of the heist. And there it was: *unbelievable.*

Someone had gotten to the bank ahead of him. Someone had flipped his gene bits.

The parent chromosomes had started reproducing and creating the children who would provide better routes for the transfer of cash. That had worked just fine.

But then, the children had inherited unsuitable gene bits from their parents. The children hadn't been strong enough to survive. They had been weaker than the parents. In analyzing their environment, the children had determined that the parents offered stronger paths for the heist. The children had realized that the parents stored the correct amounts for the electronic transfers, whereas they, the children, now stored incorrect amounts.

The children had killed themselves.

The parents remained alive.

But the parents only knew that they were to go to the First International Bank of Switzerland. They had no other destination. So they fizzled out and died, too.

It was a major programming bug. One that Cal had never considered. Chromosomes without a destination. The digital cash accumulated so far had no place to go, no route on which to continue. Stopped in midstream, the chain collapsed. The whole thing ground to a halt.

Ingersoll moved his face close to Cal's. "Whatever is wrong, fix it." No threats, no mention of Harry's fate. He merely stared Cal in the eyes and issued his ultimatum. *"Fix it now."*

"I need time to think," Cal said. "Time to figure out what to do."

"There's no time, Calvin," Ingersoll said. "It's your code. Make it work."

Not knowing what to do, Cal aborted the program. He slapped in a couple of hasty lines of software. He made the parent chromosomes into read-only snippets of code. This way, nobody could write to them; nobody could change them or flip their bits.

He recompiled the code, tested it once—not a very thorough way of debugging—then touched the EXECUTE icon.

There was only one person who could have screwed with Cal's code.

TerMight.

She was out there, working against him. She was still alive. And maybe so was Dan.

* * *

"That probably got their attention," Judy said. It was five minutes past twelve. "Now, for the clincher."

Knowing Cal would be forced to try to modify his code, Judy
got back to work. She knew some of Cal's prime hit spots: major
banks and Top 50 XXX-rated porno sites. So she copied the debugger program into all of those Net sites. No matter what Cal
did to his program, the debugger would flip the gene bits as soon
as the code reached any of those nodes. There was no way the
chromosomes could avoid the automatic debugging system.

Even if Cal made his code read-only, it wouldn't matter. The
debugger could access any bit of data, and dramatically alter it.
Rather than move to the next destination, the altered chain
would break, dissolve into nothingness.

She had found the fatal flaw in Cal's bank heist code. Each
robbed bank became the termination node.

CHAPTER 32

"When do you think the cops will arrive?" Dan asked.

"Any minute," Judy said. "Cops, firefighters, and every other authority figure within driving distance. Maybe even a few by air. Should be quite a procession."

"One thing I don't understand," Dan said. "Satellite scans will show that Barrington's estate isn't damaged. The cops in town won't be fooled. What makes you think all those big guns are actually going to show up because of a fake disaster message?"

She grinned. "Because I sent those transmissions as if I was Bradley Barrington. It's a county, state, and federal crime to hack into police bands. Reporting a false disaster over the Net is extremely serious business. The ISD treats it the same as yelling fire in a crowded movie theater. Can't imagine the authorities are going to be in a forgiving mood with that size computer fraud, especially after that billion-dollar heist over the Internet last night."

Dan smiled, shifted forward in his seat. "Man, you are a hotshot. You and Cal have a lot in common. You'd make some team."

"Well, don't get any funny ideas. Let's just get your brother out of there alive, then worry about teaming up and that sort of thing *later*, okay?"

"Well, sure. Didn't mean anything."

She kept silent. Why try to explain? He'd never understand anyway.

Even in the darkness, they could tell the view was flat. Foothills were dark shapes poking up in the distance. Here and there, scruffy growths clawed the desert sand. It was bleak, dead.

"What about the murders?" Dan asked. "Rescuing Cal's not going to wipe out the charges against us."

"It's all still a mess, Dan; I can't deny that. But right now, my main worry is freeing Cal. Once he's safe, the rest of this junk will fall into place."

"I hope so," Dan said. "I'd hate to spend the rest of my life stealing rental cars."

Judy closed the netpad. She pointed to the glow of headlights not far distant. "Jackpot time. Must be a dozen cars and trucks. Everybody wants a piece of the action. Anybody asks, remember we're with Internet Security. Flash that phony badge. But I don't think we have to worry. It's going to be mass confusion."

Sirens blaring, lights flashing, the long caravan of police and fire vehicles blasted past them, heading for the Barrington compound. As the last car zipped by, Dan shifted their car into gear and eased onto the road. No one in the procession seemed to notice they had gained another member.

"They probably figure that, if we're here, we belong," Dan said. He eased on the brake as the lead car came to a stop at the estate's front gate. Impatiently, he tapped his fingers on the top of the steering wheel. "Think Cal will be in the mansion?"

"Doubt it," Judy said. "I don't think Cal is Barrington's idea of good company. The old man hates hackers. Ingersoll probably kept your brother isolated in a cabin or some place like that away from the main building. Maybe there's a guest house. Once we're on the compound, we'll find it quick enough."

"Well, start looking," Dan said, "because here we go."

Evidently, the two men guarding the entrance had objected to admitting the caravan. Judy had been right about the police wanting to slap down Barrington and his flunkies. The guards stood at the side of the open gate, their hands raised high in the air. A pair of rugged cops stood nearby. One casually held a gun pointed at the guards, while the other was busy reading them their rights. No one gave Judy and Dan a second glance. The ISD sign did the trick.

Almost immediately, Judy spotted a cottage fifty yards off to the left of the mansion. "That's it, that's got to be it."

"I don't think anybody's going to worry why we're stopping," Dan said. Horns were honking, sirens wailing, men were yelling, red and yellow lights flashing. Judy could even hear dogs barking. "Place is a madhouse."

Dan jerked the steering wheel and swung the car onto a dirt path. "No cover here at all. Leaving this place might be a problem."

"Stop worrying so much," Judy said, as Dan pulled the car alongside the cottage. "Those jerkoids at the gate aren't going to be on duty for the rest of the night. They picked the wrong people to start an argument with. Cops in the Mojave don't take any back talk, especially from these right-wing lunatics. No one will notice us when we drive off. Come on. Let's just find Cal and make tracks."

They hurried out of the car and up to the front door of the cottage. The door wasn't locked. They entered the front room. No one was there. The place appeared deserted. "Hell," Dan said, "he's *got* to be here. Cal! Cal! Where are you?"

No answer. The cottage was silent.

"Don't give up. Let's search the place." Judy headed down the hall, noticed two doors on the left, one on the right. The walls held framed prints of the Old West. The pony express or something similar that she vaguely remembered from her childhood.

She pushed open the first door on the left. It didn't hold much—two black leather chairs, a bed, a sofa, and a makeshift desk with a computer on it. Machine off. No Cal.

"This must be where Cal's been working, and living," Dan said. "Maybe Barrington and Ingersoll took him up to the mansion when the cops arrived."

Something hard thumped against the door of what looked like the lone closet. Judy wrenched open the door. Lying on the floor, arms and legs tightly bound by loops of gray duct tape, was a much thinner, younger version of Dan. A large piece of tape covered his mouth. He'd been using his head to beat on the door.

"Cal!" Dan was on his knees, ripping the tape off his brother's hands and feet, anxiously at first, then a little more gingerly. "Thank God you're alive. Thank God, thank God."

With Dan's help, Cal wobbled to his feet. He pulled the tape off his lips, yelped as the last inch ripped off a small patch of skin. He looked just like his photo.

"TerMight, right?" Cal said, his voice shaky, face turning red. "Judy Carmody?"

"Would you ever have believed this—meeting in person, and all? That was a maximum meltdown tonight, don't you think?" She was chattering like crazy. Here she was, talking to *Griswald*. Part of her wanted to say, I've studied your code, you're a hacker legend, and all the stuff that Tarantula and Grouch had said to *her*. But he probably wouldn't like it any more than she ever did. He'd probably be uncomfortable with guys like Hector Rodriguez and Steve Sanchez, probably feel like a fool taking five hundred bucks an hour, probably feel left out, though he was a guy himself, when the businessmen shook hands and twittered about sports and cars and beer and their wives.

He grinned, and some of the nervous flush drained from his cheeks.

His ribs stuck out over a concave stomach. His shorts were baggy and hung on his hips. Had they been starving him, forcing him to slave away without giving him food?

"You found a fatal flaw in my code." Cal's voice was soft, low. He wasn't used to speaking much to strangers, any more than Judy was.

She said, "You fought back, but not a lot. I thought you'd put up more of a struggle."

"No time," Cal said, shaking his head. "They didn't give me any time. And you know what you've done, don't you?"

Yeah, Judy knew, all right. "I don't know how to fix the mess, Cal," she said. "All I knew was that I had to stop the theft, buy you time, get you out of here, and save your neck."

"Speaking of," Dan said, "this Ingersoll, the NSA honcho, did he toss you in the closet?"

"It was Greg," Cal said, rubbing his face, "Ingersoll's flunky.

You'd just screwed up my chromosomes, Judy, wrecking the heist. Ingersoll was furious. He really wanted that fifty billion. I was trying to rewrite the program, find a method of avoiding the flip-flop, when we heard the sirens. He told Greg to keep watch while he went to investigate. Two minutes after Ingersoll left, Greg taped me up and threw me in the closet. Guess he figured it was time for a quick exit. Didn't want to kill me for fear of what Ingersoll would do, or that somebody would catch him."

His eyes grew wide. "Hey, we gotta get out of here. Before Ingersoll gets back. He'll kill you."

"Grab whatever you need," Dan said, "and let's *move*."

"One second," Cal said. Stepping over to the makeshift desk, he booted up his computer. Using one finger, he typed in a single word. *Atomic.* A small mushroom cloud appeared on the screen. Then, the monitor went blank.

Judy recognized the same technique Cal must have used to destroy his computer in San Jose: f parm, with 0:0 fff 0. Infect the machine with an atomic bomb, instantly destroy all files, then blitz the operating system.

"That ends that," Cal said. "Hate to do it. No trace of where that money was stolen from. But I'll be damned if I'm letting this code get into *anybody's* hands. It's bad enough what I've already done."

"Cal, if you and I can do what we've done, to that many innocent people—"

"Yeah, I know," he said. "If you and I can do it, somebody else out there will figure out how to do it, too."

"Maybe someone like that Jose character," Dan added.

Yeah, a guy who didn't even know *how* to destroy things—not on purpose, anyway. An innocent mistake, that's all it would take, at the hands of any programmer.

The world would fall to its knees.

Cal grabbed a large green glob of what looked like kid's putty. It smelled like ammonia.

"Lucky charm," he muttered. "I'm ready."

They tumbled out of the room and into the narrow hallway. Five steps took them back to the small living room—where they came to a sudden halt, confronted by a lean, middle-aged man with slicked-down black hair. Dressed in a suit and tie, looking as fresh as a cologne ad. He stood beside the door that led outside. The gun in his right hand was pointed directly at them.

As he stared at them, a slow smile formed on his lips. "TerMight, I believe." His voice was smooth, relaxed. "And I suppose that you must be Calvin's brother. Daniel Nikonchik. The chili dog king."

"You're Ingersoll," Dan said, grabbing a lamp off the table by the sofa. "The son of a bitch who kidnapped my brother. And sent those killers to murder me and Judy."

Still smiling, Ingersoll nodded. The gun in his hand didn't waver. "Guilty as charged. Robert Ingersoll, National Security Agency, at your service. I had a feeling—when this amazing convoy arrived—that TerMight had to be behind it. I left poor old Bradley Barrington up at the mansion and hurried down here as quickly as I could. Made it in the nick of time, it seems."

He gestured with the gun. "Calvin, get over here. Now."

"No way," Cal said. "I'm not moving. You're crazy, Ingersoll, just plain crazy."

"Five seconds, Calvin," Ingersoll said. "Start walking. Or I blow a hole in your brother's stomach and you can watch his guts spill on the floor. You know I'm not bluffing. Remember Harry. Five, four . . ."

"I'm coming," Cal said, his voice turning shrill. "I'm coming."

Judy couldn't believe what she was hearing, what she was seeing. After all that she'd been through, everything she'd done, this couldn't be happening. She couldn't fail now. She wouldn't let it happen.

"It's over, Ingersoll," Dan said. "You're finished. Judy stopped the heist. Nothing you can do now. Why the hell don't you just let it go?"

Ingersoll's laugh was short and bitter. He hardly seemed to notice Cal, standing at his side, nervously kneading the green glob in his right hand. "Give up fifty billion, chili man? That wouldn't be very smart, would it? Not with Calvin still alive. And two murder suspects dead. Once TerMight is out of the picture, Cal can run his code again. And fatten my anonymous bank accounts."

"That's what you think!" Cal screamed, and he slammed the

green glob into Ingersoll's eyes. Caught completely off guard, the NSA agent howled in pain. With his left hand, he desperately tried to peel the ammonia glob from his eyes. His right hand jerked, squeezing the gun's trigger. A bullet whizzed across the living room, through the window, and shattered the glass. An instant later, Dan slammed the lamp against Ingersoll's right hand. The gun dropped to the floor.

The two men grappled, crashed into the back wall of the room with a thud, then tumbled to the floor, arms flailing wildly.

Déjà vu, Judy thought, as she scrambled forward. One of Dan's hands was flattened across Ingersoll's face, keeping the green blob over his eyes. His other hand had the lamp cord. He was trying frantically to wrap the cord around the NSA man's neck.

Cal hopped back and forth, screaming incoherently. Judy, laptop held with both hands, searched for an opening.

Ingersoll's palms whipped to Dan's chest, shoved him back. He grabbed Dan's shirt and shoved again. Dan fell back onto the sofa.

Green glop clinging to his face and dripping, the NSA agent rose to his feet. As did Dan.

"I'm going to rip out—" Ingersoll began. Fury was replaced by surprise when Dan punched him solidly in the stomach, then followed with a brutal left and right to the head.

The NSA agent struck wildly at Dan, who stepped aside and smashed Ingersoll in the face with a savage uppercut. Face bloody, the agent tried grabbing Dan by the shoulders, only to be met by a knee to the groin. With a screech of pain, Ingersoll dropped to his knees, close to Judy. She didn't hesitate. Ingersoll was the man responsible for murdering Trev, Jeremy, Larabee, Mercy, and Hailstorm.

Raising her laptop as high as she could, with both hands, she smashed it into the back of Ingersoll's head. With a grunt, his features went slack and he collapsed face first to the floor.

"Grab his gun, Cal," she commanded. There would be no murder tonight.

"Your—your laptop," Cal said, grabbing the gun off the floor. He held it gingerly by the barrel, as if it were alive and might bite him. "You hit him with your laptop!"

"Just a little blood on the carrying case," Judy said. "It'll wash off. Anyway, all my stuff is backed up on the netpad and at Bren and Carl's place."

"Nicely done," Dan said, grinning. "You really know how to use that computer, TerMight."

"I—I hate violence," Cal mumbled.

"Time to go," Dan said, grabbing Cal's arm.

"One second." Judy pulled the nylon cable ties from her laptop case. She stooped to wind the cable around Ingersoll's ankles.

"Sorry to interrupt, folks," a voice said from the cottage door, "but I'm afraid that won't be possible."

Three state troopers stood in the opening. Big, powerfully built men, they all carried guns. They were looking at Cal. "Son," the lead man said, the one doing all the talking, "please put that weapon on the floor. Right now."

"Sure," Cal said. Kneeling, he gently put the gun on the floor. "I hate guns."

One of the troopers cautiously moved forward, plucked the gun off the floor, and dropped it into a plastic bag. The trooper wore tissue-thin gloves. To prevent fingerprints.

Judy rose from tying Ingersoll's ankles, dropped the cable.

"Seems like you folks had some sort of disagreement here." The lead trooper—Sergeant Evans, according to his name tag—glanced at the bloody computer case, then at Ingersoll. "Argument over a computer game?"

"Officer, arrest these people," Ingersoll whispered, his voice slurred. He slowly shifted into a sitting position, pried the remnants of the ammonia blob from his eyes. "They're fugitives, wanted in Los Angeles and San Jose for murder. They just tried to kill me."

Evans nodded, his face expressionless. "Murder, huh? Los Angeles and San Jose. Now the Mojave? Sure cover the miles." He made no effort to assist Ingersoll in any way. "And who are you, sir?"

"Robert Ingersoll." He couldn't open his eyes. Tears coursed down his cheeks, spurred by the ammonia. "Damn, that hurts."

"Robert Ingersoll?" the cop said.

"Yes, sir. National Security Agency, United States government."

"Yeah, NSA," Cal said. "He's the maniac behind a billion-dollar heist off the Internet. And he tried to steal another fifty billion tonight."

"Not to mention," Judy added, "that he's the man behind all the false disaster reports submitted tonight over the *illegally tapped* police communications lines."

"Ridiculous," Ingersoll said, struggling to his feet. "This woman is—"

"Enough jawing," Evans said. "I've heard enough. You'll have your chance to talk up at the big house. That's where we're going."

He turned to one of the other troopers. "Calhoun, you and Ames check the cabin for any more surprise guests. Then seal the place. We don't want to be accused of OJing the evidence. I'm heading up the hill with these three. I'm sure Captain Sawyer's going to be thrilled to make their acquaintance."

Judy felt a flush rise to her cheeks. Despite having rescued Cal, they were *still* in deep trouble. She stood accused of murder, without any evidence to offer in her defense. She was trapped, and there was no place left to run.

Her spirits hit rock bottom; then she looked at Cal. He lifted his eyebrows, gave her a quick grim smile.

Cal had a trick up his sleeve.

Though TerMight had played all her cards, maybe Griswald held a final ace.

CHAPTER 33

Sergeant Evans marched them up a stone path to the house on the hill. It was a huge white building, a mansion in the style of the plantations of the Old South. Even in the dark, Judy could see that the gardens were opulent. Flowering succulents, rose bushes: the air was fragrant with perfume. It was a garden of Eden, a place that should have satisfied anyone, but this place held greedy men who always needed *more*.

No guns showed; there was no need. The sergeant hadn't said she couldn't talk, so Judy asked the obvious question. "Dan, where did you learn to fight like that?"

"My parents were weirdo neohippies, Judy," Dan said, chuckling, "but I never said they were pacifists. Growing up in a commune, but attending a public high school, I had to learn how to defend myself. My dad was a pro boxer before he went back to nature. He taught me how to use my fists."

Dan looked down at his bloody knuckles and smiled. "Guess he wasn't that bad a father."

Inside the mansion, they were steered down carpeted hallways, past mahogany bookcases and more paintings of the great frontier. They filed into a large office, already filled with people.

Judy stood close to Cal and Dan, and the three of them huddled by a glass case that held crystal goblets and vases. On the walls were framed portraits of an old guy standing with past presidents and other famous people.

Ingersoll, accompanied by Sergeant Evans and another state trooper, was ushered to the center of the room. He stopped before an immense desk. Sitting behind the desk was the old guy from the photos. Except he was even older in person, and it seemed to Judy his eyes were those of a deranged man: baffled, and burning with a passion that made no sense.

Nothing about this man made sense to her.

He was Bradley Barrington.

Judy's father probably hated him. Judy's mother would have fallen to the floor and kissed Barrington's feet.

Judy glanced at the other people in the room. A woman in a skirt suit sat in an antique chair alongside Barrington's desk. Her brown hair was tied into a bun on top of her head. This woman was trying to look as if she was all business: her clothing and demeanor practically screamed, treat me like a man. But there was an undercurrent, perhaps the way she glanced at Cal and Ingersoll, that betrayed her facade. Judy figured her for a man-eater in businesswomen's garb.

On the other side of the desk stood a short, muscular man. A long scar stretched down his neck. He was trying to appear totally disinterested in what was happening. The skirt-suited bimbo was glancing at him, too, trying to catch his eye.

A half dozen additional men and women, several in uniform, stood by the closed door. None of them looked happy.

One was a tall, lanky state trooper, clean shaven, with sandy hair and blue eyes. Captain Sawyer, according to the name badge on his shirt, walked across the office and confronted Barrington. "Okay, here's your man. Ingersoll. My men found him at the guest house. Now, we're ready for some answers."

Sawyer turned to one of the men by the door. "Everything's being taped. Right?"

The man nodded. "No sweat. Got our unit running. Plus, Barrington's got the whole place tapped and running on continuous video. Everything in this room is always taped."

Barrington's eyelids fluttered. His voice was surprisingly loud and clear for a man in such frail condition. "I like to keep informed. Nothing illegal about that."

Ingersoll, his face bruised, with a tinge of green across the bridge of his nose, was cool and calm. "Can we get on with things, Captain? There's a simple reason for this entire incident, if you'll just let me explain."

"Bob," Barrington said, "where have you been? Please, explain to these . . . these bureaucrats that we had nothing to do with their stupid emergency transmission. They refuse to believe *me*."

"Please be quiet, Mr. Barrington," Captain Sawyer said. He stared at Judy and the others. "Okay, now who are these people?"

"Found these folks in the guest house, Captain," Sergeant Evans said. "They were engaged in a fairly violent argument with Mr. Ingersoll. A weapon had been discharged. No injuries other than those resulting from the tussle. Mr. Ingersoll claims to be working for the National Security Agency. Says the others are fugitives, wanted for murder. They say he's the man who sent the illegal signal. And stole a billion dollars."

"NSA?" the captain said, staring at Ingersoll. "I didn't realize there were any unaccounted-for government agents in the area."

"Captain," Ingersoll said, his voice calm and level. "Captain, I demand you arrest these people—"

"Robert Ingersoll?" a middle-aged woman interrupted and stepped next to Captain Sawyer. Dressed conservatively in navy skirt and matching jacket, she stared closely at Ingersoll, as if trying to place him. "MIT graduate, class of 1978? Encryption specialist, recently *retired* from NSA after thirty years' service? That's what the gold ring on your finger means, correct?"

"Bob," Barrington said, his booming voice beginning to shake, "you told me you came from the government. Y-you're not a member of the National Security Agency?"

Ingersoll drew in a deep breath, appeared momentarily uncertain. Then he addressed the woman. "Yes. I'm that Robert Ingersoll. Didn't mean to imply I'm still with the agency. Just a figure of speech. Old habits die hard. Doesn't change the facts. This woman is Judy Carmody, also known as TerMight. She's wanted in both Laguna Beach and San Jose for murder."

"It's a lie," Judy said. "I didn't kill anyone."

"Of course not," Ingersoll said, with a contemptuous laugh. "The man next to her is Dan Nikonchik, her accomplice. His brother is—"

"Calvin Nikonchik, also known as Griswald," the woman said. She pulled a badge out of her purse. "I know all about TerMight and Griswald. I'm Susan Dexter, Internet Security Department."

She pointed to a short, stocky man, who was talking softly into a netpad. "Riley Marx, my partner. He's keeping our office informed of developments here. We're well aware of the crimes Ms. Carmody is accused of committing. Lately it seems that there's some question as to their validity. That's something to be settled in court, not here.

"We were on the road, on our way to the compound from the Los Angeles office, when Riley picked up the emergency brush fire report. I arranged to rendezvous with Captain Sawyer at the estate. What a pleasant surprise. It seems like everyone we wanted to interview is present."

"Internet Security?" Ingersoll said. Suddenly, his calm voice betrayed a note of uncertainty. Los Angeles was three hours to the west. "On your way here *before* the emergency bulletin?"

"Have you been on the Net anytime in the last few hours, Mr. Ingersoll?" Susan Dexter asked.

"No," Ingersoll said. "I've been busy with Mr. Barrington, discussing business plans. Nothing to do with the NSA. I'm here advising him on future investments."

"I'll bet," Dexter said wryly. She smiled at Cal. "And I can guess where the money comes from. For the past three hours, Mr. Ingersoll, on hundreds of Web sites across the country, a quite spectacular video has been running. Shot with a microcam that uses the latest digital technology. The picture and sound are nice and clear. I received a copy early, from a professor friend at UC Berkeley. That video clearly shows you, Mr. Ingersoll, ordering an unseen hacker—" Susan Dexter smiled pleasantly at Cal. "—to steal a billion dollars off the Internet. While such information is not admissible as evidence in a court of law, Mr. Ingersoll, I'd say you and your rich friend have a great deal to explain."

"Yes!" Cal cried. "All right! It's about time!"

"My God," Barrington said. The big man slumped back in his armchair, his expression numb. "Oh my God."

"Internet video," Ingersoll said. "That—that's impossible. It's a fraud. Completely fake. You—you can do anything with digital photography. Nikonchik doesn't even own a video camera."

"Yes, I do," Cal said, "and the officers here can find it hidden under my mattress in that prison hole you called a bedroom. It's a wrist cam. The latest model. The original video is still on it."

"Where the hell did you get that?" Ingersoll said. Silent for a moment, the ex-NSA agent turned slowly and stared at the skirt-suited brunette with the prim bun on the top of her head.

"Gloria? You bitch," he said, his voice rising in anger. "You deceitful, lying bitch!"

"Hey," Captain Sawyer said, "watch that."

The brunette—Gloria—rose from her chair. "Don't talk to me about lying," she said, sneering at Ingersoll. "I'm not stupid. Greg told me how you were planning to double-cross me. Nobody plays *me* for a sucker."

"Gloria," Barrington wheezed. "How could you? I've always treated you like one of the family."

"Sure," she said, "installing a camera in my room so you could watch me undress, taping my phone calls. Just like one of the family, you old bastard."

"Greg told you?" Ingersoll said. His hands clenched in fists. "Greg? The two of you, screwing around, scheming behind my back? You told her about my plans?"

The man with the scar shrugged. "Don't give me any holier-than-thou crap, boss. Didn't take a rocket scientist to realize you weren't planning to split the cash with anybody. I'm not stupid. I'm not Harry."

"Shut up, you idiot," Ingersoll said. "Don't say another word." Then to Dexter, "We've done nothing wrong. There's no evidence, nothing that will hold up in court. We need a lawyer. Now."

"Your privilege," Captain Sawyer said. "Sergeant Evans, read all of them their rights. Looks like we're taking the entire crew into custody."

"I refuse to say another word without receiving counsel from my attorney," Ingersoll said. He looked at Barrington, then Gloria, then Greg. "I advise you all to do the same."

Judy looked at Dan. He appeared as stunned and baffled as she was. She couldn't resist asking. "Who's Harry?"

Cal laughed. "Captain, I'll tell you why Ingersoll wants Gloria and Greg to shut up. Because they know that Mr. Ingersoll shot and killed his other assistant, Harry, yesterday. Shot him point-blank in the head. I saw the whole thing myself. Greg dumped the body in the desert. He probably—"

"You little son of a bitch!" Ingersoll roared, leaping forward suddenly. He grabbed for Cal's neck.

His hands never connected. Sergeant Evans stepped forward, caught Ingersoll by the shirt collar, swung him around, and threw him into a chair hard enough to make the wood frame shudder. "NSA, huh?" the state trooper said contemptuously. "Big deal."

"Thank you, Sergeant," Captain Sawyer said. "What a can of worms. I suspect we're better off at police headquarters. Ms. Dexter, do you agree?"

"Definitely," the ISD agent said, "though I suspect this mess will wind up in federal court. Ingersoll and his rich buddy may have violated just about every Internet security law on the books. Should make for an extremely interesting trial. And there's murder to consider."

"You'll never pin this theft on me," Ingersoll said. He pointed a finger at Cal. "He's the one. Calvin Nikonchik, the hacker. He wrote the code, executed the operation. Not me."

"What do you say to that, Griswald?" Ms. Dexter asked. "Seems like tonight you're the one with all the answers."

"I say, send your assistant down to the guest house to check my computer. See what he finds," Cal responded.

"Riley," Susan Dexter said. "Go ahead. The main office can survive for a few minutes without your bulletins. Look for the watch with the minicam, too."

Riley Marx, accompanied by one of Captain Sawyer's men, hurried from the room. He was back in less than ten minutes. In one hand, he held a wristwatch.

"Computer's wiped clean. Absolutely blank." The ISD agent shrugged his shoulders, grinned. "Almost as if someone *nuked* the whole machine. Not to mention all backups stashed on the server."

Dan laughed. "Damn! I always thought you needed me to protect you, Cal. Looks like it's the other way around."

"No code?" Ingersoll shrieked. "But, but . . ."

If there was no trace of the genetic code on Cal's machine, then there was no proof to link him with the bank heist. All Judy's computers contained was the original code done for Dan's restaurant, and fragments of the heist. Nothing that could be used as evidence. Her name, inserted in the looted bank files, wasn't proof that she had committed the crime, either. Without the actual code, there was no hard evidence that a robbery had even taken place.

"Enough fooling around," Captain Sawyer said. "Time we got these people out of here. It's going to be a long night, so we better start working."

The state trooper looked at Ingersoll, then Greg. "We'll come back in the morning, with bloodhounds. To see if they can find a body."

"Lies," Ingersoll said. "All lies."

"Sure," Captain Sawyer said. "That's what they all say. Sergeant Evans, you take these three—" He pointed to Judy, Cal, and Dan. "—in your car. I'll take Mr. Ingersoll and Mr. Barrington with me. Stransky can have the pleasure of the two lovebirds. Agreed?"

"Sounds fine, Captain," Evans said. "Everybody up. Time to go bye-bye."

Wearily, Judy let the troopers take her arm. It had been an incredible evening. One she would never forget. It wasn't quite over, but finally she felt as though things might work out.

She hoped they'd let her shower at the station. She'd be happy even to wear some clean prison clothes. And maybe they'd finally give her a decent bite to eat, too.

Cal waved a hand at Captain Sawyer, like a little kid in school, anxious to speak. "Mind if I say something to Mr. Barrington before you take him away? Won't take long, nothing secret."

"Free country, kid," Sawyer said. "But, no profanity, okay?"

"Never," Cal said.

He walked up to Barrington, who was being helped out of his chair by one of the policemen. "Mr. Barrington, I just want to say that you're dead-on right."

"Right?" the old man said, scowling at Cal. "What do you mean?"

"Computers *have* changed the world, and there *is* no truth in the digital age. Facts and figures can be altered, changed by one touch of an icon. Nothing's safe; nothing's sacred. Records, files, data. *Not even the digital keys of secret bank accounts.*"

Barrington's jaw dropped. His ruddy features turned bleach white. Ingersoll, a few steps to one side, groaned and covered his face with his hands.

Judy laughed. Despite having stolen a billion dollars, Barrington and Ingersoll weren't a dime richer. The money had disappeared into anonymous bank accounts across the world. Digital cash, it could only be accessed electronically over the Net. And Cal had changed the digital keys.

The robbers had been robbed.

Unfortunately, there was still that mess back at Laguna Savings to clean up.

Worse, a stream of electronic cash, billions of dollars— hijacked from corporations and Joe Homeowners all over the world—had been stopped dead cold in transit by the termination node. The money had dissolved into nothingness, disappeared without a trace.

How would they ever get the billions back to their original bank accounts? Who even knew where the original accounts were, where the money had been stolen from?

Cal had spoken the truth. Barrington, the right-wing radical, was right. Though he hadn't gotten any richer, he'd proven the inevitable point: in the digital world, nobody was safe. Even Judy's money was gone, possibly forever. The Net was one hell of a dangerous place.

A frightening thought, but it was true. And what Judy had told Dan back in San Jose was equally true.

Hackers rule.

He walked up to Burghature, who was now halfway to the

E P I L O G U E

Judy stooped by the ocean and lifted a washed-up sand dollar.

"I used to collect those as a kid," Cal said. "Kept them in jars next to my bed. They always crumbled, though; took only a few weeks."

Cal pushed his sunglasses higher on his nose and hopped back as ocean froth curled up to his ankles. A salty spray whipped the hair around his face.

He looked pretty silly in tiger-print bathing trunks and a zoid T-shirt. His nose was slathered in cold cream.

"Everything crumbles, Cal. Sand dollars—" She smiled. "—even digital dollars. It's the pattern of life. Like the waves." She pointed, and he nodded, as the waves rose and peaked, then collapsed and died.

"I know," he said, "but I wanted my sand dollars to last. I thought they were pirate treasure."

"Maybe you think too much. Or maybe you think too little." She rose and took his elbow, gently steered him down the beach. The sand was coarse and cold beneath her feet. "For example," she said, "if you got rid of the cold cream, maybe your glasses would stop sliding down your nose."

He laughed. It wasn't a shrill and hysterical laugh. Not the laugh of a man fleeing in terror, not the laugh of someone trying to convince murderers that the building superintendent was just there to do repairs. It was a calm and mellow laugh, as gently rounded as waves far out to sea, where they just brushed the horizon.

Cal stopped walking. He stared at a couple of girls sprawled on a blanket near a palm tree. "Wow," he said, "would you look at *them*."

Even this late in the season, the hard-core sunbathers were out in full force. Skin glistened in oil. Microbikinis barely covered their bodies.

"Those two look fried, Cal," Judy said reproachfully. Yeah, they sure did, lying motionless on their stomachs, baking under the December sun, their limbs perfect, their brains probably containing about as much as the dead sand dollars.

"Think they might want to meet a celebrity?" Cal asked.

Judy laughed. It felt good to laugh. It felt good to be alive, not on the run. It felt good to have a friend, even if it was a girl-crazy geek like Cal.

"Only one way to tell," she answered. "Why not go over and introduce yourself. They've probably seen you on TV. Maybe they have a thing for hackers."

"Well, I don't know," Cal said, sounding slightly nervous. "You're right. They're probably vacuum heads. I want a girl with brains. Someone perfect, like you."

"That's sweet, Cal," Judy said. She reached out and squeezed his shoulder. Slowly but surely she was learning to interact with people, to deal with them on a personal basis. It was a difficult but steady process.

Cal was her friend, a kid. But a friend, like Dan Nikonchik and Steve Sanchez. Men she liked, whose company she enjoyed, but they didn't interest her romantically. Sooner or later, she'd meet the right guy, but she was in no rush. Life was much more interesting taken one day at a time.

Cal shifted his gaze back to the ocean. Midnight blue water laced with pink and yellow threads from the sun. Gulls cawed overhead, diving for fish. It was beautiful, tranquil, but though she was clad in jeans and a T-shirt, Judy wanted to keep moving. The spray was giving her a chill.

"Come on, Cal," she said, "let's finish our walk, and then I'm teaching you how to Rollerblade, like you promised."

"Me, Rollerblading. I'll probably fall down and kill myself."

"No, you won't, because you'll analyze it to death before you even take your first step."

He laughed again. "That's why I like you, Judy. You push me to do things I've never done before. You've opened up a whole new life for me. Like that Sanchez contract. It's fun sniffing out those security leaks. Easy way to make good money. And Steve reminds me of Dan. Same high-pressure sales pitch. Makes me feel right at home."

"I'm just glad it's working out so well for you," Judy said. At the moment, she considered herself retired. No computer work, no security jobs, nothing of any significance. It was nice just being Judy Carmody for a change, not TerMight. Someday, she hoped to work with Cal on finishing his Dozong project. But, that was in the future.

"I like your earrings," Cal said. "Bren give them to you?"

"Sure did," Judy said, fingering the NORs dangling from her ears. "She insisted I take them when I visited her and Carl last week."

It had been nice seeing Bren under normal conditions, not worrying that the police might break down the door any minute. They had talked for hours, about code, about people they knew in common, about life in general. A good visit. Afterward, though, Judy realized that as much as she liked Bren, and in many ways, admired her, she had no desire to *be* like Bren. She wanted a life that wasn't hooked into a computer day and night. There was more to living than work, and Judy meant to find it. No matter how long it took.

The cold cream was melting on Cal's nose. He wiped it on his sleeve. "There. Better?"

"Much," Judy said.

"And when are you going to take *my* advice, and get into one of those microbikinis? Something tells me you'd attract a lot more attention."

"Not the kind of attention I want, Cal."

They sauntered farther down the beach toward the edge of the boardwalk, then climbed the stone stairs that led to the wooden walkway, where Cal would get his first Rollerblade lesson. His pace was slowing. "I can see it's gonna take a long time to change you," he said.

No. Some things would never change. Judy would never strut her stuff in a microbikini, hoping to attract studboys with her suntanned thighs. She'd never be able to expose that much of herself to anyone.

Cal panted from the upward climb. He wasn't used to exercise. He kept pausing to examine the flowering succulents and palms, pretending to be fascinated by the plant life. "By the way," he said, "Dan sends his regards. Told me to tell you the next time you come to town, he'll take you for a ride in his new Porsche. A silver one."

"Not in a million years," Judy said. The thought of another car ride with Dan made her shudder. "How's he managing? Any problems with those friends of his?"

"Nope," Cal said. "Loan sharks don't like dealing with people in the limelight. And once he sold the restaurant to one of their stooges, they lost all interest in Dan. Believe it or not, he's talking about investing the money from the sale, putting it into a summer camp."

"A camp? You're kidding."

Cal shook his head. "Don't laugh. Dan knows his way around the woods. Never liked to admit it, but he learned a lot growing up on the commune. When I talked to him on the phone, he actually sounded pretty excited about the idea."

"Probably serve sausages and potato chips for lunch," Judy said. It was good news. Dan had finally begun to make peace with his past.

"You see Gloria on the Net today?" Cal asked. "Man, did she look hot. I thought the news guy was gonna attack her, right there during the interview."

"Ever figure out why she gave you that microcam?" Judy asked. "Never made much sense to me."

Cal shrugged. "Don't know for sure. But, I suspect she guessed that Ingersoll planned to double-cross her and she wanted the tape for blackmail. Figured she could twist me around her little finger." He grinned, looking goofy. "Greg must have told her I had a weakness for girls."

"You have a weakness for *bimbos*," Judy said, laughing again. "Is the trial ever going to start? Seems like all they do is interview juror after juror. Amazing how many people they've dismissed."

"Newsgroups on the Net are already calling it the trial of the new century," Cal said. "Even before it starts. It's got everything: rogue government agent, crazy millionaire, antitechnology, hot-looking babe, and her jealous boyfriend. Throw in a billion-dollar robbery, a bunch of murders, and it makes great entertainment."

"Not so entertaining," Judy said. "The economy's still a freaking mess. It's hard enough just buying food these days. Thousands of people still can't access their digicards, their credit accounts, their savings. Even corporations. No way to do payroll. No clue who owes what on mortgages. I hate what we've done, Cal."

He glowered. "I didn't do it on purpose."

"We were both forced into it. It was that, or be murdered. Not much choice."

"The freak thing is that they've shut down VileSpawn," Cal said. "Closed most everything interesting on the Net. Just simple entertainment stuff running, like news shows and Mistie Lane."

"Well, I'm not looking forward to testifying," Judy said. "I'd be happy if I never saw Ingersoll or Barrington again. They made their point good and hard. They nearly destroyed the Internet and everyone connected to it."

"Look at the bright side. Lawyers might not even call you. Hard to pin the murders on Ingersoll, especially with Tony Tuska, Paul Smith, and Ernie Kaye all dead. Ms. Dexter says that she thinks the prosecutors will probably concentrate on Harry's death and the billion-dollar heist. The other stuff will come later. One trial after another. It'll take years."

"Been seeing a lot of Ms. Dexter, huh?" Judy asked.

"Plenty," Cal said. "She's pretty sharp for ISD. We're almost done transferring the stolen billion back into the right accounts. Taking longer than I thought, but it's working out okay."

"She's lucky you're honest," Judy said. "Not many people would return a billion dollars."

"A billion is nothing compared to what the second heist blew away, Judy. The ISD can't trace those thefts. I doubt we'll ever recover all *that* money. Maybe some of it, thanks to daily bank backups, but how do you unravel the millions, maybe billions, of bank transactions that I pulled within a few minutes? Banks are pulling out of electronic cash. People everywhere are scared to death. I don't know. I feel like Satan."

"Well, Satan has decades of computer security contracts ahead of him. You'll be rich. Anyone in our business, Cal, will be in business for a long time. Face it. Next time some lunatic tries to loot the Net, it'll be much worse than what we did."

They reached the top of the stairs and sat on a wooden bench while Judy strapped on her Rollerblades. Cal's pair had training wheels.

"I don't know about this, Judy."

"Oh, come on. It's not going to kill you."

He slipped one foot into a skate. Tentatively tightened the Velcro straps. "Well, I suppose it'll build up my leg muscles. And it might attract the chicks."

"Cal, what it'll do is give you a sense of freedom from all the computer work. Trust me on this. I *know*."

She was already on her feet, skating in tight circles, feeling the old rush. She was anxious to get moving, feel the wind in her ears.

"Why is freedom so important?" he called, struggling to stand, then wobbling and clutching the bench.

She looked over her shoulder at him, gave a mighty push with her right hand, and sent herself soaring down the boardwalk past a young mother with a baby. The baby looked up, startled. The mother smiled.

"Because freedom is all we have, Cal."

He grimaced, then rolled forward on both skates. His back arched. His arms waved wildly. "Wait up!"

She streaked over the boards. They clattered beneath her skates. She crouched, crossed her legs, aiming for maximum speed as she zoomed around the volleyball nets.

Freedom. It was worth anything. She'd wheel back and retrieve Cal. But not quite yet.

ACKNOWLEDGMENTS

Special thanks to Steve Saffel at Del Rey for believing in us and giving us the opportunity to write *The Termination Node*; to Shelly Shapiro, Kuo-Yu Liang, and Tim Kochuba at Del Rey for continued support and advice; and to Lori Perkins for making things happen.

Many thanks to Ron Lewis and Marillyn Cole for answering some desperate phone calls. To the late Sam Peeples, for words of wisdom and encouragement. To Cynthia Manson, Marty Greenberg, and Dean Koontz for good advice when it was most needed.

—Lois H. Gresh and Robert Weinberg

In addition, for a lifetime of adventures in computer science:

Deep gratitude to Bob Miller, Claude Marini, and Pete Tieslink, who let me work in my bedroom as Sister System Slayer. To the many wizards I've been fortunate to know, in particular: Rob Fitter, Chris Homan, Steve Miller, Steve Smith, Mike Scaglione, Michele Seitz, and Sue Semancik. To the people of Color Science: David McDowell, Larry Steele, Pete Weishaar, Dick

Bucknam, John Maurer, Tom Ashe, Chris Heinz, Sam Swartz, David Smith. To the people of Virtual Reality: Errol Naiman and Amos Newcombe. To Arthur Carrol, Otto Eckstein, Ted Sweere, and Wayne Donnelly, for giving me breaks when I was a kid. To George Slack, for electronics. And especially to Bob Campbell and Ed Covannon at Kodak, for showing me the future.

—Lois H. Gresh

A CONVERSATION WITH
LOIS H. GRESH & ROBERT WEINBERG

DR: How did the two of you come to collaborate on The Termination Node?

Bob: About five years ago, I edited a series of anthologies. I bought a number of spectacular stories from Lois, an author I had never met. When we did finally run into each other at a convention, we talked, and in casual conversation I asked what she did for a living other than write SF short stories. She told me about her computer work. When I heard about some of her experiences, I immediately asked why she was writing short stories instead of high-tech thrillers. And a new writing team was born.

Lois: We met at a biker bar near Las Vegas. I'd just finished hacking the coin-ops and needed to mellow while my partner, Paul W-----, buried our stash behind Old Maw's Denture Palace. The biker joint wasn't exactly an Internet café. There was nothing to do. So I drank rotgut and was on my fourth when I heard a mellow voice spinning tales. It was Bob. Legs: four feet long. Cowboy boots. Spurs. Yet beard of a computer guru; and thick glasses. I listened carefully. He spoke of Internet terrorism, vacuum tubes, Donald Duck, Mi-Go, and Virgil Finlay. I immediately asked why he was editing anthologies rather than writing high-tech thrillers. And a new writing team was born.

DR: Have you always been interested in SF?

Bob: I've always loved SF, and have been reading it since I was a kid.

Lois: I must point out that Bob read five to ten SF novels per week throughout his teens. And spent his childhood reading stuff like André Norton and Edgar Rice Burroughs. In terms of fiction, my father read nothing but SF, so I've been immersed in SF since childhood.

DR: Without giving away any major plot twists and turns, what can you tell us about The Termination Node?

Bob: *The Termination Node* is the first thriller of the twenty-first century. Being coauthored by someone who has spent her entire adult life in the computer field, it's the first book that portrays the computer world in a totally accurate manner. It's fast-paced, scientifically accurate, and a lot of fun. And it's also pretty damned scary, in a subtle but quite meaningful way.

Lois: *The Termination Node* is a computer technothriller about the Internet theft of billions of dollars. It's about hacking—how it's done today, how it'll be done tomorrow. And yes, we believe that it's the first near-future computer technothriller that uses accurate hacking techniques, right down to the code.

DR: Could someone use TTN *as a hacker's handbook?*

Lois: No. For example, someone today can hide binary images in other files. However, the novel doesn't explicitly provide the technique. If you want to hide files as we do in *The Termination Node*, read Dr. Dobb's. Another example: password hacking. Very well known techniques to anyone in the programming community. Or phone freaking boxes. Very well known techniques. What we do in *The Termination Node* is take all the methods that I know and push them five to ten years into the future—that is, change them to reflect a forward thrust in technology. Then we add what I believe the future's bringing in terms of new net technologies, and we provide hacks of our projected techniques.

DR: TTN has been described as "bleeding-edge." Do you consider it a science-fiction novel, or is it something else—something new?

Bob & Lois: The term "bleeding-edge" is very appropriate for our book. *The Termination Node* is just a heartbeat into the future. It's our world, projected a step beyond today. Our biggest worry has always been that much of what we predict in the book would come true before it's published. *The Termination Node* is science fiction now, but in ten years, it'll be science fact.

DR: For example?

Bob: Internet hookups in new cars. Most TV shows being broadcast over the net. It's coming, sooner than people realize.

Lois: Financial transactions over the Net. Digital cash. The key point about *The Termination Node* is that the Net heist of billions of dollars could be done today. The only difference between today's method and the one used in our novel is the coding technique. But such a heist could occur right now, tomorrow, and the money could be stashed, digitally, anywhere in the world.

DR: SF has always been predictive of the future (albeit wrong much of the time!). But when the time lag between what SF predicts and what technology achieves is measured in months or years rather than decades and centuries, does SF lose the qualities that distinguished it from mainstream fiction in the first place?

Bob: Good SF not only predicts the future, it extrapolates the effects of science on the future as well. SF will always be different from mainstream literature in that mainstream fiction describes what is—SF describes what might be.

Lois: At its best, SF prompts us to think about how scientific advances will change the human condition. As Bob points out, this factor distinguishes SF from mainstream literature. When we measure technical advances in terms of years rather than centuries, we're still wondering how the advances will change the human condition. Think of it as looking through a camera lens with zoom focus. Our focus in a near-future technothriller is tomorrow. Frankly, I view *The Termination Node* as a thriller, the computer scientist's version of something that might be written by Michael Crichton or Tom Clancy.

DR: So TTN *doesn't really belong within the cyberpunk tradition.*

Bob & Lois: Actually, while we enjoy cyberpunk fiction, *The Termination Node* doesn't fit into that category. Gibson et al. envision a world that someday might exist. Our book describes a future that's hurtling at us like an express train. It'll be here awfully quick, whether we like it or not.

DR: A future that itself owes a lot to science fiction in the sense that many of those who are shaping it were themselves shaped by a deep familiarity with specific ideas drawn from SF and, more generally, by science fictional ways of thinking in the abstract. Tom Disch talks about this in his new book, The Dreams Our Stuff Is Made Of. *Can you address this in terms of* TTN *and your own work with computers?*

Lois: Perhaps the best way to address this question is to use the example of virtual reality. To design and program a VR world requires two strands of thinking: (a) the highly abstract and (b) the purely logical. First, I envision a world that doesn't exist. It's populated with creatures and people, constructed of any architecture or even nonarchitecture, filled with textures and materials, lighting and shadow . . . I envision an entire 3-D world that simply doesn't exist outside of my head. And it happens instantly. This is very similar to how I write fiction. It's a very abstract "what-if" way of thinking. The purely logical side, of course, is programming the VR world. In its present state, virtual reality code is all numbers with a few words tossed in, so we can fool ourselves into thinking we have a nonmathematical language. Somehow, the best of science—as well as the best of science fiction—fuses the highly abstract with the purely logical.

DR: To what extent can we control the direction and speed of these advances? Do we drive them, or are they driving us?

Bob: The human condition drives everything. Technology advances because of demands of business, the military, and civilians. War and peace and profit and loss are the cornerstones of research and development.

Lois: I disagree somewhat. Sure, R&D requires that someone with lots of cash sees a moneymaking angle in fueling scientific advances. But I think we're seeing something different with the Internet and some of its coolest technologies. I agree that there are plenty of people making plenty of money via Net technologies. However, the Net itself was conceived by people who wanted everyone, and anyone, to be able to hook together, converse across the seas, exchange scientific ideas, etc. The Netscape browser has always been a free download. Ditto, a lot of plug-ins, such as the Cosmo player for VRML and Shockwave for Flash. What fuels the real advances on the Net is the drive by individual programmers and artists to do things that haven't been done before. To be the first to break new boundaries. To be creative, to let loose, to be free to combine the abstract with the purely logical, to know no boundaries. Individuals around the world, hooked together, exchanging information and ideas. This is the Net, and the individuals are driving the technology forward.

DR: For many people, one of the most worrisome aspects of advances in computer and Internet technology is the loss of privacy. Do you see privacy becoming a commodity available only to the very rich and/or powerful as the free flow of information becomes ubiquitous?

Bob & Lois: Not even the rich and powerful are protected in a world hooked to the Internet. After reading our book, we think everyone's going to realize that not only is Big Brother looking over your shoulder but he's brought along all of his friends as well.

DR: Who is Big Brother?

Bob: Big Brother is a lot of people. It's the government—ours and foreign ones, including both our allies and our enemies. Big Brother is also big corporations. Big Brother is anyone who wants to know more about us—what we eat, what we drink, what we watch on TV, how we think. Big Brother in the electronic age is everyone.

DR: We are clearly living more and more in the paranoid world of the Pynchonesque. What, if anything, can people do to protect their privacy?

Lois: Nothing. We're all doomed. Just kidding. Honestly, I don't think there's much we can do to protect our privacy. If foreign terrorists are cracking into the Department of Defense computers—which they are—and if hackers are scouring Social Security files—which they are—then how can Joe Citizen remain anonymous? Everything's stored in a computer somewhere.

DR: What about the popular image of the hacker as Robin Hood for the information age? Do hackers even the playing field between Big Brother and Joe Citizen or are they really helping Big Brother to diminish privacy, whether they admit it or not?

Lois: A hacker is neither Robin Hood nor Big Brother. He's just a really good programmer who specializes in cracking and/or protecting systems.

DR: Some argue that an evolutionary advance has already taken place in our species thanks to the expansion of human capabilities and capacities via computers (which they view more as mutations than tools). This process will only accelerate with the advent of AI, virtual reality, etc. What will it mean to be human in twenty years? Does this future frighten you, or do you look forward to it?

Lois: Well, of course, humankind has changed dramatically since computers came along. At first, most people were afraid of computers, and the computers themselves were locked behind fireproof glass windows and serviced by elite engineers. During the past two decades, the PC explosion brought computers into houses, and lots of people use computers at work—lay people, who don't program, build hardware, etc. But they use spreadsheet software, word processing programs, send and receive mail, conduct sales from distant locations, and so forth. Computers have become extensions of us. On the flip side there's a large component of the world population that isn't hooked to the Internet or to computers, in general. Already, the world economy is shifting. Geographic boundaries don't matter on the Internet; intercountry business differs little, if at all, from intracountry business. I trade technical information with people I've never met, and they live all over the world. I've had some long-term customers via the Internet; I shipped projects and invoices via the Net, and, in turn, they sent me project changes and more work via the Net. I don't think that the computer work mutated me, though I am a bit worried about this fuzzy green growth on my fingertips.

So do AI and VR frighten me? Heck, no. I play with AI for fun: it's my hobby. And I program VR projects professionally. I'd love to experience total VR immersion. I'm ready for nanotech implants, too. But full-scale AI, total VR immersion, and nanotech implants probably won't be realities of everyday life within the next twenty years. Too bad. Sure, I'm ready.

DR: But is there a danger of losing whatever it is that makes us human? Or will our humanity shape whatever future spaces, virtual and otherwise, we inhabit?

Bob: Are we losing what makes us human? Never. Man is master of his own destiny. Machines might enhance our understanding of reality, but they are not people. They are not replacing men and women. At least, not for a long time yet.

Lois: Eventually, our humanity may indeed evolve into something different due to fusion with technology. But this is not necessarily a bad thing. Evolution is simply that: evolution. Who knows? We may require fusion with technology to survive on an increasingly contaminated planet. In one or two hundred years, we may require nanotech implants to determine our fate. We'll still be human, no matter what happens. As for less radical technologies, such as VR spaces, even total immersion won't mutate our humanity into something else. Someone who prefers Internet relationships or voyeurism today may prefer VR immersion for his or her relationships tomorrow. No change in human thinking there.

DR: Are you working on another collaboration? What about upcoming individual projects?

Bob: Lois and I finished *The Computers of Star Trek*, a hardcover nonfiction book published in March 1999. As for the future, let's just say that we're writing in a new genre: cyberthrillers. *The Termination Node* is the first believable computer science thriller. Lois and I want to remain in front of the crowd that's sure to follow.

Join us online
to find out more about

THE TERMINATION NODE

by Lois H. Gresh and
Robert Weinberg

Visit us at

**www.randomhouse.com/delrey/
promo/terminationnode/**

for a list of special hacker, Internet banking, and cryptography sites; to read more
about the authors; and to consider
whether *The Termination Node* is science
fact or science fiction . . .